THE CHINESE PUZZLE

Charles Dickens Investigations
Book Eight

J. C. Briggs

SAPERE
BOOKS

THE CHINESE PUZZLE

Published by Sapere Books.

20 Windermere Drive, Leeds, England, LS17 7UZ,
United Kingdom

saperebooks.com

ISBN: 978-1-80055-211-1

For Tom with love, remembering Hong Kong and China days

CHARACTERS IN THE SERIES

Charles Dickens
Catherine, his wife
Georgina, his sister-in-law
Superintendent Sam Jones of Bow Street
Elizabeth Jones, his wife
Eleanor and Tom Brim, their adopted children
Sergeant Alf Rogers of Bow Street
Mollie, his wife, (formerly Spoon) who runs the stationery
shop for Eleanor and Tom Brim, whose parents are dead
Scrap, shop assistant, messenger boy, and amateur detective
Constables Stemp, Feak and Semple of Bow Street
Fikey Chubb, known fence and criminal
Doctor Allen Woodhall, a pathologist

IN THIS NOVEL:
The Politicians:
Lord John Russell, the Prime Minister of Great Britain
Sir George Grey, the Home Secretary

The Police:
Richard Mayne, Commissioner of Police
Colonel Hay, his deputy

The Police in the East End of London:
Inspector Bold of the Thames River Police
Constable John Gaunt, godson of Superintendent Jones
Constable Sleat

The Chinese Connections:
Mr Cornelius Mornay, retired banker, formerly merchant of Canton
Jonathan Mornay, his son
Fanny Mornay, his daughter
Mr Francis Hope, tea dealer and nephew to Cornelius Mornay
Michael Spencer, James Spencer, and Jane Spencer, children of Mr Cornelius Mornay, born in Canton
Mr Alexander Mattinson, banker, formerly merchant of Canton
Mr John Fullerton, formerly of the East India Company
Mr Li Shen, his land agent
Captain Bright, formerly of Canton
Miss Anne Palmer, former missionary of Canton
Captain Hesing, of the Chinese Junk
Mr Cheng, opium seller
Mrs Cheng, his wife
Lily Cheng, his daughter
Ah Say, deceased sister of Mr Cheng

The Aristocrats:
Sir Marmion Grex, peer of Ireland
Paul Grex, his son, fiancé of Fanny Mornay
Mrs Monthaven, Sir Marmion's sister
Lady Julia Boyle, Cavendish Boyle, related to the Irish Earl of Cork
Viscount de Montclair Frankland, Irish peer
The Duke of Devonshire

The Theatrical Connections:
Mark Lemon, editor of *Punch*, actor in *Not So Bad as We Seem*
Wilkie Collins, author, and actor in *Not So Bad as We Seem*

John Forster, writer, and actor in *Not So Bad as We Seem*
Mrs Stirling, actress at Drury Lane
Mr Buckstone, playwright and actor at The Adelphi Theatre
Kitty Lovell, sometime actress, mistress of Viscount Frankland
Maggie Chester, her sister

The Ragged School:
Mr John Macgregor, teacher and barrister
Smike, a shoe-black boy, sponsored by Charles Dickens
Toby Quick, a shoe-black boy
Sally Quick, his sister, a prostitute

The Criminals:
Uncle Dag, receiver of stolen goods, petty thief
Captain Blood, thief
Horsemeat, hard man and thief
Bendy Butler, thief
Milk, or Millikin, opium dealer and all-round bad lot

Extras:
Josephine, a charwoman who really did work for Charles Dickens
Doctor Grafton of Ramsgate
Mr Pickle, an undertaker
Captain Flint of the Ramsgate Coastguard Station
Captain Heavisides of Ramsgate
Phineas Phelan, a lawyer of Lincoln's Inn
Mr Silas Goodbody, lawyer to Cornelius Mornay
Mr Ajax Cheese, a shopkeeper
Mr Ernest Holiest, a clergyman
Mrs Locke, landlady of The Spaniards Inn
Mrs Rose, a guest at The Spaniards Inn

PROLOGUE

The man on the bed, a decrepit four poster, tossed and turned under the grimy blanket, and mumbled over and over, 'Ah, say, say, say…'

The grey-haired woman stroked the man's brow and murmured to him in a sort of rattling whisper as though she were choking. 'Soon, soon, now, smoke will make you better. Plenty of smokes. Soon.'

In the corner, a man with a pigtail was tending to a skillet placed over a few miserable coals in the tiny fireplace. Something liquid like black treacle bubbled in the pan. The smell in the room was of burnt sugar and laudanum and the grease of tallow from the candles. He paid no attention to the man on the bed or to the whispering woman. He took what looked like an iron skewer, dipped the pointed end into the liquid and held a drop over the flame until it hardened, repeating the process by adding another drop and another until he had a piece the size of a pea, which he handed to a dark-haired girl in a black gown. She fitted the little object into a clay bowl on top of a bamboo pipe and offered it to a man who was standing near the half-open door.

He shook his head and continued to watch the man on the bed who no longer mumbled, but whose breathing seemed more laboured and hoarse now. The girl gave it back to the man with the pigtail.

'Sleepy now, sleepy now,' the grey-haired woman crooned. 'Cheng brings smoke — make better later.'

The dark-haired girl watched the man at the door from under lowered eyes. He frightened her. She couldn't see his face, which was partly concealed by a muffler. On a hot summer's night? He stood so still that she felt he had no pity for the man on the bed. He was waiting, she thought. She saw him glance at the man smoking the pipe and caught a glimpse of eyes that glittered momentarily, as if they were made of ice. Eyes that she had seen before. The pipe-smoker just nodded back. His face was wreathed in smoke, so she couldn't tell what had passed between them, but there was something that they knew. Something about the old man on the bed. She knew him, too. He came from time to time. She liked him. There was kindness in his eyes, never contempt, and he often slipped her money. He hadn't seemed well when the man had brought him in. She hadn't asked any questions. She had been told often enough that it was Cheng's business. It was, and she couldn't wait to get out of it.

The man on the bed made a noise, a long drawn-out moan, as if he were in despair, as if he had no hope left. The grey-haired woman mumbled again; then there was just the sound of the bubbling liquid and the whistling of the smoke drawn through Cheng's pipe.

The dark-haired girl looked to the door, but the man was gone. The door was wide open and river mist came in to mingle with the smoke from the fire and the pipe, and from the tallow candles that were snuffed out, one by one, by the grey-haired woman, who lay down on the bed.

The girl took the pipe that Cheng offered. There came again the sweet burning smell of the opium fumes, and the room was wreathed in dreams of a country far across the seas where the girl had never been. The man on the bed did not stir.

1: SHOE-BLACK BOY

The Crystal Palace, May 1st, 1851

Toby Quick came out of the exit into the courtyard where the boiler house stood. He passed the great lumps of coal and the huge granite column and went out into the park. He looked up at the bright blue sky. It was hot, but he felt a pleasant breeze, pushed back his cap, and wiped the sweat from his brow with his dirty hand, where it left a black mark. The green of the park stretched away on one side to a group of trees, and on the other there was — well, who could say what it was? It didn't look real to Toby Quick. *A palace built o' glass with trees in it — trees growin' in a palace! A wonder, that's what it iz.*

But the trees outside didn't look real to him, either. Even the folk had looked unreal in the shining light. Crowds of them had streamed towards the turnstiles, showing their tickets. *Day for the toffs*, he thought. The Queen had come. He'd sneaked out to watch the carriages and all the shining horses, the glittering helmets, the plumes, the red jackets, and he'd heard the roars of the crowds outside the park, and then the trumpets and the bands playing. But he hadn't seen her — he'd scuttled back to his place before anyone missed him.

The Queen had gone and he'd heard the cheering as her carriage procession had left the park. And now, he was free for a while, free to look up into that cloudless sky. Not a thing he'd done much before. Toby Quick had looked down most of his life when roaming the streets. He'd learned to keep his eyes open, because you never knew what you might pick up. Folk were careless. They dropped things — things you could sell.

It 'adn't bin a bad life, Toby reflected, out on the streets, free as yer like, no ol' busybodies to tell yer when ter come an' go, but it wozn't so clever if you woz caught out. Toby had been free — until — well, until he'd been supposed to act as snakesman for a robbery. 'Just get in an' open the door — nothin' to it,' Uncle Dag 'ad said. Toby had done it before. Easy money, usually, but no one 'ad said about guns an' it woz 'im, Toby Quick, wot got it in the neck — right in the neck when the gun had gone off.

Toby felt his neck as he remembered. The bullet was still there. He'd woken up in a hospital bed, glad to be alive, and wondering where Uncle Dag was. Once, he thought he had woken and Uncle Dag was there, a shadow at the bottom of the bed, but it must have been a dream because Uncle Dag never came back. Then there was Mr John Macgregor of Field Lane Ragged School who, when Toby had recovered, had found him a lodging and offered him a job.

Which was why Toby Quick was in the Crystal Palace on May the first, 1851, shining shoes in one of the gentlemen's retiring rooms where men came to relieve themselves and to have a wash and brush-up — a shoe-black boy, part of Mr. Macgregor's shoe-black brigade — and making some money. He'd made a few bob already. He had plans for his savings.

He had a pie and a bottle of beer in his pocket. He wandered through the crowds until he spied an empty spot under some trees. *We could 'ave it there*, he thought, *get a bit o' shade*. But there was someone there. Some old cove leaning against a tree who didn't look too good — unsteady on his pins, and red in the face, loosening 'is cravat as if 'e couldn't breathe. *Toff*, Toby thought — topper fallen off.

Toby wondered if he should offer to help, but someone else appeared — someone the old cove knew, p'raps, 'elpin the poor old cove, pickin' up 'is stick an' topper, an' offerin' something from a stone bottle. The old man drank and the other led him away through the crowds, the old man leaning on his stick.

Toby sat down under the trees and took out his pie, which he cut into two equal parts. And when he saw the slight figure coming towards him, he took out the bottle of beer — bit on the warm side, but it would do. He looked up and laughed. 'Blimey, I wouldn'ta known yer if I 'adn't known yer woz comin.'

From *The Morning Post*, May 2nd, 1851

THE OPENING OF THE GREAT EXHIBITION

The Duke of Wellington conversed with the Marquis of Anglesey when much to the amusement of everybody, a Chinese Mandarin, with a tail of fabulous length, appeared before them. He saluted them both in the Oriental style. This live importation from the Celestial Empire managed to render himself extremely conspicuous.

After the gracious reply of her Majesty to the address read by his Royal Highness, the Prince Consort, the Mandarin approached the throne, and had the high honour of saluting her Majesty by a grand salaam.

When the procession formed, the diplomatic body had no Chinese representative and the stray Celestial friend was quietly impounded and made to march in the rear of the ambassadors. Hundreds of people wondered where the new Chinese ambassador, of whom no one had heard, had sprung from.

2: STORM

Charles Dickens stood at the cliff's edge to watch the sea heaving and swelling under a sky black with heavy tiers of wildly rolling cloud, so dark that in the distance sky and sea seemed one. The wind blew so hard that he stood back from the edge, fearful of being tossed by some giant hand to be dashed on the rocks below. He could feel the spray on his face and taste the salt, and flakes of sea-dashed foam whirled about his head like snow.

He had been woken because of the wind rattling at his window and the weird hollow cry it made in the chimney. In his dream he had heard a child crying. He thought it was Dora, his baby girl, and he had been following the cry along dark corridors and up twisted staircases that led only into empty rooms. Still the child cried — the loneliest sound in the world. It spoke of terror, loss and unspeakable grief, and he kept stumbling on, trying to hurry, but just as he thought he had found her in a room where a light flared, he woke to the shriek in the chimney and a flame of light which showed briefly in a gap in the curtains, and he had remembered that Dora was dead. Twice, thrice, and more lost, for every dream of the dead brings as acute a pang as that first recognition that death closes all.

He had got up then, knowing that sleep would not come again, and looking out of the window, knew that the light had been a distress flare. Out there in that heaving sea, battered by the roaring wind, there must be a ship foundered on the

Goodwin Sands. Then he heard signal guns and knew that the lifeboats would be setting forth. He went out to see.

The guns were louder now, booming in the great darkness broken only by the light of the North Foreland Lighthouse, the great eye looking out from above the village, and the knowing eye of a floating light winking back its message that Death was abroad. And then there was a bell — the ship's bell, most likely, but here on the lonely clifftop it sounded like the death knell. He thought of the lifeboats plunging into the wild water and the stricken ship engulfed and all the souls aboard dragged down a million fathoms deep.

An extraordinary sight greeted him on the beach very early the next morning. The sea was still very rough, blowing in straight upon the shore, which was strewn with hundreds of cattle and sheep, lying with their stiff hoofs in the air, tumbled and beaten out of shape. It wouldn't be long, he thought, before the plunderers would be here to take away what they could to sell. In the meantime, the beach looked as if a great battle had taken place, the defeated combatants being the poor shapeless creatures now dead after a victorious army had departed.

He walked about, looking down at the beasts, thinking that there was a sort of goblin humanity about them which made him shudder. He hoped at least that some of the passengers and crew had been saved. He would walk to the pier and find out. That bell last night had sounded such a lament and the storm had been so raging that he hardly dared believe that anyone could be saved, though miracles did happen. The Broadstairs lifeboats had saved seven passengers from the brig *Mary White*, which had foundered back in March in such a storm as had happened last night.

He picked his way through the carcasses, going away from the sea's edge when something caught his eye, something black sticking out near a dead cow. Surely it was an arm — a human arm. He went closer and saw that half-concealed under the carcass was a body. Not a seaman's arm — the sleeve was wet, of course, but of black cloth, the sleeve of a man's coat. The face was down in the sand, but the hair was short and black and by the shape of the neck and the smoothness of the hand, he guessed the body was that of a young man. A passenger, then, who had perhaps thought to save himself by clutching at one of the beasts, hoping to be carried ashore, but who had drowned as he floated away and was tossed here by the incoming tide.

Dickens resisted the temptation to move him from under the cow. It seemed such a terrible thing to die thus, accompanied only by a beast. He looked about him to see if there were any more unfortunate victims, but he decided he should not linger. There was nothing he could do for the dead man except to report his find to the harbour master in town. And he should go back to Fort House first to make sure that his children were not let on the beach this morning.

3: SUPERINTENDENT JONES FEELS THE HEAT

Superintendent Sam Jones of Bow Street looked contemplatively at his top hat — his best one — and he felt the tightness of his best black frock coat. It was the heat — more than eighty degrees yesterday and it felt like it today. And, he admitted to himself, he felt the general tightness of his chest at the thought of what might be to come.

He was sitting on a bench in Hyde Park before the shimmering astonishment of the Crystal Palace towards which streams of visitors were making their way. The Great Exhibition had opened a few days ago, and the crowds were not just the middle classes and those of the higher echelons; there were also agricultural labourers in their smocks being herded by the parish clergymen who had brought them; there were country women in Sunday dresses; there were workers from manufacturing towns, who had come by train, having saved their sixpences and shillings in the travelling clubs established in their districts; and there were children being rounded up by hot and harassed-looking schoolmistresses. There were some top hats, too, and some silks and parasols. Many visitors returned again and again to see all the wonders of the world.

Jones had seen them, too, accompanied by his wife, Elizabeth, and their two adopted children, Eleanor and Tom Brim, and their great friend, Scrap. They had seen the little working colliery, the steam engines, the fossils that glowed in the dark, a colossal bronze lion from Germany — fifteen feet long — and a vast statue of an Amazon on horseback being

17

attacked by another lion. They had seen the Koh-I-Noor, the much-vaunted priceless diamond belonging to the Queen. Scrap had not been much impressed by 'a piece of ol' rock', as he had deemed it, much preferring the Sheffield pen knife with its eighty blades and Samuel Colt's repeating revolvers. Elizabeth had enjoyed the Sevres porcelain and the Lyons silk; Eleanor had loved the velocipede — she'd have loved to ride one. Tom had loved the dinosaurs in their swamp, and they'd all enjoyed the stuffed elephant bearing an ornate golden howdah on its back. Five shillings each, but worth every penny to see the children's faces. And there had been ices, bath buns and the cold drinks of Mr Schweppes to be bought in one of the refreshment rooms. And, to cap it all, free eau de cologne and chocolate.

They'd be there again on one of the shilling days which opened in a week or so. He'd promised, though he felt he'd seen enough, for he'd been there in his official capacity, too — on the very first day — which was why he was feeling the heat and the tightness of his coat. He had had a glimpse of the Queen in her pink and white; he had seen the Prince Consort and heard a few words of his address; he had caught sight of the Duke of Wellington, but his eyes had been mostly on the crowds inside and out. And on the uniformed police and plain clothes men detailed to keep safe the great and the good who had been present by invitation only. There had been thirty thousand people there — the officials and diplomats, of course, and the season ticket holders, and it had all been splendid except for the Chinese Mandarin.

Jones had seen him in his turquoise silken robes with his pigtail hanging down his back, and he had seen his curiously clumsy shoes as he made his obeisance to the Duke and his kow-tow to her Majesty. He had seen him in the grand procession, assuming, as everyone else had, that the Mandarin was an envoy from the Celestial Emperor.

Only he wasn't. He was, so it was found out later, Hesing, the captain of the Chinese junk, the *Keying*, moored on the Thames since 1848, and offering entertainments for visitors. And he had got as close to the Queen and the Duke of Wellington as any assassin might. No one could explain how he had done it without official sanction.

The newspapers had been amused; the Queen had been amused; the supposed Mandarin had been amused. However, the Home Secretary had not — not at all.

How, Sir George Grey had thundered, had such a breach of security arisen? He had been beset for a year by questions in the House about the adequacy of police at the Exhibition; whether hordes of invading foreigners would be armed to the teeth; whether he had considered the possibility of spies, revolutionaries, reds, chartists, anarchists of every nationality infiltrating the Exhibition, possibly, probably, prepared to bomb the Crystal Palace into eternity, or to shoot the Queen. Had they — meaning Mr Richard Mayne, the Police Commissioner, Colonel Hay, the Assistant Commissioner, Superintendent Nicholas Pearce in charge of policing the Exhibition, and the various Superintendents detailed to keep their vigilant eye on proceedings — had they heard of the conspiracy in Europe?

Well, Sir George had, and of the branch of the Committee of Central European Democracy here in London. He had been informed by the Honourable Member, Mr Wortley, that the aims of this organization were to promote insurrection and — and... Here Sir George slapped his papers onto his desk and ignored the unfortunate result, which was that they fluttered to the floor. A startled secretary gathered them up and scuttled away at a gesture from the aristocratic hand. And — Sir George repeated — and — to exterminate existing sovereigns.

As no one answered the question buried somewhere among the anarchists, Sir George went on to remind them how he had been at considerable pains to reassure the House that he was confident that all necessary measures had been taken and precautions adopted against the anarchist threat, and that an ample sufficiency of police would be present in the Exhibition, at the gates of the park, and in the nearby streets. He had assured the House and the Queen and the Prince that he had every confidence in the vigilance and professionalism of the police force to keep the sovereign and her people safe.

And yet, a tuppenny-halfpenny man from China, a cook, forsooth, a dancing master from a preposterous sailing vessel moored at the mouth of a sewer had been able —

Just as Jones had been thinking of the unlikelihood of the dancing master role — those clumsy shoes — one of the Superintendents blurted out, rather unwisely, that the man was the captain of the junk.

Junk, indeed, Sir George had continued. Junk was the word. Sir George — somewhat geographically muddled in his rage — did not care if the man was Ali Baba himself and in pantomime at Drury Lane, or even if, as the newspapers had it, an amusing sideshow in the Queen's procession, he had got in and he had come within an inch of Her Royal Majesty — and he might have been an anarchist in disguise. Had they thought of that? In full flow, he had adverted to the lunatic, Robert Pate. He supposed they remembered him.

Of course they remembered — all too vividly. Last June, Robert Pate, a former soldier, had struck Her Majesty with his stick as she had been entering the gates of Cambridge House. The noble forehead had been bruised and the royal blood had been spilt. Richard Mayne's patrician, high cheek-boned face — normally most composed — turned rather pale at the name of Pate. Colonel Hay turned red. He had thought that his military experience should have put him in command of the Exhibition's security — no dancing man from China would have got within a mile of Her Majesty.

In the silence that followed, Jones had watched the pulse beating time at the noble lord's temple. Sir George, he had thought, had no need to mention William Hamilton, who, in 1849, had fired a pistol at the Queen's carriage. Everyone remembered that, too. Both would-be assassins had been sentenced to seven years' transportation. Perhaps the Chinese man and his junk would be towed into the Thames and sent on their way back to the Celestial Empire.

And the Commissioners and the Superintendents had also thought of anarchists in disguise. They had been mightily relieved that no harm had been done, and no harm had been done, as far as Jones knew, in the days that had passed since the opening. Security had been tightened. Plain clothes policemen had been on the lookout for the spies and revolutionaries — the branch of the Central Committee for European Democracy had been infiltrated and other potentially dangerous types had been watched and followed. Monsieur Henri Galbie and his men of the Paris Police had kept known French criminals under surveillance and members of the German Police had kept a close eye on a public house in Great Windmill Street, where German and Polish agitators gathered. Three policemen from New York had come to look out for their own particular villains.

Perhaps it was the heat, Jones had thought. Rather than boiling up the blood of the revolutionaries, it had maybe enervated their passions, for nothing dreadful had happened.

The Queen had visited the Exhibition again in private, and Mr Mayne had made sure that she was carefully, if discreetly, spied on.

Naturally, there had been arrests — a few pickpockets, some of the swell mob with their eyes on the jewels and furs, prostitutes plying their trade in the refreshment booths. One or two old acquaintances had been followed and quietly ushered from the premises, and the foreign policemen had collared some of their own pickpockets and runaway fraudsters, but the crowds of all classes had been extremely well-behaved — stunned and astounded by what they had seen.

Captain Hesing had gone back to his junk. No wonder he was amused. His advertisements were in every newspaper: *The Mandarin* — not cook, therefore — *Hesing begs to announce that in consequence of the brilliant success that has attended the Chinese Festivals* — there would be plenty more attractions nightly — all for a shilling. And the irrepressible blighter ended his advertisements with the words *Under Royal Patronage*. No one had wanted to make any great fuss about him. Better to go along with the prevailing opinion that his presence had been a comical novelty.

But — and it was a big but, which troubled Jones at this very moment when he was perspiring on his bench, waiting to go to his appointment in Westminster — what had become of the other Chinese man? The newspapers had reported that Captain Hesing had arrived with his secretary, and there had certainly been seen another Chinese man in the crowd when Hesing had been bowing to the Duke of Wellington, but Hesing had denied any secretary. And after Hesing's royal progress in the procession, the presumed secretary had vanished. Of course, Sir George had ordered a search. The Chinese booth had been searched — the items on display had not come directly from the Celestial Emperor but from Hewitt's Furniture store on Fenchurch Street, and many were lent by merchants who had made their fortunes in China. There was a young Chinese man manning the booth. He had been questioned closely, but declared that he had not left his station, and there was no would-be assassin hiding in any of the immense jars, nor, indeed, in the sandalwood chests, or within the huge rolls of silk.

In short, it had been impossible. Who could describe him? Short of stature, slight of build, dark-haired with a pigtail, wearing a drab coloured robe and a black hat of a peculiar shape, a Chinese look about him, so said those who had noticed him.

'Well, he would, wouldn't he?' Sergeant Rogers had opined. 'If he was Chinese. Could be anywhere now.'

Rogers was right, Jones reflected, but the police had been back and forth to the Chinese junk where, not surprisingly, there had been a good many slight young men resembling the supposed secretary, performing as acrobats, jugglers and musicians. They had been to the Chinese Exhibition, which was a separate show near Albert Gate, under the management of a Mr Ellis, where again there were pigtails, peculiar hats, and robes aplenty. The Chinese family who were exhibiting there had no English, though the Lady, Pwan-ye-Koo, gave them a song — not much help, charming as it was. Mr Mayne had sent some plain clothes men down to the docks to search the few opium dens, but what with the language difficulty and the vagueness of the description, there had been no results, and since nothing of any note had happened subsequently, Sir George Grey had had to be satisfied that the man had been a harmless stray.

Now, however, it seemed he might not be satisfied again, for in half an hour Jones was to present himself at the office of the Home Secretary — a matter of security, so Richard Mayne had told him. Something was afoot, but why he should be called in, Jones had no idea. He thought of Richard Mayne's thin-lipped mouth and that hawkish stare. Perhaps they needed a scapegoat. Perhaps the lapse of security on the opening day had been found to be his fault, or at least one of his men's, or there had been another mistake on his watch. A head might have to roll. Perhaps someone thought it might as well be his.

Jones looked at his watch. Time to go. It was too hot to put on his hat. He would put it on when he was closer to the Palace of Westminster. Although if his head were to roll, he might not need it at all.

4: NEWS FOR MR DICKENS

'Attending a funeral?' asked Dickens after he had greeted Jones, who was making a rare visit to Dickens's office in Wellington Street. Jones was wearing a smart black frock coat and carrying a top hat.

'Summoned to Sir George Grey's office,' Jones corrected him.

'The Home Secretary, indeed; my, my — promotion? Greatness thrust upon you?'

'I have been in a most secret conclave with Sir George Grey, Lord Russell, and Mr Mayne.'

'Great Heavens! Knighted?'

Jones grinned. 'Not a chance, but a confidential matter — of state.'

'And you're telling me because —'

'Ah, well, your name was mentioned.'

'Now I see it. The Queen has conferred your knighthood on me — for services to literature and the drama. She will be in attendance at the new play. Not so bad as we seem, eh?'

Jones laughed. Dickens was to play in Sir Edward Bulwer-Lytton's comedy of that name before the Queen at the town house of the Duke of Devonshire on Piccadilly. The Prime Minister, Lord John Russell, had mentioned it when he had discussed the possibility of Dickens assisting with enquiries.

'Changed her mind about me, I wonder?' Dickens continued his theme.

'Alas, no title for you, either. This is a mystery of a peculiarly sensitive nature — a Chinese puzzle, you might say. You read about the Mandarin at the opening ceremony of the

Exhibition?'

'I did — he turned out to be the captain of the Chinese junk. I must say, I did laugh when I read about his kissing her Majesty's feet, but how the devil did he manage it?'

'He was assumed to be a representative of the Emperor. No one questioned him in the crush.'

'Ah, breach of security and your head's on the block, or just transportation?'

'No, thank the Lord. I've been asked to investigate another matter which is connected in the security sense. No expense spared, of course. The Home Secretary was naturally horrified that a stranger approached the Queen — he could have been anyone disguised as a Chinese man. There was a lot of fuss about anarchists and conspirators using the occasion to do something dangerous —'

'Bringing plague and pestilence — fear of the Black Death stalking the land — I read about that M.P., Sibthorpe, making a to-do. But the press reports have all been very good-humoured —'

'And that's the way Sir George wants it, which is why my matter is to be kept absolutely secret. Something else happened on that opening day — a man disappeared, a man of substance, a banker, a man who was formerly a merchant in Canton.'

'China!'

'Exactly, and in the press about Her Majesty there was seen another Chinese man, less gorgeously dressed, and presumed to be an attendant or secretary to the supposed representative of the Celestial Empire — which he wasn't, according to Captain Hesing, who denies most vehemently that he was accompanied. No one knows who he was or where he went — and extensive enquiries have been made to no avail. Hardly surprising, since the descriptions were so vague. You can imagine — little fellow, dark hair, pigtail, Chinese look about him —'

'There are dozens of 'em. I went on the junk to see the show — a more preposterous vessel I have never seen — like a floating toy shop and with the most preposterous crew — all pigtails and pinafores, and I've been to the Chinese Exhibition at Albert Gate. Impossible to find him, I should think.'

'Exactly. Now, all this is highly secret. The papers would have a field day, and every Chinese man in the city would be regarded as a potential assassin.'

'The Canton merchant — they think there's a connection to the missing Chinese man?'

'Might be, but we don't know. However, the Canton man has been missing since May the first. He was an exhibitor — a lot of the exhibits in the Chinese booth were on loan from collectors. That's why he was there on the first day. Now, the odd thing is, that was ten days ago, and it is only two days ago that he was reported missing by his daughter.'

'Where did she think he was?'

'Well, they parted in one of the refreshment booths — they had iced drinks and the daughter was ready to go; her fiancé was to take her home to his aunt's house and then she was going to the seaside. Mr Cornelius Mornay — he's the man from Canton — was to stay in London, where he had business with his bank. He often stayed away from his country house down in Kent. She went away on her holiday. Came back — no letters, no news. And nothing heard of him since.'

'And my role in this very fascinating tale?'

'The Prime Minister spoke very highly of you — mentioned your dining with him.'

'I did last year. I talked to him about the shilling days —

there were those who opposed cheap tickets for the workers, of course, but the Commissioners saw sense.'

'Well, he thinks that since you know a great many of the great folk who were there on that day, you might make some discreet enquiries about Mr Mornay — find out if anyone saw him, knew him, that kind of thing, and if anyone saw the mysterious Chinese man at all.'

'I'm much obliged to Lord Russell, I'm sure. What did Mr Mayne think of this — er — unconventional notion?'

Jones smiled. 'Not much, I could tell, and Sir George was not impressed, either, nor by me, as a matter of fact. They seemed to think that a man of the detective force would be much more likely to succeed. However, Lord John pointed out — very courteously — that the newspapers might very well sniff out detective enquiries, but that a Superintendent from Bow Street would be simply doing a job — of no particular interest to the state — other than the usual interest in crime. And, Mr Dickens, who was not, he regretted, at the opening, would be asking about the opening day of the Exhibition — as any man would. Indeed, he rather thought that Mr Dickens might be writing about it for his periodical magazine.'

'Very wise, Lord John; so I'm just to ask questions — I daresay I can manage that amongst my many other avocations. And as to great folk, Miss Coutts was very much there — swathed in golden silk, according to the newspapers. I can certainly approach her, and now I think of it, Douglas Jerrold and Charles Knight were at the opening — and are in the play at Devonshire House. What could be more natural than that I ask about the Chinese man — he would have appealed to Jerrold, I know. I'll start with them — I've to meet them tomorrow night about the play.'

'I'm obliged, Charles, and there's something else I thought

you might be willing to do.'

'Oh, yes?'

'I'm to report only to the Prime Minister, and I have complete freedom as to how I investigate. I may use such trusty men as I see fit — Sergeant Rogers, for example. Now, I'm thinking that the equally trusty Mr Dickens might be useful in other ways —'

Dickens's eyes gleamed. 'For example?'

'For example, I propose a visit to a banker. Mr Mornay was once a partner in Mornay and Smith of Lombard Street — now Johnstone and Mattinson.'

'Ah, the China Merchants of Hong Kong.'

'Yes, and a Mr Alexander Mattinson, formerly of Canton, is the chairman of the bank and lives in Upper Belgrave Street. I want to see him first to find out the history of the missing man. I should like to know as much as I can about him before I visit the daughter.'

'Any other children?'

'A son who lives abroad.'

'Prodigal?'

'I don't know yet — he works at Antwerp, I'm told.'

'Not come back to search for his missing father?'

'Apparently not. It would seem that the daughter's fiancé, Mr Paul Grex, has been making all the enquiries — relatives, friends, clubs, hospitals — even the river — all the usual things. A young man with connections — son of Sir Marmion Grex. A captain in the Light Dragoons — presently on leave from his regiment.'

'When do you wish to go to see the banker?'

'I have an appointment this afternoon.'

'And how do you explain me?'

'No one could possibly do that. You are appointed by Lord

John as a most confidential adviser to the police, as you were closely involved in the setting up of the Exhibition.'

'I was only appointed to the Central Working Classes Committee to try to widen the access to the Exhibition. Anyway, I called for it to be disbanded because the Commissioners didn't want the lower orders agitating — as if. The Commission's Chairman didn't want Prince Albert to be perceived as heading some sort of democratic movement, so they wouldn't acknowledge us under the Royal Commission. Feeble lot — I tell you —'

Sensing a tirade coming on against the general feebleness of the politicians, Jones interrupted, 'I know, I know, but Mr Mattinson will accept your presence, especially when I explain to him that all is being done most confidentially to find his colleague — the bank won't want a scandal. There were rumblings a few years ago about the opium trade, if you remember.'

'I do. Lord Ashley was very hot against it — and others.'

'There you are, then — they won't want any talk of a China opium trader being kidnapped by the Chinese.'

'You think he was?'

'The idea was discussed with regard to the unknown man thought to be the secretary. And, if it's true, think what a mare's nest that might open up. Questions in Parliament about the trade.'

'Ah — now I remember, there was a debate about India in the House in April. We covered it in the current events bit in *Household Words*. Anyway, an MP called Anstey was waxing hot about the East India Company's role in the government of India. The Company Directors manage the collection of revenue and taxes, and have a monopoly on opium production — and other goods — tea, salt, cotton — but what he said was indefensible about opium was that the Company forces the Indians to cultivate it and buys it at one fifth of the market price. Then the Company and other merchants connive at the smuggling of opium into China. Lord Ashley said something similar a few years back — talked about the religious and moral objections to the trade, though he withdrew his motion against it last time, but there are still a lot of people with a bad conscience about pushing the noxious substance onto the Chinese population.'

'What was the result of this latest debate?'

'Well, Anstey wanted some sort of Commission of Inquiry sent to India, but Lord John expressed his confidence in the East India Company directors, though there's to be a committee of inquiry into the renewal of the Company's charter — fat lot of good that'll do.'

'But add that dimension to the security question, and you can see why it's all to be so secret.'

'Veels within veels, Samivel.'

'Precisely.'

'So, when are we to present ourselves at Upper Belgrave Street?'

'Two o'clock. I'm going home to tell Elizabeth that I have been spared the sentence of death. I'll collect you at two o'clock.'

5: A MARBLE MONUMENT

'I have come a picture of respectability. Heavily disguised as confidential adviser to the Prime Minister.' Dickens's face took on an expression of humility and seriousness, rendered ridiculous by his tapping his nose and winking behind a pair of spectacles.

Jones chuckled. 'Don't — just watch and listen and keep your hands in your pockets. And do without the specs. You can't see anything with them anyway. I'm going to tread carefully. I don't want to suggest any ideas about the opium trade or kidnapping Chinese men. I shall treat the matter as a disappearance — Mr Mornay might be the victim of robbery, that sort of thing.'

A cab took them along the Strand and round St. James's Park up to the elegant, white-stuccoed houses of Upper Belgrave Street and number six.

'Plenty of money in the China trade,' observed Dickens as they waited under the pillared portico. 'A million in opium in each pocket, as someone once said.'

'Disraeli.'

'Mr Jones, you astonish me!'

'Elizabeth quoted it when I was telling her about where we were going.'

Dickens raised an eyebrow. 'Mr Jones, your wife astonishes me even more — she's read Disraeli's *Sybil* when she should be reading one of mine — did she venture an opinion on that work that calls itself a novel?'

'No, she went on to read someone else's — can't think who

now. Thackeray, perhaps.'

Dickens opened his mouth to retort, but a Chinese manservant was opening the door. They were expected and waited in the marble hall while the young man glided away on silent feet to tell his master. Jones looked at the Chinese lacquer cabinets, the huge porcelain jars and paintings on silk, and thought about the Chinese servant. No one had mentioned him.

Dickens contemplated a particularly severe-looking Roman head perched in an alcove. A senator with a cold lofty brow and a long nose under which the marble lips curled in disdain, as if the senator smelt something noxious — a faulty Roman drain, perhaps — he should be in London in high summer.

The Chinese man returned on his silent cat's feet and motioned them towards an open door, bowed slightly, and disappeared along a corridor. They went into the library, where the living replica of the marble bust stood to greet them — *as cold and formidable as the monument*, Dickens thought. He noted a portrait above the mantelpiece — fond of his own image, this tall, rather supercilious man.

Alexander Mattinson expressed his concern about his missing friend. Jones explained the confidential nature of the investigation, emphasizing his understanding that the bank would not wish a great deal of publicity, skilfully introducing Mr Charles Dickens in his role as adviser to the Commissioners, touching on matters of security, and ending by expressing his desire for information about Mr Cornelius Mornay, which, he suggested, might help in his enquiries.

Quite the diplomat, thought Dickens, admiring Jones's tactful deference, though he had noticed Mr Mattinson's disdainful glance at him. Didn't like novelists, maybe. Perhaps he remembered Disraeli's naming James Mattinson — his uncle

— as "one Mr Druggy, fresh from Canton", but Dickens merely bowed and took one of the seats to which Mr Mattinson had invited them.

Watch and listen, he told himself, taking in the face of the banker. The face of a successful man, certainly. A man who was used to command, a hardness about the eyes, which were pale grey under the lofty brow from which the light brown hair grew sparsely, but there was something bad-tempered about the mouth, as if he were not satisfied. Yet, he had immense wealth, so what was the cause of his ill temper? Perhaps it was the inconvenient interruption to the even tenor of his ways by a policeman — and that radical, Charles Dickens, always going on about the poor, and, forsooth, a novelist like Disraeli.

Mattinson's tone was sharp. 'I really must emphasise, Superintendent Jones, that I cannot think of any reason that Mr Mornay might have vanished so mysteriously — one reads of robbery and — well — kidnapping by thieves. I can only assume that Mr Mornay might have met such a fate. It is the only explanation.'

Not quite, thought Jones, but he proceeded courteously. 'It may well be the case, of course — very likely, I'm sure, but I do need to know about Mr Mornay, his contacts, his role in your bank, even his history may help me.'

'I do not see how, but if you insist, I will summarise. I knew Mr Mornay first in Canton, when his was one of the foremost trading companies — dealing in clocks at first. His father, Francis, was a French Huguenot goldsmith of Clerkenwell who made clocks and watches for the Chinese market. It was a very lucrative trade, and he sent Cornelius and his brother, Henry, to look after the business in Canton, where Cornelius met William Johnstone and my uncle, James Mattinson, both of whom expanded the company, trading in raw cotton and opium from India. Cornelius Mornay left Canton in 1830 and the company became Johnstone and Mattinson, eventually moving to Hong Kong, though I was attached to the company before 1830 in Canton. Mr Mornay put his considerable wealth into the banking company Mornay and Smith, which in 1848 became Mattinson and Company, of which I am now the chairman.'

'Mr Mornay is retired?'

'More or less — naturally, he keeps an interest in banking matters, though, as I said, I am the head of the bank. We do meet occasionally to discuss his investments, though Mr Mornay resides in the country at his home, Pole Court, near Faversham in Kent. He leads a quiet life — his health is not good.'

'Where does he stay when he comes up to London?'

'At a hotel — I have dined with him at Brown's sometimes, but I understood enquiries have been made there.'

'Yes, indeed, the initial search instigated by Mr Mornay's daughter led to that hotel. But he had not booked any accommodation there for the first of May. I wonder if you know of any other place he favoured?'

'You have tried the Oriental Club?'

'Yes, we have.'

'Then I am at a loss, Superintendent. I cannot think of where else he might have stayed.'

'You know his family — you mentioned a brother.'

Mattinson looked surprised. 'Dead, many years ago in Paris, on his way back to England.'

'Had he a wife, children?'

'He was a mere twenty-four years when he died.'

'Do you know Mr Mornay's son and daughter?'

'Not well — Miss Mornay lives in the country. Mr Mornay's

wife died several years ago. Miss Mornay is now engaged to be married to Mr Paul Grex, son of Sir Marmion Grex — an old Irish family. She will be Lady Grex.'

'As to May the first — were you at the opening of the Exhibition?'

'I have a season ticket, of course, but I was there by invitation — from my uncle, Mr James Mattinson — the Member of Parliament.'

'You didn't see Mr Mornay there?'

'Superintendent Jones, the crowd was far too thick. I hardly saw anyone beyond the people next to me on the gallery.'

Jones hardly dared ask the next question, but he had to, for he could hardly ask the person whom it concerned. 'And your Chinese manservant, was he with you?'

Mr Mattinson's eyebrows rose. 'Really, Superintendent, what an extraordinary question. Of course not. Why would I take my servant?'

An enamelled clock struck the quarter hour. Mattinson glanced at it and Jones knew that they would get nothing more. He thanked Alexander Mattinson for his time, told him that they would visit Miss Mornay at Pole Court, and he and Dickens retreated into Upper Belgrave Street. The Chinese servant closed the door without a word.

They walked down to Chelsea Road, where they would pick up a cab. 'Well?' Jones asked.

'Really, Superintendent, what an extraordinary question!'

Jones smiled. 'I wanted to know. I could hardly ask the man himself. Not that Mattinson would have admitted it if he had taken him for some nefarious purpose.'

'Suspicious of him?'

'You tell me what you heard and saw.'

'An irritable man — not given to elaborate explanations. On

the terse side, I'd say. He didn't seem overly concerned about a man he'd known for perhaps twenty-five years, and he didn't seem to know much about Mornay's life in London beyond the bank. It was almost as though he put up with Mornay coming in from time to time — how, I wonder, did Mornay and Smith become Mattinson and Company?'

'And why?'

'Some financial skulduggery? Mornay knew something about Mattinson and Mattinson had his Chinese servant bump him off?'

'Lord, Charles, I don't know how we'd find out that. You heard him mention the M.P., Mr James Mattinson — I don't think I'm supposed to uncover a political or financial scandal.'

'What if you do?'

'I report to the Prime Minister, but it's worth a bit of discreet digging. Could Miss Coutts help?'

'Actually, I've just written to Thomson Hankey, deputy-governor of the Bank of England.'

'Loan?'

'I daresay he'd oblige, but, no, he asked me for a favour. I was able to help him and I asked him if I could be of more service. I wrote yesterday, so I could go to see him and make enquiries about the change of proprietors. How much do I tell him? He's of the Liberal persuasion, knows Lord John, too.'

'Then you can tell him about Mornay's disappearance. He'll be discreet, I'm sure.'

'Safe as the Bank of — well, safer, I should say.'

'But let's wait until we have seen the family, and talking of which, there was something else — another question I asked—'

'About the brother — he didn't answer you directly when you asked if the brother, Henry Mornay, had a wife or children.'

'Might be something to ask Miss Mornay about. And Mattinson didn't say whether he knew Cornelius Mornay's son — just the daughter and her forthcoming marriage.'

'Something fishy about the son?'

'Possibly — we'll try to find out. Can you come to Kent tomorrow?'

'I can, and I'll see Charles Knight and Jerrold tomorrow night — find out if they noticed anything, though I doubt it. Mattinson mentioned the crush and you saw it yourself.'

'True, but it's worth asking.'

6: A WOMAN OF FORTUNE

The afternoon train took them to Faversham, from where they hired a trap to take them the three miles to Sheldwich and Pole Court, where Cornelius Mornay had lived in splendid isolation from the village until his disappearance. There were wrought iron gates at the entrance, fastened back beyond two stone pillars topped with rather disgruntled-looking eagles. The long drive was lined with lime trees and went through a large park to the great house.

Dickens whistled. 'My word — Mornay must have made a very sizeable fortune to have bought this. Positively ducal.'

'I wonder if he actually owns it — mortgaged to the bank, maybe, and Mr Mattinson wants it for himself — money, Charles, is a very powerful motive.'

'Or, he has vast debts — suicide, maybe.'

Pole Court was an eighteenth-century house built in the Italianate style of pale limestone. The windows overlooked extensive parkland and woods as far as the eye could see. They alighted from the trap before a grand portico upheld by eight Doric columns under which they went to the glass double front door. There was a bell at the side, which Jones pulled, and they heard the sound of its ringing echoing through the large hall. Dickens stepped back, not wanting to be found peering through the glass. Eventually, a liveried footman came, and Jones explained that Miss Mornay expected Superintendent Jones from Bow Street and Mr Charles Dickens.

The wait gave them the opportunity to look at the portrait over the mantelpiece, which showed an undistinguished, bearded face under white hair, dressed in his conventional suit of black. Who was the man within? He was there, thought Dickens. This was the outer man behind his varnished casing, frozen in time, his hands stilled forever, his face unmoving. Only the globe on a table on which his right hand rested told anything. Dickens could see the vast expanse of China spread out on the painted surface — as mysterious and remote as Mornay himself. The grey eyes were fixed on the viewer, but they weren't telling any secrets.

They were shown into a small, panelled boudoir where Miss Fanny Mornay waited with her fiancé, Mr Paul Grex, who came forward to meet them. Miss Mornay was no beauty, but she was an heiress. No doubt a great one, thought Dickens, noting how handsome was the young Mr Grex. However, her extreme pallor was probably to do with her missing father — a wan face, drawn into plainness by her anxiety. Her eyes were a pale indeterminate colour and her hair, rather unbecomingly frizzy at the temples, was a nondescript brown. She seemed very small and thin beside the tall, robust, blonde-haired Mr Grex.

Jones explained again about the confidential nature of the investigation, how he had been instructed by the Prime Minister to be most discreet in his enquiries, and how Mr Charles Dickens — of whom they had heard, no doubt — they had — a close friend of the Prime Minister, would be assisting Superintendent Jones.

Miss Mornay just looked anxious. Mr Grex seemed to accept this admittedly sketchy explanation, and was eager to express his and Miss Mornay's complete bafflement as to what could have happened to Mr Mornay. Mr Grex had made extensive enquiries. Did Superintendent Jones think that his future father-in-law had been kidnapped and robbed? It was the only possible explanation, he thought, they thought. He glanced at his bride-to-be. Miss Mornay did not speak.

Superintendent Jones was ready to accept that the theory of robbery might well be the case, but he had come to ask Miss Mornay if there was anything she could tell them about the visit to the Exhibition on the opening day which might throw some light onto the mystery. Perhaps Mr Grex would care to outline the events of the day. Had Mr Mornay met any acquaintance in the time preceding the arrival of the Queen, when, no doubt, the family party had looked around the exhibits, including the Chinese booth, where he understood Mr Mornay had exhibited some of his treasures?

Mr Grex could tell them that Mr Mornay had spoken to an old friend, a Captain Thomas Bright, whom he had known in Canton. Both men had looked about the Chinese booth while he and Miss Mornay had wandered about some of the other displays nearby. Miss Mornay had seen a great many Chinese treasures in her life, so she was more interested in the exhibits from France. They had seats in the gallery for the opening ceremony. No, they had not met any other acquaintance. Yes, they had seen the Chinese Mandarin. Mr Mornay had been most intrigued as to his identity. No, Mr Mornay had not commented on any other Chinese man, though Mr Grex thought he would have spoken to the young Chinese man at the exhibition booth. Oh, yes, he remembered, he had seen Mr Mornay speak to Mr Hewitt, the furniture man of Fenchurch Street — he had supplied all kinds of Chinese artefacts.

They had all felt the heat after the opening ceremony and had gone to the refreshment room, after which he and Miss Mornay had parted from Mr Mornay, who had other business in London — and that was all he could tell them.

Dickens had kept his eye on Miss Mornay throughout this

recital. She had mostly looked down, and he had seen her thin fingers working nervously. When she did look up, she looked only at Mr Grex and nodded from time to time.

Jones wanted to ask another question, but it was a delicate one which a lady might not wish to hear. Miss Mornay, however, solved his difficulty. She wondered if they would care for some tea. Dickens said that they would be most obliged, and she went out to order some. Why didn't she send for a maid? There was a bell pull by the side of the mantelpiece.

Jones took his opportunity. 'May I ask, Mr Grex, if Mr Mornay took advantage of the new retirement rooms?' In other words, had Mr Mornay used the new water closets — had he spent a penny? The water closets — referred to in polite society as retirement rooms — cost a penny to use.

'Yes, he did, just before we bought the iced lemonade from Schweppes.'

'You bought the drinks from the counter?'

'I did, and when I returned, Mr and Miss Mornay were sitting together at a table.'

'For how long did you queue?'

'Long enough — ten minutes, I should say.'

'So, you don't know how long Mr Mornay was away in the retiring room?'

'No.'

'I shall have to ask Miss Mornay — it is the only time we know of that Mr Mornay was alone on that day.'

'But he vanished after we had our refreshments.'

'I see that, but I am wondering if he may have met or spoken to someone we don't know about. He may have mentioned a meeting to Miss Mornay.'

'I see — but this is very distressing for Miss Mornay — you do see that.'

'We do,' said Dickens. 'Perhaps I might talk to her privately while you speak further to Superintendent Jones.'

'I hardly think — Mr Dickens —'

'I shall be very careful not to distress her, Mr Grex.'

'I need to know, sir,' Jones said firmly.

Paul Grex looked from Dickens to Jones, saw that the policeman was determined, and nodded his assent.

Dickens went out just as a maid came with a tray, Miss Mornay following. He opened the door to let in the maid, closed it again and turned to a surprised Miss Mornay. 'I wonder, Miss Mornay, if I might speak to you privately. There is something the Superintendent wishes to know. He thinks you might prefer to tell me.'

Her eyes widened. She looked suddenly frightened, but she allowed him to lead her away into the hall where the footman stood.

'Outside, perhaps?'

She nodded and the footman opened the door, and they passed out under the portico and onto a terrace, where they walked in the sunlight. He heard her take several deep breaths, as if she had longed for air. She didn't look at him, but he was aware of her trembling, and her hands still worked together, betraying her unease.

'It is only that Mr Grex tells us that your father went into one of the retiring rooms before you took refreshment, and Mr Jones wishes to know how long you had to wait for him.'

Her face still averted, she said, 'It was so hot — I just wanted to sit down. My father said he would — retire — and find us in the refreshment room. Mr Grex went to buy the drinks and I waited for them. It seemed a long time — I hardly know — perhaps fifteen minutes, perhaps longer. My father came back before Mr Grex.'

'He did not mention having met anyone outside the refreshment room?'

'No, he simply came back and found me at a table.'

'How did he seem? Mr Mattinson, to whom we have spoken, mentioned that your father's health is delicate.'

'He has trouble of the heart. He felt the heat. We both did. He looked very flushed and rather tired. I was worried that he was staying in London. I thought we should come home, but he insisted that I should go with Mr Grex to his aunt's home, and then to the seaside. He said we should not upset the arrangements. When Mr Grex came with the drinks, my father said he felt better and so he departed.'

'And you stayed with Mr Grex?'

'Yes, he went to purchase another drink for me, though I felt better by then. Eventually, we went home. I mean, to Mrs Grex's house.'

Miss Mornay turned and they began to walk back along the terrace. There wasn't much time. Dickens stopped, seeming to look across the park. Miss Mornay stood beside him.

'Your father had not reserved a room at his usual hotel — where was he to stay?'

Miss Mornay stood still. Eventually, she looked up at him, but he could not tell what she was thinking. She looked back at the open front door and then she retraced her steps along the terrace to the end, where she looked out at the dark woods.

Dickens followed. She was going to tell him something, he was sure. He stood with her and waited.

'My father,' she began, 'had secrets. When he worked in London, he did not often come home. I hardly knew him. After my mother died and he retired, I thought — I thought he might not be away so often, but he often went up to London and stayed — for a week or sometimes two as before. I couldn't understand it — nor could my brother. I do not know where he went — only that sometimes he stayed at Brown's Hotel.'

'Not always?'

'He sometimes said that he could not say where he would be.'

'Your brother could not come back to help you over this matter?'

'No — he is in Antwerp — he works — he did not wish to go into the banking house, nor did he wish for an opening in Hong Kong with Johnstone and Mattinson — he — he didn't like —' they heard voices — 'I'm sorry, I can't — find my father, Mr Dickens, find him, I beg you —' Miss Mornay turned to walk back towards the open door.

Dickens didn't follow. She looked exhausted. He saw her go in and heard the murmur of voices. He waited, looking out to the empty park. There was smoke in the woods, a thin stream rising as if from a small fire. It was the only thing that moved in the still landscape.

He turned to look up at the house, imagining the vast rooms inhabited by their silent, meaningless treasures. It was a dead house, like a museum — meant for display, not for family life. Cornelius Mornay was dead, he felt certain. He thought of the house in some distant future, Miss Mornay and her father long gone. Was it possible that her anguish would linger in some corner of that boudoir where the future lady of the house, bent over her embroidery, would feel a momentary chill on a hot day like this, or play a wrong note on the little piano and not know why?

That little boudoir — a little room in all that vast house — where Miss Mornay felt safe, perhaps. She seemed a lonely figure, a mother dead, a distant father, and a brother —

estranged possibly. What was it the brother did not like? He had not returned to seek his missing father. That was odd. Mr Grex had done all that — Mr Grex who seemed too large and vital in that lady's boudoir. She seemed to depend on her fiancé, yet she had told a stranger about her father's life and she had stopped when she heard voices. She had not wanted Mr Grex to know what she was telling. What was it she was sorry about? Something she couldn't tell him, something in her father's life that she was ashamed of?

Jones came out and they walked back down the drive to where the hired trap was waiting. They didn't speak, thinking of windows of the house watching, and of the driver who would be able to hear anything they said.

At the station, they stood at the end of the platform. Dickens told Jones about the mysterious life of Mr Cornelius Mornay, whose daughter felt she hardly knew him, and of her brother who had not wanted to join the bank or go to Hong Kong.

'She didn't finish her sentence. She wanted to tell me something, I'm sure, but I think she was frightened she would be overheard.'

'By Mr Grex?'

'They seem an ill-matched pair. Like many young couples, I suppose, brought together by circumstances. A young man, rather heedless, knowing nothing beyond school and the officer's mess — in debt, perhaps, regarding a wealthy wife as a necessity. A young woman with nothing but her riches to recommend her. The title might well attract her father and the money, his.'

'Hm — money wanting in the Grex family, maybe.'

'There's a deal of money swishing about this case, Mr Jones.'

'There is, but I'm interested now in those minutes before Mornay went into the refreshment room to meet them. Ten?

Fifteen? Twenty? You said she felt it was a long time.'

'When you're waiting, hot and tired, it does seem a long time.'

'Still, he was missing for a length of time, and that's the first I've heard of it. And the first time I've heard of Captain Bright — he shouldn't be hard to find. Mr Hewitt's name came up in connection with the Chinese booth, but I'll see him again.'

'And the retiring room — someone might have seen him —'

'Nearly two weeks ago and thousands of people in and out — I don't know, Charles.'

'Unless there was something unusual — she said she was worried about him. We know he had heart trouble — Mattinson said. He might have needed assistance. He seemed very tired, Miss Mornay told me.'

'I was tired when I went round the Exhibition, but we can ask. There are attendants in the retiring rooms. Someone might remember a man feeling ill. But what about this mysterious life he led? Mattinson said he dined with Cornelius Mornay occasionally. Now, when Mornay was full-time at the bank, I can understand his being in London very often, but afterwards?'

'And why couldn't he tell his daughter where he was staying? What secret life was he hiding? I wondered if she knew something that frightened her — that might ruin her chances. Money worries, perhaps? I mean, if Grex was attracted to her fortune.'

'I asked Mr Grex about other relatives, but he said that there were none, which gave me the opportunity to ask about Mr Mornay's brother. He thought he had heard that there was a brother in Canton, but that he had died years ago, and when I asked him if the brother had any wife or children, he repeated that he knew of no other family.'

'What about Clerkenwell, where the Mornay family came from? His father must have been in a prosperous way in the clock-making business.'

'That's an idea worth following up, and I was thinking that this Captain Bright might know something about the secret life of Mr Cornelius Mornay. I'll bet Mr Hewitt knows him. Hyde Park tomorrow morning?'

'Early, if you will, before the Exhibition opens. Shall I come to Bow Street?'

'No, come up to my house.'

'Top secret, eh?' Dickens tapped his nose.

7: DISAPPEARANCES

At the *Household Words* office in Wellington Street, where Dickens was camping out in what he called his gypsy tent when he needed to be in London, he was reflecting on the conversations he'd had that evening. His whole family was in Broadstairs until October.

He had dined with Charles Knight and Douglas Jerrold. It was Jerrold who had coined the phrase "Crystal Palace" for *Punch* magazine — Mr Punch had had a great deal to say about the Exhibition. Of course, Knight and Jerrold had seen Captain Hesing kow-tow before Her Majesty and they had been much amused. Dickens had said that he had heard that the ambassador from the Celestial Empire had brought his secretary. Had they heard that? They had, but they had not seen a secretary with him.

It was difficult to find out information by asking questions in a general way. He found that he did not quite know how to winkle out information about a missing banker without arousing suspicion, but, he supposed, the fact that they had all enjoyed the story hugely meant that they had seen nothing which aroused their suspicions.

There was not much to tell Sam Jones. That was the trouble with something that was supposed to be hush-hush. You hardly dared voice your thoughts for fear you gave too much away, and you didn't want to lie outright to your closest friends. His friend, Lord Lytton, however, had been a bit more forthcoming on the subject of Sir Marmion Grex — lived a retired life on his estate in Ireland — much embarrassed, it was said, son in the army, engaged to a fabulously wealthy heiress, daughter of a banking man whom nobody knew. And that was about it — the nugget about Sir Marmion Grex's financial embarrassments was useful, though. Certainly a motive for marriage — perhaps a motive for murder.

The more Dickens thought about Cornelius Mornay, the more he thought that it was something in the man's own life that had brought about his disappearance — something in that secret life he carried on in London. Perhaps he was dead — but he couldn't have died at the Exhibition. He must have gone voluntarily to meet someone — someone he knew — someone who had killed him? Otherwise, why had he not reappeared? If he had been ill and collapsed somewhere, he would have been found, surely. An innocent somebody would have reported Mornay's death.

And he must have gone somewhere out of the way, or a body would have been found by now. Even if he had fallen into the river, returning to wherever he had stayed, he would have been washed up somewhere after nearly two weeks. And Sam had said that enquiries had been made about that — there were always bodies turning up. *Found Drowned*, as the newspapers had it. Like that poor fellow from the *Mercury* on Broadstairs beach. Dickens wondered if he had been identified.

John, his manservant, had left some letters. Dickens opened the first and saw that it was from Mr John Macgregor, barrister and teacher at the Field Lane Ragged School — wanting money, he supposed, and he deserved it. Dickens had written an article about the school in its early days, hoping that it would gather support for those children too ragged, too wretched, too filthy and forlorn to be welcomed in any other place — and his article had helped improve matters, even at Field Lane. The ragged school had moved to larger premises in Farringdon Road, but money would always be wanting. When he had first visited the classrooms, as close and foetid as Fagin's den, he had felt how little could be done, but Lord Ashley, Mr Macgregor, Miss Coutts, and others had determined to battle on. The shoe-shine brigade had been Macgregor's idea.

Wash, brush-up and shoe-shine — the words came back to him from an advertisement for the Exhibition. There could have been a shoe-shine boy in the retiring room — if that's where Cornelius Mornay had actually gone. Smike! Dickens had sponsored one of the boys — he had been nicknamed Smike by the others.

Mr John Macgregor had been delighted, not knowing that it was more than just a kindness. Dickens was doing it for himself — a secret gift to the boy from Warren's Blacking. Smike, his own shoe-black boy with his pot of blacking, no doubt from Warren's blacking factory at Hungerford Stairs. Later, in Chandos Street, where the boy Charles Dickens had sat at the window, pasting on the labels and tying up the string. He could do it now, he supposed, tie up so many bottles in five minutes — he couldn't remember how many, but passers-by would stop to look and point. His father had come in once and that boy had wondered how his father could bear it. Well, John Dickens had borne it, and now he was dead. They had never spoken of his childhood labour again.

Do what you can for the living. He thought of Smike — a bright lad — wanting to get on — a sharp lad who might have seen something if he were one of those working at the Exhibition.

Now, while Sam was seeking out Mr Hewitt at the Chinese booth, he could have a look in those retiring rooms. And, he remembered, there was a retiring room for the exhibitors. Surely the Mornays had used that — that would be the place to start.

His eye went to the pile of articles submitted to *Household Words* — there should be something from Mrs Gaskell. There was: "Disappearances", it was titled. Coincidence. That would be worth reading.

What an extraordinary tale the article began with. A most respectable working man had left his old father in the sunshine and had gone haymaking with his wife — when they returned, the old gentleman had vanished. Only his chair remained. He could not have walked away, for he was paralysed. Extensive searches had been made, but the old man was never found.

It would be exactly suited to the journal — a curious and interesting tale. And how coincidental. It was late, and Dickens was exhausted. He could do the rest tomorrow, after he had been to the Exhibition. He went to bed to ponder on the mystery of the old man and to think if Cornelius Mornay would be another such case — never found. A man who had bade his daughter farewell and walked out of his life — or been taken out of it.

8: THE OLD COVE

There was a policeman already at the turnstile at the entrance. He recognized Superintendent Jones, and they walked in, parting at Osler's dazzling crystal fountain perfumed with eau de cologne. The Chinese booth was situated in the right-hand walkway next to the exhibits from Tunis. Dickens would come to meet Jones there.

Dickens turned the other way to walk along the north transept towards another fountain and the Coalbrookdale iron gates, behind which he knew there was the exhibitors' dining room and a gentleman's retiring room. There was no one there yet, but he thought of something else. The refreshment area into which he'd gone when he'd visited was at the end of an aisle by the fountain he'd just passed. There were tables in various open courts. The Mornays might have gone there as they were feeling the heat and there were retiring rooms for ladies and gentlemen.

Dickens's boy Smike was not in the retiring room, but he found one Toby Quick, a sharp-looking lad who knew who Dickens was and greeted him cheerfully.

'Lookin' fer Smike, sir?'

'I am — I was wondering if he had been working here on the opening day — on May the first.'

'Not Smike, sir, I woz workin' 'ere that day — chosen by Mr Macgregor. See, I'm the best an' so I gets the best spot. Dint see the Queen, though, but I sees the 'orses an' carriages an' the soldiers.'

'You didn't come across anyone in here who looked ill at all? I'm thinking of a gentleman who was taken ill on that day — a friend of mine.'

'Not in 'ere, sir, but I sees a cove outside when I goes fer somethin' to eat — the speeches an' that woz over an' the Queen 'ad gone, so I goes out ter try ter cool off —'

'Are you able to come out with me now to show me where he was?'

'Yer can ask the gent wot's in charge. Best tell 'im yer wants me to 'elp yer with somethin'.'

Dickens approached the superintendent of the retiring room and gained permission. Toby took him out through the exit he had used on the first day and into the park. The boy led him to the trees and told him of an old cove whose hat had fallen off and whom another man seemed to be assisting.

'Can you describe them?'

'Old cove — gent, as I said, tallish, white 'air, long 'air, red in the face — 'ad 'is hand to 'is throat — like 'e couldn't get 'is breath. Not steady on 'is pins — leanin' on a stick. An', I remember, 'e 'ad a beard.'

'And the other man?'

'Dunno, sir — just ornery —' Toby screwed up his eyes, trying to remember. 'Not as tall as the old cove — a jacket — sort of a dark colour an' dark trousers. Dint really take much notice 'cept ter think 'e woz doin' the toff a good turn. He gave the old cove a drink an' off they goes. There woz 'undreds, thousands o' folk, sir — it woz just a minnit or two.'

'Was he wearing a hat?' Dickens was thinking of a top hat — a hat that might give an indication of the kind of man who had helped the old cove.

'Dint notice, Mr Dickens.'

'You didn't see where they went?'

'Nah, jest sat down over there ter eat me pie.'

Dickens gave Toby a shilling and was rewarded with a grin

before the boy went back inside to prepare for his customers, and Dickens went back inside to find Jones at the Chinese booth.

'Let's get out of here,' Jones said, 'and we'll talk somewhere quiet out of this infernal heat and these crowds.'

'I know — the whole thing makes me feel exhausted. I can't take it in — it's all too much. I know where we could go — St George's Chapel up on Hyde Park Terrace, just in front of the burial ground — the corpses won't tell your secrets.'

They walked up to Cumberland Gate, weaving their way through the crowds that were coming in, out of the park and along to Hyde Park Terrace. Inside the chapel, a gloomy little place that smelt of damp and of the grave, it was blessedly cool, if not blessedly consoling. Not a place you would wish to take farewell of your nearest and dearest, but it was quiet and deserted. They sat in a pew and Dickens reported his conversation with Toby Quick. 'Could be,' was his conclusion.

'Well,' said Jones, 'we know that Mornay was quite tall, white-haired and bearded — wore his hair quite long, so Mr Grex told me, and his daughter said he wasn't feeling well, so did he go under the trees to rest and meet someone who took him away? This fellow that Toby Quick saw?'

'Mornay might have known him, I suppose, someone who was at the opening — not one of the dignitaries — a season ticket holder —'

'Thirty thousand of 'em all pouring in at nine o'clock, all eager to find a good vantage point. And thousands, hundreds of thousands of onlookers in the Park. Someone could have slipped in, I don't doubt, if he was dressed as a gentleman.'

'Someone from his country home, maybe? Someone with a grudge?'

'Mayne told me that Cornelius Mornay was involved in a law

case — his gamekeeper was attacked by a couple of poachers who gave him a bad beating. They were sentenced to seven years' transportation — couple of years back. Mornay gave evidence. I'll get Rogers onto that — see if there's anyone in the village of Sheldwich who knows anything that might suggest someone harbouring a grudge.'

'What did Mr Hewitt tell you?'

'He spoke to Mornay and he saw him with a Captain Bright, for whom we'll enquire at the Oriental Club, but there's something else — a neighbour of yours —'

'Mine?'

'A Mr John Fullerton of York Gate — know him?'

'I don't, I'm afraid.'

'Pity — he was formerly a merchant in Canton.'

'Another one — and he was at the Exhibition?'

'No, it's more interesting — he has a Chinese servant who is not really a servant anymore. A man called Li Shen, who runs Mr Fullerton's farms in Minster in Kent — married to an English woman, has children, and is quite a pillar of the community. Mr Fullerton does not come to London very often, but when he does, Mr Li Shen accompanies him, and it was Mr Li Shen whom Mr Hewitt saw with Cornelius Mornay at the Exhibition. Dressed, however, in the clothes of an English gentleman — so not the mysterious Chinese man, but maybe the man seen by Toby Quick.'

'He didn't say a Chinese man.'

'But the connection is there — to Canton.'

Number 23 York Gate, overlooking Regent's Park was a large, handsome white stuccoed house, and as they arrived, a gentleman was standing at the top of the steps, carrying a bag. There was a carriage waiting.

'Mr Li Shen, I imagine,' Dickens observed as the man came down towards them.

Jones approached to ask if he might speak with him about Mr Cornelius Mornay, whom they had been told was an acquaintance of Mr Li Shen.

'He is,' Mr Shen said, 'but I'm afraid I cannot delay now. I am going home to Minster in Kent — my train leaves very soon.' His English was very good, although Dickens detected a slight foreign intonation as he looked at the pleasant face of the Chinese man whose hair was cut short.

Jones introduced himself as a Superintendent from Bow Street and explained that Mr Mornay had been taken ill on the opening day of the Exhibition, had not been seen since, that his family was most concerned, and he, Superintendent Jones, was making enquiries of friends and acquaintances who had seen Mr Mornay at the Exhibition. Mr Hewitt, who supervised the Chinese booth, had directed them to Mr Li Shen.

'I see — that is concerning, but I can only say that Mr Mornay seemed just himself when I spoke to him. He complained of the heat and the crowds... I don't know what else...' He looked at the waiting carriage.

'It is rather urgent, Mr Shen. I would be much obliged if you could delay your departure and speak to us inside the house —'

Mr Shen looked at Dickens then. 'I know you, sir, I have seen you before — you live about here?'

Jones stepped in. 'This is Mr Dickens, who is assisting me.'

'You know Mr Mornay?'

'I know his family,' Dickens replied — somewhat evasively.

Mr Shen looked at Jones again. 'I don't know how I can help—'

'If you could spare some time.'

Mr Shen went to speak to the driver of the carriage and let

them into the house, where they saw that in the hall pieces of furniture were covered in dust sheets. 'Mr Fullerton, my employer, will not return to London. His health is very delicate. I will be joining him in Dover, where he has gone for the sea air. I am shutting up this house. It is to be sold.'

They stood in the hall. Mr Shen did not invite them further into the house. 'What do you wish to know?' he asked.

'You didn't see Mr Mornay outside in the park?'

'No, only at the Chinese booth — we spoke only for a few minutes.'

'You knew Mr Mornay in Canton?'

'No, sir, I did not. I was in the service of an East India Army Major. I came to England with him before I entered Mr Fullerton's employment.'

'Mr Fullerton knew Mr Mornay in Canton, then?'

'Yes, Mr Fullerton worked for the East India Company, but he returned to England many years ago — more than twenty years. His health was not good. Mr Fullerton sometimes visited Mr Mornay at Pole Court, but not in recent years. As I said, Mr Fullerton is not a well man.'

'But you had met Mr Mornay?'

'A few times. I recognized him at the Exhibition. He knew me and we spoke of the exhibits he had loaned, but that is all I can tell you. It was just a passing encounter. I know very little about him except that he established the bank in Lombard Street, which is now Mr Mattinson's, but he is retired now.'

'You know Mr Mattinson?'

'Not at all. He is Mr Fullerton's banker.' Somewhere, a door banged. Mr Shen looked along the corridor. 'The cleaning woman — just leaving. She came to finish her work in the kitchen. We do not come up to London very often, but Mr Fullerton knew that my wife and family wished to see the

Exhibition — I have two unmarried daughters still. My eldest son serves in the East India Company Army; my second son is an army surgeon. I have been here for a few days to shut up the house.'

Dickens observed Mr Shen while he was speaking. The smooth skin gave no indication of his age, but he must be in his forties, he thought. His sons were grown up, and he had been in England for perhaps thirty years. His dark eyes gave nothing away, and his expression didn't change even when the door banged. A smiling face, a pleasant face, but somehow unreadable. His voice was low, the words like flowing water. Keeping his secrets, Dickens wondered.

Jones was asking if Mr Shen knew Mr Mornay's family, but, no, he did not. He knew that Mr Mornay had a son and daughter who lived with him in the country. He was very sorry he could not help more, but he must be on his way to Minster. He did not think — in answer to Jones's question — that Mr Fullerton could assist, for he rarely went into society and had not, as he had explained, seen Mr Mornay for many years.

Mr Shen still smiled, but Jones knew he would get no further and he and Dickens went out into the hot street.

'Your thoughts?' asked Jones.

'He showed the right amount of concern — pleasant, amiable, but hard to read. An unusual story, but it could all be true — he knows Mr Mornay slightly and noticed nothing out of the way.'

'Probably nothing to be gained from him. Captain Bright, then. Who do you know at the Oriental Club?'

'Why don't I just go in and ask? I could do it now.'

'Right — I'll send a message to Sergeant Rogers to go to Sheldwich and see what he can find out about those men who assaulted the game-keeper.'

9: CHINESE WHISPERS

Money, thought Dickens as he went up the steps of the Oriental Club in Hanover Square. He pictured the old men with faded tanned faces, burnt long ago by the suns of India — and China — folded into deep armchairs in front of fires which never warmed them, eating their hot curries in the sumptuous dining room, exchanging wistful stories of tiger hunts and shooting jackals, and counting their fortunes in their heads.

He offered his card to the porter whose yellowish pallor spoke more of London fogs. 'Mr Charles Dickens to see Captain Bright.'

The porter went away to see if the captain was in. Dickens waited in the hall, hoping that no one who knew him came out. Henry Austin, his brother-in-law, was a member. Thackeray dined here occasionally. His father had died in India and his stepfather had been a Major in the East India Company Army. It would be embarrassing if Captain Bright emerged with someone he knew and he had to explain that there was no appointment.

He concentrated on the Duke of Wellington's nose in the portrait above the mantelpiece and thought of the noble Duke looking down it at the Chinese Mandarin kow-towing at his feet, and he thought about Sam's responsibility for this case — Sam couldn't afford to fail, that was certain, and it was his own job to assist where he could. What was he to say to Captain Bright, though? He supposed he would have to explain some imaginary connection to Cornelius Mornay.

The porter returned with the news that Captain Bright was not in the club. Dickens apologized — perhaps he had mistaken the time of his appointment — very foolish of him. Would the porter have any idea of when Captain Bright might come in? Ah, for dinner, this evening — no, Mr Dickens would not be able to return. Might the porter know where Captain Bright could be found?

Dickens waited hopefully. He could hardly ask for Bright's address, but the porter was obliging enough to tell him that the captain went to the Jerusalem Coffee House most days. 'To hear the seafaring news, sir.'

Cowper's Court, Cornhill then. Dickens went to find a cab.

The subscription room of the Jerusalem Coffee House was famed for the availability of news and shipping intelligence from all over the east: Canton, Hong Kong, Macau, Penang, Singapore, Calcutta, Bombay. The merchants and sea captains gathered there to hear of the arrivals of ships and cargoes — and fortunes — of departures, pirates, mutinies, tempestuous seas, storms — *ships of rich lading wrecked on the narrow seas*, as that of Antonio, the Merchant of Venice, whose ship had been wrecked on the Goodwins like the *Mercury* a few days ago. Dickens wondered again about that body on the beach and who he might be.

Murder, too. Dickens paid his cab driver at Cornhill near the sign for the Jerusalem Coffee House. The Salt Hill murder. In 1845, John Tawell, having poisoned his lover with Prussic acid, had fled from the scene of the crime to London and the police had traced him to the Coffee House. He had been hanged by Calcraft — who had made a sickening business of it with his use of too long a rope, which had strangled the prisoner. That gave Dickens a jolt and he paused at the door. Hanging. Was he looking for a murderer?

The place was crowded, smelling of tobacco smoke, coffee,

brandy, and gravy; men stood or sat with their newspapers, deep in clipper ships for sale, chronometers, coal, capstans, captains, missing mariners, missing ships, stocks, shares, exports and imports. Snatches of talk came to him on the waves of smoke: sugar was coming in at twenty-six shillings a ton; *The Paradise* had sailed for Calcutta; *The Coromandel* was in from Macau; *The Emperor of China* had reached the downs from Hong Kong; a tea merchant had gone bankrupt; long timber was eleven shillings and ninepence a load; *The Confucius* was missing in China waters — a solitary man turned away at this and stumbled out. *Story there*, thought Dickens, momentarily distracted by the haggard face.

Just as he was thinking that he would ask one of the dextrously skimming waiters about Captain Bright, a heavy hand clapped him on the back and a voice boomed, 'Mr Charles Dickens.' So much for discreet inquiries. He turned. Ah, he should have known. The well-named Captain Heavisides, whom he knew in Ramsgate. A good many people turned to look at the sound of his name. Dickens smiled vaguely at faces he did not know.

'Up from Ramsgate, Mr Dickens. My son's ship, *The Ariel*, has just come in from Calcutta so *The Shipping News* tells me. Safe and sound.'

'I am heartily glad for that, sir.'

'Rum, Mr Dickens, you'll take a drop?'

'By all means — let us sit down — over there.' There was a table just vacated in a corner. *Get him out of hearing*, thought Dickens, *and ask about Bright. He might know him.* Heavisides was often up in London, and this was his favourite haunt.

Captain Heavisides ordered the rum and talked about his son, a lieutenant on a merchant ship, and at last, asked Dickens what brought him to the coffee house. 'Going off to sea?' he asked, his burnished face beaming.

Dickens laughed and told him that he was looking for Captain Thomas Bright, whom Heavisides pointed out and offered to introduce him to.

Captain Bright was delighted to meet Mr Dickens and the talk was of sons and sailors and ships and seas, and eventually of China — to which country Dickens navigated the old sailor, all the while hoping that Captain Heavisides would go there himself, or at least to the docks to greet the good ship *Ariel* — of the Blackwall line, Heavisides told them — bringing raw cotton, indigo, spices, tea. At long last, he looked at his watch, an object fastened to something which might have been mistaken for an anchor chain, and departed to meet his son.

Captain Thomas Bright turned his face to Dickens — the face of a seafaring man, lines like a map of the world criss-crossing his cheeks and forehead, deepening at the eyes which were a pale faraway blue as if bleached by the eastern sun. They were wise eyes in a wise face. 'You wished to speak to me of something?' he asked.

'I do, sir. It is about Mr Cornelius Mornay — a confidential matter.'

Captain Bright looked wary. Did he know about the missing man? However, Bright asked, 'About his family?'

'No, no — I am afraid that he is missing. He vanished on the first day of the Exhibition — you spoke to him.'

'I did speak to him — but Mr Dickens, what is your interest?'

Dickens explained the details of Cornelius Mornay's day at the Exhibition, his daughter's holiday, his failure to return home. He referred to Captain Hesing's unorthodox appearance before the Queen, the young Chinese man who was thought to be his secretary but could not be found.

Captain Bright smiled. 'I think I see — the government wishes to keep quiet the disappearance of a merchant from Canton.'

'Yes, and Superintendent Jones of Bow Street has been asked to make discreet enquiries — with my help. The Prime Minister is a close acquaintance of mine. It was thought that I might —'

'Find out things that a policeman could not.'

'Quite so — and I met Mr Mornay's daughter — she is most worried about her father. I think she is glad that the matter should be investigated with discretion. She told me that her father had secrets — that his life in London was a mystery to her.'

Captain Bright gave him a sharp look. 'How did you find me?'

'Mr Hewitt at the Chinese booth at the Exhibition saw you speaking to Mr Mornay. I wondered if you might be able to tell me about him. I went first to the Oriental Club.'

'Ah, the porter told you where I would be. Let us walk, Mr Dickens, down to the river.'

They passed out of Cowper's Court into Birchin Lane, down towards the Thames. Neither spoke. Captain Bright walked swiftly — he knew where he was going — and with a roll in his gait like a man on the deck of a ship. Dickens kept up with him until they slowed and went down to Old Shades Pier, where they stood to watch the steamers chugging away to Greenwich and beyond, to Europe. Further down across the river was St Saviour's Dock; he could see the entrance which led into the notorious Jacob's Island where Bill Sikes had died by hanging, and he and Superintendent Jones had ventured across the filthy stagnant water in pursuit of a very real murderer.

The captain gazed down towards St. Katharine's Dock, where the sails and tall masts of some ocean-going ships could be seen in the Pool of London. 'Nothing beats sail,' he said. 'All the way to Canton and not a puff of steam — just the wind and the stars and the swell of the sea.'

'Canton,' Dickens murmured, imagining the word carried away on the wind into the estuary and away to the east, but the captain heard.

'You want to know about Cornelius Mornay.'

'It may help.'

'It may not. I will tell you about Canton in those early days of Mornay and Sons. We lived as single men during the trading months between September and March at the factories — that's what the Chinese called them — the Thirteen Factories, warehouses, really. Then we had to leave — by order of the Cohong merchants. They were the Chinese who controlled our trade into China from Canton. We went to Macau to spend our summer months. It could be — it was — a lonely life, and there were many men who took — mistresses, sometimes wives, Portuguese or Chinese ladies, but marriage was frowned upon. A blind eye was turned to mistresses.'

Captain Bright turned to the river again, perhaps remembering someone — a delicate girl like a flower whom he had loved and left. He continued, 'There were children, of course. Cornelius Mornay's brother, Henry, married a Chinese wife who had a son, Francis Hope —'

The dead brother about whose wife or family no one knew, thought Dickens, but he did not comment. The captain would tell his story in his own thoughtful way.

'The boy was sent to England to be educated for the Indian Civil Service — out of the way, you see, for Henry Mornay, his father, was forced to resign from the company in 1815. It was still Mornay and Company then. Henry Mornay died at sea on his way home. I don't know what happened to his Chinese wife.'

'Mr Cornelius Mornay?' Dickens asked tentatively.

'Did not marry his Chinese mistress, but he had three children, born before he married his English wife, two sons and a daughter, who were sent to England in the charge of a former missionary, Miss Anne Palmer — the arrangements made by the new partner, Mr James Mattinson. The company always looked after the affairs of its partners.'

Affairs, thought Dickens, *apt word*. 'Did Mr Mornay see his children when he returned to England?'

'I cannot tell you that. I knew Mr Mornay twenty years ago. I met him very occasionally at the Oriental Club, but we did not talk of those things, and I saw him at the Exhibition, as you know.'

'How did he seem? His daughter was anxious that he was not well. Heart trouble, she said.'

'He complained of the heat, that is all. We talked of the exhibits he had loaned — a matter of minutes.'

'Mr Hewitt at the Chinese booth mentioned a Mr Li Shen.'

'I know him, of course, and Mr Fullerton, formerly of the East India Company, for whom Mr Li Shen is land agent. Mr Shen is married to an English lady and manages Mr Fullerton's farms. Mr Fullerton is an invalid who lives a retired life. He rarely comes to London and Mr Shen is very much with him, I believe.'

'Is there anyone else who could tell me about the children? Mr Alexander Mattinson, for example?'

'You have met him?'

'I have.'

'Then you will know that he won't tell you unless he is

forced to, and I hardly think your policeman will be able to do that. Mr Mattinson is a powerful man — chairman of his own bank, a director of the Bank of England, and with powerful political connections. Mr James Mattinson is a Liberal Member of Parliament. And a great friend of the government.'

No, thought Dickens, *Sam could not afford to embroil himself in political matters* — he had been ordered to be discreet, and though Lord John, the Prime Minister, was an honourable man from what Dickens knew of him, his Liberal party was not entirely secure. He would not want awkward questions in Parliament from the Conservative side about his own members. And since Alexander Mattinson was a director of the Bank of England, it might be unwise to go making enquiries of the Deputy-Governor, Mr Hannay. Dickens shuddered at the thought of Sam as the scapegoat policeman who had far exceeded his duties. Still, the matter of the children was of the greatest interest, and he had the name of the missionary lady. It was something.

He was about to shake Bright's hand and thank him when the captain said, 'Francis Hope, Henry Mornay's son, did go to India. However, he did not stay with the civil service. He is a tea dealer now in Fenchurch Street. He is married to the daughter of Mr Bathe, proprietor of the London Tavern.'

'I know him, of course — I have attended many dinners there. Indeed, only in April I was…' Dickens paused there, for that night, the night of April 14th, when he had finished speaking, his friend John Forster had come to tell him that the baby, Dora, had died suddenly, of convulsions. He felt the east wind off the river then and shivered.

'Mr Dickens?'

'Oh, I do beg your pardon. I was thinking back — yes, yes, I know Mr Bathe very well, and, of course, I have met his daughter, though I cannot recall her husband.'

'He might be able to help you, though I do not know if there are any connections between Mr Mornay and his brother's son. It would be as well, Mr Dickens, if you could avoid mentioning my name if you do see him. I have told you what I know for the sake of Mr Cornelius Mornay who is missing, and to whose secret life you alluded, but I should not like Mr Hope to believe that I have told his secrets.'

'Indeed, I see that, Captain Bright. I will tell Superintendent Jones what you have told me, and he will work out a way of pursuing this. I am obliged to you, sir, for your confidence.'

Dickens left Captain Bright still staring out at the river where the water glittered under the summer sun, revolving many memories, no doubt.

Memory. That evening in April, seared into his memory, and that dream of a child crying. Dickens thought of those children sent to a strange land, torn from their mothers. How lost and bewildered they must have been. Unless Cornelius Mornay had kept in contact with them.

He made his way to find a cab and directed the driver to Bow Street. Then he changed his mind. He shouldn't go asking for Sam at Bow Street. He didn't actually know where Sam was, and Sergeant Rogers was in Kent pursuing the tale of the attackers on Mr Mornay's gamekeeper. No help from him.

'Norfolk Street,' he told the cabbie. Sam might well be at home. He hoped so — his own heart quickened with the cab wheels. Three secret children.

10: CHINESE CHARACTERS

'Keep the cab.' Sam Jones had come out of his house just as Dickens was paying the driver. He turned to see Sam already opening the door of the cab and telling the cabbie, 'Waterloo Pier, and quick as you can.'

Dickens stood on the pavement, gaping as the driver took up his reins again, and he heard the hooves ring on the stones of the street.

'No time to hang about — get in.'

Dickens stepped in and the cab wheeled round so fast that he hardly had time to close the door. He sat down heavily as the cab rolled on at a smart trot. 'In a hurry, I take it.'

Jones grinned. 'To Wapping to see our friend Inspector Bold of the River Police. I had a message — about a corpse in the river. Well, it's not there now, o' course.'

'Dear Lord — not Cornelius Mornay?'

'Don't know yet — unidentified, but a gentleman and with something interesting in his mouth which prompted Bold to send a message by John Gaunt — my favourite godson. He is very well, by the way.'

'I am always interested in your favourite godson, Mr Jones, but not at the moment — what was in the mouth?'

'Some coins and a piece of filthy rag.'

'That's a grim idea.'

'Chinese coins —'

'Good Lord, that is interesting.'

'John brought one to show me. Round, made of copper, with a square hole in the middle surrounded by Chinese characters.'

'But how was it that Johnno came to you?' Dickens always

69

called him Johnno after John of Gaunt, and Gaunt, a most amiable young man, always enjoyed the joke, but then he admired Mr Dickens, who had been involved with them in a case about a murdered sea captain.

'Inspector Bold knew that there was a hunt on for a Chinese man. I spoke to him when I went down with Superintendent Pierce — he was in charge of security at the Exhibition — so when the body was found, Bold, I'm glad to say, thought to ask my advice as to whether it was worth reporting to Pierce. I sent John back with a message for Bold to wait for me. He doesn't know about Mornay, of course.'

'After all this time, Sam, will you be able to identify — or to ask someone to? That'll be difficult.'

'I know — we only saw that portrait, but there might be something on the clothes, tailor's label, handkerchief, shoes.'

On the steamer to Wapping, Dickens told Jones what he had found out from Captain Bright about Cornelius Mornay's Chinese mistress and his children, and Francis Hope, the tea dealer of Fenchurch Street.

'Son of the brother Mr Mattinson had nothing to say about,' Jones said.

'Exactly — I know Mr Bathe of the London Tavern and have met his daughter, but Captain Bright did not want his name mentioned. Didn't want to be known to be revealing family secrets. I'll have to think of a way in — other than buying orange pekoe or something.'

'And we must find the lady missionary, Miss Palmer. Shouldn't be too difficult.'

'Not so much as telling two lots of children that their father is dead.'

'Maybe,' said Jones. 'Let's see the body first and think about the rest later.'

Dickens and Jones got off the steamer at Wapping Stairs and walked to the police office, where burly Inspector Bold greeted them as old friends, for they had all, including Constable John Gaunt, worked together on the case of the murdered captain.

'You'll want to see the body first, and then I'll show you the clothes.'

At the end of a yard behind the police office, there was a square brick building where the drowned bodies were taken when they were given up by those who had found them. There were those, Dickens knew, who made a profession of dragging bodies from the river. Nearly always, nothing was found of any value on the corpses, but no one could prove that coins or watches or jewels had been stolen. It was always possible that the pockets had been emptied by the rush of the water.

Within this somewhat makeshift mortuary, the air was chill and damp; it smelt of the river and of putrefaction, of course, and was only lit by Inspector Bold's bull's eye lamp, which cast a feverish light on the sheet-covered thing on a rough trestle table and threw their shadows on the walls, where they hung crouching over the table like hunchbacked witches. *The three Fates*, thought Dickens, *the Apportioners*. Who, he wondered, had apportioned this death at this time?

Inspector Bold was characteristically brisk and called Gaunt to bring in his lamp. The shadows diminished and Bold pulled back the sheet to reveal what had once been a man until the water and the fishes, and the rats had done their work. The face was horribly bloated and a livid green in colour, a greenish blue which they could see on the neck and chest, all of which, Jones knew, was evidence that the body had been in the water for some time, but it would not be possible to know yet if he had been dead before being in the water. The surgeon had yet to do his full post-mortem.

As to identification, the face no more resembled the portrait than a hideous gargoyle, but the hair was long to the collar, the dead man had a beard, all tangled and muddy from the river, and he had been tall — about five feet ten inches. *He was not a young man*, Jones thought; the hair and beard were a dirty white.

'Thank you, Inspector Bold,' Jones said, covering the face again. 'Let's have a look at the clothes.'

They went out of the mortuary, closing the door on the man who may or may not have been Cornelius Mornay. Inspector Bold took them into a room where there was a black frock coat, a pair of black trousers, much torn and stained with water, and what had been a white shirt. There was a torn black silk cravat.

'No watch or purse or jewel?' asked Jones.

'Nothing on him except the coins Gaunt told you about. I questioned the man who brought him in — known to us, of course. Jonah Crabbe — makes a living from what he fishes out, but I doubt he'd do murder and leave Chinese coins in the mouth. He might have taken money, but there's no way I can find out that.'

Jones and Dickens examined the clothes. Jones thought of all the frock-coated, black-trousered men he had seen at the Exhibition. He fingered the cloth — expensive — and looked for the tailor's label: *John Graves of Covent Garden*. He noted, too, that there were stains on the coat — water, probably. And he saw that the undergarments were stained.

'You know who he is?'

'I know who he might be. I can tell you the name, but it is not to be asked about — only if you hear it spoken, and then you can send to me. It is a confidential matter, I'm afraid, and I'm to investigate with the utmost discretion.'

'I see — well, I don't — but I know you, Superintendent Jones, and I'll accept what you say.'

'The name is Cornelius Mornay, and he has been missing for two weeks.'

'I don't know the name, but I will listen for it. There is something — the rag which stopped his mouth has dried out. Here.'

Jones took the rag and examined it. There were brownish stains — not water, he thought, something darker, the colour of treacle. Blood, perhaps. It was just a piece of rough cotton with a tear at the corner, as if it had been ripped from a bigger piece.

'I'll have to take all this, and the coins,' he said.

Inspector Bold handed them over. Dickens and Jones looked at them. Dickens looked at the Chinese characters. What message did they have? They told of murder, he thought, and hatred, perhaps. He saw for a moment the dark shadow of a man opening his victim's mouth and placing the coins there, then shoving a dirty rag in to stop up the coins. Cold-blooded.

'Chinese hereabouts?' asked Jones.

'A few — mostly sailors come off the ships, but there are a few shopkeepers scraping a living, selling bits of marine stuff. There's a so-called tobacconist in Bluegate Fields —'

'So-called?'

'Opium for the Chinese sailors and others wanting to smoke themselves into a stupor. Owner is one Cheng — lives with an English woman — one daughter. No violence — they're all too drugged up. Want me to ask about?'

Jones put the coins in his pocket. 'Not yet — until I'm sure who he is. The body will have to be taken to University College Hospital. I'll arrange for collection — late tonight when it's dark. Can you be here at eleven o'clock? Is there a way out by the yard?'

'Very cloak and dagger, Mr Jones,' Bold observed.

Jones smiled at him. 'I know, but I can't take any risks. What can you tell your men?'

Bold smiled back. 'Toff — some high-up — family don't want a scandal. That happens sometimes, especially when a body's found hereabouts. Suicide most like, I'll say. No, I didn't get a name.'

'You might tell Gaunt — he'll be discreet for —'

'Your sake, I know, and so will I, Mr Jones. I'll be outside the mortuary at eleven.'

'Until then, and I'm most obliged to you, Inspector.'

With that, they bade farewell to Inspector Bold and went to take a steamer back to Waterloo Bridge.

'Do you know, Sam, this case frightens me — if that is Cornelius Mornay, of course — who brought him to Wapping, of all places? And the coins in the mouth? Some ritual thing, do you think?'

'Chinese, you're thinking?'

'I don't know, but it's sinister somehow — it is bad enough to kill a man, to roll him in that horrible water, but to stop and deliberately place the coins there, and that filthy rag, there's a cold kind of hatred in that.'

11: NEWS FROM THE MORTUARY

In the morning at Wellington Street, Dickens made himself concentrate on his work while waiting for Jones to come from the mortuary. There was the rest of Mrs Gaskell's article to edit. What came after the story of the paralysed old man who had vanished without trace?

As he read, Dickens put down his pen — he was too engrossed to think about his editorial task. He read to the end and sat back in his chair. It was extraordinary.

'The mystery of Garratt Hall,' he said to himself. He looked down at it again, feeling the hairs prickle on the back of his neck:

The owner of this estate, Garratt Hall, married young; he and his wife had several children, and lived together in a quiet state of happiness for many years. At last, business of some kind took the husband to London. He wrote and announced his arrival; I do not think he ever wrote again. He seemed to be swallowed up in the abyss of the metropolis, for no friend (and his wife had many and powerful friends) could ever ascertain for her what had become of him; the prevalent idea was that he had been attacked, and had resisted, and had been murdered...

London — from the country — vanished without a trace — thought to be attacked and murdered — it had all struck Dickens powerfully, but what had made him shiver was the outcome of the story, which Mrs Gaskell averred was a true one. The heir to the missing gentleman had finally found his father — he had been taken to a mysterious house in London, which never after could be found, where the missing father told him that he had found lasting love and married a shopkeeper's daughter by whom he had more children.

Cornelius Mornay and his secret life — what might a son feel were he to find out that his father kept a second family? Mrs Gaskell's heir had accepted it rather meekly, Dickens thought, but then he had come into his substantial estate and prospered without his absent father. Had Cornelius Mornay upped sticks and gone to live with his other children?

He thought of Cornelius Mornay's son and Miss Mornay's hint that all was not well between that father and son. Did he know of his half-brother and sister, and was he filled with jealousy? Had he followed his errant father and done away with him in fit of rage?

Francis Hope, the tea merchant — also the son of a Chinese lady. He needed to see him — he would have to approach Mr Bathe of the London Tavern. It was the only thing he could think of. Francis Hope might not even know that Mr Mornay was missing, but surely he would know of Mr Mornay's other children — they would be his cousins. Drawn together, perhaps, by a shared history — their Chinese mothers. The missionary lady, too — they had to find her.

And those coins — perhaps Captain Bright could tell them whether coins in the dead man's mouth meant anything.

The more he thought about it, the more he was convinced that Mornay's disappearance — or death, if it were he in Doctor Woodhall's mortuary — had to do with this second family. Now, the young man in Mrs Gaskell's tale had inherited his estate and fortune, but suppose Mr Mornay intended to divide his and someone had found out. The truth would come out after his death and scandal would ensue. Had someone tried to prevent that?

Jones came in.

'What news?' Dickens asked.

'It is Mornay.'

'How did you find out?'

'I went to the tailor's first, Graves in Covent Garden, and he told me that Mornay was a customer and that he been fitted for a new frock coat some weeks before the Exhibition. The measurements of the coat I showed were the same as Mornay's — Graves checked his book. He knew it was Mornay's. Then I went to Upper Belgrave Street to see Mattinson —'

'Mattinson!'

'I wanted an identification —'

'But the face —'

'I know, but I wanted to see how Mattinson reacted — whether there was anything to suggest guilt. He was not exactly pleased to see me, but he could hardly refuse. I told him that I couldn't ask Miss Mornay and, as there were no other relatives...'

'How did he take that?'

'Gave nothing away, nor did he at the mortuary. He looked, but the face, of course — hugely disfigured. He was very indignant — said I'd wasted his time. He couldn't tell. I showed him the clothes. Of course, he said that they could have been any gentleman's. I told him about the tailor and asked him if there was anything singular about Cornelius Mornay that might help.'

'Was there?'

'Scar on the back of his neck — he'd been attacked years ago in Canton, by some Chinese robber. He was bashed on the head with some spiked thing that broke the skin. Woodhall looked and there it was. It's Cornelius Mornay, all right.'

'Think Mattinson's involved?'

'I don't think so — once we'd seen the scar, he really did

seem shaken, as if it had all become real to him. He was quite ashen. And he understood the need for a discreet investigation, because Doctor Woodhall told us that Mornay was poisoned — opium. The signs were there — on the rag. That treacle colour — Woodhall's sure it's the stain of opium. And under his microscope, Woodhall detected stains of vomit on the shirt, and the stained undergarments suggest evacuation of the bowels — all signs of poisoning —'

'Toby Quick said that the other man he saw gave Mornay something —'

'Could be — opium would make him giddy, certainly, but he must have been given more than one dose, and a hefty one, because Woodhall found other signs — the vessels of the head were unusually congested, bloody points on the cut surface of the brain —'

'Good Lord, Sam — Woodhall knows his stuff. However, I'm not sure I want to know about Mornay's brain.'

'I know; it's grim. Fluidity of the blood is an almost sure sign of opium poisoning.'

'How much would he have to have been given?'

'Our unknown man gave him a drink — enough to make him dizzy and confused. Taken to a carriage, maybe, given another dose — say five grains — whisked off to Wapping, dies on the way and is rolled into the river at night.'

'Good God —'

'Well, Wapping is very suggestive. Woodhall thinks he was probably dead before he was put in the river.'

'What next, then?'

Before Jones could tell him, there was a knock at the door and Dickens's sub-editor, Harry Wills came in to tell them that a shoe-shine boy wanted to speak to Dickens.

'Name of Toby?' asked Dickens.

'Smike, he said — your boy, I take it. Said it was urgent.'

'Bring him up, if you will.' Dickens turned to Jones. 'What's this about, I wonder? What's so urgent?' Smike appeared at the door. 'Smike, what brings you here?'

'Mr Macgregor sent, sir — Toby ain't come back — not last night, not yesterday teatime. Mr Macgregor wants ter know if yer sent 'im on an erran' or somethink. Toby tol' me yer give 'im a shillin' yesterday mornin' at the park. Ain't seen 'im since.'

Dickens felt another chill at his neck. Cornelius Mornay murdered, and the last person who had seen him alive was Toby Quick, who had seen Mornay go away with a stranger. And now Toby Quick had vanished. 'No, I didn't send him. I'll come to see Mr Macgregor — he's at Farringdon Street?' The boy nodded. 'Go back now and tell him I'll be along very soon.' Dickens turned to Jones. 'I hope to God that this is nothing to do with Mornay — Toby saw him go away with someone and now Mornay's dead — murdered.'

'Let's not rush at it — you don't really know what kind of a lad he is. He might have run off with his takings. Not all of them can stick to proper employment.'

'I know, but he seemed pleased with himself — proud of what he was doing. And you must admit it's a devil of a coincidence.'

'Then get along to Farringdon Street and find out what you can. I'll come with you, but I won't see Macgregor — let's not alarm him. I'll wait in The Magpie and Stump.'

Dickens gave him a rueful grin. 'Not the place I'd have chosen — just across from Newgate, but it will serve.'

12: THE RAGGED SCHOOLMASTER

They hurried across Drury Lane into a muddle of alleys which took them a quick way to the ragged school and the dormitory next to it. Jones left Dickens, who went in to find his protégé, Smike, who took him to see John Macgregor. He was standing beside Toby Quick's rough cot and looking at his few belongings.

'I beg your pardon, Mr Dickens, for troubling you, but it was just that Smike said Toby had spoken of your meeting and the tip you gave him. I thought — I hoped —'

'No, it's quite all right. I asked him about an acquaintance who had been taken ill at the Exhibition, and who is missing from home — I thought Toby might have seen him in the retiring room.'

'Had he?'

'No.' Dickens didn't dare say any more. He'd have to wait for Sam to consider the matter. 'You don't think he has just gone off — sometimes, these boys are tempted back to the streets — if he had some extra money —'

'They are rough and uncouth, Mr Dickens, you know that — brutal, some of them — but with Toby I was sure we'd made progress, as with your Smike.' Smike had already been sent downstairs to wait. 'Toby was proud of his work — I asked him to demonstrate to the other lads, and since March when we began, he has come back faithfully with his money.'

'Tell me about him — how you recruited him, where he came from.'

'I came across him in the hospital. I was visiting another lad who had been knocked down by a carriage. The nurses didn't know who he was — only that he had been shot.'

'Shot!'

'Yes, I don't know how, but the bullet is still in his neck — he's quite proud of that, and the others look up to him for that bullet.'

'Which hospital was it?'

'The infirmary at the Wapping workhouse, off Old Gravel Lane.'

Dickens thought of Cornelius Mornay, drowned in Wapping, but he only asked, 'Any visitors to see the boy?'

'According to one of the nurses, she saw someone at the end of his bed — just for a few moments, but she was busy with another patient, and when she turned again, he was gone — a man, she thought, or a lad. However, in his fever, Toby mentioned an uncle whose name seemed to be Dag — if that's possible — but when I spoke to him about the name, he said he didn't know a Dag. He'd had an uncle, but he was dead, and Toby said he had been living on the streets. He could not remember anything about the shooting.'

'He didn't say where he'd come from originally?'

'I had a feeling it was near docks — certainly, the riverside — he talked of mudlarking, scraping a living in watch houses, living in a boat.'

'Toby might have said something to the others — Smike, for example.'

'I'll call him back.'

'What do you know of Toby's life before here?' Dickens asked the boy when he came in.

'Not much, sir, only 'e lived near London Docks — mudlark, 'e was, an' 'e lived with 'is Uncle Dag wot's dead now.'

'And the bullet in his neck?'

'Said 'e'd bin shot durin' a robbery — Uncle Dag went off,

an' someone took Toby ter the 'ospital. Dint wanter go back ter Wappin', though, cos 'e'd be wanted by them robbers — dint want another bullet in 'im.'

Dickens gave Smike sixpence and the boy went off. He turned to John Macgregor. 'I've a good friend at Bow Street. I'll make some enquiries about this Dag and the robbery. When, approximately, do you think it happened?'

'I met Toby back in January, and he'd been in the hospital a day or so — January the fourth or fifth, I should think.'

'I'll let you know what I find — he might be back, of course. This might be just an aberration, but I should discourage the other boys from speculating too much or looking about for him themselves. It might be dangerous if Toby was in with some ruffians.'

Macgregor asked, 'Is this connected with your missing acquaintance, Mr Dickens? If you know anything, I think you ought to tell me.'

John Macgregor was a barrister as well as a ragged schoolteacher — a good man and a sharp one. Dickens trod carefully. 'I don't know, Mr Macgregor. I hope not. I should be most distressed if the two events were connected. However, I promise you that I will tell you what I find out. Do you know Superintendent Jones of Bow Street?'

'Your good friend? I do — you were involved in the case of that poor lunatic who was accused of murder late last year. You found the dead girl, I believe.'

The word 'dead' somehow hung in the air between them. 'I did, and now Superintendent Jones is investigating the disappearance of a man whose name I cannot reveal, but be assured, sir, that Mr Jones will tell you about it — if it becomes necessary.'

'I hope it does not. I hope you have not, however

inadvertently, embroiled my boy in something dreadful.'

The words stung, but Dickens could not answer. He felt bad enough about Toby Quick. He thanked John Macgregor and went across to the Magpie and Stump to tell Sam all that had been said about the boy, the bullet in his neck, the visitor to the hospital, and Uncle Dag who was apparently dead.

Jones thought about what he had heard. 'When was he shot? And where?'

'I asked about that — back in January, fourth or fifth, Macgregor thought. He and Smike thought the boy had lived by the docks. He was taken to Wapping Infirmary. I thought instantly of Cornelius Mornay, but I didn't say anything to Macgregor; however, he's a lawyer and sharp. Asked me if I thought Toby's disappearance had to do with my missing friend —' Dickens saw Jones's alarm — 'I had to tell him why I'd wanted to talk to Toby —'

'I see that — still, no name mentioned. Wapping, though, that complicates things. Let me think. Two possibilities: the boy was spirited away by the robbers, or went back to them, or —'

'It's to do with Mornay —' he gave Jones a bleak look — 'and it's my doing.'

'Our doing, Charles — but if it is, why did whoever took Mornay away go back to the Exhibition where he saw you with Toby? That was a risk —'

'But maybe he thought Toby was a witness who could recognize him?'

'But if he did see you, why would you have anything to do with Cornelius Mornay? You could just have been chatting to the lad.'

'So, it has to be someone who knows that I'm involved: Alexander Mattinson, Miss Mornay — and Paul Grex. They are the only three closely connected to Mornay.'

'Two weeks he's been missing, Charles; we don't know who knows. I spoke to Hewitt at the Chinese booth — we don't know who saw me, heard me, saw me with you, saw you with Toby — any number of possibilities, and the boy might have simply gone off with a former associate, or, as you said, been taken. This mysterious visitor at the hospital, for example.'

'I thought of Bold.'

'Yes — he'll know about a shooting. We'll go down there and ask.'

'I know the surgeon at the infirmary, and I spoke to a nurse there a while ago — research for *Household Words* — she was a good soul, very upset about a child found in the street. She looked after him, but he died. I could talk to her — she might know something about Toby.'

'Right, you go to see the nurse and I'll see Bold. We'll take a steamer from London Bridge.'

13: SHAKESPEARE'S HEAD

'Anything?' asked Jones as Dickens came into Inspector Bold's office at the Thames Police Station.

'A Lascar sailor said he'd found the boy bleeding in an alley at the back of a house in Wellclose Square, scooped him up and took him into the infirmary. A good Samaritan, the nurse seemed to think. "Poor boy", he said, and then he went off. No one asked his name. They just wanted to save the boy. I asked about Uncle Dag. She just remembered some man standing at the end of the bed one time and then he was gone.'

'Well, Inspector Bold here knows Uncle Dag, and he is very much alive.'

'He is that,' said Bold. 'Did the nurse describe the visitor?'

'Just a man in a dark jacket and peaked cap — smallish, she said, but nothing remarkable about him — a lad, maybe, she thought.'

'Not Dag, then, she'd have remembered. He's a great hulking fellow — wears a red kerchief round his bull neck. Sailor once, I believe.'

'Is he the boy's uncle?'

'He's everybody's uncle — kidsman — runs a gang of lads — bit like your Fagin, but better-natured. These lads have no homes and Dag takes 'em in — mudlarks, odd-jobbers, sell what they can pick up in the street or on the shore, run errands, mind horses, sweep crossings —'

'But the shooting —' Dickens said.

'Ah, well, Dag knows a lot of folk, of course, and most of 'em not so savoury — quite prepared to use a lad as a snakesman for breaking and entering. Now, we questioned

Dag about the shooting, but he knew nothing — well, he wouldn't — told us the boy wasn't one of his, and we heard nothing more about it. Doctor said the lad couldn't remember anything. No robbery occurred involving guns, so we left it. There's so much crime, you know that, Mr Dickens, and unless there's evidence…'

'Is it possible for us to question Dag?'

'I've sent a man to find him — Constable Sleat. Dag's favourite pub is The Shakespeare's Head, top of Old Gravel Lane. Not a safe place. Gaunt had better take you. Landlord, Mr Sherriff, knows him. And there'll be a man outside.'

The Shakespeare's Head, thought Dickens wryly as they made their way with John Gaunt, threading their way through the seething street, though it would have been much the same in Shakespeare's day, he supposed, packed with sailors from all over the great globe: swarthy Lascars, Africans, Chinese, tall Finns and Norwegians all shouting, singing, roaring in a cacophony of tongues, vying with the screeching women plying their trade at the doors of tumbledown lodging houses, or selling their wares from the slop shops, the grog shops, the dram shops, and everywhere there were grubby little shops with doorways festooned with sailors' caps and jackets and Brobdingnagian trousers which seemed to be made of sails. There was everything for sale: parrots, pots and pans, clocks and caps, saveloys, shells and oysters, and opium, no doubt. Dickens noted the barefoot, ragged children darting everywhere, grubbing in the mud like little animals, and grieved to think of Toby Quick brought back here from his shoeshine station in the glittering palace.

They picked their way through the mud; the road was very nearly a swamp with filthy water streaming along the gutters, and the smell of the river, mud, sewage and fish permeated everything, trapped in the heavy air. They passed Milk Court and Rance Alley and he thought of that hot air which poisoned the food, turned the milk sour, incubated disease, cholera and typhoid and smallpox, all infecting the close dark courts. Fever in the very air, in the vapours rising from the gutters, in the stagnant pools, fever creeping from the river, slinking in at doors — where every door was death's door — secreting itself in corners, in cupboards, in cellars, and in the bodies of all the wretched beings condemned here to die. Rancid Alley, more like.

The Shakespeare's Head looked a bit grim as did the head of Shakespeare, a peeling, somewhat faded image of the poet looking down with a melancholy eye upon the teeming citizenry of Wapping, the houseless poor, the rank-scented many, wrecked on a sea of filth. No, not much had changed, Dickens thought, depressed suddenly by the sight of a drunken man lolling in the gutter, heedless of the stink and sewage, but Gaunt and Jones had gone inside.

The tavern was crowded with seamen. All the Jacks of all the world: British Jack with his cross-eyed lady love and her pint of gin; Jack Tar with a silver-haired mermaid in grubby white satin — no teeth, but that was to be expected of mermaids, Dickens supposed. Spanish Jack with curls of black hair and his black-eyed girl with curls, too; and Jack of Sweden with his mother on his knee — she was old enough. And Jacks of all trades: coal-whippers, watermen, lightermen, lumpers from the docks, draymen, butchers with bloodied aprons, and a man with a face covered with tattoos. Several customers were propped against the wall, clearly imbibers of the advertised gin: *The Real Knock Me Down* — it certainly did. Someone was playing a piano accordion — to the tune of "Jack's Delight, His Lovely Nan"

— not that lovely Nan was anywhere to be seen.

No one heeded them, but Dickens noticed some eyes slide away from John Gaunt as he shouldered his way through. Some faces stared sullenly at Dickens and Jones as they followed Gaunt towards a corner table. Then someone stood in front of Gaunt, a swarthy-faced man with a twisted nose. The music faltered. Someone laughed, but Gaunt stood his ground — he was bigger. The man turned away and the music came again. A wizened, little, hump-backed man seemingly made entirely of bones started up a grotesque dance which was greeted with jeers, catcalls and the stamping of feet.

Someone spat. Dickens didn't know if it were the swarthy man, but he saw the gob of spit glistening on his own boot. He looked up into a pair of the coldest, palest eyes he had ever seen — a glance like a falling blade, ice sharp. He saw a red mouth pursed up as if ready to spit in his face. Dickens dodged aside. He didn't want to look back — those eyes had seemed inhuman, frightening because so.

As he moved forward again, he saw Gaunt talking to a shabby man who had risen from a table, half obscuring another whom Dickens took to be Dag, judging by half a large head and one broad shoulder and a flash of red. Gaunt was turning back, motioning Jones and Dickens to go out. He didn't see the dark man or the man with the glittering eyes, but there was a woman with a small, pert face, very pretty, who looked at him and winked, but as he passed, she put out her foot. Dickens avoided tripping and looked her full in the face. Her smile was mocking. What was in that hard black stare? Did she know him? She lifted her hand, and he caught a glimpse of gold. Then he felt a hand at his back. Sam Jones was hurrying him on. They went out.

Gaunt explained, 'Not the right moment. We'll meet Constable Sleat round the corner. That dark man knows Dag.'

'Who is he?' asked Jones.

'Irishman — Blood by name. Fancies himself as Captain Blood.'

'Oh,' said Dickens, 'he who stole the Crown jewels.'

'The very same. Bold knows him. We haven't managed to pin anything on him, but Dag looked frightened.'

'To do with that shooting?'

'I wouldn't be surprised. He's a reckless devil, Blood, and into all sorts, I don't doubt.'

Constable Sleat was waiting in the alley just off Gravel Lane. He guided them through a tangle of alleys where daylight hardly ever came, and the stench of sewage was even stronger. They came to a shabby house with a battered door through which Sleat took them. They went past the tumble-down staircase and came to a door beneath it, which Sleat opened and down they went into a lamp-lit cellar where Dag stood waiting, his great feet planted in the earth floor as if he had grown from the very dirt. He seemed to fill the room, but his smile was amiable enough, even with the blackened teeth.

Jones went straight to the point. 'The boy, Toby Quick, missing from his employment as a shoe-shine boy. Is he here?'

Something flared in the man's eyes: fear, alarm, surprise? Dickens couldn't tell, but Dag knew something. However, he only said, 'Ain't seen 'im.'

'Since he was shot, you mean?'

Now there was alarm. Jones stepped forward. He looked menacing in the dim light and the big man shrank away. 'Don't know nothin' about that. 'Eard about it, tha's all.'

'What is Toby Quick to you? He mentioned an Uncle Dag.'

'Wot the lads call me. I ain't their uncle.'

'What lads?'

'Just lads — makin' wot livin' they can. They brings their stuff an' I sells it on — shares out the takin's.'

'Regular thieves' kitchen,' Jones said, looking round at the rickety deal table covered with odds and ends of rope, bits of metal, pieces of coal, broken bottles, stubs of candles in blacking bottles, tin cups, a loaf of bread with a vicious-looking knife next to it, and some vile-smelling tripe in a cracked dish. Not that there was anything worth stealing.

'Honest business, this,' Dag said.

'I believe you, I'm sure. Now, Toby Quick also told his pal that you were dead.'

'Well, I ain't dead —' Dag attempted a grin, an unholy attempt that revealed the blackened teeth and breath as foul as ditch vapour. Jones — heroically, Dickens thought — did not recoil, though Dickens could smell it from where he stood near the door.

'So I see, but why would Toby Quick say so?'

'Dint wanter know me. Some lads is like that. They jest goes off.'

'Frightened of whoever shot him?'

''Tell yer, I dunno — plenty o' villuns round 'ere. Toby mighta —' Dag stopped himself, but Jones was too quick for him.

'Might have what?'

Dag looked around helplessly. Gaunt was inside the entrance door, Sleat was posted against the only other door and was fingering his truncheon, and the big policeman was very close. There was no way out and Dag was thinking about who might have seen him at the pub, and who might turn up uninvited.

'Sometimes — sometimes — a lad gets taken up — by a gang, say, if they needs a little 'un ter get in some place.'

'Where, for example?'

'Places — workshop, coal yard, shipyard, ships… I dunno nothin' about it.'

'You think Toby Quick was taken up?'

'Could be.'

'Who?'

'Anyone, mister, you ask Inspector Bold — tell 'im ter find out. Can't tell yer nothin' else.'

Jones thought he would make sure of what the nurse had told Dickens. 'One last thing — did you visit Toby Quick in hospital?'

'Ain't nothin' ter me. Why should I?'

'One of your lads, you said.'

''Oo buggered off. Not the first.'

'Well, if you hear anything of him, be sure to tell Inspector Bold, won't you?'

Uncle Dag did not answer, but he looked relieved to see that they were going, and they were relieved to be out of the foul cellar — not much relieved, for the alley was as close and dark as a ship's hold.

They worked their way back to the top of Old Gravel Lane, where Jones stopped to look at the two constables.

'He knows all about it,' Gaunt observed. 'He half told you, but he's too frightened. I'll bet he was there when Toby Quick was shot and he's been told to keep his mouth shut. I can't blame him, if I'm honest.'

'No,' said Jones, 'I realized that. I don't want his murder on my conscience, but I'd like to know who he is frightened of. This Blood, do you think?'

Sleat answered, 'Dag seemed pretty worried in the pub, especially when Blood squared up to Gaunt. That's when he said he couldn't talk there. We slipped out the back way. Honestly, Mr Jones, he ain't a bad sort an' what are them lads to do, eh? You saw them straw beds an' the bits o' blankets. They'd be sleepin' in the gutter otherwise.'

Jones looked at the constable's honest face. 'A timely thought, Sleat. You know Dag better than I, and I'm willing to be guided by you.'

'These boys, Sleat, could one of them have visited Toby in the hospital? Do you know any of them who might talk?' asked Dickens.

'I shouldn't think so — I doubt 'ospital visitin's in their line. One of 'em might talk ter you, sir. Sorry, Mr Jones, I think they'd be a bit scared o' the police. There's a lad I know, a mudlark — if Mr Dickens'd come at low tide, he might.'

'Thank you, Sleat, but if you and Gaunt here can find the lad, then you might ask about Toby Quick. Tell him that Toby's left the ragged school — don't mention the shooting. Just that the teacher wants to know if he's come back here — the lad will understand that. Mr Dickens and I ought to be getting back. If you hear anything, let me know at Norfolk Street, John, if you will. And give Inspector Bold my compliments. I'll come down if he has anything.'

The two constables went on their way back to the police station. Dickens looked at Jones. 'A rather hurried farewell, Superintendent —' he saw that Jones looked worried — 'what — what is it?'

'I want us out of here. We'll talk when we're well away.'

They walked quickly across the main road and went by the Church of St George's in the East into Cannon Street, going north, not stopping or speaking until they reached the

Whitechapel Road, where they found a cab to take them back to Wellington Street.

Inside the cab, Jones let out a deep breath. 'I didn't much like what I saw in that pub — that girl who almost tripped you up. She was very well-dressed for that kind of place.'

Dickens thought. 'By God, Sam, so she was, now I think of it. Good teeth, too. What are you thinking?'

'Something wrong about her. Why'd she pick on you? And she was with someone — not Blood, but another. I saw her laugh with him. Youngish, black hat — well-dressed, too. He's the one who spat.'

'I know — I looked him in the eyes and never more cold eyes did I see.'

'That's why I don't want you hanging about the shore in search of mudlarks. For once, I'd have welcomed those damned specs.'

'You think they recognized me? I wondered for a second if she knew me. There was something about her eyes.'

'Could be — they didn't belong there, but they were — well, comfortable enough, whereas we got a few sidelong looks, and that young man, he was standing right next to Blood. I wonder if Bold knows them — I'll have to write him a note.'

Dickens was thinking. 'You know I said that someone might know I'm involved.'

'I thought of that when I saw that girl. I wonder if we've been a bit rash charging off to Wapping and asking questions.'

'My fault — rushing you into the Toby Quick disappearance. Macgregor put the wind up me — not that I blame him. He's done such fine work for those boys.'

'It's done now. We'll leave Toby Quick to Bold for now. He knows what he's about down there — more than we do. They'll find him.'

'If he's to be found — even if it is nothing to do with Mornay, I don't fancy his chances if he was involved with Blood and those other two. I suppose they might have recognized me — but there's not a lot we can do about that.'

'Well, you won't be hanging about Wapping on your own.'

'You never shall desert —'

'Not in Wapping, certainly.'

14: READING THE TEA-LEAVES

They ate a lunch of cold salmon, pigeon pie and pale ale which Dickens had ordered in from the nearby Albion pub, and over a cup of tea, he told Sam about Mrs Gaskell's story of the husband with two wives and two sets of children.

'Mornay led a double life?'

'Miss Mornay said he had secrets — she never knew where he had gone.'

'A double life that brought about his death?'

'Captain Bright didn't know whether Mornay saw his children, but suppose he did? Money and scandal, I'm thinking. Suppose the son from Antwerp had found out that half his inheritance was going to the Chinese children — or had gone.'

'Suppose the Chinese children resented his English heirs. Chinese coins, opium.'

'Can you dig into Mornay's financial affairs?'

'Ask Mattinson, you mean? Not without Lord John's say-so. I'll mention it. I've to see him later this afternoon at his home. I wrote to ask for an interview — no names, of course, but I need to tell him about Mornay's death. See what his instructions are.'

'Will you tell him about Toby?'

'I will. I'll have to mention the shooting and the boy's background. I'm going home now in the hope that Rogers will come to tell me about the poaching people at Pole Court.'

'What do you want me to do?'

'Write to Macgregor telling him about Dag, the robbery and that the Wapping Police are investigating. And then go and buy some tea in Fenchurch Street.'

95

'Francis Hope.'

'Yes, find out what you can about the second family. Come to Norfolk Street at five o'clock. We'll give you a chop — or two.'

Dickens contemplated the leaves in his teacup. Divining the tea leaves had come from China, so it was said, but there didn't seem to be any news to be read at the bottom of his cup — unless that blob there meant a dark stranger with a pigtail. Perhaps the thin strips of leaf were Chinese characters. A warning? No use if he couldn't read it. He put down the cup.

China tea, though. Ought he to see Mr Bathe of the London Tavern? Tell him he wanted to meet his son-in-law, Mr Francis Hope — thinking about writing something on the tea trade for *Household Words*. He'd done it before to effect introductions. That was how he had inveigled himself into a lunatic asylum to identify the daughter of a prominent politician. It had worked, too, but he had told the truth to his close friend, Doctor John Elliotson. He could hardly tell Mr Bathe that he wanted to question his son-in-law about his murdered uncle.

And to think of telling Francis Hope that his uncle had been murdered in Wapping. That was a horrible thought. He stood up, not really knowing whether he was going to Fenchurch Street or not. But they had to find Cornelius Mornay's other children. What about the missionary lady? But then he would have to tell her. And those two children might be there, though they wouldn't be children now. They must be — he didn't know. Captain Bright had said that Cornelius Mornay had left Canton in 1830. He had gone out as a young man — perhaps in his early twenties more than thirty years ago. Perhaps those first children were in their thirties now.

But the daughter might still be with the missionary lady. He thought of poor Miss Fanny Mornay. Sam would have to go back to Pole Court. Surely Lord John would sanction that. She couldn't be left in the dark.

Fenchurch Street it would have to be. Deal with it head-on and improvise. He reached for his hat. Wills put his head round the door. 'A Mr Mornay to see you. Shall I send him up?'

Dickens sat down. Mornay? The son from Antwerp? Must be. It couldn't be … a warning in the leaves. Unless it was the Chinese son. Unlikely. He thought of Francis Hope, who had been given a new name — not Mornay.

'If you're too busy?' Wills ventured.

'No, no, I beg your pardon, Harry. Yes, send him up by all means. No interruptions, if you please.'

This was a turn-up. If his visitor were Jonathan Mornay, then Dickens would have to tell him. The door opened and Wills ushered in a young man. It was he — very like his sister, but not plain, just an ordinary young man who looked very anxious indeed, and burst into speech as soon as the door closed.

'My sister sent me. I didn't come back at first —'

'My dear Mr Mornay, please do sit down and get your breath, then you can tell me about your sister.'

Mornay sat down and took the advised breath. 'I'm sorry, Mr Dickens. I will try to be clear. It's just so upsetting. I've just come from the Antwerp steamer. I didn't come back before because I thought I knew where our father was, but I couldn't tell Fanny — Miss Mornay. I thought he would turn up — he had done before. Then Fanny wrote immediately after you visited Pole Court with the policeman. She said I ought to see you — that you would help. She had told you about father's—'

'Secrets?'

'She has no idea what they are. I do and I don't know how to tell her.'

'Before you go any further, I must tell you some very grave news —'

'He's dead, isn't he? Died there, I suppose, with them. Heart, was it?'

So, young Mr Mornay knew. The words "there" and "them" suggested that, and the bitter tone, but Dickens didn't think he knew anything about murder unless he was a remarkable actor. Still, he would have to test him.

'I'm sorry to say that your father was found dead in the river at Wapping.'

'Wapping! But they live there.'

'Who, Mr Mornay, who lives in Wapping?'

'His other daughter — and her brother — he had another family. That is the secret.'

'I see — then that may explain why he was there. I'll tell you all I know, and then you can tell me about this other family if you wish to.'

'Was it suicide? I — he — we were estranged — a bitter row.'

'Superintendent Jones and I went to see — him. There is no doubt that the dead man is your father. A post-mortem has been carried out. The doctor thinks that your father may have died of opium poisoning.'

Jonathan Mornay looked stunned. 'Someone gave him opium?'

'We don't know. Let me give you some brandy. Just a drop. It will steady you. This is a very great shock to you.'

As Jonathan Mornay sipped his brandy, Dickens told him everything from the beginning, including his father's illness at the Exhibition, the man seen with him, and the involvement of the Prime Minister.

'They thought it might be some Chinese — something to do with the opium trade — and wanted to keep it quiet. Money, I suppose. I know, Mr Dickens, I know where our fortune comes from —'

'I wonder now, though, Mr Mornay, whether it is a more personal matter. Are you willing to tell me about —'

'His other life — who else has to know?'

'Superintendent Jones has been ordered to investigate very discreetly. He will have to know, but he reports only to the Prime Minister. What happens depends on whether someone gave your father that opium, or whether he took it by accident. If the former —'

'It would be murder, and that would lead to — oh, God, Mr Dickens, how could he? How could he have left such a tangle — not that I don't feel — perhaps it was suicide — perhaps my fault — I was very angry —'

Mornay buried his head in his hands, and Dickens saw his shoulders shaking. His mind had been filled with the betrayal of his sister and himself — their dead mother, too, probably. Anger and hurt had propelled him from Antwerp, but now the fact of his father's death and the possibility of suicide or murder had hit him. Dickens didn't dare tell him about the rag and the coins. He was sure that Jonathan Mornay was not guilty, but Sam would want to be certain. He could check the passenger lists to find out if Mornay's story were true.

Dickens poured more brandy and waited for Mornay to recover himself. Eventually, Mornay looked across at Dickens. His face looked haggard.

'I found out about the other family — I quarrelled with him. That's why I went to Antwerp. It was at the beginning of the year. I didn't write. I didn't want to see him — I was so angry when he disappeared. I thought he'd gone to them.'

'Will it help if you tell me how you found out — to share the secret? Perhaps I can advise you.'

Mornay looked at him, the tears wet on his young face, and then the words came as if he were relieved to tell someone the thing that he had kept secret, the secret he had not known what to do about — except to flee.

'In January, I was in London, and I was to meet him for dinner. I turned up early and asked for him. The porter told me that he had gone out with the young lady — I knew it wasn't Fanny. She was at Pole Court. I couldn't help wondering — you know — when he said "the" young lady, as if he'd seen her before. Then my father came and over dinner we talked. He said he had been at the bank and at the China Association meeting some business acquaintances, but he didn't mention any young lady. Anyway, the next day I went to the hotel, saw him come out with his portmanteau, and followed him — to a house. A young woman came to the door — I thought she must be... She looked young. She took his hat off his head — intimate, somehow... Then a young man came. I thought they looked — well — not English. My father went in and the woman hung on his arm. They were all laughing. I couldn't understand it. I thought they might be a Chinese family that he knew — but they were so familiar with him. It was never like that for Fanny and me. Fanny would never have taken his hat — a footman would always — it was all so different — such a little house —'

'How did you find out?'

'I waited for him to come out — I waited until nightfall. I saw the lights come on in the room overlooking the street and I went to look. I saw him — by the fire and the woman sitting on the floor leaning back against his knees. The young man saw me and said something. My father looked at me and came to the door. He came out into the square and he told me that they were his son and daughter, born in Macau — their mother was Chinese. She was dead, he said. He had looked after them ever since they had been sent to England —'

'A double life.'

'You read about such things —' *you do, indeed*, thought Dickens — 'I couldn't believe it. He said it would make no difference — no difference — a happy family — obviously happier than ours. He said I would still be heir to the house; that Fanny and I had been well provided for — as if that was all I cared about. He didn't have a clue — how Fanny might feel — how I might feel about our mother.'

'She wasn't alive then?'

'No, no, but he'd betrayed her all the same, and us. I never knew him at all. He was my father — I trusted him. I don't understand. Tell me what to think —'

Dickens looked at the young man's wretched face and at the indeterminate eyes where the tears still gathered. An ordinary face, but a suffering one, and a very young one. And if the features were an index of the heart, an innocent one. 'I cannot, Mr Mornay, I can only say how hard it is to read any man's heart under his waistcoat — most of us are a mystery to others and to ourselves. Only time and experience can teach you what to think, but for now —'

'I left him there in the dark. After what I said... I didn't know that I would never see him again and now — I don't know what I feel —'

'You are cut to the heart, I know, torn between your anguish at the injustice done to you and your family and the horror — and grief at your father's death.'

'But he didn't care for us —'

'Perhaps he did — in his way — and at the same time felt a

responsibility for those other children. He tried, perhaps, to balance the two, spending time with each.'

'But they looked so happy together. It wasn't like that at home.'

'Wealth, Mr Mornay, great riches — what a burden they can be. In one house he kept up appearances — a country squire's life with all its responsibilities, and a smaller life in which he could be at his ease.'

'That is not good enough. He lived a lie. I cannot see how to forgive him.'

'Look a long way off and not under your nose. You are young, my dear sir, and your whole life and fortune are before you, but responsibility comes with that fortune. My counsel is that you must leave now for Pole Court where your sister waits. You have heavy news for her, and only you can break it. It is your duty, and you must face that duty with a resolute and steady heart. The investigation you must leave to Superintendent Jones. He will come to you at Pole Court, I am certain, and tell you what he finds, but to carry out his investigation he must know where the house is to which you followed your father.'

'I don't know that I wish to tell you — why can't they just be forgotten? I don't want to see them, and if he's provided for them, then they shall have it and be done — I can forget about them...' He looked away from Dickens's penetrating gaze.

'Let your heart be softened by your own affliction and have some sympathy for them — they are bereft, too.'

Dickens saw the fluctuations of feeling chasing across young Mornay's face — resentment, shame, and sorrow contended there, but he did not speak.

'I understand your feelings, sir, and they are natural, but it is possible that your father was murdered. Whatever he has done, the murderer must be found, and these other children — surely they have a right to know. They are not at fault. It is another duty — hard as it is.'

'The sins of the father,' Mornay said, still with that trace of bitterness. After a few moments, he looked at Dickens again, something clearer in his eyes. 'But you are right... Duty, you say... And I ran away — like a spoilt child —' he shook his head — 'I think, Mr Dickens, that in this half hour —' he gave Dickens a shaky smile — 'I may have grown up — a little. Though I can't forgive him — yet. The house is in Princes Square, number twenty-six. James and Jane Spencer.'

'Good man — now, take that train without delay. You will hear from Superintendent Jones. Stay with your sister.'

When Jonathan Mornay had gone, Dickens sat looking at his teacup again. Not so much a dark stranger, but a stranger nonetheless, and he knew now where the second family was to be found — or part of it. Captain Bright had said there were two sons and a daughter, but Jonathan Mornay had mentioned only a man and a woman at the house. What did that mean? One dead, perhaps? He hadn't dared question the lad — he had been distressed enough. Nor had he dared mention Francis Hope. It was too late to go to Fenchurch Street now. But he had much to tell Sam Jones.

15: SUPPER AT NORFOLK STREET

It was after seven o'clock in the evening when Jones returned. Dickens had played with Jones's adopted children, Eleanor and Tom Brim, whose father had died of consumption a year ago. The stationery shop he had owned was run by Mollie Rogers, the wife of Sergeant Rogers — he who had gone down to Pole Court in search of information about poachers, and whose report Dickens would very much like to hear, but he bore his impatience and his trepidation about Sam's absence with fortitude and concentrated on Tom Brim's wooden horses and toy soldiers. And when Tom Brim had been whisked off to bed, it was Eleanor's turn to show him the cardboard panorama she had got from the Exhibition. He forbore to look at his watch — but where was Sam?

The chops lay uncooked in the kitchen, and Elizabeth Jones watched as Dickens was taken through the exhibits and booths and invited to smell the handkerchief which Eleanor had dipped into the perfumed waters of the crystal fountain. He was so good with children, she thought. He must have seen it all. She knew that he had been to the Exhibition with Sam about that missing man, and yet he expressed astonishment and awe in a satisfactory manner.

'You don't mean to say that Scrap wasn't impressed by the Koh-I-Noor — a diamond as big as that.'

'It wasn't very interesting — it didn't sparkle very much. I suppose the Queen liked it — but then a Queen would have to say she did if it was a present, even if she didn't. I preferred the velocipede — I should like to ride one in the park, but then I'd have to wear bloomers — you know about Mrs Amelia

Bloomer, I suppose,' Eleanor said, giving him a straight look.

He glanced at Elizabeth, whose lips were twitching. No help there. 'I surely do.'

'Mama and I saw the ladies with their trousers under their skirts at the Exhibition — people were laughing. Some boys were laughing and some men, but the ladies looked very comfortable. Scrap laughed, but I told him not to.'

I'll bet you did, thought Dickens, feeling a momentary pang for Scrap, Eleanor's best friend. He'd have regretted that incautious moment. He wondered what Sam thought, but Eleanor was continuing her lecture. 'We read about Mrs Bloomer in the paper. She says, how would men like to wear long skirts and all those petticoats?'

'Hm — well, a fair point,' Dickens temporized. The advocate of women's rights, however, clearly expected more, fixing him with a steely eye. 'I mean, when the velocipede comes in, of course ladies will have a special outfit — as they do to ride horses.'

'I should like to do that, too. I've been painting the coalman's horse, but he had to move on when the coal went down the chute.'

'Oh, I'd like to see that.'

Eleanor hastened to get her portfolio. 'Very fine,' Dickens observed with some relief, preferring the topic of horses to bloomers, and when he had finished looking at her sketches and drawings, Elizabeth said it was time for bed and Dickens was left alone to look at his watch and wonder anxiously where Sam could have got to. 'Miss Eleanor is growing up,' he said when Elizabeth came back.

She laughed. 'I'm not sure Sam would have coped with that conversation, either.'

Dickens raised an eloquent eyebrow. 'Surely, my dear

Elizabeth, you wouldn't —'

'For such a radical, you're on the conservative side about women's dress, I see.'

Dickens was indignant. 'I have plenty of women writing for *Household Words* — independent women, too.'

'But not wearing bloomers.'

'They look like Turks to me. Rational dress, forsooth!' He saw that she was laughing at him and he laughed, too.

'It's an extraordinary world, Charles. When I think of the Exhibition — all those engines, those machines, all those inventions, all that progress, and yet little Chinese ladies with bound feet. I asked someone at the Chinese Exhibition — the one at Albert gate — about it. Little girls' toes bandaged and broken because tiny feet are a sign of beauty.'

'It makes me shudder to think of it — better Miss Eleanor in bloomers than with bound feet, I suppose. We old-fashioned men will come round to it, I daresay —' he grinned at her — 'in a hundred years.'

'You look better than when I saw you last in April,' Elizabeth ventured, 'quite brown.' Though he did look older, she thought, more lined, thinner hair, but his youth was there in his eyes, still bright and searching.

'It's the fresh air of Broadstairs…' He looked away for a moment, and when he looked back, she saw sadness in that searching look. 'I haven't forgotten, you know, despite what people say. Someone said — about the play — that I was acting with a dead father in one pocket and a dead baby in the other —'

'Cruel.'

'It was. I walked and walked all night for three nights after my father's death, and then dear little Dora… Someone sent flowers one night, and I couldn't get up the stairs. I felt —

even I felt as if I could have given up. It was very nearly insupportable, but poor Catherine... I did my best, and I have to work, Elizabeth — to play my part, fulfil my duties —'

His eyes filled so she took his hand. 'You need not explain. I know. It was the same for us when our daughter Edith died. Sam had to go to work. I know you, too, I think. In your heart, she is there, and it is painful. It wants time — you said that, do you remember, about Eleanor and Tom when their father died. It wants time, and even then, the loss is still as acute when the memory comes.'

They heard the front door, and Jones came in to see his wife with her hand on Dickens's hand. *Something amiss there*, he thought, hoping that nothing more had happened to Dickens who had borne much in the months of March and April, but he only said, 'Dear Lord, this heat, the traffic.'

'You've been a long time with our political friend. Sorted the national debt, have you?' Dickens asked.

'I've been in Wapping with Inspector Bold — and our good Constable Stemp, heavily disguised as a seafaring man. He'd be a match for anyone in that get-up.'

Elizabeth interrupted. 'I'm going to cook those chops — if you both still want them. We'll have to eat in the kitchen, however — despite your hobnobbing with the Prime Minister, Mr Jones. I'll leave you to talk for half an hour.'

'Stemp?' asked Dickens when she'd gone.

'Yes, you'll remember that Lord John said I could enlist a few trusty men if I needed to, and after this morning, I thought that my fearless Stemp would be just the man. You'll enjoy his disguise. Dressed as a common sailor — with an earring, too, knife in his belt. He frightened me. Rogers is down there in plain clothes — he came back from Pole Court. Nothing doing there, though. Cornelius Mornay seems to have been a decent landlord to the farmers and labourers. They are not averse to a bit of poaching, but the attack on the gamekeeper was not regarded well — not that they approved of transportation, either, but Rogers didn't get a feeling of any bitter resentment against Mornay. So, we can discount that. Miss Mornay told him about her letter to her brother.'

'Yes, he came to see me.'

'She hoped he would. However, tell me over supper. I'd rather tell you about Wapping while Elizabeth is busy. It's grim stuff, but whether it bears on Mornay's case, I don't know yet. I asked about the well-dressed pair in the pub. John Gaunt has seen them about and wondered. And there are some odd cases — unsolved, but possibly connected, Bold thinks now he's started to put them together.'

'Tell all.'

'You remember a police constable was killed in Wapping a few months ago?'

'Yes,' said Dickens, looking grave, 'beaten to death, wasn't he? But they were caught, I read.'

'Yes, they were. A gang of drunks had been moved on by two constables, only for four of the men to come back and attack them with bricks and bits of metal. The murdered man went down, and his head was kicked in. The second constable managed to sound his rattle and they fled. He remembered the four from the first encounter, but he also saw a fifth man looking on and then scarpering with the four. He was never found, but the second constable was struck by an unusual thing —'

'He was well-dressed. That's why you're telling me this.'

'Quite so — square-rigged, as Constable Sleat put it.'

'Colourful.'

'So it is, and the man's face was concealed by a scarf. Of

course, the police wondered if he were just a bystander. Yet it might be expected that a well-dressed bystander might have sought help. The attack was pretty ferocious. But he was never seen again.'

'And the other cases?'

'Somewhere round Bluegate Fields a gentleman was found in a cellar, quite naked, all his clothes, money, and his watch gone. No idea how he had got there, but when the police were called, he said he'd been attacked from behind and thought he'd been drugged.'

'What was a gentleman doing in Bluegate Fields — that wilderness of savagery and lost souls?'

'Lost, indeed, lost his way, he said, having been on some business at the docks. John Gaunt found a witness who said she'd seen the gent with a pretty, well-dressed woman. However, the gentleman denied that, said he was only too glad to be alive, and he just wanted to get home to his wife. Of course, it's a common thing for prostitutes to drug their clients and make off with their money.'

'Wife, eh? But a pretty young lady, not one of the usual sort. Well-dressed, too. Makes you think.'

'As does the case of a robbery near Princes Square —'

'Princes Square — good Lord, that's where Mornay's second family lives.'

'Is it now? Well, a gentleman's elderly housekeeper was found dead in her kitchen. No sign of violence, but a sharp-eyed constable found a bottle of laudanum under the kitchen table. The gentleman said he hadn't laudanum in the house. However, there was no sign of the drug from the post-mortem, so it was concluded that she had died of fright — from the effects of sudden terror.'

'She would, had she seen those eyes I saw. Any witnesses?'

'A neighbour saw a well-dressed couple pass by the house. It was a quiet Sunday morning and the housekeeper's employer had gone to church. Course, no one ever saw the couple again. Silver, jewellery, and money taken from the house.'

'What does Bold think?'

'He's willing to accept a connection — and to have Stemp and Rogers make their enquiries. He thinks as I do that we don't want to alert them with official police enquiries, but his men will be aware of Stemp and Rogers and where they are.'

'Nasty lot of violence, Sam, and that poor old woman. I wonder what they threatened her with.'

Before Jones could answer, they heard Elizabeth calling and they went into the kitchen for a supper of chops, potatoes and beer, during which Dickens told them about his visit from Jonathan Mornay.

'And he came straight from the boat? Not been in London recently?'

'He came because of Miss Mornay's letter, he said. You can check if he was on the Antwerp boat, but I don't think he did it, though he was very angry. He was upset, too. He quarrelled with his father and never saw him again.'

'Understandable,' Elizabeth said. 'He must have felt a horrible sense of betrayal — a second family, a brother and sister he knew nothing about.'

'What made the whole thing worse was that he got the impression of a happy little group, all at ease together.'

'Which wasn't the case at that barn of a place, Pole Court. Footmen and maids everywhere.'

'I'll bet that little family ate in the kitchen, too. Apple pie, anyone?'

'Delicious,' said Dickens, breaking into the pastry and letting out the fragrant steam, 'better than Simpson's at the Albion.

They send in my meals now I'm camping out.'

'I'll feed you any time you want. You are always welcome here.'

'I know, Elizabeth, and I thank you.'

'What did you tell young Mornay to do?' asked Jones after polishing off his pie.

Dickens smiled at Elizabeth. 'Told him to go back to Pole Court and look after his sister — do his duty and remember that his half-brother and half-sister are not to blame.'

'Bracing — how did he take that?'

'Promised to get the first train.'

'Two, you mentioned. I thought your Captain Bright mentioned three children.'

'He did, but I thought it was too much to ask of Jonathan Mornay. I thought of Francis Hope.'

'Who's he?' asked Elizabeth, getting up to take the dishes to the sink.

Jones stood. 'We'll talk while I wash the dishes. You and Charles can dry.'

Dickens repeated what he knew about Francis Hope whose father had married his Chinese lady and had sent his son to England.

'Another Chinese lady — what happened to them, I wonder? Poor things — their children taken away, and those children deposited among strangers.'

'Just what I thought, Elizabeth, though Cornelius Mornay looked after his. Francis Hope's father lost his job and died on his voyage back to England. Hope never knew what happened to his mother. And, Sam, Francis Hope lives in Montague Street. Tea broker and not short of money. I wonder if his father left him provided for.'

Elizabeth left them, having heard a cry from upstairs. 'That'll be Eleanor,' she said.

'Bad dreams?'

'Sometimes she dreams of her father — still sick in his bed and she cannot help him.'

'Poor little girl. Too young to see what she saw when he was so ill.'

'I know — too many children see such terrible things. One could weep. I must go up.'

'All these children, Sam — do you know, I read in the paper about a boy called George Ruby, a crossing-sweeper brought up before the magistrates to give evidence. He couldn't read, didn't know what an oath was, didn't know what prayers were, didn't know what God was, nor the devil, didn't know nothing — didn't know nothin', he said, 'cept a-sweepin' the crossin'. Nothing will come of nothing.'

'Except that you'll continue to write it all down — it must do some good.'

'I hope so, Sam, else what's the use of it all?'

'That boy, Smike — your shoe-black — he's doing all right.'

'He is, but Toby Quick, eh? What's become of him?'

Back in the parlour, Dickens took a brandy from Jones and asked, 'What's next for you? I'll see Francis Hope tomorrow after lunchtime.'

'I can go back to Bow Street.'

'Heavily disguised as — soldier, sailor, beggarman, thief?'

Jones was glad to chuckle. 'No need, as I am investigating the disappearance of boys missing from ragged schools —'

'Boys?'

'Lord John's notion — nothing to be said about the man from Canton, and I'm in Wapping or anywhere about these boys. I'm sending Feak to Hyde Park tomorrow to ask about Toby Quick — and one Tommy Cobb.'

'Ah, I think I might know him.'

Jones kept a straight face. 'And poor little Dick — once of a certain workhouse.'

'No other name?'

'Dick Oliver, I'm told.'

Dickens laughed. 'No little Billy Sikes?'

'That might be going too far.'

'What about using Scrap — as a shoe-black boy, I mean? He could ask about his friends, Dick Oliver etcetera. Scrap knows what he's about. He'd shout the glass out of the Crystal Palace if anyone tried to take him.'

'Why didn't Toby Quick?'

'Different kind of lad — he could be tempted away, I daresay, for a bob or two, especially if someone told him they wouldn't be long — keep an eye on my horse — that sort of thing — get back to your work in no time. Scrap won't fall for anything.'

'All right. I'll call at the shop first thing tomorrow. Mollie Rogers can find him some brushes and a cloth.'

'He'll need a red jersey — I'll find one at home, something of Charley's or Walter's.'

'Right, I'll meet you at the shop. Give me a chance to talk to Rogers on the quiet and Scrap can go down to Hyde Park with Feak. Then come to Bow Street after you've seen Mr Hope, if you will. Then we'll think about the family in Princes Square.'

'As I am a man and brother. Now, I'll get back to my gypsy caravan. Tell Elizabeth goodnight and thank her for supper.'

'I will — and come again. You're a good hand with the drying cloth.'

Time it rained, Dickens thought, feeling the heat still. Suffocating, this weather, the air full of grit and dust, and depressing to the spirits. He looked up at a black sky as close and heavy as a coffin lid. The street was fairly quiet now, the hum of the night-time city at a distance, and the sound of horses' hooves coming his way. Too slow for a cab. Perhaps some weary carter going to his rest. But as the sound came nearer, Dickens saw emerging from the dark two horses with black plumes on their heads, and driving them, a man in black, likewise plumed, and with black streamers dangling from his hat. The driver looked neither right nor left and the spectral hearse passed on into the dark, vanishing as Dickens looked back.

The things one sees, he thought, shivering despite the heat. Dust, ashes, waste, want, ruin, madness, and that fell sergeant Death — all abroad in the London night.

16: CHINA TEA

Orange Pekoe, Mild Pekoe, Black Leaf Pekoe, Congou, Souchong, Singlo, Hyson, Gunpowder tea. Dickens stared in at the window of Mr Francis Hope's broking house, wondering at the Chinese inscriptions decorating the canisters and tea caddies. Enough Gunpowder tea to blow the lid off a washerwoman's copper.

And here he was with a kind of gunpowder news in his mouth, ready to blow a man's peace to smithereens. He had kept to his resolution of simply going to see Francis Hope without any mediation with Mr Bathe of the London Tavern, but still he hesitated. For all the tea in China, he wouldn't be here. He looked in through the glass door to see a young man in a canvas apron stirring the contents of a tea chest with a bamboo cane.

But when the young man turned round at Dickens's entrance, he saw that he was only a pimple-faced English lad who said politely, 'Can I help you, sir?'

'I wonder if I might see Mr Francis Hope — here is my card.'

The lad said he would see, and Dickens was left to take in the fragrance of tea leaves and to gaze at the shelves with their enamelled jars, delicate porcelain tea sets with their little figures scurrying over bridges, and at the names on the chests: Pekin, Nankin, Canton. Canton.

The young man took him behind a counter to show him into an inner office where the man he presumed to be Francis Hope stood. He was about thirty-five, Dickens estimated, a handsome man with his smooth skin and dark hair. He had a letter in his hand at which he was looking with an expression of alarm. Did he know already? However, he put down the letter and turned to Dickens with a smile that seemed half-distracted.

'Mr Dickens, I am very glad to meet you. Mr Bathe, my father-in-law, speaks of you often. I have hoped to meet you. How may I help? A matter of tea?'

Dickens sat down on the chair indicated by Francis Hope. 'Not today, thank you. I have come on a matter of some delicacy, and if you would prefer not to tell me anything after I have told you, then I shall quite understand.'

That look of alarm reappeared. 'What is it?' His eyes went to the letter.

'It is to do with a Mr Cornelius Mornay.'

Francis Hope looked astonished. 'Mr Mornay? I don't understand. How do you know —?'

'There is no easy way to tell you, but he is dead, I'm afraid — he was found murdered in Wapping — in the river.'

'Murdered! Good God, Mr Dickens — I don't know what to say. I am entirely shocked — and bewildered. Murdered?'

'I am afraid so. The case is being investigated by a Superintendent Jones of Bow Street. Mr Mornay had not been seen since the first day of the Exhibition, and the Superintendent made enquiries there, of course, at the Chinese booth.'

'But why are you here — did Mr Bathe send you?'

'No, no, Mr Hope — it is all very complicated, but I learned that Mr Cornelius Mornay was your uncle and we — that is, the Superintendent and I — thought you might be able to tell us something about him.'

'Do his children know?'

Dickens evaded that question. 'Superintendent Jones has

been to Pole Court, and Mr Jonathan Mornay has been to see me to ask my assistance.'

Francis Hope looked shocked again. 'Surely he did not mention me?'

'No.'

Francis Hope let out a long, rather ragged breath. 'Then how — oh, at the Exhibition, I suppose. I know Mr Hewitt — his warehouse is just down the road. He knows that I am acquainted with Mr Mornay. I would rather Cornelius's family did not know. I have an English wife, and a child, Mr Dickens — a son who looks English, and I am a naturalized citizen. I submitted a denization petition, which gives me rights to reside here and to hold property. I was brought up here and have lived here nearly all of my life. China — is but a faraway dream. A man sometimes wishes to leave his past behind…'

So he does, thought Dickens. How often the past haunts the present — a boy with blacking in his nails, his father in a prison cell, the memory of a song, a girl in pink silk, little blue gloves, the scent of a flower, a letter — dreams splintered in neat copperplate. A stranger coming with dreadful news. The Ghost of Christmas Yet to Come, pointing to a grave.

'I understand that very well, Mr Hope, and as I say, I do not wish to distress you. I can walk away and leave you in peace.'

'Too late, Mr Dickens; you have mentioned murder, and I know the victim. Of course, you must ask. I owe a debt to Mr Cornelius Mornay.'

'He kept in contact with you?'

'We met from time to time — last year at the Chinese Exhibition. When I was at school, and later, he wrote to me and looked after my interests. My father left me a good deal of money. It was intended that I should go to India, but Cornelius Mornay knew that I wanted to settle here — a man wants to belong somewhere when he has no parents, no home, and was born in a foreign land. He understood that. He felt responsible — about my mother and his — children's mother... However, in later times, he came only a few times to see me — his wife and family did not know about me, or about...' Francis Hope faltered and looked at the letter on his desk.

'His other family — Jonathan Mornay found out.'

'I see. And do they know about Cornelius?'

'Not yet — I thought I ought to see you first. Of course, I did not know if you knew them.'

'I do. I see them sometimes. Cornelius brought Jane — his daughter — here once or twice. We have a shared history, of course — our mothers — not that we talk about them. Hope is my mother's Chinese name character — which means something, I suppose. They were married, which is why my father lost his post. He died on his way back to England.'

'Your mother?'

'I have no idea. Cornelius Mornay did not marry his Chinese mistress — not in the usual sense of the word. Such liaisons were a kind of marriage in that the Chinese fathers of these young women entered into an arrangement. My mother was probably sent back to her family — provided for, of course. That was the usual thing. Married off then to a Chinese man because they had dowries. I don't know what happened to Cornelius's mistress — I never talked to him about her. I didn't want to know.'

'Do you remember your mother?'

'Just vaguely. I try not to think of her, though in dreams sometimes, I can see the old house, the promenade and the sea. I can feel the humid air blowing in at the window. I am in Macau, and there are women dressed in jewel-coloured silks, laughing and singing — and the smell of spices and oils — but it is a dream, Mr Dickens. It is past and gone. This is all I have from that time.' He took something from his desk and handed it to Dickens. 'A Chinese puzzle ball — perhaps it was my mother's. I don't really know.'

Dickens took the ivory ball. It was about four inches in diameter with intricately carved scenes on the outer ball which featured a garden scene, complete with tiny human figures and dragons. Inside he could see more carvings on an inner ball. 'A beautiful thing,' he said.

'From Canton — gui gong qiu — the devil's work ball.'

'Why?'

'Because it was thought to be made by spirits. It is a puzzle, of sorts. You're supposed to align the holes with something like a toothpick and then you see into the heart of the mystery. There are nine layers of balls in that one. Some have forty layers — mysterious things — unfathomable.'

As China itself, thought Dickens as he handed it back. 'Jonathan Mornay mentioned James and Jane, but I had an impression there were three children of Mr Mornay. Perhaps I am mistaken.'

Francis Hope looked anxiously at the letter. 'No, Mr Dickens, this is an extraordinary coincidence. This letter is about the third child, Mr Cornelius Mornay's eldest son.'

'Where is he?'

'This letter tells me that he is missing.'

Dickens looked at Hope in astonishment. 'From where?'

'From the asylum at Fort Pitt in Chatham — where he has been confined these last ten years.'

'He is mad?'

'Michael Spencer — that is the name Cornelius Mornay gave his children — it was his mother's maiden name — joined the East India Company Army — he was invalided out, suffering from fever and congestion of the brain. He returned to Broadstairs where Miss Palmer, a missionary lady and the children's guardian looked after him until —'

'What happened?'

'He attacked Miss Palmer and she nearly died of her injuries. Their lawyer sent for me and I sent for Cornelius Mornay. Michael was declared insane and confined to Fort Pitt, the asylum for army men and now —'

'When did he vanish?'

'Mr Cornelius Mornay took him away on April twenty-ninth. Apparently, he thought he might move him to an asylum in London and wished him to be examined by another alienist —' he looked at the letter again — 'a Doctor Forbes Winslow in Hammersmith.'

'I have heard of him.' *That might be useful,* Dickens thought. Doctor Forbes Benignus Winslow had been a key witness in a case concerning the murder of several young women which Dickens and Jones had investigated the previous year.

'Michael Spencer is not a raving lunatic, Mr Dickens — he is perfectly calm, but he cannot look after himself. His mind is — not as yours and mine are. However, it was the opinion of the doctor at Fort Pitt, according to the letter, that, though he could not recommend release, it would be in order for him to be moved.'

'But nearly two weeks have passed. Have they not communicated with you before?'

'They have written to Mr Mornay care of the bank, but I know now why there has been no reply. My uncle is dead, and his son is missing.'

17: FAMILY MATTERS

'Attacked Miss Palmer!' Jones interrupted Dickens's account of his meeting with Francis Hope.

'Yes, no police, of course, in the circumstances. Michael Mornay — Spencer, of course — was bundled off to the asylum at Fort Pitt in Chatham — he'd served in the East India Company Army, so Mornay got him in. Contacts, no doubt. Mornay wasn't far away, near Faversham.'

'When was this?'

'Ten years ago. Nothing untoward since — no violence, no raving, though the doctors wouldn't sanction his release. He can't look after himself. Cornelius Mornay brought the two other children — who were twenty or so then — to live in London, wanting to put a distance between them and the asylum. Then, according to the letter Francis Hope received from Fort Pitt, old Cornelius decided to bring Michael to London to see if Doctor Winslow would take him —'

'Forbes Winslow?'

'I knew that'd make you sit up.'

'It does.'

'Francis Hope wondered if Cornelius had concerns about his own health — worried about the future — and maybe the other two children pressed him to bring Michael nearer.'

'Did Cornelius Mornay see Winslow?'

'No, that's why the doctor at Fort Pitt wrote to Francis Hope. Winslow had enquired about the missed appointment. The Fort Pitt doctor wrote to Cornelius Mornay at the bank — several times, but no answer. He had Francis Hope's name as second person to contact in the event of an emergency. He wondered if something had happened to Cornelius Mornay — and was concerned about his patient, Michael Spencer. The doctor's letters will be there, I suppose, waiting in some box.'

Jones nodded. 'So, the question is: where were Mornay and his eldest son on the nights of April twenty-ninth and thirtieth — hold on — I've assumed — everyone's assumed that Mornay came to town from Pole Court. Suppose he didn't —'

'But Miss Mornay —'

'Was staying at the house of Mr Grex's aunt. I remember I was told that Mr Grex was to take her home to his aunt's after the Exhibition — home to his aunt's — perhaps that suggests she was staying there already.'

'So it could, and Cornelius Mornay may well have been in London on those two nights before with his son. I remember now that Miss Mornay said she was worried that he was staying in London — because he wasn't well. I assumed she meant the night of May the first, but it could mean he was already there.'

'The son — this Michael Spencer — Mornay wouldn't have taken him to the Exhibition. He was meeting Miss Mornay. So, where the hell was he?'

'The stranger that Toby Quick saw? The missing Chinese man?'

'Are we on the wrong track? Michael Mornay kills his father — no, no, why take him to Wapping? If he's mad or half-mad, he couldn't take a dying man in a cab, surely. It doesn't make sense.'

'Unless he isn't — mad, that is. We don't know why he attacked the missionary lady. Remember, Francis Hope told me that he was suffering from fever and congestion of the brain. A fit of madness, maybe, but not necessarily insane, but kept in the asylum for ten years because his father didn't want a scandal. Think how bitterness, anger, resentment build up, and then he's to be confined again at Winslow's asylum.'

'The opium?'

'He was in hospital for ten years. He might know how to get it.'

'So, where is he now? And what has any of this to do with Toby Quick?'

'Perhaps Toby Quick is in the hands of the robbers.'

'But Michael Mornay could still be in Wapping —'

'Lord, Sam, Princes Square.'

'Then, we'll have to see them. We'll check at Brown's Hotel on the way — see if Mornay reserved a room there for the nights of April twenty-ninth and thirtieth — though I daresay someone has checked. Still, I'd like to be sure. And we'll see Bold while we are down there in Wapping.'

'What a coil this is — this will be the third time I've told his family members that Cornelius Mornay is dead.'

'Unless they know already.'

Jones thought that they didn't know. It was he who, having announced himself as a Superintendent from Bow Street, told James and Jane Spencer, that their father was dead — had been murdered in Wapping. Their shock was so great that he and Dickens were convinced. The brother and sister accepted that Jonathan Mornay had told Charles Dickens and that was why he was involved. James Spencer had looked very grave at the name of Jonathan Mornay, but both were too stunned to ask questions.

In the small parlour of twenty-six, Princes Square, the beautiful daughter of Cornelius Mornay wept. She was very beautiful, Dickens thought, comparing her to Miss Fanny Mornay. Her hair was dark and shining, her face and features very delicate, though marked now by her tears. James Mornay was a handsome young man, too, tall, like his father and with the same expressive dark eyes as his sister. When Jane Spencer had taken some wine and was more composed, Superintendent Jones told them what they knew, and that Dickens had spoken to Francis Hope.

'Did you expect to see Mr Mornay after the Exhibition?' asked Jones.

'We knew he was coming to London for — for the Exhibition —' Jones noted the pauses, but he and Dickens had agreed not to rush to the matter of Michael Spencer. He wanted to know why these two young people had not come forward about their absent father.

James Spencer continued. 'This is difficult, Superintendent — ours is an unusual situation. Our father — came when he could. We did not always know when, and, of course, we did not write to him at Pole Court. I would send a note to the bank —'

'And if you did not hear from him?'

'Then we assumed that he was in Kent— it was an arrangement that has worked well — we never expected...'

'And on May first you assumed that he could not come?'

'Yes, and then we went away to Dumpton for a few days — it is near Broadstairs. Our former guardian, Miss Anne Palmer, lives there. Mr Mornay — our father — knew that. We thought he might come down. He had done so before. We came back — but Wapping, you say, Superintendent Jones — was he coming to us and — attacked, robbed — what?'

'That is a possibility which is being investigated, of course. Have you left any messages at the bank?'

'Yes, Jane wrote yesterday — I must confess, we were beginning to feel alarmed. Jane wondered if he were unwell.'

'There is another matter of which Mr Hope spoke — it

concerns your brother.'

'Michael!' Jane Spencer was alarmed. 'What has he to do with all this? He is —'

James Spencer interrupted. 'He is unwell — has been for many years — after he left the East India Army.'

'He is at Fort Pitt,' Dickens began carefully. 'Mr Hope told me that.'

'You know that he is confined.'

'Yes — however, Mr Hope had just received a letter from the hospital to say that your father brought Michael to London to see Doctor Forbes Winslow —'

'But he did not tell us that. It is what we wanted — to have Michael nearer. Dr Winslow's asylum is a benevolent place, and Michael is so much better — but how can he be missing?' Jane Spencer was much distressed again.

'Have you any idea why Mr Mornay did not tell you?'

James Spencer spoke up. 'Perhaps he thought to see Doctor Winslow first — he would not want to build up our hopes... We hoped ... we believed that Michael was well enough to come home. We wanted to care for him. Perhaps Doctor Winslow would eventually have agreed.'

'The appointment was not kept. Nothing has been seen of Mr Mornay since May the first, and nothing has been heard of your brother since he left Fort Pitt on April twenty-ninth with your father,' Jones said.

'You are not suggesting that Michael —'

'No, Mr Spencer, I am not suggesting anything, but I should like to know about your brother and if you have any idea where your father might have taken him — where they might have stayed. We know that he often stayed at Brown's Hotel, but he made no reservation for the two nights — I have just called there to enquire.'

'I have no idea, Superintendent — unless our father went to some friend —'

Jane Spencer spoke up. 'It is impossible — Michael — he couldn't hurt anyone. He is very gentle now, very quiet. He is like a child. He needs care —'

Dickens saw the tears well up in her eyes. He spoke gently. 'Would he know how to get here?'

James Spencer spoke sharply. 'He is not here, Mr Dickens — we are not hiding him.'

'No, I did not mean that. I just wondered if he had your address and might try to find you.'

Jane spoke again. 'I don't think so — he would not know. He had no need. He cannot survive alone in these streets, in London. You must help us — a search surely can be made.'

'That will be done, I assure you, Miss Spencer. You do not think he would be able to make his way back to Fort Pitt?'

'Take a train? A steamer? He would have no money. Our father must have left him — somewhere at an hotel. What about somewhere near Doctor Winslow's in Hammersmith? Surely that would make sense — I could go there, see Doctor Winslow and ask him if my father told him where they might stay.'

'No, Mr Spencer —' Jones was firm — 'I would prefer you to stay here. I will certainly enquire in Hammersmith, and you shall have any news as soon as I get it. You have my word.'

James Spencer gave Jones Miss Palmer's address and saw them to the door. They went out of Princes Square and into the churchyard of St George in the East where they stood to mull over what they had heard.

'What do you think?'

Jones thought. 'Hard to say — I'm inclined to think they are innocent, and that Michael Spencer is as meek as a lamb, but he did nearly kill a woman.'

'So he did — but there's planning in this. I could understand if Cornelius Mornay had been found in a hotel bedroom or lodging, even in a dark alley, stabbed to death in some kind of frenzy. I know I said he could have had access to opium, but after what we have heard...'

'Hotels, lodgings — you went to Winslow's asylum about the Venice murders. What's about there?'

'Terrace of houses opposite — could be lettings there, the Bell and Anchor on the Hammersmith Road at North End and a pub called the Red Cow — oh, and there's a hospital.'

'I'll send Rogers. He can have a look at the likely places, and he can see Forbes Winslow. He'll remember us, I'm sure. Stemp can manage on his own for a day. He'll be careful. Now let's go and see Inspector Bold.'

18: AN EYE FOR AN EYE

The corpse's face was dreadful — more dreadful than anything Dickens had seen at the waxworks or on the stage. Two words sprang to his lips, 'Out vile', and he felt a horrible bubbling of hysteria rise in his throat, but he mastered it. "Out vile jelly", indeed. Someone had put out the eyes. Not a thing you saw close-up on stage. Gloucester's blood-bandaged eyes were quite enough to suggest the horror that had been done to him. This was hideous. Dickens stepped back, feeling the sweat on his back and the bile in his mouth. Rogers gave him a sympathetic glance.

They knew who it was. The straggling grey hair and red kerchief gave it away. It was blood-soaked now.

'When?' asked Jones.

'Last night, I should think. One of those lads found him in the morning — screamed blue murder and someone fetched Sleat. No sign of a struggle. Left to die. Done with his own dagger.'

'Cruel,' said Dickens, thinking of a glance that fell like a blade from two cold eyes.

'It is, Mr Dickens,' said Inspector Bold, 'and no one's talking. Gaunt and some of my men have been out and about and to The Shakespeare's Head. Those lads of Dag's have scattered.'

'Not long after we went to see him,' Jones observed.

'Right, and you two and Gaunt were seen in that pub.'

Dickens was glad to go outside of the mortuary, not that there was any fresh air there, only heat and the stench of the river. *Poor Dag*, he thought. A rogue, no doubt, but he hadn't deserved that. And those wretched lads — what would become of them? Dag's had been some kind of home for them, however squalid. He thought about the Chinese coins in Cornelius Mornay's mouth, a policeman battered to death, a rich man drugged and stripped naked, and a man who had seen something whose eyes were put out. And he thought of Toby Quick who had seen a stranger with Mornay.

Rogers was waiting for him. 'All right, Mr Dickens? Horrible business.' Rogers had seen a good deal of death — but never this.

'I'm all right. A shock, though.'

They followed Bold and Jones into the station house. Jones asked, 'The so-called Captain Blood and that pair we saw in the pub? Any sign?'

'No, but we'll find Blood —' Bold paused — 'Blood's a reckless devil as I told you — but what we've seen in there, I don't know, Mr Jones, there's something in that — something different. Blood would thump a man, beat him, even, shoot him — but those eyes. That's nasty. Those other two — they don't belong here. We're looking at those other cases. If we hear anything, I'll send, and about the lad, too.'

'We'll leave it to you, Inspector. I'll have to take Sergeant Rogers with me for now. I need him to follow another lead. We've found some family of our murdered man — a son and daughter living in Princes Square. Name of Spencer, but I don't think they've anything to do with the murder. However, there's another brother missing — one Michael Spencer. These children are half Chinese so there might be something, but only if you hear the name. Don't ask, but you can tell the name to Gaunt and my lad, Stemp.'

Bold went to find Gaunt, and Jones told Rogers about Michael Spencer and the enquiries he should make in Hammersmith.

'Find Stemp now, if you will, and fill him in. Tell him to be careful and on your way back to change into something respectable. If you get to see Doctor Winslow, tell him I sent you. Mr Dickens and I will take the train. You go back by steamer — I don't want anyone seeing you with us.'

'I'll go out by the back, down onto the shore. Stemp'll be about somewhere.'

'There's something devilish about this,' Dickens said as they sat on the train. 'Robbery I can understand. I can even cope with two young well-dressed people dabbling in the sordid life of Wapping, stripping a man of his clothes and valuables, but that policeman and the old woman — and what we've just seen.'

'I know and nothing yet to connect these two to the crimes. Of course, they could have gone — vanished into the night. Let's hope Bold finds Blood — they were together in the pub. Blood might be able to tell Bold something about them.'

'Toby Quick — he saw something. Dag saw something. His eyes, Sam — the putting out of eyes. Such naked cruelty. That part in *King Lear* when Cornwall puts out Gloucester's eyes — I thought of that when I saw poor Dag. Dear Lord, and Regan, Lear's own daughter. Her own father. What might those two do to a child?'

They fell into silence then. What was there to say? Dickens looked out at the passing landscape, the tiles and chimney pots, backs of squalid houses, desolate strips of waste ground, narrow courts where children played in gutters and dirty washing hung on straggles of line, and just for a moment a white face turned to the train and a hand waved. A farewell, a signal of distress, a cry for help? He thought of the dark river. Toby Quick's hand above the water and then gone, and no one to return a farewell.

Jones turned his mind to the missing Michael Spencer. He thought about the people they had seen, the people connected with Cornelius Mornay. He thought about the Exhibition, Hyde Park, Regent's Park. York Gate. An empty house where they had stood in the hall. A door closing and a Chinese man who told them that the cleaner he had employed was leaving. A man in a hurry. Two days ago — the day Toby Quick disappeared.

'York Gate,' he said.

'Yes?'

'Two days ago, Toby Quick disappeared, the same day that Mr Li Shen told us that a servant was just leaving — but he was already locking the front door when we arrived.'

'Oh, Lor, Sam, so it was but … I suppose he'd have to leave a key with someone. I mean, it could have been quite innocent.'

'He wasn't keen on our going in.'

'Oh, you're thinking — but Mornay had been missing for nearly two weeks when we saw Mr Li Shen —' Dickens looked at Jones — 'you don't think Michael Spencer could have been —'

'There? I know it's unlikely, but the connections are there: Cornelius Mornay in Kent; Mr Li Shen farming in Kent —'

'Minster in Kent — not that far from Broadstairs, where the missionary lady lives.'

19: JOSEPHINE

There was a for sale sign outside the house in York Gate —
Mr Li Shen had told the truth about that. *Still*, Jones thought,
seeing that the door was open, it was worth asking.

There were boxes piled high in the hall. The doors of the
other rooms were open, and a breeze came from somewhere.
Someone airing the house.

'Anyone here?' Jones shouted.

'Comin',' a female voice answered, and a woman appeared at
the nearest door.

'Good Lord,' Dickens exclaimed, 'Josephine.'

'Lawks, sir, I thought you was the pantechnicon. They're
comin' terday ter take the furniture.'

'What are you doing here?' Dickens asked.

'Well, it ain't my day fer Devonshire Terrace. Yer knows
that, sir.'

'No, no — are you working for Mr Li Shen?'

'Yes, I came in ter clean an' 'e asked me ter see about the
movin' men.' She looked at Jones hopefully. 'You ain't the
pantechnicon, are yer?'

Jones laughed. 'No, I'm Superintendent Jones of Bow Street
— friend of Mr Dickens.'

'Mr Jones, meet Josephine, who is keeping her eye on the
dust of Devonshire Terrace while we are in Broadstairs — and
the dust flees I know not where before her gimlet gaze.'

'I knows where it goes, Mr Dickens, but where it comes
from only the Lord knows, I daresay, an' 'e ain't tellin'.'

'Can we sit down somewhere?' asked Jones. 'I want to ask
about Mr Li Shen.'

'As nice a gentleman as yer'd meet, Mr Jones, sir, for all he's a furriner.' Josephine removed a couple of dust sheets and they sat. She looked anxiously at Dickens. 'Ain't in trouble, is 'e?'

Jones answered, 'No, I just want to know a few things. Can you think back to the opening day of the Exhibition?'

'Yes, sir — dreadful 'ot, it was, an' all them crowds. Streets was packed. I'd 'ave liked ter see the Queen, though. All in pink, they said. Might go on one o' them shillin' days. My lad's wild ter see them ingines.'

'Were you here that day?'

'I came in ter tidy up. Mr Li Shen asked me special. I 'elped 'im out the day before.'

'How?'

'Mr Li Shen 'ad guests — fer lunch. Some folk 'e knew from China —'

Dickens felt a tightening in the air. The very dust motes seemed to be stilled, and he sensed as if by some telegraphic message Sam Jones's anticipation, but Jones was patient. He liked to give his witnesses time.

'Chinese, Mr Li Shen, yer knows, Mr Dickens — fancy that — China. Mind, there's a lot of 'em about fer the Exhibit. Funny clothes, some o' them, an' pigtails. Mind, Mr Li Shen dressed as an Englishman. Lives in Kent, see.'

'Were the guests in their Chinese costume?' Dickens asked, serious-faced.

Josephine laughed. 'No, bless yer, sir, they wasn't Chinese as such. Just came from China, I thinks — on that boat, I suppose — in the — a junk, it's called. Yer knows, the one on the river.'

Josephine always had a tendency to wander into uncharted waters, Dickens thought, remembering an accident with the kitchen copper, but he only said, smiling encouragingly, 'So it is, a junk. Now, what can you tell us about Mr Li Shen's guests?'

'Very perlite gent, the old man. Mr Mornay, 'e was. Now, the young man was very quiet. Dint say anythin', jest nodded when I served 'im some food. I thought, sir, if yer don't mind me sayin' it, 'e want all there. Looked Chinese — mebbe 'e dint speak English, I dunno. Like a child, 'e was. Mr Mornay was 'is pa an' told 'im wot ter eat an' when.'

'They didn't stay the night?' Jones asked.

'No, sir.'

'And you came the next day.'

'Yes, I went ter Devonshire Terrace first, Mr Dickens, ter check on things an' came 'ere ter do the dishes, tidy up an' that cos Mr Li Shen was goin' ter the Exhibit and then ter Kent, an' I was ter come terday fer the pantechnicon.'

'And have you been in between May the first and today?'

'Once a week, sir, jest ter keep an eye on things. But I came in on Wednesday ter see Mr Li Shen, an' Thursday to get ready for the pantechnicon.'

'Mr Li Shen was here alone?'

'Yes, sir, though I 'eard voices in the lobby as I was leavin' — dint want ter disturb Mr Li Shen, but I locked up the back door, Mr Dickens. I'm allus careful.'

'I know, Josephine. Nothing to worry about.' Dickens gave her two shillings — for the Exhibit, he said. 'You might see the Queen, you never know.'

They left Josephine on the front steps, waiting for the elusive pantechnicon. Dickens had a wild thought about a body secreted in an old coffer and sent down to Kent for Mr Li Shen to dispose of in some secret woods, but he didn't share his idea with Jones, who was already making his way to cross the New Road out of York Gate.

'Minster in Kent, then,' he said as Dickens caught up with him. 'Mr Li Shen lied to us.'

'Ramsgate train from London Bridge. When?'

They crossed the road and went down into Devonshire Place where it was quieter. 'It'll have to be tomorrow. I need to get back to Bow Street and see Rogers. Though I doubt we'll get anything new from Hammersmith. Mr Li Shen's the man we want.'

20: A GLINT OF GOLD

Dickens woke from a dream of a gentleman in a top hat, top boots and nothing else at all, and who seemed perfectly unaware of that embarrassing fact. He was telling Dickens, 'But we all must die, Mr Dickens, sooner or later.' And then the gentleman took his hand and they jumped from a high cliff into the boiling sea below. Dickens was fighting his way to the surface when he woke.

Cornelius Mornay, he supposed, not that he had drowned, but someone had left him in the river. Who was the naked man? Mr Li Shen? Mr Li Shen who had lied about his acquaintance with Cornelius Mornay. Why should he do so? Perhaps it was to do with Michael. Perhaps Mr Li Shen knew about the attack on Miss Anne Palmer and Mr Li Shen did not want to tell that story. Captain Bright had not mentioned it. He had told Dickens as much as he thought Dickens needed to know.

As he mused, he got ready to meet Jones at London Bridge. Three hours or so to Minster. Then he remembered that Mr Li Shen was joining his employer, Mr Fullerton, in Dover. Mr Li Shen's family would surely know where he was staying in Dover with Mr Fullerton.

Wherefore to Dover? *King Lear*, again. Rather how to get to Dover from Minster. There was a train to Deal, and they could get a steamer to Dover and back to London by train in about three hours — depending on what Mr Li Shen could tell them about Cornelius Mornay's eldest son and where he might have gone on May the first. Or, he wondered, could they get back to Broadstairs and seek out Miss Anne Palmer? That would take hours. However, they could stay overnight at Fort House — it wouldn't matter how late they were.

Broadstairs. Standing on the cliff top, watching the roaring sea on a stormy night. Drowning. The body of a young man with dark hair who had been washed up from a ship — a ship from Antwerp, so he had heard. Great heavens — could he be wrong about Jonathan Mornay? Jonathan Mornay who knew that his father had another family. Did young Mornay know about the half-brother who had attempted to kill someone and who was confined in a madhouse?

He took his hat and stick, and the basket Mr Simpson had sent with sandwiches and beer for himself and Jones. The train to Ramsgate left from London Bridge in half an hour. He'd have to hurry.

Dickens was never late. Jones looked at his watch anxiously. He wanted to get this early train. Three hours to Minster and then somehow, they'd probably have to get to Dover if that's where Mr Li Shen was with his employer. Jones had remembered that last night. The important thing was that they should get back to London from Dover — if, of course, Mr Li Shen had any idea of where Michael Spencer was.

Then Dickens was beside him. 'Sorry, Sam, I left it a bit late.'

'Not like you. Late night, was it?'

'Dreams, Samivel. I'll tell you on the train.'

'Dover,' said Jones when they were settled in their carriage. 'We'll have to get a train from Minster to Deal. What's the best way to Dover from there?'

'Steamer, I should think,' Dickens said, vaguely it seemed to Jones.

What on earth's on his mind? Dickens looked distracted, Jones thought. No one was more eager when they were travelling to some destination in pursuit of a witness or evidence. He'd brought a basket, so there couldn't be much amiss. That play, probably. Someone backed out? Jones hoped he wasn't to be roped in. Dickens had hinted that a valet's part might be going. 'Breeches, white gloves, powder in your hair — suit you. Valet to me — Lord Wilmot,' he had jested — what seemed a lifetime ago.

'Broadstairs,' Dickens announced, interrupting Jones's musings about the stage.

'Oh, Miss Palmer — how on earth do we get to Broadstairs if we have to go to Dover?'

'No, not that. Last night — or rather early this morning, I was dreaming of drowning.'

'Cornelius Mornay on your mind.'

'You remember that ship that foundered on Goodwin Sands earlier this month? There was a body on the beach the next morning — drowned among all the dead cattle and sheep —'

Jones stared at him. 'It was the *Mercury* — all the passengers were saved. I read it.'

'What!'

'Elizabeth pointed it out to me because she knew you were in Broadstairs — wondered if you'd seen it. But all saved.'

'Good Lord, Sam — I found a young man dead on the beach, a young man with dark hair, wearing a suit. A gentleman, I thought. I assumed he had been on that ship.'

'You reported it?'

'I did, but I was coming to town — I didn't want to be in the story. I know the coastguard. I just said that I thought I'd seen something that might have been — you don't think —'

'I don't know what to think. Except that Miss Palmer lives near Broadstairs and Mr Li Shen is not so far off and we did wonder if Michael Spencer might have somehow found his way there — though James Spencer thought it unlikely.'

'I thought of Jonathan Mornay — whether he had come from Antwerp before he got his sister's letter. It was the fact that the ship came from Antwerp, but since the body was not that of a passenger, I think we can discount him.'

'I sent Feak to St Katharine Docks to check the passenger list of the boat that came in on the afternoon two days ago. Jonathan Mornay was on that boat. The *Mercury* was wrecked on the night of May the fourth — he could have come to London without anyone knowing, I suppose. I'll need to contact his employers — see if he was absent. Michael Spencer's been missing since April the twenty-ninth. Mornay was taken on May the first, so why the delay between April twenty-ninth and May the fourth?'

'I don't know if he knew about the third child — my guess is that his father wouldn't have told him, given the story of Fort Pitt.'

'All right, let's leave him out of it until we get some evidence. I suggest that we carry on to Minster, find out where Li Shen is in Dover, go on to Ramsgate — then Broadstairs — see if we can learn anything about this body, and then to Dover. If need be, we could stay in Dover and get the first train to London tomorrow morning.'

'What about Miss Palmer? Howbeit, if we see her while we're there — it might save us a trip to Dover. I mean, if Michael Spencer is the dead man —' he looked at Jones's sceptical face — 'I know it's far-fetched, but Kent, Sam, and a young man's body. And we know a young man is missing —' he hurried on — 'or he might be at Miss Palmer's.'

'Now that is a point — all right, Ramsgate first.'

'The Seaman's Infirmary will have received the body. Oh,

Lor, Sam — he may be buried already, but I do know the surgeon there, Mr Grafton. He might be able to tell us something.'

'I still want to see Mr Li Shen. He lied to us.'

At Minster, Jones thought to enquire at the post office for Mr Fullerton's address. A servant there would surely know where the master was in Dover and that would save alerting Mr Li Shen's family. It was easy enough. The post mistress was quite ready to oblige a Superintendent from Bow Street who was enquiring about a robbery at Mr Fullerton's house in London.

The train took them on to Ramsgate where Dickens took them first to the coast guard station.

'At the hospital mortuary, Mr Dickens,' Captain Flint told them. 'Nothing on him to say who he was, and we've advertised. It was assumed that he came off the ship, but Doctor Grafton had doubts about whether he'd drowned, so the magistrate said there'd be a second inquest after enquiries had been made.'

'I read that all the passengers were saved,' Jones said. 'He couldn't have been a stowaway?'

'Well, the enquiries were made of the captain and crew. Course the police traced as many of the passengers as was possible, but no one knew him. The captain was adamant about no stowaways and he came to look with some of the sailors, but no one recognized him. I don't know, Mr Dickens, he could have been a stowaway, but we'll never know unless someone comes forward. The second inquest took place a few days ago — cause of death unknown, according to the doctor. They'll have to bury him on the parish.'

At the Seaman's Infirmary, they were directed to the mortuary where the porter told them Mr Grafton was showing the body to someone who had come to enquire about a missing relative.

'Few minutes ago, Mr Dickens.'

Downstairs there was an open door, and Dickens heard the voice of Mr Grafton and then a lady's rather impatient voice asking, 'How did he die, sir?'

Jones knocked and went in, followed by Dickens. An elderly lady stood facing the doctor.

'And who might you be?' the lady asked sharply, turning to look at them. *Betsey Trotwood*, Dickens thought, noting the sharp eyes and rather angular face. She wore a close-fitting lavender coloured dress which emphasized her angles rather than softened them and like the redoubtable Miss Trotwood she wore a gentleman's gold watch pinned to her gown. She stood very straight under her old straw bonnet which looked oddly like a helmet to Dickens. Quite ready to do battle — with boys or donkeys, or any man or woman at all, or doctor. The surgeon looked a bit cowed.

'Superintendent Jones of Bow Street, London, and Mr Charles Dickens.'

She didn't blink. 'Hm,' she said, looking at Dickens with a steely eye, 'oh, I know you. And you know me.' Dickens felt somewhat hot about the collar. Had she read his thoughts? 'Well, here's a story for you, sir. My sometime ward, Mr Michael Spencer, is missing. I find out a body's been found on Broadstairs beach — possibly Chinese — and I want this man to tell me how he died.'

'I should —' Jones began.

'I'm sure you should, sir, but you'll wait your turn. Now, Mr Surgeon Grafton, what have you to say?'

Jones, very wisely, did not interrupt.

'I — er — well, he didn't drown,' Mr Grafton began nervously.

'And he wasn't on that ship — he can't have been, because he was in London with his father, so how did he come here and how did he die?'

'I cannot tell you the answer to your first question, madam, and as to the second — I can only tell you that he did not drown. I cannot establish a cause of death.'

'Fiddlesticks,' the lady said. 'You're a doctor.' She shook her head. 'Imbecility.'

'I assure you, madam —'

'Where is he now?' asked Jones.

'At the undertaker's — Parson and Pickles — he's to be buried today.'

'Fiddlesticks — I must see him first. I must know if it is Michael.'

She turned to go, but Jones stopped her. 'I must come with you to ask some questions, Miss Palmer, for that is who I think you are. I have come from London in search of Mr Spencer. There is a good deal I must tell you.'

'Very well, but I must see him, or they'll have him in his grave before I have time.'

Mr Parson was not in evidence — saying his prayers, perhaps, but Mr Pickle emerged from behind his mahogany counter, rose, as it were from the grave. *An unfortunate name*, Dickens reflected, while composing his face. He always had a desire to laugh when he met an undertaker. Still, the theological Parson cancelled out the comedy of a pickle. Mr Pickle was a well-preserved elderly man in his suit of black, its solemnity rather belied by his sun-browned face and wings of white hair which gave him the look of cheerful cherub. His tone, however, was suitably melancholy as he told them he would be with them in a few moments.

He bowed to Miss Palmer and said, 'I will show you his face. Fear not, my dear lady, you will recognize him if you know him.'

They waited in silence. Fearless Miss Palmer stood erect, unmoving. Dickens watched her sharp, unflinching profile. A missionary lady from China — she would have seen a good deal. A strong woman who had survived an attack by poor mad Michael Spencer, but she had obviously forgiven him.

They went in and Miss Palmer looked at the waxen face. The dead man looked very young. His face was smooth and peaceful, all marks of suffering erased by death. The eyes were closed in that long sleep which ends all strife. But, if he had not drowned, how had he died?

'It is Michael,' Miss Palmer said. She touched the brow with one finger, and they heard her say, 'Poor boy.' She turned and seemed to falter. She sat down suddenly on the nearest chair.

Jones turned to Mr Pickle. 'Where can we go?'

'There is a quiet parlour next door for the bereaved.'

'Thank you. I will come to find you when we have finished.'

Miss Palmer allowed Jones to help her up, but that's all he did, sensing that she must compose herself. She straightened her shoulders, lifted her rather long chin, and went out, followed by Jones and Dickens.

In the next room Anne Palmer listened to the Superintendent's account of the death of Mr Cornelius Mornay, the disappearance of Michael Mornay, the meeting with James and Jane Spencer, and Jonathan Mornay's knowledge of the second family. She sat straight on another hard chair and looked directly at Jones, unblinking. The only thing that indicated any emotion was the soft, continuous beating of her hand on her lavender skirt.

'Now, Mr Superintendent Jones from Bow Street, you must answer me a question — and no prevaricating.'

'If I can —' Jones began.

'Already prevaricating. I thought you looked a decisive man. One question: are you thinking that that poor benighted creature lying dead there — of who knows what — has killed his father?'

'No, I am not.'

'Very well, now that's out of the way, I'll tell you what I can. You know why Michael Spencer was at Fort Pitt?' Dickens and Jones nodded. 'He was a very sick young man when he came from India, and I nursed him. Nightmares, he had — of bandits, of ghosts, of beasts, snakes — all sorts of wild things, all coming for him, and in the night he thought I was some dreadful spirit come to harm him. That is how it happened. Not the boy's fault. I'd have kept him with me — lunatic asylum, forsooth — but Cornelius Mornay was frightened — that it might happen again, and of scandal, of course. Not a bad man, Cornelius, but he'd married an English woman. Many of them did when they came to England, and they wanted to forget the children they had sired. Cornelius supported them — it wasn't until he took them to London that he got to know and — love them. He regretted what he had done, but — that's the way of things — too late. But, sirs, none of them would have harmed their father. You can put that idea out of your heads at once.'

'Mr Li Shen?' Jones asked.

'What has he to do with anything?'

'Cornelius Mornay took Michael to see him on April thirtieth, but he did not tell us that.'

'No, he wouldn't — if Cornelius had asked him not to.

144

Loyal, Mr Li Shen, and he won't have brought Michael here.'

'Unless Mr Li Shen took him home and Michael wandered away.'

'Fiddlesticks —' Dickens did want to laugh. He hadn't heard Jones addressed so roundly before, but he kept an expression of becoming seriousness — 'Li Shen would have told me. Loyal, I said. He knew Cornelius in China, you see.'

Jones let pass the question of Mr Li Shen and his loyalty. 'You did not think it odd that Cornelius did not contact you about Michael for almost two weeks?'

'James and Jane were here with me. Cornelius knew that. He would not write to me about Michael when they were here. They were not to know about the London doctor. Cornelius wanted Michael kept at Fort Pitt — he worried that the story would get out. His brother and sister wanted him nearer. I was waiting to hear from Cornelius and then James wrote to tell me about his father and Michael being missing. This morning I heard about a young man found on a beach — a gossiping fool of a neighbour told me he was a Chinese sailor. I was coming into Ramsgate and I looked at the posters. Not a sailor, the bank clerk told me, a young man in his thirties with a Chinese look about him. A mystery, he said. It had been in the newspaper. Never read 'em, but I came to look, of course. Now, Mr Superintendent Jones, what do you propose to do?'

Jones hesitated a fraction too long.

'Come, come.'

'Michael Spencer's death must be connected to his father's death. I need to find out why he came here and how.'

'And who brought him — Michael could not have come here on his own. You may take my word for that. Someone brought him here and left him to die — or killed him. And it wasn't his brother or sister — nor Mr Li Shen — I can swear to that, sir. You need to question that quivering thing that calls himself a doctor about how he died.'

'I will — now, what do you propose to do?'

'I'll go to London — to tell James and Jane that Michael is dead. It should come from me — not you. You'll find me there if you want me —' she consulted her gentleman's watch — 'There's a train at half-past four.'

'How did you come from Dumpton?' asked Dickens, wondering if they might take her home to pack her things.

'Walked. I needn't go back. My girl, Janet, will not worry. She's used to me. I have all I need here.' She pointed to a capacious bag — very like the one Betsey Trotwood had always carried.

She stood up then and adjusted her old bonnet, seized her umbrella, and made ready to go. Jones wasn't going to stop her.

Dickens went upstairs to see her off. He offered to accompany her to the station.

'Fiddlesticks, young man —' it was his turn now — 'no need. I can board a train without assistance. Get along with you and find who left that poor boy on that beach.'

He waited at the top of the steps as she went down. She turned to look back at him. 'I know you,' she said, 'you'll do your best. Betsey Trotwood, eh? You know me, it would seem.'

Then she was on her way, a brisk, solitary figure, stalking along, shoulders high, wielding her umbrella like a weapon.

Jones came out. 'I've told the undertaker that the body must be returned to Doctor Grafton. I want another word with him.'

Doctor Grafton looked relieved to see that Miss Palmer was no longer with them. Jones asked about his findings.

'It was assumed at first that he had come off the ship, but his clothes, though damp, were not sodden. He had not drowned — the lungs were of normal size and not distended; the cavities of the heart were full — in a case of drowning, the left cavities of the heart may be empty or contain much less blood than the right; and there was no water in the stomach which is an indication that the subject has swallowed water during the struggle for life, and the skin was perfectly normal — there was no evidence of cutis anserine — that is commonly called goose-skin —'

Dickens interrupted. 'I remember that — I looked at his hand.'

'You were there, Mr Dickens?'

'I was — the morning after the storm. I assumed he had been a passenger on the *Mercury* and reported it to the harbour master at Broadstairs, but the hand — it was perfectly smooth and dry.'

'To go back to the clothes, Mr Grafton, I should like to know if there were any stains of vomit or evacuation of the bowels.'

Grafton gave him a sharp look. 'Poison, you're thinking?'

'This young man's father was murdered in Wapping. I am investigating the case. The father was found in the river, but our doctor found evidence of opium poisoning.'

'I see — there was certainly evidence of vomiting on the jacket, which I put down at first to his having been in the water. As far as the undergarments were concerned, yes, they were stained, but again that is not unusual. I must say I did not think of poison. My thoughts were natural causes — shock, heart failure…'

'It would be helpful if you could examine him again — the head —' Jones was thinking of Doctor Woodhall's conclusions about Cornelius Mornay.

'Yes, yes, the vessels of the head would be unusually congested. You wish me to recover the body from the undertaker.'

'I have already taken the liberty of instructing the undertaker to return the body to you immediately. I need to know if there is a connection between the two deaths.'

'Very well.'

'I am much obliged, Mr Grafton. Now we will leave you to your further examination. What time would you want us to return?'

'In not less than two hours.'

Dickens and Jones went out to breathe in the sea air and look out at the water, serene and sparkling under the summer sun. Dickens thought of the night of the storm and of someone taking a bewildered young man onto a deserted shore and leaving him to die.

'Dover?' he asked.

'I wonder. Given what your Miss Trotwood said —'

Dickens laughed. 'Just what I thought — lavender gown and all. She knew, too. She said "Betsey Trotwood, eh?" when she left me.'

'Well, I get the impression that she's just as wise, and despite her somewhat bracing manner, she's a kind heart beating time under that gold watch. I think Mr Li Shen will be there when I want him. In any case, I'm thinking of the time if we have to come back here to see Mr Grafton.'

'Broadstairs, then — we'll go to Fort House, have something to eat and I'll get Georgina, my sister-in-law to drive us back in a couple of hours, and we can have a look at the beach.'

Anne Brown, Catherine Dickens's maid, told them that Mrs Dickens and her daughters were in Ramsgate, but the boys and their Aunt Georgina were down on the beach. 'Building castles,' she said. They would go down, Dickens told her, and come back in fifteen minutes if she could get some sandwiches made and some tea.

Great acclamation greeted the unexpected arrivals. Jones was amused to see so many boys swarm up, demanding to show castles, to play leapfrog, cricket, to paddle, to shout for "Pa". He watched with Georgina as Dickens went the rounds of the various fortifications.

'You are not staying?' she asked.

'I am afraid not. We have to return to Ramsgate in a couple of hours — on some business.'

Georgina didn't ask what, but she observed that the children would be disappointed. 'They love it when he is here — like the sun coming out for them. They are very good boys, all of them, but he's the one who tells the stories, sings to them, and invents all kinds of games. Catherine and I miss him, too.'

She adores him, thought Jones, hearing the wistful note in her voice, and then a little boy came up to him and said, 'I can show you our things, if you like, at the house — what we find on the beach. Treasure.'

Dickens came back and they went back up to the house, the small boy, Sydney, holding Jones's hand — he wasn't going to let go now that he had a companion all to himself.

'Treasure,' he said, 'the man wants to see my treasure.' *Not quite true*, thought Jones. It was just the kind of stratagem that

Tom Brim used — his desire translated to his chosen subject's. It was usually Poll, the dog who wanted the biscuit.

Dickens laughed. Four-year-old Sydney was quite adept at getting his own way. Jones was taken upstairs immediately to see the treasures and Dickens followed, keen to see the exhibition which last time he had been up in the nursery had comprised a good many pebbles of apparently fabulous worth, a piece of pyrite, the gold of which was priceless, several pieces of old rope, some dried seaweed, some curious pieces of dried wood — from a pirate ship, it was firmly believed — and a shell in which, as had been demonstrated many times, you could hear the sea. It was, as Sydney gravely told his captive, their Great Exhibishun. The sound of running feet on the stairs heralded the arrival of another curator who was equally determined not to be left out. Alfred, aged five, came in.

Dickens looked at the new exhibits — more seaweed, more shells, a shiny black stone with a hole in it which reminded Dickens of the Chinese coins that had been in Cornelius Mornay's mouth, an intact green bottle, and the centrepiece which Alfred picked up with great reverence to show Pa.

'A pirate's bone,' he said, 'from that wrecked ship — the pirate ship. A pirate drowned — an' this was his leg, I bet, Pa. Blackbeard, Pa.'

The bone — probably the remnants of some poor drowned beast — was thoroughly examined, found to be, undoubtedly, some desperate pirate's arm or leg, and put back in its place of honour. Something gold caught Dickens's eye. Not the pyrite, but an odd conical-shaped piece of metal about an inch and a half long, tapering to a point and chased with some design. Dickens picked it up and asked where they had got it.

'On the path, on the way up. I saw it shining in the sun. It's gold, Pa, pirate's gold. See, you can wear it on your finger.'

Alfred put it on. Then Dickens knew exactly what it was. Alfred was right.

'A Chinese man's fingernail, Alley, my boy, and a great treasure, indeed.'

At the words "Chinese man", Jones turned to look and saw Dickens wearing a golden fingernail exactly like the ones he had seen worn by the Lady Pwan-ye-Koo and her musical entourage at the Chinese Exhibition.

'Now, Alley, this piece of gold is very important to my friend, Mr Jones —' Dickens squatted down and put an arm about each of the boys — 'and this is top secret —' he looked about him in the manner of one who fears to be overheard and lowered his voice — the boys gazed at Pa with great round eyes — 'Mr Jones is a policeman who has come down with Pa to look for clues because, and you know all about these things, there is a pirate who must be caught. A desperate rogue who has stolen treasure from — the Queen!'

'Will she chop his head off?' Alley had an imagination of the sanguinary kind.

'No, but he must be put into the Queen's dungeons so dark and deep that he can never come out to sail the seven seas again. Now, Mr Jones must have this clue if he is to catch this ruffian. Will you let him have it?'

Alley and Sydney looked up at the policeman. Sydney was not now quite so sure of his new friend. Alley looked thoughtful. Then he took the golden treasure from Pa's finger and offered it to Jones. 'For the Queen,' he said.

'God blesser,' added Sydney, for that was what Pa always said, and Sydney liked the last word.

'Good boys, and now you must show us where you found it, Alley, and not a word to anyone. Cross your hearts, lads.' Which they did, most solemnly.

Later, Dickens and Jones stood on the clifftop. The pony and trap had come back with Mrs Dickens and her daughters and they had all had tea. Georgina would drive them back to Ramsgate.

They looked down at the sands below where Dickens had picked his way through the corpses of cattle and sheep to find a dead man. Now, children played there, building their castles, tossing balls, running into the little waves that crept up and retreated. They could hear, borne on the breeze, the laughter and the shrieks of joy. It was hot, but the sea breeze was fresh and salty. They both felt they could breathe, as if in the thickened air of Wapping, which stank of sulphur and sewage and stale fish, they had not been able to.

'Oh, to have to go back to that wilderness of darkness,' Dickens said.

'Stay here — play with those children, entertain your guests, write your book … take care of your wife.' Jones had thought that Catherine Dickens seemed very anxious. He had talked to her about her little dead baby because she knew about his dead daughter, Edith, though that had been many years ago. She had been glad to hear about Elizabeth's feelings.

'Bracing, Superintendent,' Dickens gave him a crooked smile.

'Well, you look tired, Elizabeth said so.'

'So do you.'

'It's my job.'

Dickens walked to the edge and breathed in a great gulp of air. Jones followed and touched his arm. They looked out at the placid ocean and saw far away the steel grey band of the horizon, the faint smoke smudge of a steamer off on its voyage to the distance. Dickens looked down. A child looked up and waved. Sydney? He squinted into the light. No, it was Alley. He waved back. He could make out his wife and the girls. They were shadows in the sunlight. He felt the distance, caught between two worlds, and somehow always walking away, taking a train, a carriage, a boat — travelling on. The steamer had vanished over the horizon.

He looked at Jones. 'We'd better go.'

'Sure?'

'I never shall desert —'

'I know, and I'm grateful.' Jones looked at him gravely. 'But, if it's too much — after all that's happened.'

'The battle of life, Samivel, always to be fought — to the end. Come down — when this is over. Bring Elizabeth and the children. Bring Scrap. Make a holiday. Catherine would like it.' Of course, those searching eyes had missed nothing.

'I will — when it's over. When. That young man was murdered. Someone took him down that path.'

'In the dark. In that storm.'

Alley looked up. But Pa was gone. A cloud covered the sun. And when he turned round, his sandcastle had collapsed. Built too near the water.

Mr Grafton had examined the head and brain and had found the enlarged blood vessels and the tell-tale bloody points on the cut surface of the brain. It was enough. They spent time asking at various hotels and pubs. Jones was convinced that the murderers — there must have been two, he thought — had come from London — by train, surely, but there was no trace of them, and they had not time to investigate every house with lodgings to let for summer visitors, and there were many of those.

'There were those posters of which Miss Palmer spoke,' Dickens said as they waited for the train. 'Someone would have remembered them here. They could have come from Minster

— any station on the route from London. The North Kent line, too, from Strood —'

'But where was Michael Spencer between April thirtieth and May fourth when he was left on the beach? Cornelius Mornay must have left him somewhere, and who brought him to Broadstairs?'

'Only Miss Palmer, Francis Hope, Jane and James Spencer knew about him.'

'And Mr Li Shen.'

'But Miss Palmer said she would swear —'

'So she did, but I still want to see him.'

'Bluegate Fields first.'

'You're right. The frustrating thing is that until I see Lord John again, I can't ask about Cornelius Mornay at that opium den —'

'But you could ask about a Michael Spencer.'

'So I could — and this —'

Jones took the finger guard from his pocket. A shaft of sunlight caught the gold. It was a beautiful thing, but sinister, too — cruel, even. And Dickens remembered suddenly a pair of impudent black eyes and a glint of gold in a seedy pub in Wapping.

21: OPIUM DEN

Bluegate Fields was a foul narrow lane skirting by St George's Church; whether there had been a blue gate sometime in the distant past, Dickens did not know. Now it seemed the black gate to hell. The fields had long gone. Here was a wilderness built of brick and stone, with the meanest shops, their cracked windows patched with sacking; outside one a collection of old clothes, by another a few wizened-looking potatoes and carrots. Somewhere in this blighted place must be the tobacconist's to which Bold and Constable Sleat were leading him and Sam Jones. Two other invisible constables were somewhere behind them.

There were the most wretched lodging houses and brothels, but the denizens of this squalor were not yet abroad. They kept late hours, preferring the dark in which to conduct their business: thieving, whoring, fighting, stabbing, garrotting, boozing. The sailors called it Tiger Bay after the tigresses, savage hoydens who'd strip a man of everything he had, even his life if they had a mind to. All alike in their sodden hideousness with misshapen, aged faces and toothless mouths, and their garish shabby satins and feathers.

A tiger's heart wrapped in a woman's hide. Not all alike. Dickens thought of a pretty young woman who had stripped a gentleman of his money and clothes. She must have a heart of adamant to venture here. Perhaps she had not been alone; perhaps there had been a well-dressed man with eyes like ice.

They turned in to Angel Court. The church, he supposed. Hawksmoor's great church with its soaring tower had perhaps inspired the name. There were no angels here now. The tobacconist's shop was closed. There was no one to be seen through the bleary window.

'Round the back,' Sleat offered, and led them along a tiny passage where the door to a yard was open and a young, dark-haired girl was emptying a bucket of dirty water into the alley. She looked alarmed when Sleat approached. She knew him. She glanced fearfully at the men following, two tall, grim-faced men. More police, she thought. She couldn't make out the third.

'Your pa in?' Sleat asked.

The girl stepped aside, and the men went into the yard where a back door was also open. Dickens looked at her as he passed. A paler, shabbier version of Jane Spencer, a faded sketch of the more beautiful girl, but the same dark eyes, the same high cheekbones, and a similar height. She was very thin, especially in the face, and he noticed her short hair, which looked as though it had been chopped about with a knife. She looked at him for a moment. She seemed scared, but then she turned away.

Sleat was in the house with Inspector Bold and Sam Jones. Dickens looked through the gap between them and saw a small room with a large, dilapidated four-poster bed covered in a grimy blanket. There was a tiny fireplace on which was placed a skillet over a few coals.

'Get up, Cheng, up, up.' Sleat had dealt with Cheng before.

There were two humps in the bed. The smell was of unwashed bodies, stale cooking, smoking coals and something sickly, burnt and sweet at the same time. *Opium*, thought Dickens. Samuel Taylor Coleridge, poet and opium addict, had written that he had "drunk the milk of paradise". *Dear Lord*, he thought. *Paradise.*

Sleat snatched the threadbare blanket and pulled it back to

reveal the sleeping forms beneath. 'Chop, chop, Cheng.'

The Chinese man sat up and looked about him blearily. He was fully dressed in a drab tunic and trousers and wore a nightcap. The effect was ludicrous, as if a Chinese Scrooge had been woken by the Ghost of Christmas Past — or Marley in his pigtail, more like. The hump beside him did not stir, but they could hear the laboured breathing and snores.

'Wake her up,' Bold ordered.

Cheng gave the hump a sharp poke with his skinny elbow. Another poke. More grunting and snuffling and the hump in a filthy nightgown stained with brown sat up, and Dickens saw a grey-haired hag. Two more bleary eyes gazed at them, and the mouth opened in an unlovely yawn.

'Know what this is?' Bold asked, showing Cheng the finger-guard.

Cheng nodded vigorously, the tassel of his nightcap shaking in time. 'Chinese,' he said, smiling at Bold, 'for finger — for Mandarin — not Cheng's.'

'Know whose it is?'

'No, sir, not know — for Mandarin. Rich man — emperor.'

Bold showed it to Mrs Cheng, who shook her head. 'I know what it is. It's nothing to do with us.'

Dickens was astonished at her voice. It wasn't a London voice — more a country voice, like the voices you heard in Kent, but not uneducated. When she looked at Bold, he saw that though her face was a ruin, there were remnants of youth. She wasn't as old as she looked, but that was the way with addicts, whether drinkers or drug users. Mrs Cheng might have been beautiful once. He could see it in her broad brow and finely modelled nose, even in her large eyes. He imagined a well-made farmer's daughter with a rosy face and blue eyes and strong teeth. But the mouth was toothless now, and the lower face fallen in. Who had she been?

'Captain Blood,' barked Bold, 'know him?'

'Come for bacco sometime. Bad man. Not nice man,' Cheng answered.

'Why does he say that?' Jones asked the woman.

'He's a brute and he doesn't always pay.'

'What about his friends? A man with pale eyes and a pretty dark-haired woman. Both well-dressed. Customers of yours?'

'Not know, not know,' Cheng insisted, but Dickens saw his eyes slide towards his wife.

'Lots o' customers — I don't remember them all. People are always coming by for their tobacco.'

'And opium,' Jones said, 'customers come for opium.'

'Achey, achey,' Cheng chanted, 'headachey, toothachey. Cheng cure them. Sailors come with achey.'

Jones looked at Mrs Cheng. 'A missing young man — half Chinese — name of Spencer, Michael Spencer. Have you heard of him?'

'No, I haven't — customers don't give their names, you know — they only want their tobacco and a pennyworth of opium. It's not illegal,' she said sullenly.

It wasn't. They all knew that. Opium could be bought anywhere: from barbers, confectioners, druggists, of course, ironmongers — even stationers sold it — and tobacconists, certainly. A penny for as much as thirty grains — cheaper than gin, and for many, a means of suppressing hunger as well as pain, and everyone took laudanum for aches and pains. Dickens had taken it himself for neuralgia.

They went out of the door through which they had entered. The girl was sweeping the yard, but she didn't turn round. Dickens noticed that she was wearing a white cap now, the sort a maidservant would wear.

'Is she the daughter?' asked Dickens as they went into the alley.

'Yes, poor thing,' said Sleat. 'Those two are hopeless.'

They made their way back to the police station, not wishing to loiter any longer than they had to in Bluegate Fields.

'Do you know anything about the woman?' asked Dickens when they were safely back in Bold's office.

'You noticed,' said Bold. 'She's not from round here, that's for sure. I don't know, but they've been around for ten years or more. I don't know where they came from. Could be anywhere. Cheng off a ship, Mrs from the country. You know how it happens — a girl abandoned by her parents, comes to London — poverty makes ruin of them.'

'How old do you think she is?'

'That girl's about sixteen, I should think. Mrs might be in her thirties. Looks a hundred, I know.'

'They were nervous about Blood and that pair we mentioned. The gentleman that was robbed and stripped. Found in Bluegate Fields, wasn't he?' Jones asked.

'They were and he was. I've no doubt they know them — but as to criminal involvement, hard to say, and as to the gentleman — he thought he'd been drugged, but nothing to say Cheng had any part of it. Opium, no doubt, but there was no way of telling, and the man wasn't willing to take it further, and there are plenty of similar cases. Usually sailors drugged and robbed.'

'But not so many gentlemen.'

'No, indeed, Superintendent Jones, but I'm thinking about Dag, too. Cheng's a mess, and his missus, but I don't want them on my conscience by going in too hard on them. We'll keep a discreet eye on who goes in and out. Captain Blood's the man I'm after — he's in with that young man and woman,

I'm sure of it.'

'And if you hear anything about Michael Spencer, let me know — he died of opium poisoning and someone dropped that finger guard on the path down to the beach where he was found.'

Bold nodded, then a knock came at the door and Constable Stemp came in. Dickens saw what Jones had meant. He did look frightening with his black stubble, his filthy face, his earring and his knife at his belt.

'Stemp,' Jones greeted him, 'all well?'

'Yes, sir, I came to say that I found one of Dag's lads — name o' Ned — down on the shore. Gave him some bread and cheese, an' he had a tale to tell about Dag's murder.'

'Where is he now?'

'Not in any danger, sir.' Stemp looked at Inspector Bold. 'Constable Gaunt, sir, said to tell you that 'e's taken the lad to the Seaman's Orphans — said you'd know about it.'

'Yes.' Bold explained to Dickens and Jones, 'The Merchant Seaman's Orphan Asylum up on Bow Lane — the lad'll be safe there. Gaunt has — a friend — one of the nurses there. What did he tell you, Stemp?'

''E didn't see it, but 'e heard them an' didn't dare come out. 'E was that frightened cos 'e knew who they were. Name of Milk — well-dressed cove with very pale eyes, the lad said. Knew 'is voice. Toff, 'e said.'

'And the girl?' asked Jones.

'She was there, too. Would you believe it — called Puss.'

'Did he hear any exchange with Dag — why they did it?'

'Police, the lad said, ter do with Dag an' the police. Dag told 'em that 'e 'adn't said anythin', an' they wanted ter know 'oo the toff was — I wondered if they meant you, Mr Dickens. Dag 'adn't a clue, o' course. Not that they believed 'im. Lad 'eard what went on — ol' Dag pleadin' with 'em, but, thank God, 'e didn't actually see 'em do the killin'. Bad enough what 'e saw after they left. Lad 'ooked it fast an' 'e's been 'idin' in an old boat. 'E was so terrified that he left it to someone else to find Dag, but Gaunt an' me, we persuaded' 'im that 'e'd be safer well out of it.'

'The girl — what did he say about her?' Jones asked.

'Not much 'cept that she wasn't like the others. Like a lady, 'e thought, though what 'e knows about ladies…'

'Does he know what the connection is between Dag and this pair?' Bold wanted to know.

''E'd seen 'em with Dag in that pub — they was payin' Dag fer somethin', the lad thought. 'E thought it mighta been to do with a robbery. 'E knew that Toby Quick was shot an' disappeared, an' that Dag was a frightened man after that, but then Dag 'ad money an' all seemed well, till the police came an' Dag was frightened again. Lad 'eard 'im tellin' this Milk that 'e 'adn't squealed.'

Dickens asked, 'Did they say anything about Toby when they were attacking Dag?'

'Lad didn't say.'

'Now, we need to find them, Superintendent Jones, now we know they did it, but I wonder — Milk's some kind of toff, so have they cleared out? No one's seen them since Dag was killed. But we'll keep looking. As I say, Captain Blood's the man I'll start with.'

'And Stemp here can keep looking for Toby Quick. I'll send Rogers, Stemp.'

This time, Dickens and Jones slipped out of the police station the back way to make their way to the steamer pier. On board, they stood in the lee of the funnel.

'Milk,' Jones said, disgust in his voice.

'Milk to gall,' Dickens replied, thinking of Lady Macbeth, 'hardly the milk of human kindness.'

'They gall me, I can tell you. Milk and Puss — who the devil are they?'

'Cheng and his wife — they knew them, I'm sure. I wonder if Cornelius Mornay had been there. I mean, he was often in Wapping. Might he have known Cheng? Was Mornay an opium addict? Picked up the habit in Canton, maybe?'

'Could be, but you can get opium anywhere. Mornay wouldn't have to go to Wapping for it — unless he smoked it, I suppose. I can see that he might have known Cheng, but is there any link between Cornelius Mornay and this Milk?'

'There has to be. Someone took Mornay to Wapping.'

'Maybe they didn't — maybe Mornay intended to go off to Princes Square in Wapping.'

'And the stranger that Toby Quick saw?'

'Just a stranger — Mornay feels faint. Good Samaritan helps him, takes him to get a cab to Wapping. Seen by Milk and Puss and the rest we can guess at. Opportunists.'

'Michael Spencer?'

'Suicide. Coincidence.'

'You don't like coincidence.'

'No more I do — I was just testing the possibilities, trying to find a reason for Milk and his girl. A toff, that lad, Ned, told Stemp — who the hell is he?'

'And how can we find out?'

'Captain Blood — let's hope Bold finds him. He's the only connection we have.'

They looked at the bank as the steamer chugged by the docks. Dickens contemplated the great warehouses where tobacco, ivory, silks, spices, opium — all the goods of the world were stored. They passed the Tower, the great Custom House and up to London Bridge, past Old Shades Pier where Dickens had stood with Captain Bright who had told him about Canton.

'Dover,' he said, 'Mr Li Shen, who is married to an English woman — from Kent, presumably. Mr Cheng, who is married to an English woman. What did you see when you looked at her?'

'An old hag — same as Bold saw, older than her years, of course.'

'And?'

Jones looked at him narrowly. 'Come on — what did you see? You always see beneath the surface.'

'I saw what she might have been before the opium destroyed her — a country girl, Bold said, and I thought so because I heard a country voice and I thought of Kent. It's a voice I hear all the time.'

'Kent, hmm —' Jones looked away towards the water — 'loyalty, Miss Palmer said, because he knew Mornay in China.'

'Perhaps Cheng and his wife are connected to Mr Li Shen and to Cornelius Mornay. I don't see how, of course — through a glass darkly —'

'And he lied to us. Dover, then, tomorrow morning and back as soon as we can.'

The steamer took them to Waterloo Bridge from where Jones walked with Dickens to Wellington Street.

'I'll have to see Lord John. I've been thinking about Mornay's death. He must have made a will — his death would bring it all out if he's named these children in it. His murder would be pointless.'

'He was ill — suppose he was thinking about making a will

in favour of his first family to provide for them in case of his death. I mean, that's why he was concerned about Michael Spencer's future. Maybe he would have to name Michael Spencer in some sort of trust — if someone got wind of that...'

'You could be right — I want to know who gets what. And only the Prime Minister can sanction a visit to Mornay's lawyer.'

'I'll walk round to the shop to see if Scrap's found out anything.'

'If he has, come up to my house with him later.'

At the counter in the stationery shop, Scrap was in a truculent mood. Sent on a fool's errand to Hyde Park — in a red jersey — askin' fer folk wot didn't exist, an' no one comin' ter ask wot 'e'd found out. Not much, granted, but Mr Jones might 'ave asked. Coulda sent Mr Dickens. Sergeant Rogers all tight-lipped an' Constable Feak shruggin' 'is shoulders. *An' me*, he thought, *left ter mind the shop an' murder done. Must be murder. So wot's the big secret?*

Thus he greeted the smiling Mr D. with unusual brusqueness. 'Where you two bin? I went ter Bow Street with Mr Feak, but Mr Jones want there, an' Mr Rogers ain't back neither. Wot's goin' on? Mystery, is it?'

Dickens knew exactly what was wrong. Their chief assistant left out in the cold — and rightly so when he thought of what he had just seen in Wapping. He'd have to be careful what he said. 'It is, Scrap — we've been down in Wapping, trying to find out about the shoe-black boy, and other things.'

'Like that, is it? Me an' Mr Feak ain't allowed to know any more.'

'You'll have to ask Mr Jones, Scrap. I daren't tell you too

much — it's all top secret, and Mr Jones, well, he's gone to see the Prime Minister.'

'About a shoe-black boy? Blimey, Mr D., think I was born yesterday?'

'I know exactly when you were born, Mr Donnelly —' Dickens had discovered Scrap's origins and his real name when the boy had wondered who he was — everyone else he knew had a proper name — and that had made him miserable — 'but, I'm serious; he has gone to see Lord John Russell —'

'But 'e oughter 'ave 'is best coat on — Mrs Jones'll be that annoyed — yer means it?'

'I do — about a missing banker — well, we've found him —'

'Murdered, I serpose, an' yer didn't tell me.'

'No, no one was supposed to know — it's a tricky case for Mr Jones, Scrap. He'll have to watch his step, and we've to follow orders on this one. He'll tell us what he can — but not everything.'

'Oh, I serpose.'

'What have you found out about the shoe-black boys?'

Scrap looked at him knowingly. 'No one's 'eard o' the lads Mr Jones mentioned — yer Dick Oliver an' that — pair o' fools we woz, lookin' fer kids wot don't exist —'

'All part of Mr Jones's master plan, see, because if you'd known —'

'As if I'd 'ave given it away — Mr Jones an' you knows me better than that.'

'We do, we do, but think about it, Scrap, Mr Jones working for the Prime Minister — if anything went wrong and he was dismissed — well, it makes me feel ill, I can tell you. Think of Mrs Jones, too, and —'

'Eleanor and Tom — I knows — sorry Mr D. I was jest —'

'Feeling out of it. I understand, Scrap — I'm a bit out of my depth, too, on this one. The two of us have different things to do for him, but we have to do what he wants — for all their sakes. Toby Quick exists, though —' *I hope*, he thought — 'did you hear anything of him?'

'There woz a shoe-black boy 'ad seen Toby Quick wiv someone out under some trees —'

'A man?'

'Or a lad — 'e couldn't see. Not a woman, anyway.'

'When?'

'Day Toby Quick vanished. An' also Toby Quick showed this lad somethin' 'e'd found under the trees — a thimble.'

'When did he find it?'

'Lad couldn't recall, but not on the day 'e disappeared.'

A thimble, Dickens thought. Anyone could have dropped it — any woman taking advantage of the shade under the trees. He couldn't imagine Miss Puss at her embroidery, but he only said that they ought to report to Mr Jones. Scrap bustled to shut the shop with all speed. At least he'd cheered up.

22: WHERE THERE'S A WILL

'There's a family,' Dickens said.

'What?'

'I was thinking aloud. Where there's a will, there's a family — as some cynic once said.'

'Picking over the corpse. Grim thought. Well, we're about to find out, I hope. I was just wondering who it was that the lad saw with Toby Quick on the day he vanished,' Jones pondered as they walked to Lincoln's Inn to find Cornelius Mornay's solicitor.

'The person who took him away.'

'Very likely, and all we know is that it wasn't a woman.'

'Miss Puss in disguise? The same person who visited Toby in the hospital?'

'I can believe anything at this moment.'

'A mandarin's golden finger guard, Chinese coins, a thimble — are we searching for a seamstress disguised as a Chinese man who happened to be sewing under the trees?'

'I know, it all sounds mad —'

'As if we've found ourselves in some impossible story — the Thousand and One Chinese Nights.'

'Lord, Charles, don't. I just hope that this solicitor is not out of some fairy tale.'

The singularly and inaptly named Mr Silas Goodbody — a man of particularly sparing appearance, but an ordinary human being as far as Dickens could tell — read the letter from Lord John Russell which the Superintendent from Bow Street had handed him. His long thin hand tapped at his narrow forehead as he did so. Then he looked from one to the other very gravely.

'This is very dreadful news, Superintendent. This letter tells me you believe that Mr Mornay was murdered, and his eldest son, also.'

'I do, and I take it that you know all about Mr Mornay's two families.'

'Not until very recently. Mr Cornelius Mornay was not a well man — his heart was weak, and he had fears for the future, which is why he came to see me. He wanted to make a new will.'

'When did you see him?'

'In the middle of April. He told me he was coming to London for the Exhibition and would come to see me then to make the changes. However, as I had advised against such changes, I assumed that he had changed his mind. I wrote to him, of course. I thought he must be mulling it over.'

'Did he say he was coming for the opening day, May the first?'

'He did — he said that he would come to see me after that date to discuss the matter further. He had some provisions he wished to consider further.'

'Had he a copy of the new will?'

'He had.'

'And those changes, Mr Goodbody — you see that Lord John asks that you share the information with me and Mr Dickens — who is acting for Mr Jonathan Mornay and his sister, Miss Fanny Mornay.'

Mr Goodbody went to his shelves from where he picked out some papers from a box. 'The first will is dated twenty-one years ago — the birth of Mr Jonathan Mornay meant that Mr Mornay needed to secure his heir's position. By this will, Mr

Jonathan Mornay would inherit Pole Court, its contents and the bulk of Mr Mornay's fortune when he came of age. Of course, Mr Jonathan Mornay was a mere babe at this time. In the event of Cornelius Mornay's death before his son reached his majority, Mrs Constance Mornay would continue to live in the house and manage the estate, and Mr Mornay's daughter, Fanny Maria, was to inherit fifty-thousand pounds and some other property.'

'Other bequests?'

'Miss Anne Palmer to inherit ten thousand pounds to dispose of as her Christian values dictated. She was a missionary in China —'

'We have met her,' said Dickens.

'Then you will know her relationship to — er — Mr Mornay's other children.'

'Yes, we do — and the phrase "Christian values" suggests, does it not, that Mr Cornelius Mornay trusted her to provide for those other children?'

'Indeed — at the time, I thought the wording curious, but Mr Mornay merely said that as a former missionary, she would understand his meaning.'

'And the new will?' asked Jones.

'Is very specific — rather too much so, I thought. I was greatly surprised by the information Mr Mornay imparted when he came to see me towards the end of April. I understood then the true significance of the bequest to Miss Palmer. Mr Mornay explained that he feared for his own health and that Miss Palmer was not a young woman. He wanted to secure the futures of the legatees specified, namely Mr Michael Spencer, Mr James Spencer and Miss Jane Spencer.'

'You thought that the names would cause distress to Jonathan Mornay and his sister?'

'Not necessarily — they might be explained away as connections linked to his time in China, but Mr Mornay insisted on a more particular wording —' Mr Goodbody looked down at the paper and read aloud — 'my sons, Mr Michael Spencer and Mr James Spencer, and my daughter, Miss Jane Spencer — born in Canton, children of my Chinese wife.'

'Wife?' Dickens exclaimed, glancing at Jones, whose mouth was forming the same word. 'I was told that Mr Mornay had not married his Chinese — er — lady.'

'Well, it would seem he did.' Mr Goodbody's tone remained quite even — but then he was a lawyer and was no doubt familiar with the many cases of disputed inheritances that were so often in the papers — to sensational effect, usually. He merely gave a lawyerly dry cough before he continued. 'Mr Mornay told me that he had married Miss Ah Say, but that she had died. He wished to make amends to his children by acknowledging their legitimacy — the brand of illegitimacy is a hard thing to bear, he said. I asked him to think about his children by his English wife.'

'He said only that he would give the matter consideration?'

'He did. I told him that I foresaw very great difficulties ahead, especially for Mr Jonathan Mornay, whose title to the estate might be in doubt if the eldest legitimate son made a claim, and even for Miss Fanny Mornay, whose marriage is forthcoming. Though, there must be a delay now, I presume.'

'Is there proof of the marriage to Miss Ah Say?' asked Jones.

'Only in the wording of this will. I have no proof of the marriage as an absolute fact. A case in court would hinge on the question of the marriage in fact. In a case heard only last year — the case of an East India Company officer married to an Indian lady — it was ruled that no legal marriage had taken place; therefore, the children of that relationship were declared illegitimate. You see why I was very reluctant to approve this document.'

'May I ask, Mr Goodbody, what sums of money are involved in this proposed second will?'

Mr Goodbody looked rather pained at Jones's question. 'Hm — yes, indeed — Mr Cornelius Mornay envisaged the sale of the house and lands which are estimated at sixty thousand pounds. Other properties, farms and so on, estimated at twenty thousand pounds. There are bonds and securities valued at another forty thousand pounds, shares in the bank of Mattinson and Smith valued at twenty thousand pounds, cash available in the bank account at fifteen thousand pounds — an inheritance of some one hundred and fifty thousand pounds.'

'Divided as?'

'Twenty-five thousand pounds for each child — a trust established for the care of Michael Spencer. Mr Mornay told me about the — er — circumstances pertaining to his eldest son.'

'What would happen to Michael Spencer's legacy?'

'That would depend on whether Mr Mornay has provided for that eventuality — another difficult point of law, Superintendent — in the hypothetical event of there being a dispute — though now that Mr Mornay is — er — dead — the first will stands unless —'

'Mr Cornelius Mornay had signed and attested the new will.'

'I am afraid so, sir, and I do not mind saying that I hope he did not.'

'The fortunes of Mr Jonathan Mornay and Miss Fanny Mornay would have been much reduced,' Jones said.

'It would have been a hard blow to them.'

'Not so hard, perhaps, as having the whole of their father's secret life made public,' Dickens said, thinking of Fanny Mornay's thin, anxious face, and Jonathan Mornay's guilt at his quarrel with his father. He wouldn't be able to forgive him this if Cornelius Mornay had signed the second will.

'Indeed so, Mr Dickens, and there are other bequests to servants and various charitable institutions. However, Miss Palmer receives five thousand pounds without the reference to her Christian values, but her role as guardian to his older children is specified. There is a bequest of five thousand pounds and certain, specified Chinese works of art to Mr Alexander Mattinson.'

'Did Mr Mattinson inherit by the first will?'

'I understand that Mr Cornelius Mornay's shares in the bank were left to Mr Mattinson under the first will. He is named executor in both wills —' Mr Goodbody cleared his throat — 'and now I come to some other bequests which frankly I cannot understand. The names are mystery to me.

'There is a bequest of two thousand pounds to a Mr Li Shen of Downs Farm, Minster in Kent, in acknowledgement of his loyal friendship, and the bequest of certain, specified Chinese works of art to Mr Fullerton, of Downs House, Minster in Kent, who is named as another executor in the second will. There is a legacy of two thousand pounds to Mr Mornay's nephew, Mr Francis Hope, tea broker of Fenchurch Street — and one final one — about which, I may say, Mr Cornelius Mornay gave no explanation — a legacy of two thousand pounds to a Miss Lily Cheng, of Angel Court, Wapping.'

'These are people that I have met, Mr Goodbody — the connection is obviously China. I think I understand the bequest to Mr Li Shen — he is the agent of Mr Fullerton, who knew Mr Mornay in Canton. Friends, I believe.'

'And the nephew — I confess that I had no idea that Mr

Mornay had a sister or brother.'

'His brother died many years ago, but he did marry and have a son — his wife was Chinese. It was Mr Francis Hope who told me that Mr Mornay had not married Miss Ah Say,' Dickens said.

Mr Goodbody sighed. 'I see — and Miss Cheng — Chinese, I presume — I hope not another —'

'She is the daughter of a Mr Cheng who owns a tobacconist's shop in Wapping, but why Mr Mornay should leave her such a sum of money, I cannot say.'

'Tobacconist,' murmured Mr Goodbody, a faint look of anguish about his mouth. He picked up Lord John's letter again and gazed at that, his long hand tapping at his brow as though to stir his brains. When he looked up again, Dickens saw the question in his eyes — the question he did not want to ask. He gave his little dry cough again. 'I take it, Superintendent Jones, that you do not believe that Mr Cornelius Mornay was a victim of some random attack.'

'Of course, I cannot be sure, but what you have told us naturally makes me wonder who might have known about this second will — who might have wished to prevent its being signed?'

Jones's words hung in the air with all their ominous implications. Mr Silas Goodbody suddenly looked paler and older. There was nothing else to say.

Outside, Dickens and Jones looked at each other. A slight breeze rustled the trees — a sound very like whispering. They walked away to find a secluded bench.

'Well, Mr Dickens, what a turn-up. Fairy tales, eh? Imagine the sensation if that will were to be proved.'

'Chinese wife, mad son, secret children, disinherited heir, a fortune at stake, a suit in Chancery, opium dens — it's the stuff of a three-volume novel.'

'Sharpening your quill, are you?'

'Truth, Sammy my lad, as the poet says, is stranger than fiction.'

'So it is in this case — but it gives us our motive. Who wanted to stop that will being signed?'

'Any of 'em: Jonathan Mornay, Fanny Mornay, Mattinson, even Francis Hope who was very keen to keep his past a secret.'

'Fullerton? Li Shen? Not Fullerton himself, I suppose —'

'Li Shen stood to gain.'

'Perhaps the money wasn't important — they didn't want to be dragged into the story by that will. Who knows what secrets they have?'

'If they knew about the second will.'

'Then every reason to see Mr Fullerton and Mr Li Shen.'

'Therefore to Dover.'

They walked on through the quiet precincts of Lincoln's Inn. 'We've missed someone out, of course,' observed Jones.

'Paul Grex — set to marry his heiress. When I spoke to Bulwer-Lytton, he said that Grex was rumoured to be marrying the daughter of a wealthy banker whom nobody knew.'

'Well, they'll all know if that will has been signed — and nearly half the fortune gone.'

'Twenty-five thousand and property's not bad for a young man whose family is financially shaky — it's a lot of money, Sam, and surely no need to commit murder to get it.'

'What about the scandal?'

'I remembered that Indian case that Goodbody mentioned — it was in the papers, of course, and I read it as eagerly as the next man, but it's old news. People forget, and money smooths the path through the marble halls of society — and Grex will have the title, remember. In any case —'

'Milk and his lady love — what's Grex to do with them?'

'Or them to do with anybody we've mentioned?'

'A motive and a gaggle of suspects — none of whom seem particularly convincing to me at this moment, I have to say…'

'Mattinson? Loses his shares in the bank in exchange for five thousand and a few trinkets.'

'I saw his face when he realized that it really was Mornay's body. He did look shaken.'

'What might a man look like if he were gazing upon the man whose murder he had connived at?'

Jones looked at him. 'I rather wish you hadn't said that.'

'You look quite ashen yourself.'

'If only your Lord John hadn't —'

Dickens looked at Jones. He did look pale and strained. The thing was a knotted tangle, true enough. He put his arm through Jones's and gazed up at him.

'You're in a nice state of confugion, Mr Jones. Nothing but what a stroll in a pleasant afternoon, though warm as we must expect when cowcumbers is three for twopence in Kent —'

Jones couldn't help laughing as he looked down. It was Mrs Gamp, nodding her head waggishly in a hideous parody of sympathy.

'— wouldn't set you up again as right as a trivet. First train from London Bridge for Dover — three hours and a bit — time to interrogate the suspects — back on the one o'clock. London by fourish — a fresh cowcumber in each pocket — pickled salmon at six.'

'Much obliged, Mr Bradshaw.'

'Bradshaw's book of spells — *The Arabian Nights* of the railways — and I'm the conjuror.'

23: THE MANDARIN'S TALE

Mr Fullerton, as frail as a faded piece of parchment and with a thin pale face that might have been carved from ivory, sat in his wheeled chair in the garden of his Dover lodgings in the best part of town where he had taken three very well-furnished rooms in the house of a widow. From the garden, Dickens could see the sea and feel a cooling breeze on his hot face. He felt the sweat at his neck. Mr Fullerton looked cool, however, his knees covered in a rug despite the warm weather. He wore a quilted silk jacket and velvet slippers which gave him the look of a Chinese Mandarin. Mr Li Shen looked every inch an English gentleman in his light suit and straw hat. He rested a protective hand on the back of the chair.

Mr Fullerton greeted them courteously enough, but there was steel in his eye, Dickens saw. Clearly, his fragility was a matter of the body not the mind.

Jones began with a challenge to Mr Li Shen. 'Mr Cornelius Mornay had lunch with you at Mr Fullerton's house on April thirtieth — with his son. You did not tell me, Mr Li Shen.'

Mr Fullerton answered, 'Superintendent Jones and Mr Dickens, may I suggest that you sit down — you will see that I cannot easily converse with you standing. Mr Li Shen will get us some tea or something cold, perhaps? In the meantime, I will tell you what I think you need to know about poor Cornelius and his unfortunate son — Miss Palmer has written to me.'

Mr Li Shen went before Jones could answer. They sat, but Jones was determined not to be outmanoeuvred. A good night's sleep and a journey away from London had restored his spirits. He was not prepared to mince his words, as he had told Dickens. 'Make 'em sweat, Superintendent, eh?' Dickens had teased.

'We know a good deal, sir, about Mr Mornay's Chinese family and the reason for Michael Spencer's confinement in Fort Pitt. We have visited an opium den in Bluegate Fields. It is my belief that Mr Li Shen, Cornelius Mornay and Mr Cheng are all connected — Mr Cheng of the opium den.'

'I divined, on hearing her voice, that Mrs Cheng has her origins in Kent,' Dickens put in.

The steel sparkled momentarily. 'Very observant, Mr Dickens, but that is to be expected. You are a keen student of dialect and accents.'

'I know Kent very well.' There was no sign of Mr Li Shen or any tea. Mr Fullerton was the protector, perhaps, not the protected.

Jones was not to be diverted. 'If you will explain, sir.'

'Cheng was a servant of mine. Unlike Mr Li Shen, he came from China with me more than twenty years ago. I was fond of him, but he proved a disappointment. He became involved with a local girl, Mary Comfort. In short, she was with child and they ran away. I assumed to London. That is where Cheng longed to stay. I had taken him to London sometimes.'

'And Mr Mornay?'

'There are not many Chinese in London, Superintendent — sailors, of course, and servants of those who served in Canton.'

'Mr Alexander Mattinson, for example, whom we have met.'

Mr Fullerton showed no surprise. 'Yes, indeed, Mr Mattinson has two Chinese servants and some of my old Canton colleagues have their Chinese servants. However, to answer your question about Cornelius Mornay, I presume you know that he was a frequent visitor to Wapping.'

'His children James and Jane Spencer live there,' Jones answered.

'He met Cheng and recognized him and his wife. Mr Mornay wrote to me. I felt responsible. Mary Comfort was the daughter of one of my tenant farmers — simple folk and good ones who lost their only daughter. I tried to persuade them, through Mr Mornay, to come back, but they refused. I set them up in the tobacco shop, but —'

'Opium,' said Jones.

'Mr Mornay knew that they sold it, but what could he do? It is sold everywhere.'

'And then they began to smoke it. I suppose that was awkward, too.'

Mr Fullerton gave Superintendent Jones another steely look. 'You mean because his own fortune came from the opium traded into China.'

'He felt guilty, perhaps. Lord Ashley, whom I know, has made some very strong arguments against the trade, strongly refuted by Mr James Mattinson, the Member of Parliament,' Dickens said.

'Yes, I am aware of the controversy. I should point out that the Mornay Company started out dealing in clocks. I, myself, was President of the East India Supercargoes Committee, dealing in a great many goods.'

Jones pressed the point. 'But the bank, Mr Fullerton, Mattinson's, that's built on opium. You are a shareholder, I imagine.'

A guess, but it went home. 'Very well, I admit that our fortunes are made from the China opium trade, but so are many others in London — there is an opium trade there in Mincing Lane supplying opium from Turkey throughout this land for the greatest lord and the meanest labourer.'

'No doubt, Mr Fullerton, but Mr Cheng and his opium den are my concern here.'

Mr Fullerton nodded. 'I will admit that the degradation of Cheng and his wife — Mr Mornay described it vividly — made me feel responsible for them. I sent money, of course.'

'For how long have you supported them?'

'For ten years — it was when Cornelius moved his children to Princes Square that he met them. There was a child, of course, a little girl. They were living in poverty — Mary doing laundry. She had been educated for something better. Cheng was working at the docks when work could be had. I thought I was helping — what an irony —'

'Do you think that Mr Cheng had any reason to conspire in the deaths of Mr Mornay and his son?'

'I cannot think so, Superintendent. It was Cornelius who kept an eye on them — and their daughter. They could gain nothing from his death.'

Two thousand pounds, thought Jones, if that will were known about, but he wasn't ready to mention that yet.

'And Mr Li Shen's part in all this?'

Mr Fullerton looked across to the open garden windows, but there was no sign of Mr Li Shen. 'He did it for me and I did it for Cornelius... You know that he and his son were to see Doctor Forbes Winslow?'

'Yes, we know about that.'

'Cornelius would have preferred to leave Michael where he was, but Jane Spencer wanted — believed that he could go to live with her and her brother. Cornelius, who had enough secrets from his English family, was terrified that Michael might repeat his crime, or that the first would be discovered. He hoped that Doctor Forbes Winslow would be of the opinion that Michael Spencer should stay at Fort Pitt. Those were the reasons for secrecy, and I asked Mr Li Shen to give Cornelius any help he needed — and when you came, he —'

'Lied for my master and benefactor's sake.' Mr Li Shen had come upon his silent feet behind Dickens and Jones. 'I am sorry, Superintendent and Mr Dickens — I know you now, of course — but those were not my secrets to tell.'

'Did Mr Mornay and his son stay in your house on the nights of the twenty-ninth and thirtieth?' Josephine had said not, but Jones wanted to be sure.

'No, I offered to accommodate him, but he came only to lunch. He wanted me to see Michael — to observe him. He wanted a stranger to —'

'Tell him that his son could not live a life outside Fort Pitt,' said Dickens.

'He told me that was his hope. The young man was like a child, Mr Dickens. Mr Mornay thought that he would be a burden to his other children.'

'Where did Mr Mornay stay on the nights before the Exhibition?'

'He usually stayed at Brown's Hotel,' Mr Fullerton interrupted.

'He did not stay there. Mr Li Shen?'

'I thought near Doctor Winslow's asylum — Mr Mornay was to take Michael on May the second.'

'Would your knowing about Mornay's visit to my house have made any difference?' asked Mr Fullerton.

'I doubt it, sir; Mr Mornay was already dead by the time we questioned Mr Li Shen.'

'And you don't know who killed him — or Michael?'

'I have a very good idea, but I do not know the connection between the murderers and Mr Mornay except, I am afraid, that opium den. That brings me to another matter — Mr

Cheng's daughter.'

'That poor child — Cornelius did give her money from time to time, but he could tell that she was taking the drug.'

'Cornelius Mornay was thinking about making a new will before he died. He was going to leave the girl two thousand pounds. Have you any idea why?'

Fullerton exchanged a glance with Li Shen. *Another secret to be told*, thought Dickens. A Chinese puzzle, indeed.

'For the sake of Ah Say — you know that she was his Chinese wife?'

'The lawyer, Mr Goodbody, told us.'

'Cheng was Ah Say's brother.'

'What happened to her?'

'She died. Cheng and his sister lived in Macau, where we had our summer residences. Cheng was my house boy, and his sister became — Cornelius Mornay's mistress. She was very beautiful, and he fell in love and married her secretly when she became pregnant with Michael. She died when Jane Spencer was a small child, and they were sent to England in the care of a missionary lady — it was easier that way. I brought Cheng to England because —'

'It was easier, too — he wouldn't tell about the marriage,' Dickens said.

Another steely glance. 'It was.'

'This two thousand pounds, Mr Fullerton, might well be a motive for murder, don't you think?'

'But you said that Cornelius was only thinking about —'

'The will is in the hands of Mr Goodbody and Mr Mornay had a copy. We do not know if he signed it, but, according to that will, you and Mr Li Shen are beneficiaries.'

'I did not know anything of this, Superintendent, and I can assure you neither I nor Mr Li Shen murdered Cornelius

Mornay for an inheritance. We have more than enough.'

'I see that, Mr Fullerton, but all these secrets brought out into the open — an opium den, murder, a secret marriage and your name dragged into it.'

'Only if that will is found and has been signed. I'm an old man and not a well man, Superintendent; why should I care?'

'One last thing, Mr Fullerton —' Jones took the Chinese coins from his pocket — 'These were found with Mr Cornelius Mornay's body — in his mouth.'

The coins caught the light in the silence that followed. Mr Li Shen spoke. 'Revenge.' He looked pale in the bright light as he stared down at the coins. 'A Chinese legend tells us that those who are wronged place a coin in the mouth of the wrongdoer, whose death is retribution.'

24: SERGEANT ROGERS HAS NEWS

Dickens wiped his brow as they descended the hill for the railway station. 'You made me sweat, never mind them. Torturs of the Impostion, an' I'm a witness for the persecution.'

'Inquisition, my foot —' Jones was more than familiar with Mrs Gamp's vagaries of expression — 'anyway, I wasn't going to be messed about by a man who's made his fortune in drugs. "We have more than enough" — so he does, and more than he deserves.'

'Not a murderer, though.'

'Not in his state of health, nor Li Shen — and I do understand why he lied, except that we might have got the information sooner. But we got some things clear. Mattinson, for example, is he any more likely than Fullerton to have murdered Mornay for his inheritance? He's another that has more than enough.'

'True, my Torquemada, not but what I'd like to see you in your present mood, turn the screws on him.'

'Very funny, but I am going to ask him about that will — I had a thought that Mornay might have left it at the bank rather than at Pole Court — and we could look at all the other letters he may not have answered, like Jane Spencer's.'

They arrived at the station in time for the drink which Dickens observed that they had not been given at Mr Fullerton's lodgings.

'A penny bun, Mr Jones?' he asked as they stood at the counter.

Jones contemplated the buns which looked like museum exhibits. 'China tea will do.'

'Don't,' Dickens said, 'I think I've had quite enough.'

'Two lemonades, then. We'll drink it on the train.'

'Cold comfort,' Dickens replied, getting some coins from his pocket.

'Mary Comfort, eh?'

When they were settled in the carriage, they drank the lemonade, after which Dickens asked, 'Cooled down, 'ave yer, Mr Jones, sir?'

'Positively cucumberish, Mrs G. Drink up, and let us consider what else we now know.'

'Or what we don't — where the devil was Mornay on those two nights?'

'Near the asylum, Li Shen said, but Rogers found no trace of them. I'll have to send another man, but more important now is this link between Fullerton, Mornay and the opium den.'

'No chance that he took it himself?'

'Not that we ever thought so, but it's good to be sure.'

'You know you said that someone must have given Mornay a hefty dose after he'd been taken from Hyde Park — could he have been taken to Angel Court because that someone had seen him there?'

'Milk, I'll bet. He's in this, and he killed Dag because —'

Dickens thought about a tall, heavy man rolled into the murky depths of the river. 'Dag put him in the river — paid to shift the body. They'd need someone big and someone who knew the river.'

'Easy money — what would Dag care about a dead toff?'

'Nothing until Milk came calling after he'd seen Dag with the police.'

'Those coins, though —'

'Stuffed in his mouth by Milk, I'm sure. I don't believe in this revenge stuff. I'll bet Milk knew what the coins meant — wanted to muddy the waters to throw suspicion on Cheng or to make us think Mornay was the victim of an attack by some Chinese sailor, but he got it wrong, Sam. Overreached himself.'

'How?'

'Mr Li Shen said a coin — not a handful. The coins are Milk's bit of theatre.'

'And a filthy old rag with opium stains. He didn't think of that.'

'In love with his own artistry — couldn't resist the extra meaningless flourish. That finger guard — I'll bet they meant to leave that by Michael Spencer's body for the same reason — killed by some Chinese man, but they dropped it going down in the dark. On the other hand, you don't think Cheng —'

'For his sister's sake — no, I don't think so. Mornay married her and she died and Mornay kept his eye on them for old time's sake — and for Fullerton. If, as we speculate, Milk took him there, they'd be frightened to death when he died — they'd not want a body on their hands and if Dag came to take it away, they'd be relieved to get rid.'

'If they understood anything at all in their state of stupefaction.'

'As for the inheritance, I hardly think Mornay would have told them. He was too secretive for that.'

'What about Cheng's daughter? She seemed a bit more alert — she looked frightened when we arrived. Perhaps she'd tell.'

'We'll go to see her. I daresay you could persuade her.'

The train chugged on past the high Shakespeare Cliff named after that cliff in *King Lear*, down from which the blinded Gloucester thought he had leapt. Dickens thought of poor Dag and in the darkness of the tunnel under the cliff he thought of Toby Quick. Out in the light they rolled through the green fields, the cornfields, the orchards and hop gardens; a couple of oast house chimneys flashed by, some cows stood motionless in a field like farmyard toys, a row of headstones in a churchyard, a glint of a distant river, all peaceful under the summer sun until the map of Kent was rolled up and the sky darkened as if it might rain. But it was London with its great lead canopy of smoke lowering over the housetops.

'There has to be a connection between Mornay and Milk,' Jones said as they got off the train. 'That's the key to it all — someone paid to have it done.'

'To stop him signing that will.'

There was someone waiting at the door in Wellington Street, a someone who was looking anxiously up and down. When he saw the Superintendent and Mr Dickens, Sergeant Rogers in his plain clothes came to meet them.

'News of the boy, sir, Toby Quick — he was seen alive by the lad Gaunt took up to the Orphan Asylum. Gaunt talked to him again.'

'When did the lad see him?'

'Couple of days ago, he thinks — he saw him going into a shop in a place called Dry Salt Alley — off Cinnamon Lane down in Wapping —' Rogers looked at Dickens — 'name of Cheese.'

'Monger?'

Jones looked at them both. 'What's cheese got to do with anything?'

'Sorry, sir, owns the shop.'

'Couple of days, you say — after Dag was killed.'

'Can't be sure, sir, you know these lads — never know what day it is. Gaunt's waitin' for you. He thought Mr Dickens might —'

They were both weary. Jones looked at Dickens, who said, 'If there's a chance —'

25: A FALLEN MAN

Cinnamon Lane throbbed with heat, and reeked — not of spices — but of fish, sewage and the smell of the river lying still and sluggish brown under a sulphurous sun. Dry Salt Lane was the home of various hardware merchants who manufactured and sold paint, sugar of lead, and saltpeter — you could smell those, too, in the closeness of the narrow lane. Somewhere down here was the grocer's shop where the boy, Ned, had seen Toby Quick. They passed a little shop where in the window Dickens glimpsed a selection of bottles advertising cordials and medicines — opium in every one, no doubt.

What a place this is for poisons, Dickens thought. Kill yourself for a penny any day of the week — or be murdered for the same sum. Sugar of lead to sweeten your tea; arsenic in your cake; opium in your wine; or you could blow yourself to bits with saltpeter. Or just throw yourself in the river for nothing.

Gaunt was turning by a pub called The Pear Tree. Or someone could bash your head in with a maul or rip out your throat with a chisel — The Pear Tree Pub was where the infamous John Williams, the Ratcliffe Highway murderer, had been arrested. There must have been a pear tree growing hereabouts in some pleasant orchard before John Williams had made it infamous. Like the cinnamon, the fragrant pears were long gone.

Dickens heard the hollow note of a shop bell. Evidently this door led into Ajax Cheese's grocery shop. *Cheese, forsooth.* Jones and Dickens went in, leaving Gaunt to keep watch outside. Stemp would be somewhere, Dickens knew, fingering his dreadful cutlass, and Constable Sleat and Rogers in their plain clothes — Inspector Bold didn't take chances.

Not with Charles Dickens, he didn't. A nuisance, Bold often thought, shuddering on the quiet at the idea of a murdered author on his hands, but Superintendent Jones must needs bring him, and Gaunt, of course, regarded the man as a genius, especially after that murder on *The Redemption*.

Ajax Cheese stood at his counter in his grey shop coat, with his grey face, his wisps of grey hair standing about his head, and surrounded by dust particles caught in a stray beam of light which had followed them through the open door. He looked very like a ghost and when the light caught his spectacles, his eyes had the appearance of two spectral moons gazing at them.

Jones closed the door, and the bell sounded eerily hollow again as they were plunged into gloom. The shop looked like a cave with its barrel-vaulted roof from which hung an assortment of hams, candle sconces, and fly papers. As his eyes adjusted to the gloom, Dickens noted the flies swarming at the papers. Greedy for the arsenic. The shelves and floor were piled with vegetables, eggs, bread, candles, oil flagons, gin bottles, soap, starch, shoe blacking, sacks of coal and flour, and tea, of course — all jumbled together. And cheese — though whether the smell came from that round of Dutch or Mr Cheese himself, it was hard to tell. Strong cheese, however. Pickles somewhere, too.

A sign bearing the legend *Children's Draughts* pointed a black finger at various earthenware bottles labelled *Godfrey's Cordial, Paregoric, Liquorice Syrup*. All guaranteed to soothe your restless infant — into the grave more often than not. A box labelled *Arsenic* nestled in with the sugar and salt. Dickens thought of those moonish spectacles and wondered. The ghostly apparition spoke to ask if he could help. Pickles on his breath.

Human, then.

They went nearer and saw the knife in his hand. Reassuringly, it didn't look very sharp. On the counter was a block of something dark which he had been cutting into short lengths. Penny Sticks — raw opium.

Jones introduced himself and asked about the boy, Toby Quick, who had been seen entering the shop two days ago.

'Bright lad, Mr Cheese,' said Dickens, 'light brown hair — a lot of it, dark eyes, red mark on his neck — possibly wearing a red jersey.' Toby Quick probably wasn't wearing his shoe-black's jersey. It would be too conspicuous, but it was worth a shot.

The grey eyes looked at him searchingly. 'I know you,' Ajax Cheese said slowly. 'I should like to shake your hand. I have been reading this —' he fetched a familiar green-backed book from under the counter and set it down — 'David Copperfield — a rise and fall — what a fall — but a rise again to fame and fortune. I, myself, have risen — and fallen — to this, the blossom blighted, the leaf withered, forever floored, my dear Mr Charles Dickens. A warrior yet a comestible. An unfortunate juxtaposition. "What's in a name?" asks the Bard. Much, I say, much.'

He seemed to require an answer. Clearly, it was up to Dickens to provide one — a task to which he felt unequal in the circumstances. 'Cheese,' he said in as melancholy a tone as he could muster.

'Cheese does not pay. Corn does not pay. Coal does not pay. You recommend Australia? The heat, though, very trying just now, and in those Antipodean regions, what heat may come?'

Dear Lord, thought Jones, a literary critic and a philosopher, and he'd thought Dickens had made up Mr Micawber and here he was.

'Quite so, Mr Cheese, quite so —' Dickens didn't quite know what to say. The man seemed hardly fit for a sail on a steamer to London Bridge, never mind Australia. A melancholy man, Mr Ajax Cheese, but an educated one. What catastrophe had brought him here?

'Too late — it is always later than you think —' *It certainly is,* Jones reflected, but he was too late to interrupt — 'Procrastination is the thief of time —'

'Collar him,' Dickens couldn't help saying. After all, it was what he had written.

'He is gone. Too late, too late —' the words seemed to rise and mingle with the dust, but Ajax Cheese seemed to cheer up suddenly — 'I will shake your hand, Mr Charles Dickens, and I shall feel a rise, of sorts — to the empyrean of the literary world.'

Dickens offered his hand. 'The boy,' said Jones.

'Ah, the boy — now there was a rise and a fall. Such is the way of things. We are but straws on the surface of the deep.'

'You know him?'

'I do. I thought he was to rise — a shoe-black boy he became in the great world of the city, but then the fall —'

'He came back,' Jones said flatly.

'Yes, his mother — poor, benighted creature, lies on her deathbed not a league hence — in short, a street away beyond the sign of the Pear Tree.'

'Where exactly?'

'Second left after the sign — Hope Alley —' he looked at Dickens — 'where there is none.' There was something compassionate in his voice despite the melodrama.

'What did the boy want?'

'For me to see her, give her some opium — to ease her coughing, he told me — pneumonia, it was. Nothing to be done.'

'Just his mother?' asked Jones.

'There's a sister — fallen, I am afraid — you'll find her in Bluegate Fields.'

Dickens was looking at the block of raw opium and remembering Mr Fullerton's words about the London trade. 'Does opium pay?'

'A little — there is great need round here. Pain and hunger buy it.'

'Where do you get all this?' Dickens pointed at the earthenware bottles.

'My supplier, sir, from the City.'

'And he is?' Jones's voice took on a harder note.

'Mr Millikin, sir.'

Jones didn't blink, but he heard a hiss of a breath from Dickens. 'And he represents?'

'His premises are in Mincing Lane — the City, you know. The opium comes in from Turkey to the docks and thence to the City, where it is auctioned to the wholesalers like Mr Millikin who supplies the retailers hereabouts.'

'Good prices?' asked Dickens.

'Very competitive — I used to deal with a representative of Ellis and Hall, but Mr Millikin is, in short — cheaper.'

'Can you describe Mr Millikin for me?'

'A gentleman — a surprisingly gentleman-like personage — fallen, perhaps, rather lower than his birth, I hazard. Most elegantly turned out — top hat and so forth. Tall, thin, and pale eyes — rather cold, I thought, but a gentleman.'

'Did he ever have a lady with him?'

'A lady? No, indeed not. This would hardly be the place. Cheese, you know.'

'Keep an eye out for the boy, will you? If you see him, get in touch with Constable Gaunt at the police station.'

Ajax Cheese looked pained at Jones's brisk tone, so Dickens added, 'I'd like to find him. I have some connection with the shoe-black brigade. I might be able to help him. Here is my card.'

Ajax Cheese held it reverently. He bowed and the dust motes scattered from his hair. He stood up to his full height. 'Your servant, sir.' They left him gazing up into the murky empyrean of his grocer's shop. He certainly had risen.

26: THE POOR GROUND

They had no time to think about what they had heard. Gaunt was waiting and Jones said, 'Hope Alley — the boy's mother lives there.'

'I know it.'

As they walked, Dickens asked John Gaunt about Ajax Cheese. 'What an odd man — for a grocer, I mean.'

Gaunt chuckled. 'He is — always on about his ruin. He was a doctor, so he says, with a practice in Harley Street.'

'What happened?'

'He never says — just that he has fallen — his way of life in the sere — that sort of thing, but he's a decent sort. Sells his medicine cheaply to the poor —'

'He said it's all they have to ease their pain — and hunger.'

'He does visit the sick — he's all they have other than the workhouse infirmary, and they very often won't go there. The girls — in Bluegate Fields — the prostitutes — they are always being beaten up if they're not doing the beating, but he will help for a sixpence, or less, if it's a child.'

So, Ajax Cheese had treated Mrs Quick. A strange man with his orotund phrases, but beneath it, a good one — inadvertently linked to Milk, for that was who Mr Millikin, the gentleman supplier was, surely. Milk and Cheese — dear Lord — and Blood — where was he?

Hope Alley was just as hopeless as any other alley about here — as dank and dark as a cell, and probably less healthy even than Newgate Prison — where, at least, you could be seen by a doctor rather than a grocer, but then Ajax Cheese might have been a fine doctor once before his fall. Gaunt asked a woman who was coming out of a tumbledown dwelling if she knew where Mrs Quick lived.

'Dead,' she said, pointing down a set of greasy steps near where they were standing.

'When?'

'Saturday, I thinks — buryin' 'er today sometime.'

'Where?'

'Poor Ground at St. John's, it'll be — parish'll be buryin' 'er. They can't pay.'

'Who?'

'Lad an' 'is sister — she looks bad, too — not long fer this world. Whore like 'er ma. Still, the wages of sin.'

Having pronounced her epitaph, off she went, a thin, haggard woman with hard eyes and without pity for her neighbours, but why should she? It was hard enough to keep yourself alive. Dickens had noted her yellow face and toothless mouth. She might have been twenty or a hundred.

'Can you have a look?' asked Jones of Dickens. 'I don't want to frighten him if he's there.'

Dickens went down the steps to where a rotten door was propped open with a brick. He could smell it — poverty and ruin, pain and death. There was only silence within. Perhaps Toby Quick was burying his mother even now — in that Poor Ground by the church, by the workhouse, by the charity school.

He pushed open the door and called quietly, 'Toby, Toby — it's Mr Dickens come to see you.'

There was no one there.

'St. John's?' asked Gaunt.

They walked back along Cinnamon Street, making their way to Greenbank at the end of which Dickens knew there was the church of St. John. A pauper's burial. He imagined the cheapest pine coffin and the most meagre ceremony. The parish would pay for the coffin with its rough cloth pall, used before, and it would be again and again. No bells, no headstone, no plaque, no name. The coffin would disintegrate as would the others in the same grave until flesh and bone rotted into the river-dank earth. She would be forgotten, Mrs Quick, whoever she had been. Toby Quick would remember, though; remember the mother for whom he had given up his chance of something better. Well, he'd have that chance again if Dickens had anything to do with it.

Gaunt left them to go back to the station. Dickens and Jones stood at the gate. In the north-west corner of the churchyard where the paupers were buried, they saw the white surplice of the officiating vicar and two slight figures holding hands. And the coffin bearers standing by, waiting to lower the coffin into the grave. The sexton leant on his spade. Another man spat out his tobacco. Somewhere, a bird sang.

'That him?' asked Jones.

'It is.' Dickens recognized the shock of thick hair and the heart-breaking red smock of the shoe-shine brigade. It was the best thing Toby had, no doubt. The second figure was a boy's too. Someone from Dag's, maybe. Dickens wondered where the sister was — back in Bluegate Fields, perhaps.

'You'd better speak to him first,' Jones said. 'I'll wait outside the gate.'

Dickens watched as the coffin was taken from a group of three waiting for burial. Paupers, too, from the workhouse across the way. They were brief, these maimed rites, only the bird to hymn a farewell.

Toby and his friend turned and came towards him. He stepped forward with his top hat in his hand.

'Toby — I was worried about you.'

'Mr Dickens.' He seemed startled and wary. His companion stepped back behind him.

'Smike came to tell me that you'd gone — Mr Macgregor thought that I might have sent you on an errand.'

'Sorry, sir, it was my ma — I 'ad ter come. Nothin' else ter do.'

'And you will go back. I'm sure Mr Macgregor would understand.'

'Nah, it's too late. 'S'over.' Toby pulled off his red smock top and handed it to Dickens. 'I won't need this no more.'

Too late — the hopeless echo of Ajax Cheese's voice. Miss Palmer had said the same thing of Cornelius Mornay. Dickens could see the change in Toby — his eyes were dull, his hair uncombed and his face dirty. *The pity of it*, he thought. He had lost his hope of something better, but Dickens had to try. He didn't take the red top. 'I could come with you to explain.'

'I got somewhere else ter be, sir, ta all the same.'

Dickens was aware of Jones outside the gate. He had to try to persuade them to come with him. There was another gate leading into Church Lane. There was a pub by Wapping Stairs. He could buy Toby and his companion something to eat, see if he could persuade him. Jones would realize what he was doing.

'You look hungry, the pair of you — let me take you to a pub to get something to eat, and then I'll give you some money to tide you over.'

Toby looked very much as if he would prefer just the money, but he said he would come. He handed the smock to the other boy. Dickens looked at him properly. Just another urchin boy. You wouldn't notice if you didn't know who she was. He didn't comment but turned back to Toby.

'Where do you want to go?' he asked. Not The Shakespeare's Head, he hoped.

The Town of Ramsgate Pub — *Ramsgate*, thought Dickens, as they walked down Church Lane. Poor Michael Spencer in the mortuary there, his father found in the river near here.

'I'm not hungry, sir — if yer could jest give —'

It was time to be firm. 'No, Toby, I want to talk to you. Your friend can go in and buy a couple of pies and some beer, and we'll eat it down on the shore in the open air.' He fished in his pocket and found a florin. 'Go and get something, lad,' he said, keeping his eye on Toby.

They walked down the stairs and onto the shore. The tide was going out and Dickens found a couple of big stones for them to sit on. He looked at the grey water and the long stretch of shore to where Executioner's Dock lay. It was grim place, where the pirates had been hanged and left on the gibbet until three tides washed them. As a boy, he had roamed here with his friend, Kit Penney, and they'd been appalled and thrilled by the place. The shore was empty now apart from a few mudlarks grubbing in the mud — a place where dreadful things happened, but not in daylight, surely. He glanced up at the stairs to see if the girl was coming and saw the reassuring figure of Constable Sleat, who half-waved and then vanished. Toby was staring out at a passing ship.

'I told Mr Macgregor that I'd look for you. You are my responsibility. You might not want to go back, but you must consider it.'

''Ow'd yer find me?'

'Mr Cheese at the grocer's told me about your mother. Did your sister come to tell you?'

'Nah, someone came, said she was dyin' — by 'erself. They dint know where Sally woz. She'd — Ma — asked fer me. Wot could I do, sir? I could 'ardly — she mighta died afore I got there.'

'I understand, but you took a risk — I know about the robbery and the shooting.'

'Well, I ain't stayin' any longer. We're gettin' out.'

'You and your friend?'

'Yers, she — 'e's —'

'I know who she is.'

Toby looked angry. 'Know it all, don't yer? Well, yer ain't ter say nothin'. She can't stay there — 'er folks is as bad as mine.'

'I know, I saw — but I need you to tell me about the robbery. You know Uncle Dag is dead?'

'I knows, but it ain't ter do with —'

'Who?'

Toby watched the ship. He was longing to get away. Dickens could see that, but he wanted to find out what the boy knew and who came to tell him that his mother was dying.

Toby turned to him. 'Blackmail, is it? I tell you and you won't tell about Lily an' me?'

'No, Toby, I won't tell, and I will give you the money I promised. I need to know because of the old cove — he was found murdered in the river near here.'

'Blimey — 'ow'd yer get mixed up in that? T'ain't safe round 'ere, Mr Dickens — yer shouldn't be askin' about murder.'

'I know — I'm not on my own, but I beg you to tell me about that robbery.'

'Captain Blood, 'e calls 'imself — 'e 'ad the gun. Bloody fool — drunk as a fish. They woz on the lay —' he looked at Dickens narrowly — 'yer knows wot that is?' Dickens nodded. Bill Sikes had taken Oliver Twist on the lay at Chertsey —

Oliver was the boy to get through the window and open the door to let in the burglars.

'I woz ter be the snakesman ter get through the winder at the back of the 'ouse in Wellclose Square — some rich cove's — but afore we could do anythin', Blood tripped an' the gun went off an' I woz shot. Course, 'e an' 'is pals scarpered.'

'You went willingly to the robbery?'

'Done it afore — Dag, see, 'e was pals with Blood an' they worked together, shared the swag an' when they needed boys, well, we done it. Course I couldn't tell Mr Macgregor all that, an' I wanted out afore the coppers got onto me. Said I couldn't remember.'

'Who were his pals?'

'The usual — 'Orsemeat, they calls one of 'em, cos 'e deals in it. T'other's a lad called Bendy — one o' Dag's boys once. Bendy cos 'e can get in anywhere — bones made o' wax.'

Not Milk, then. Dickens didn't ask about him. 'But the shoe-shine brigade — you seemed to like it,' he went on.

'I did. I woz glad ter get away an' I woz savin' fer Lily an' me — until — well, yer knows now —'

Lily Cheng came then with the pies and beer. She kept her head down, but they both ate hungrily. Dickens waited until they'd finished, wondering if Toby Quick was still in danger from Blood. He didn't sound as if he were frightened. Now to find out if Lily Cheng knew anything about Cornelius Mornay. *Tread softly*, he thought.

'Mr Dickens knows 'oo yer are, Lily, but 'e's promised not ter tell. We can trust 'im — I 'opes.' He looked at Dickens. A challenge in those too old eyes.

'You can, I promise. I thought someone had taken you from the Park after I'd spoken to you about the old man — the one who was found murdered here in Wapping.'

'Told yer — someone came.'

Dickens realized then. 'Miss Cheng?'

'Yers, it woz Lily — she came on the steamboat. She knows my sister. It woz 'er, Sally, wot told Lily. Course, Sally couldn't come —'

'Why not?'

'Drunk or drugged — or both. She couldn't even come ter the funeral. 'Er own ma — she want much, our ma, but gonnows, she tried, an' when I knew she woz dyin', I couldn't —'

Toby's eyes filled. He looked just a boy then — not much more than a child. Lily Cheng took his hand. *Babes in the Wood,* Dickens thought. What was he to do about them?

'The old cove — the toff you saw with the long white hair and the stick — he was drugged. Opium.'

Lily Cheng looked at him as fearfully as if he had been a necromancer. She knew, even though he and Jones had not asked about Cornelius Mornay at the opium den.

'Tell me, Lily.'

'Go on,' said Toby, 'if yer knows somethin'. Yer ain't goin' back there.'

'I knew him — he gave me money — from a Mr Li Shen, he said, who knew my auntie who died in China. He gave money to Ma and Pa, too. He was kind. Then one day a man brought him — he was ill — very ill well into the night. Ma gave him smokes. He was on the bed. The man went away. I was asleep — Pa gave me a smoke. When I woke up, the gentleman was gone.'

'Did you know his name?'

'Just the gentleman, Pa said — not my business.'

'Did you know the man who brought the gentleman?'

'I knew his eyes. He brings opium to my pa. I heard him say

to Ma somethin' about milk as if that was 'is name, but I dunno.'

'And a lady with him?'

'Not to our shop, but I saw them with Sally. The lady gave her somethin'.'

'Do you know them, Toby?'

'Friends of Blood, I think, but I didn't know 'em — I ain't been about fer a few months, yer knows.'

'Did the gentleman say anything while he was ill on the bed?'

'No, he just mumbled — kept saying the words "Ah Say" — he meant my auntie.'

All those years, thought Dickens, and Cornelius Mornay hadn't forgotten Ah Say. He wanted to do right by her and her children and had brought about his own death. And Captain Bright — perhaps he remembered a girl, too. He thought of Francis Hope recalling sunlight and silks and tinkling laughter.

'Look, sir, ain't that enough? We gotter go, me an' Lily — can't do no more fer Ma — the money, Mr Dickens, please. I'm beggin' yer.'

'Where are you going?'

Toby and Lily looked at each other. 'Dunno yet, but somewhere — me an' Lily used ter meet near the school when I 'ad free time. There's lodgin's round there — if yer'll give us the money.'

'I will, but there's your money and things at Mr Macgregor's school.'

'Yer can 'ave that fer wot yer gives me or give it ter Smike — your lad. I ain't goin' back, Mr Dickens. Can't leave Lily, can I?'

'I see that — what if you take lodgings in Limehouse? It's far enough away. I know someone who'll show you where to go. Find a Mr Kit Penney at the Ship's Chandler's in Three Colt

Street. He's my friend. Tell him I sent you and get him to change this —' he handed Toby a half sovereign — 'I'll come and find you and then we'll work out what you two can do. Don't go anywhere until I come.'

An idea had come to Dickens from something Lily Cheng had said, but he'd have to think it out. Of course, they might just take his money and run, but he couldn't do anything about that. Toby and Lily were on their feet already. He wouldn't make them promise — they might break it. He'd thought of something else, too.

'Just two more questions for Lily — first, did you visit Toby in hospital?' Lily nodded. That was cleared up, then. 'And how did you know where to find Toby in the Park? Had you been here before?'

'I sneaked 'er in on that first day — dressed as a Chinese boy. No one asked 'oo she was. Loads of furriners, see. Wot a lark. Lily saw the Queen an' the Chinese cove wot bowed to 'er.'

They turned to go and then Toby said, 'Oh, Mr Dickens, I forgot — found this under them trees where the old cove was.' He handed Dickens the little ivory cup.

Dickens looked down at it in his open palm, and Lily Cheng said, 'That's an opium measure.'

Dickens watched them walk down towards the steamer pier. To Limehouse, he hoped. He went back to the stairs, half-laughing, thinking of Sir George Grey, Mr Mayne, and all those policemen desperately searching for the mysterious Chinese man. Sir George Grey had assured the House of the vigilance of the police. Oh, dear. *Mind*, he thought, *Sam might not find it funny.*

27: BLOOD WILL HAVE BLOOD

Constable Sleat was waiting at the top of the steps.

'I was glad to know you were there, Constable,' said Dickens.

'Mr Jones went back ter the station. Gaunt came ter tell 'im that they've got Blood — urgent, 'e said. Superintendent said not ter let you out of my sight.'

Who would have thought the man had so much blood in him? Well, it is his name or the name he goes by, thought Dickens as he looked at the doctor who was trying to staunch the blood which was pumping out of the man's side. His legs were thrashing and there was a dreadful gurgling sound. Blood looked a wreck — his face was almost unrecognizable except for that twisted nose. Someone had beaten his face almost to a pulp. His eyes were closed, and Dickens could see the gashes on his neck; then the doctor bent over him and the legs stopped moving.

The doctor turned to face Jones and Inspector Bold. He was all blood up to the elbows and blood dripped onto the stone floor. 'He's dead. The wound was too deep. I'm sorry.'

Bold passed him a towel with which the doctor began to clean himself up. 'Put him in your mortuary. I'll sign the paper and get onto the parish. No relatives?'

'Some girl he lived with,' said Bold. 'I'll send to the lodgings in Bluegate Fields — if she's there.'

'I'll clean him up a bit if you'll get more water.'

Dickens and Jones went upstairs with Bold, who sent a constable for the water and more towels. Then they went into Bold's office where Constable Stemp was waiting with Sergeant Rogers. He looked a bit of a sight, too, red marks on his face which would ripen into bruises, his shirt torn and his sailor's kerchief missing. His looks were not improved. Rogers looked all right.

'What happened?' asked Dickens.

'Tell him, Stemp,' said Jones.

'I was outside that pub — The Shakespeare's Head — when a fight breaks out. Blood's drunk as a fish an' some sort o' card game 'ad ended in fisticuffs. Sailors, they was. I'm guessin' Blood was cheatin' and they're not 'avin' it — all drunk, o' course. Anyways some big lad 'as Blood by the throat an' another's punchin' is face in. I thought, sir, you might be needin' Blood, so I tries ter drag 'im away. I wish I 'adn't. One of 'em starts on me —' Stemp touched his jaw — 'then there's the sound of a police rattle and they all scarpers. Two o' Mr Bold's constables appear. I thought Blood was in a mess, but I didn't know —'

'He'd been stabbed,' Bold put in. 'I didn't realize myself until we got him in the cell and saw all the blood. I sent for the doctor, but — well, too late.'

'No sign of those other two — the well-dressed ones?' asked Jones, thinking of the murdered policeman and the well-dressed bystander.

'Didn't see 'em — mind, sir, I was a bit occupied.'

'Understandable, Stemp — you look a bit worse for wear. Do you need that doctor?'

'No, sir — I'll be all right 'cept for a few bruises — an' these rags don't matter. I look the part even more now, if you still need me down 'ere.'

'No, I think you should get back to Bow Street — someone might have seen you with the constables. And you, Rogers — you should both get off. I'll see you tomorrow.'

After they had gone, Bold turned to Jones. 'There's some girl Blood lived with in lodgings in Bluegate — she might know something about this Milk and his lady friend now that he can't tell us anything.'

'I found someone who knows the lady,' Dickens interrupted, and he told them what he had found out from Toby Quick and Lily Cheng, and that he had sent them to Limehouse. 'To Kit Penney's,' he said to Jones. He didn't mention the appearance of Lily Cheng at the Exhibition. That could wait.

'They'll be safe enough there. So Milk didn't take Toby. I'm glad that's cleared up. Now, as to Cornelius Mornay —' he turned to Bold — 'he was at the opium den and the girl said Milk took him there. We found out the connection between Mornay and the opium den — he was helping them because he'd known Cheng in China — I needn't go into detail — and we also think that Milk is a Mr Millikin who sold opium to Ajax Cheese and to a lot of other businesses round here.'

'Cheng's, too,' Dickens said.

'Now, I'm wondering what sort of shady dealing was going on. Millikin was supposed to have represented some company in the city and then set up business on his own —'

'Stealing it,' Bold said. 'He'd know the ropes — it comes off the ships and goes to London — he'd know the carriers. Could be there's a deal between Milk and one of them. Take a quantity, after the bill of lading's been approved — who's to know? Thousands of pounds of the stuff come in from Turkey and Egypt. Might be more than one in it. There was a case not long ago — young fellow at the docks stole five thousand pounds worth of raw opium. He sold five hundred pounds to one Jemmy Brand, who hawked it round the pubs.'

'So you'll investigate from this end?'

'Yes, that's what we do best — not all this murdering of toffs stuff. You think those two are away from here?'

'I do. Mincing Lane's the place for the opium traders — we'll take a look there.'

'And the Chengs?'

'Leave 'em be, I'd say. We know Mornay was there and why, but it was Milk killed him. Cheng's an accessory — if you want him for that after we've found Milk, then that's up to you.'

'They won't know whether he's milk or gin — he took Mornay there because Mornay knew them.'

'We think Milk got Dag to put Mornay in the river — that's why he was killed.'

'Makes sense. If you'll excuse me, I'll have to see about that body and find the girlfriend — not that I've much hope of that.'

'Toby's sister,' Dickens said, 'is it worth looking for her? Toby Quick said Bluegate Fields and that she's an opium addict. Fallen, Mr Cheese said.'

'Oh, aye, I'd forgotten her. Sally Quick — right — she'll be in some lodgings, I daresay with her fancy man. I'll let you know if we find her.'

'Toby knew Blood — went robbing with him — could she be the girlfriend?'

'I'll look into it — Sleat knows where Blood lodged.'

The steamboat pulled away from the pier. 'Blood,' Dickens began.

'It is what Stemp thought, I should think — a drunken brawl. Bold said Blood was reckless. Transportation, the gallows, or bleeding to death in a gutter — bound to happen. What are you going to do about Toby Quick and this girl — bit young for eloping, aren't they?'

'He's about fifteen, she's sixteen — it happens round these parts. Over the broom. Old for their age — what they've experienced. Toby's a resourceful creature — they met up in Hyde Park. She was dressed as a boy for the funeral. Looked just like a young Chinese man —'

Jones looked at him sharply. 'Hyde Park? What day?'

'Exactly — Toby sneaked her in disguised in a Chinese costume. She saw the Queen — "bit of a lark", Toby said.'

Jones couldn't help laughing. 'Dear Lord, and half the police force looking for a Chinese assassin. I won't mention it to Mr Mayne or Sir George. They'd have her transported. So what's your plan? I know you.'

'I had a thought when the girl told me about Mr Li Shen. I'm sending them to Dover, to Fullerton and Li Shen. They've enough, as you said yourself, so they can do something for Miss Lily Cheng. See how they like that. I'll send a letter with them. It gets them away from here at any rate.'

'They can't be worse off — Fullerton knew Ah Say, so he might be willing.'

'I hope so. Lily Cheng told me something rather sad — Cornelius Mornay kept saying "Ah Say" over and over. His last words on this earth.'

Dickens looked back into the distance where the river flowed on to Limehouse Reach, past Greenwich, through Galleon's Reach, Erith Roads, Fiddler's Reach, into the salty waters of Gravesend Reach, turning at Lower Hope Point and entering Sea Reach, to Sheerness to meet the great ships with their white wings unfolded, waiting to cross the ever heaving sea to the lands far beyond — to China, where Ah Say lay in that sleep of death, dreaming of that English man whose children she had borne and lost.

Jones was looking, as he always did, ahead, towards Waterloo Bridge, thinking of Lord John Russell and banks, and opium brokers.

'Oh,' said Dickens, 'I nearly forgot. Toby found this under the trees in Hyde Park.'

'Not a thimble.'

'It's an opium measure.'

Jones looked at the little ivory cup in Dickens's palm. 'Mincing Lane, tomorrow morning then.'

28: THE LAND OF SPICES

Dickens found the Superintendent and Sergeant Rogers deep in *The Public Ledger and Advertiser*. Rogers was making notes as Jones read out names.

'Mincing Lane?' he asked.

'Yes, we're noting the opium brokers — no one called Millikin, however. Someone may have heard of him.'

Dickens looked at the front page of the paper — that prosaic publication with its practical black and white notices which read like a volume of *The Arabian Nights*: ivory, elephants' teeth, frankincense, myrrh, manna and mace, ambergris and amonpsiacum — whatever that was — cinnamon, cardamoms, cochineal — all for sale and sounding like magic spells.

'To be auctioned at Garraway's Coffee House,' Jones read, 'ten chests of Egyptian opium — George Brooke — oh, no, he's in Turnwheel Lane. There's Grey and Clark in Mincing Lane.'

'Jacob Mocatta,' Dickens read. 'Mocatta — must be a magician — oil of juniper, fifty sacks of otto of roses, nineteen sacks of Zeondar root — do they come on magic carpets, I wonder?'

'What's Zeondar root when it's at home?' asked Rogers.

'Love potion, I believe — very powerful. Men have died and worms have eaten them. You don't want that anywhere near your respectable premises, my dear sergeant.'

'Give over,' said Jones. 'Does he deal in opium?'

'Yes, five chests — but he's in Lime Street. Oh, wait a minute —'

'I haven't got a minute.'

'Time, Mr Jones, is for slaves of the lamp — I was about to say Mr Thomas Merry — as a grig, no doubt — is selling Turkey berries, tamarind, Dragon's Blood — very restorative, I'm told, and —' he saw Jones's face — 'five chests of opium this very afternoon from Mincing Lane.'

Jones moved the paper nearer. 'Alf, you'll have to find where some of these other concerns are, too. They don't all give their addresses. There's Ellis and Hall — that's the company Ajax Cheese mentioned. Trade Directory will tell you where it is. And look up — er — Griffin and Price —'

'Manna,' said Dickens, still reading, 'from heaven, no doubt.'

'From Lewis and Peat — they're in Mincing Lane at number eleven.'

'Several in Fenchurch Street, too, I see — where Francis Hope — oh, Lor, Sam.'

Jones put down the paper. 'Could you see him again? He'll need to know that Michael Spencer is dead. Perhaps, you could —'

'Mention Millikin — do you know, when I say it, I don't believe in it. He made it up — no one could be called Millikin — except in a novel. Miss Millikin, the abstemious young lady. Millikin, the poor curate — Millikin, spillikin — he could have made up his connection with Mincing Lane.'

'Made up or not, it's all we've got, and there's every reason to believe in Mincing Lane. He must have worked in the opium trade — for a broker, maybe. It's a lead. Anyway, time I went to see Lord John about Mattinson. You two can fly off to the land of spices.'

Francis Hope had been horrified to learn of the murder of Michael Spencer. Dickens had told him about the gold finger guard and the opium cup. He looked very pale.

'It is to do with China — with Canton? This is horrible to me, as though some shadow of the past is cast over me, as though what I wanted to forget comes back to haunt me.'

Dickens pitied him — a man who had made something of himself despite his orphan state and his mixed heritage. He wanted only to provide for his wife and his child — to have his loving home. But he had to ask about Millikin who dealt in opium and sold it in Wapping. Francis Hope did not know the name, nor did he know anything of an opium den in Bluegate Fields.

'Why do you think I deal in tea, Mr Dickens? It is because I wanted nothing to do with the opium trade. Yes, my father left me money which came from opium, but I have built my life on tea. Do you think that I — I who waited so long to be an English man — would hazard all I have to deal in opium?' There was genuine anguish in his tone as he asked his question.

I believe him, Dickens thought, making his way to meet Sergeant Rogers by the Church of St Katherine Coleman at the corner of Fenchurch Street and Church Row. He waited opposite an empty premises where a 'To Let' sign hung somewhat disconsolately. He made out the name above the door: *Henry Pigeon, Chemist and Apothecary*. Well, that bird had flown.

No sign of Rogers. He walked down to Mincing Lane, gazing in at the brokers' windows, reading the names, some of them so strange they might have been written in Chinese: bags of Myrobalans, casks of gum Sandarac, of Mahoe Bark, bales of Jalap, tins of Balsam Tolu, kegs of Jamaican Honey — countless chests of opium. He stood outside Lewis and Peat from where the manna came, and so did Sergeant Rogers who, turning round on the step, saw Dickens, and shook his head.

'No one's heard of him. Let's try Lime Street.'

'Open sesame and behold: Mr Mocatta, magician.'

Rogers grinned, 'And Ellis and Hall — the company Mr Cheese mentioned. Cheese, eh? Nothin' magic about him.'

Lime Street wasn't far, a turning off Fenchurch Street. Mr Mocatta, a smiling Portuguese man whose magic carpet was not in evidence, could not conjure Mr Millikin, nor could Mr Ellis, a stout and prosperous-looking English man who regarded them both suspiciously and snorted disbelievingly at the name Millikin.

'I don't believe it, either,' observed Dickens to Rogers. 'What now?'

'I'd best get off to Turnwheel Lane.'

'Shall I report back to Mr Jones?' Dickens suggested. He had a strong feeling that Mr Millikin would not be found there, either, and he did not fancy walking all the way to the Tower for no good purpose.

'I doubt I'll find him, either, but I ought to have a go.'

Jones, back from seeing Lord John, listened gloomily to Dickens's account of Francis Hope and to Rogers's failure to find any trace of Millikin.

'Anything useful from Lord John?'

'I have his permission to ask Mattinson about the wills — or rather, I may ask to see Mr Mornay's letters.'

'Anything in the banking way?'

'I touched on the banking crisis of 1847 — he knew what I was suggesting since I had alluded to the possibility of Mattinson's shares being denied him.'

'Daring, Samivel, I feel quite pale at the thought. What did he say?'

'Gave me a lesson in family history.'

'Good Lord, what?'

'Sir Francis Baring is First Lord of the Admiralty in Lord John's cabinet.'

'Barings Bank — yes.'

'Son of Sir Thomas Baring whose father was Chairman of the East India Company way back —'

Dickens's mouth formed a very round 'Oh.'

'— and whose brother, George Baring, founded a trading company which became Dent and Company — in Canton.'

Dickens's mouth formed an even rounder 'Oh.'

'There's more — Sir Francis Baring married first a Miss Jane Grey, now dead, but she was sister of —'

'Sir George Grey, the Home Secretary.'

'Yes.'

'I see —' Dickens looked narrowly at Jones — 'you don't think that Lord John would turn a blind eye to murder because of Sir Francis Baring's connection to The East India Company and Canton — and presumably — to Alexander Mattinson and John Mattinson, Member of Parliament?'

Jones looked at him bleakly. 'He said he would make enquiries, but, as far as he knew, Mattinson's bank was, and is, sound.'

'You know, I don't think much of that miserable dung heap at Westminster, but, Lord John, I think — I hope — he is an honest man — after all, he employed you to investigate.'

'Discreetly — for political reasons, remember. And now, I think of that debate you told me about. You quoted Lord John as having confidence in the East India Company directors. Think of the opium trade in China. Worth untold millions — and an unknown man found in the river, a body on a beach at Broadstairs, a kidsman in Wapping, and a known crook killed in a brawl, a man called Milk — and only a policeman's fancy to connect them.'

'On the evidence of a lad who was shot in an attempted burglary, a lad who had been a snakesman, and a drug-sodden prostitute — if she can be found — a Chinese man in an opium den —'

'And not a chance of bringing them to court — and if we ever did — when I think of all those names and all that power and money to be held on to — and I think of Mayne looking down his aristocratic nose as though I were a bad smell.'

'Ah, yes, a nose born to command. It's a funny thing about noses, Samivel — the nose is the man. Think of all those judicial noses in chancery — blowing their own trumpets in silk handkerchiefs, the drunkard's nose all garlanded with carbuncles, and that Inspector Wells we met once — now there was a meaning nose, especially when he rubbed it with his fat forefinger —'

Jones cheered up as Dickens meant him to. 'Lord John should have asked him to do his dirty work. Wells is the blunt sort — not put off by the lords and ladies.'

'As is his nose, as I recall. Ah, well, I daresay Sir John recognized your subtle nose for things.'

'Never mind noses — what am I to do about Mattinson?'

'You can ask for the letters and mention the will — perhaps you could tell Mattinson about the possible second will —'

'I daren't mention his legacies — dear God, Charles, it would be tantamount to accusing him.'

'I see that, but you needn't mention the details. You could just see his reaction to the idea of a second will.'

'I could. Of course, if he's guilty there will be no will in Mornay's box — he would have destroyed it.'

'Mind you, we don't know what Mornay did with it.'

'True — still, if it is there then Mattinson's in the clear — and I'm out of some very deep water.'

A knock came at the door and John Gaunt came in. 'We found Sally Quick — she was Blood's girl, and she knew Milk, who supplied her opium, and — more importantly — Puss.'

'Who is she?'

'Sally Quick was on the stage once — some penny gaff or other — and that's how she knew her. Miss Puss was an actress.'

'Real name?'

'Kitty Lovell.'

'Well, well,' said Dickens, 'that's a name I know.'

Jones laughed. 'You would — who is she?'

'You don't remember the name?' Jones and Gaunt shook their heads. 'Try this one: Viscount Fergus de Montclair Frankland.'

'You mean Lord Frankland the man who sued — oh, Kitty Lovell was the girl. He sued her for the recovery of jewels that she'd pawned. Some years back.'

'1845, I think, and she was acquitted even though she had pawned them. Said they were presents from the noble Lord with whom she had been living for some time. The jury believed her. I don't think the Viscount made a very good impression. He was separated from his wife, had at least two illegitimate children by different women, and Kitty Lovell was his current mistress — he'd picked her up in the Haymarket, it seems. The general feeling was that it was his own fault. Bad reputation all round — gambling, drinking, theatres, dens of vice — the usual things.'

'What happened to her?' asked Gaunt, to whom all this was fresh news.

'She was on the stage in no time. Some enterprising manager snapped her up — the Royal City of London Theatre, it was. Houses were packed, of course, to see the innocent girl wronged by the debauched peer.'

'Did you see her?' Jones asked.

'No, but I remember it because the play was *The Miser's Daughter*, adapted from Harrison Ainsworth's novel by Edward Stirling — Stirling adapted *Pickwick Papers* for the same theatre back in thirty-seven.'

'Any good?'

'Well, I didn't lie down in my box for shame — as I have done during some adaptations of my work — but I remember 1845 for another reason. In the same week as Kitty Lovell was bowing to her cheering audience, there was another production of *The Miser's Daughter* at Drury Lane to which I went for Ainsworth's sake. I knew him well in those days.'

'And Kitty Lovell, did she go on to star in anything else?'

'No, I don't think so — judging by what Johnno's found out, she must have disappeared into the minor theatres once her few weeks of fame fizzled out — where she met Sally Quick who is now an opium addict and prostitute in Bluegate Fields.'

'Would anyone at the Royal City remember her, do you think?'

'They'd remember, but they might not know where she went — it is a few years ago. Did Sally Quick tell you anything else, Johnno?'

'No — only that she was with this fellow, Milk, and they looked as if they had money.'

'They certainly did,' Jones said, 'from opium and those robberies we think they were involved in.'

'Witnesses in the Lovell case,' Dickens said. 'There was the pawnbroker to whom Kitty Lovell pledged the jewels. Can't remember his name, but it was in the papers. I could go and see my friend, Thomas Beard — journalist for the *Morning Herald* — he'd show me the back numbers. I might find someone who knows her.'

'I'd better get back,' Gaunt said, 'and tell Inspector Bold — we can try the theatres down our way.'

'The Effingham, Whitechapel Road, Johnno — where they do the melodramas for the sailors and their girls. That's low enough for Kitty Lovell.'

'And I'm for Lombard Street to ask Mr Alexander Mattinson about Cornelius Mornay's will.'

'Or wills.'

29: THE RIVALS

Dickens set off for Fleet Street, trying to remember the details of Kitty Lovell's cause celebre. Her defence had been that the Viscount had given her the jewels and trinkets — worth a few hundred pounds or so, he recalled. Diamond earrings and a gold watch, snuffboxes. She'd lived with the fellow for several months, so it was possible, and the jury had believed her. But Dickens did recall some sceptics who rather thought her swooning performance at the Old Bailey about as convincing as her appearance on stage.

He stopped suddenly in Brydges Street. *Mrs Stirling*, he thought, once the wife of Edward Stirling, adapter of Ainsworth's novel — now to be Lady Teazle in *The School for Scandal* at Drury Lane, and here he was passing the entrance. It would be worth asking if she knew anything about Kitty Lovell.

He went round the back to the stage door and asked. The doorkeeper told him that he thought the rehearsal was just coming to an end. He went to sit in the stalls. A delightful piece of comedy, he always thought. He had played Sir Peter Teazle in some amateur theatricals a couple of years ago to his friend Mary Boyle's Lady Teazle, the young wife caught up in a scandal. Mrs Stirling was coming to the end of her epilogue and was forswearing the lures of life in town — to be a country wife. She was very good. Charming, in fact, in her satin dress and powdered eighteenth-century wig.

He gave her a round of applause and stood so that she could see him. She gave him a curtsey and motioned him to come up. Delighted to see Mr Dickens — come to audition, had he? He might like to play Snake? He laughed, knowing that Snake was referred to as a writer and critic — forger, too, of libellous letters. She took him to her dressing room and yanked off her wig. The eighteenth-century belle was gone, and an ordinary hard-working actress took her place. 'Damned hot,' she said, shaking out her own hair and giving him a mischievous look. 'You might have asked me for *Not So Bad as We Seem* rather than Ellen Chaplin,' she teased.

'You are far too much engaged for amateurs,' Dickens said.

'Good enough for the Queen — the newspapers say she's to attend. However, I shall forgive you if you've come for tickets or a box.'

'I came to ask you something. Do you remember *The Miser's Daughter*?'

'I certainly do — Mr Stirling adapted it for the Olympic — in 1845, I believe. I try not to think a great deal about Mr Stirling.' She smiled, however, taking the sting out of the words.

'I was there — because of Ainsworth, but there was a rival production at the Royal City of London in the same week. Do you remember?'

Mrs Stirling chuckled delightedly. 'Yes, indeed, Mr Stirling was not pleased. A rival production and Mr Dunn of the Royal City was not a man of scruple. Mr Stirling was ready to shoot him — they got all the publicity because of that girl — Kitty Lovell — she was in that case against the nobleman — er — Mont- something or other.'

'Montclair Frankland — Lord Frankland —'

'Ah, yes — dreadful reputation, I recall — school for scandal, eh?'

'So it was. Did you meet Kitty Lovell— I mean — in any other theatre?'

'No, I'd have remembered. She wasn't a very good actress by all accounts — she got more applause in court than on the stage.'

'What did she play in *The Miser's Daughter*?'

'She wasn't in that — which added fuel to Mr Stirling's rage. Two productions might not have been so bad for him, but nobody paid any attention to the skinflint's daughter or anybody else's daughter for that matter. The cry was for Kitty — Kitty Lovell was in Buckstone's *The Dead Shot* — Louisa Lovetrick — very apt, I thought.'

'You don't know what happened to her?'

'Vanished — into some of the minor theatres — more disreputable than Mr Dunn's, I should think.'

'There's no one you can think of who was in *The Dead Shot* with her?'

'Old Frank Cowle was in Dunn's company, but he died last year. Oh, I don't know, Mr Dickens, it's a while ago. John Buckstone might have seen it, though — he wrote it.'

'I saw him in April at the General Theatrical Fund Dinner — I'll ask him.'

'I read your speech in the paper —' she grinned at him — 'charity for the greatest and the least — the monarch or the spear carrier — even Louisa Lovetrick, eh?'

'I think I might except Miss Lovell from the charitable avocations of the Fund.'

'What do you want her for — something criminal?'

'Theft.'

'She was good at that. John Buckstone's at The Adelphi. Devilsfoot in *The Bohemian Girl*.'

'I might find her, then, as well.'

Wherever you went in London, you trod in the steps of a murderer. Dickens was turning into a queer little dog's leg of an alley on his way to the Adelphi stage door which was in Bull-Inn Yard. There was the dark outline of a man resting his head on the wall in an attitude of despair, his arms above his head. Dickens slowed down, but the man was gone — just gone. What an odd place. *Seeing phantoms*, he thought, remembering the story of an actor murdered thereabouts back in the Regency times when the Adelphi had been the Sans Pareil. By a rival, perhaps, who'd wanted fame and fortune? Doomed forever to seek the stage door. Dickens would have told him where it was, had he stayed to listen.

John Buckstone was very much alive, though somewhat pale about the gills with powder, and was very intrigued to hear about Dickens's search for Kitty Lovell, whom he remembered as Louisa Lovetrick.

'Inaudible, she was, and yet the gallery cheered. Every time she came on. You should have seen her take her bow — almost fainting with gratitude. She did the fainting very well in court, I read. Dunn thought a deal of her — the money, of course. Miss Puss, he called her. She didn't last long. Collected the cash from her benefit show and went off.'

'Can you remember anything about her?'

'Dark hair, pretty little thing in the pert manner. Black eyes — bit too sharp for my liking. Impudent bitch, I thought. Last heard of at The Garrick Subscription in Leman Street. That burnt down in forty-six — that'd be the end of her career. Up in flames. Unless she's at The Effingham Saloon — that's a place for thieves and rogues. You don't want her for your amateurs, do you?' he asked, laughing. 'The Queen might not be amused.'

Dickens laughed. 'I've enough trouble with the cast I've got.

No — theft from someone I know.'

'That fits. Remember Mrs Mitchell? Lizzie Mitchell.'

'Of course — I've not seen her in anything recently.'

'She's in Southampton, but I mention her because she was involved in Kitty Lovell's case — always referred to as Miss Mitchell who'd taken Kitty Lovell to meet the Viscount who made the girl his mistress. He said Miss Mitchell was Kitty Lovell's hairdresser.'

'She wouldn't have cared for that. She was a good actress, as I recall.'

'She wasn't called as a witness, but there was some talk of her being given jewels by Kitty Lovell. Anyway, she survived the gossip, and she did well at The Olympic, The Haymarket, and at The Theatre Royal with Madame Celeste — she is a good actress. I'm telling you because she never talked about it except once when she confided in me — Kitty Lovell came to see her here at the Adelphi. Lizzie was appearing in *The Rivals* and getting very good notices.'

'When was this?'

'It would be the end of forty-nine, before Lizzie went to Southampton. She told me in confidence that she was glad to be going away. I imagine Kitty Lovell might have followed Lizzie's career. Anyway, she turned up and asked Lizzie what she could do for her — getting her a leading role, for example. Saw herself as a star in the making still, I suppose, a rival for Lizzie or Fanny Stirling, I daresay. Kitty Lovell was thinking of approaching Mr Webster — manager here — telling him about her old friend Lizzie Mitchell who'd had some of Lord Frankland's jewels —'

'She hadn't?'

'She said not — but she did know Frankland and she had been to his house in Southwick Terrace, and her name had been in the papers. She didn't want anyone being reminded of the case. She'd lived it down, especially the hairdressing bit and the suggestion that she was in cahoots with Kitty about the jewels. She acted with the best and she was up for a role with Macready at Drury lane. You know how punctilious Mac was — he wouldn't have liked a leading lady tainted with scandal.'

'No, indeed —' it was quite true; Dickens's old friend, William Macready, had expected high standards of his leading actresses — 'spot of blackmail, in fact.'

'Exactly — I advised Lizzie to go to the police, but she'd already given Kitty Lovell twenty pounds. I said she'd be back — that's what blackmailers do — but Lizzie decided on Southampton and gave up Mr Macready.'

'Get away before Kitty Lovell did come back.'

'Right — Kitty told Lizzie some sob story about her husband-to-be who'd lost his job and they couldn't afford the lodgings they'd signed for.'

'Did she say anything about the husband? Name?'

'No, I don't remember that. He'd been in tea, Kitty said, a broker who'd lost all his money — swindled by his partner. Lizzie didn't believe a word of it, but she gave her the money just to get rid of her.'

'No address for Kitty Lovell?'

'I can't remember that far back.'

Dickens thanked him for the information. They exchanged a few words about the Theatrical Fund. Dickens promised to come to the play and went out into Bull Yard. He didn't go back through the dog's leg alley. *Enough murdered ghosts in my life*, he thought, making straight for Maiden Lane. He would go to Fleet Street to see Tom Beard. It would be worth reading up Kitty Lovell's case and finding out the names of other witnesses.

30: A SISTER AND A DAUGHTER

'I didn't see Mattinson.'

Dickens had come back to Bow Street to tell Jones all about Kitty Lovell and the witnesses in the case, and had found him returned from Mattinson's bank, and looking less than pleased.

Dickens raised an eloquent eyebrow. 'Ah.'

'He was at a very important meeting, so his senior clerk told me — with Sir Francis Baring — matters to do with the Bank of England. I knew, of course, he pointed out helpfully, that Mr Mattinson is a director of the Bank of England.'

'Good job I didn't go sniffing about there. Sir Francis Baring — a name to conjure with.'

'Oh, I conjured all right, and out from my sleeve came —'

'A warning?'

'Could be. However, the chief myrmidon did give Mr Mattinson's gracious permission to examine Mr Mornay's papers.'

'No will.'

'Not one.'

'Ah.'

'Dead end for now. Tell me you've got something.'

'Well, I found out a good deal about Miss Kitty Lovell, called Miss Puss by the manager of The Royal City Theatre.'

'Was she, indeed?'

'Last heard of at The Garrick Subscription Theatre in Whitechapel, which burnt down in forty-six. Career gone up in flames, as my contact, Mr Buckstone, put it. And not heard of again, theatrically speaking, until eighteen forty-nine when she tried a spot of blackmail on another actress, Lizzie Mitchell, who went off to Southampton. Lizzie Mitchell was mentioned in the Frankland case as someone who had received jewels from Kitty Lovell. She had gone to Mrs Mitchell with some sob story about her husband being swindled — he was a tea dealer, so she said.'

'Tea!'

'He might have been in tea, I daresay, even in Mincing Lane or Fenchurch Street —'

'Hope didn't know him, though.'

'No — he'd have remembered, I'm sure. I was thinking more about that area — maybe where he got interested in opium — that is if the husband existed or is Millikin.'

'I think he probably is — she might have got the idea about tea from seeing the tea dealers, and it sounded more respectable than opium. Anyway, we don't know where they are now. Rogers went to Turnwheel Lane. They'd not heard of him. However, Rogers had the wit to ask about any clerks let go, so to speak — anyone fitting the description of Millikin — no one, of course.'

'I went to *The Morning Herald*'s office in Fleet Street. Tom Beard remembered it all — he was in court. It's a ludicrous tale in its way. Lord Frankland was a singular creature, picked up the girl in Haymarket, took her to live with him and locked her up — spent three hundred pounds on her jewels and dresses, and off she went to the pawn shop with her swag, the jewels and a gold toothpick, gold watch, a pendant, several snuffboxes — valuable things — and some little miniatures he'd collected.'

'Surely he didn't give her his snuffboxes and pictures?'

'The jury believed her. As I said before, they didn't take to Lord Frankland and there had been quite a to-do about his mistresses and illegitimate children. However, Tom Beard remembered that there was a sister who lived in St. Giles's where the pawn tickets were found. Now, we didn't find her name in the papers, but Kitty Lovell pawned the goods in the name of Chester and the address was Bread Yard, off Denmark Street. Did she give her sister's name? Still there, I wonder?'

'Well, for want of anything else, we'll stroll across there now, shall we?'

Bread Yard was a different planet altogether from the noble lord's apartments in Southwick Terrace and not a place where you might adorn your ears with diamonds or keep valuable miniatures on your library table — unless you were keeping them for a friend who had acquired them in the course of his professional avocations as a cracksman — a cracksman who preferred a broken window to a smartly painted front door. A dark little house in a dark little yard was just the place to store your — or someone else's — valuables.

Maggie Chester, a woman coming out of the yard, answered their query about the Chester family — lived in a house just inside the archway leading in. Their feet crunched on stones and oyster shells as they went in.

'Poverty and oysters always seem to go together,' observed Dickens, shaking a large shell from his boot.

But the Chester house looked neat enough, and there was the sound of children's voices coming from the open door. Dickens knocked while Jones stayed in the shadows. Several children spilled out to gaze up at the gentleman who was asking for their mother. Dickens could smell frying fish. He asked again about Mrs Chester, but the children still gazed upward so he knocked on the door.

'You lot, stop playing the fool and get in here — food's

ready.'

'There's a man, Ma, a man wants yer.' A girl of about ten years piped up.

A harassed-looking woman, older than Kitty Lovell, and shabbier, but with a look of her in the dark hair and black eyes, came to the door, wiping her hands on her apron. 'For the Lord's sake, I've told you, this is not the time — I haven't got anythin' to spare these days —' she saw Dickens then — 'oh, sorry, sir, I thought you was — oh, never mind.'

'Mrs Chester, I've come to ask about your sister, Kitty Lovell.'

'Oh — I don't — I haven't —'

Jones stepped forward. His large presence scattered the children. 'I am sorry to disturb you, Mrs Chester. I am a policeman from Bow Street, and I do need to speak to you about Miss Lovell.'

'Kitty!' cried the girl who had stayed by her mother. 'Auntie Kitty — she ain't 'ere — we ain't seen 'er fer years. Ma says —'

'Hush, Tilly, hush — take the others in an' give them their teas in the kitchen while I speak to the gentlemen. Now — I mean it or else —'

They all heard the threat, and the four other children went inside, only Tilly looking back curiously. She had a look of Kitty, too — innocent, though. What Kitty Lovell might have been when she was a child. Dickens and Jones followed Maggie Chester into a small parlour where they sat at a small table, and Mrs Chester asked as if she were not at all surprised, 'What's Kitty done? Somethin', I suppose, or you wouldn't be here.'

'A matter of theft.' Jones wasn't ready to discuss murder yet. He wanted to know where they might find Kitty Lovell.

'Oh — again — can't help herself, that one.'

'Have you seen her recently?'

Maggie Chester laughed a small bitter laugh. 'No, she don't come here — too good for St. Giles's is Kitty. Always had grand ideas. You know about Lord Frankland, I suppose — and them jewels.'

'We do,' said Dickens. 'Did she steal them?'

'I don't think she did — he gave her jewels to wear and clothes, but as for them other trinkets, the snuffboxes and little pictures, the gold pencil an' the watch, I think she just helped herself. See, Lord Frankland — she called him Frankie — was a drunk an' a gambler. Didn't know what he was doing half the time. He let her play with all the knick-knacks an' she'd just take 'em if she felt like it. Finders, keepers was Kitty's motto.'

'Why did she leave Lord Frankland?'

'Oh, she liked it all at first — Kitty could do the fine lady, all right. When he went out, I used to go there. She'd send a cab an' we'd try on the jewels an' the dresses, drink chocolate an' eat sweets, but eventually she got bored. The deal was that she could stay, but he wouldn't take her out. Course, his cronies came and went — gamblin' parties, mainly, but he wouldn't take her to the fancy places she wanted to go to. Kept her under lock an' key — that's why she sent for me. She had to show off to someone, but I wasn't enough for Kitty — she needed a bigger audience — she fancied herself as an actress an' thought she'd be set up in her own place — a cottage in Regent's Park she was after. An' when the lord wasn't visitin', she could entertain her own friends — her set she called it — like that Miss Mitchell — she thought she'd be a big star on the stage, but the lord wasn't havin' that, so Kitty upped an' went with the jewels an' stuff. Pawned 'em in my name to get the ready cash.'

'And after her time at the theatre?'

'Took up with a gent from the city. She had the same idea — that he'd be the one to set her up — not that she was short of money, but there'd never be enough for Kitty.'

'Did you know his name?'

'I remember it cos it made me laugh.'

'Not Millikin.'

'Millikin — now that is a laugh — sounds like a nursery maid — no, sir, I'd have remembered that. No, it was Mr Merlin. I thought she'd made it up, but it was true. He was in the papers — went to prison for forgery. Ernest Merlin — mind, that was a few years back.'

'And Kitty kept in touch with you at that time?' Jones asked. He knew the name "Merlin" very well — and the man wasn't a magician.

'Oh, yes, she sent money for —' Maggie stood up and went to the parlour door. She made sure it was closed.

'For?'

'For Tilly — Tilly's her daughter. She doesn't know and I don't want her to. Kitty had her at fourteen. She came here an' I took the baby — I hadn't my own kids then. Kitty would have — well, you know — but it was too late, and then our pa found out. He was a respectable man — just a cobbler, but proud of his work an' wantin' to keep his daughters respectable. He threw her out an' I took her in. I was married, but no kiddies then. See, I was the eldest an' I tried to look after her after our ma died, but Kitty was always a thief — and a liar, always runnin' off with lads. After the baby, I got her a job as a kitchen maid — you can imagine how she liked that. Off she goes with a silver pepper pot and spoons. I took 'em back — I didn't want the police here. The housekeeper was a good sort, but they didn't want Kitty anywhere near again. Then she took to sewin' at the theatre an' met Miss Mitchell and Lord Frankland — an' then there was this Mr Merlin an' then nothin'.'

'Nothing for Tilly?'

'Not a farthin', an' you know, sir, Tilly thought Kitty was next thing to the Queen — the odd time she came here all dressed up — best for Tilly to forget her.'

And that might not be possible — Dickens thought of what would happen if they found Kitty Lovell and proved her part in murder. Another newspaper scandal for poor Maggie Chester to cope with, and a long prison sentence — or worse. Still, the child might never find out that her mother was a murderess, or at least an accessory.

'You don't know if Kitty married?' Jones asked just to clear up the story of the ruined tea-dealer husband.

Maggie looked astonished. 'Marry? That's not Kitty's way — rich men she likes — to live off. She'll not settle down. Live like this —' she gestured round her neat parlour — and it was neat. It was not a City trader's mansion, or Southwick Terrace, or Grosvenor Square where, according to *The Morning Herald*, Viscountess Montclair Frankland had lived. Dickens wondered if she were still there. Maggie was still talking. 'Not good enough for our Kitty. She'll have found someone, I'll bet — a crook, like her. I don't know where she is — and I don't want to.'

'Merlin,' Jones said as they walked out of Bread Court.

'At your service — magic for the masses, turn your farthings into gold, boil a pudding in your hat, conjure your watch —'

'From a loaf of bread — I know, and very good it is, but I'm thinking of Mr Merlin.'

'Ah, the fraudster she mentioned.'

'I put him in prison.'

'The devil you did — and Kitty Lovell was his mistress.'

'I don't remember her. His wife was in court — a pretty-looking woman who had no idea that she was married to a crook — or an adulterer for that matter. However, as far as I know he's still in prison. He went down for ten years — forging and uttering bills — eight thousand pounds' worth. I remember it vividly because when the sentence was given, Merlin turned blue before our very eyes and dropped senseless — heart attack. I wonder if he knows anything of Kitty.'

'You're going to find out — where is he?'

'Millbank — if he's still alive.'

'When was his trial?'

'Eighteen forty-seven.'

'After the Whitechapel Theatre burnt down — Kitty's his mistress for a while then he's off to the clink; perhaps she goes back to the theatre — some penny gaff or other — and works with Toby Quick's sister, meets our friend Milk, and takes to crime full time.'

'Always a thief, Mrs Chester said, and she's abandoned them. By herself a petty thief, maybe, just stealing from her lovers, but with Milk —'

'It turns into something very ugly.'

31: PUSS IN BOOTS

Dickens went back to Wellington Street and upstairs to his own rooms. He opened a window, feeling the heat, and walked up and down, into one of the bedrooms, back into the sitting room, into the kitchen and the scullery beyond. He thought of fetching a bottle of wine from the cellar to cool himself down, but he walked back into the kitchen and contemplated the tea kettle. He couldn't face that, either. He contemplated the pile of papers on the desk. He took up his pen. "On Duty with Inspector Field" — that was to be the new article, based on his experiences with Sam Jones and all of them at Bow Street, names disguised, of course, and cases. He was not going to mention a merchant from Canton.

He listened to the clocks striking the hour, counting the chimes. *How goes the night?* St. Giles's clock was striking nine. *That's it*, he thought, *that's the beginning. A wet night, cold, not summer as now, and St. Giles's, not Wapping.* St. Giles's where they had gone to investigate a murder and they'd found the cause of a death at Hungerford Stairs. And he remembered a woman who had lost a child. There had been a kind of pity for her. He put down his pen.

Kitty Lovell who had abandoned her child; Kitty Lovell, always a liar and a thief. Kitty who'd had a taste of the high life with Viscount Frankland, who had been the heroine of the Old Bailey, who had basked in the applause from the gallery, who'd bagged a man from the city only to be thwarted again, who'd perhaps gone back to the East End. Kitty Lovell who saw herself as a great actress, only denied her success by bad luck — by the unfairness of it all. Lizzie Mitchell owed her. She should have come to court to speak for her; she should have stood by her after *The Dead Shot* had finished, but no, Lizzie Mitchell had gone on to star at The Olympic. Lizzie Mitchell did nothing for Kitty Lovell. Lizzie Mitchell should pay, but Lizzie Mitchell went off to Southampton and all Kitty got was twenty pounds. That wouldn't be enough. And then she met Milk. What coincidence had brought those two thieves and liars together so that in the crucible of their mutual attraction, something evil had flared into life?

And Milk — he'd be the same sort — a nature that could not be satisfied. An ambitious young man, but the world would be against him. Just a clerk, perhaps, in a drugs company, but seeing with envy those who made all the money, knowing the trade, scenting an opportunity, finding a career in crime and loving the power it gave him — all those poverty-stricken customers whose lives depended on his word. He could raise his prices any time he liked, leave his addicts until their craving forced them to beg, to sell, to steal, to kill, even, to get their drug. And if they died, well, too bad — there were plenty more.

Dickens thought of a story in the newspaper of a respectable woman who had said that she had sold everything because she couldn't live without her opium, and the story of a rising young merchant's clerk who had stolen from his employer to pay for his habit.

And only the other day, there had been a verdict of accidental death of an unknown man found in Took's Court. An educated man, it seemed, earning his living as a law writer, copying documents for a stationer. No one knew who he was, but his room stank of poverty, failure, loss — and opium. A fallen man.

Yes, Milk and Kitty would enjoy their power — immoral and

greedy, they'd do anything for money. But who had set them on? The murders of Cornelius Mornay and his son could not be their crime alone.

Not coincidence, or if so, some coincidence of the stars. He felt it in his bones. Some fate linked these people, formed a net of connectedness. He thought of Uriah Heep's mother, whom he had described weaving a net with her Chinese chopsticks of knitting needles, resembling in the firelight an ill-looking enchantress. A net to entangle Agnes Wickfield. Weaving a net. But who was the enchanter of the evil they had smelt in the heavy air of Wapping? Someone whose invisible power was weaving the net to enmesh them all.

Alexander Mattinson — a powerful man, indeed, with all the weight of the Bank of England behind him. Still, Sam had Lord John behind him, the Prime Minister — he hoped, remembering Sam's bleak face. Lord John had helped him get a pension for the old writer John Poole; he'd been very sympathetic to the deputation of the Sanitary Committee, which was agitating for reform of burial grounds and the repeal of the Window Tax — all meant to relieve the suffering of the poor. Surely a good man.

But then there were those high-powered people in Lord John's own party — Sir Francis Baring, Sir George Grey, the millionaire M.P. James Mattinson — Disraeli's Mr Druggy, all connected by China and opium. Who really knew what went on in the corridors of power? Money. Power. And, even if Sam found evidence against Mattinson, how could it be proved without finding a connection between him and Milk? They hadn't even proved yet that Milk had murdered Cornelius Mornay.

He felt almost as if the net were drawing tighter about him, a curious heat about his head and a sensation as if he were choking. He must have air. It would be cooler now. He could walk up to Lincoln's Inn Fields and walk about there.

There was a stillness in the gardens, pleasant to stroll through. He looked over to the houses in Holborn Row, at the windows of number fifty-eight where his friend, John Forster lived, but all was dark. Pity, he would have liked some company this evening. He might as well go back and get some work done.

He walked towards Duke Street from where he could hear the cries and shouts of those passing. In the alleys and the courts, there would be crowds of people: lodgers, thieves, tramps, whores, parents, children, unclaimed children, all packed in like oysters in a barrel, quarrelling, drinking, lolling in the gutters, tumbling about the doorsteps, leaning from windows, living their wretched, raucous lives while the lawyers and merchants, politicians and aristocrats drank their port by open windows or wandered in cool, shady gardens. What a city for contrasts London was: the Queen in her palace of many rooms and the poor Chinese man in his opium den, and nothing to link them but two beating hearts. And what more than two beating hearts connected the opulence of Pole Court and the squalor of Bluegate Fields?

And here was a sight in Wellington Street. A cart had broken down in the middle of the street, its wheel spinning towards Dickens, pursued by the carter. The cart was piled high with household goods, some of which had fallen off, a frying pan and some fire irons making a clatter. A little child sat on a mattress at the back, gazing with wondering eyes at the commotion, and a man in a threadbare suit was bending down to pick up some of his possessions from Dickens's doorstep — before anyone darted out of an alleyway to steal them. A very old woman with a look of terror on her face sat screeching in an easy chair now leaning at a drunken angle and forcing her to flail about. The painfully thin horse — more fit for the knacker's yard than for hauling goods — stood quite still, its head hanging. For shame, perhaps.

The woman continued her wailing and her waving. *Poor old thing*, he thought, about to step out to help, but stopped by the wheel which fell at his feet. A family on the move, he supposed, flitting — rent not paid, no doubt. He picked up the wheel and steadied it for the carter, a tall, rough-looking, broad-shouldered man who took it and turned away without a word. He and the threadbare man humped the wheel onto its axle and the rattling caravan began to move away, the old woman still crying out. Dickens waited to cross the road.

A woman was looking up at the window on the first floor. He wondered who she was, but then she turned away to cross the street. A dusty yellow light still hung in the street, the tired remnants of the hot day, but in that light, he saw her face. He dodged back into a doorway.

He was sure, though. It was she — Puss. She was coming his way. He put his hand to his face, tipped his hat and lounged against the door, hoping no one would come out to thrust him into the street. A not unlikely prospect, since he was lurking in the doorway of Reynolds's publishing house — not a friend of his, Reynolds. He'd probably chuck Charles Dickens into the street.

He heard the swish of her dress as she passed, and he saw briefly an arm and a gloved hand that held a parasol. He might have touched her. There was the scent of something musky, which lingered for a second or two. He heard the tapping of her boots fading away.

He peeped out and saw her walking towards the Strand. He kept his distance, but by the time he reached the junction she was gone. He stood, irresolute for a moment, and then had the chilling thought that she — and Milk, possibly — could be watching him. She might have seen him as he picked up the cartwheel. He turned back and slipped into a narrow lane which led into Covent Garden where there were still plenty of people and darting, barefoot children picking up bits of cabbage leaves, squashed fruit and offal to take to their dens under carts, in wheelbarrows, and whatever holes in the ground afforded some shelter.

He took shelter in Piazza Coffee House and sat by a window. It was dark now, but from time to time a gas lamp lit up a passing face. He didn't see her, but he conjured her in his mind's eye. A neat figure in dark red. A skirt swishing by, a glimpse of black piping near the hem. A dark red sleeve with black trim. A gloved hand. And he focused that inward eye on a figure in The Shakespeare's Head. He saw the red sleeve with its black piping. A gloveless hand raised to her mouth. A glint of gold. Not a ring, not a bracelet. A fingernail guard. That's what it was. He was certain.

And Alley had found a gold fingernail guard on the path down which Michael Spencer had been taken on a storm-filled night.

She had let him see it. She had smiled that mocking smile and raised her hand. It had been a challenge and now? She knew him. Though, why not? Lots of people knew him. Lots of people had seen his likeness. Why not Puss?

And, perhaps, his connection with Sam was known, or guessed at. His appearance during the trial of a murderer last year had been in the papers. Sam and he had been linked by their visit to a house in some woods and the discovery of a body. Logic said that Milk and Puss might well know him. Thank the Lord he hadn't stayed in Broadstairs to give details about his discovery of Michael Spencer's body — that would have been a headline.

They couldn't know that he and Sam had been to Ramsgate and Broadstairs. Sam was determined that the burial of Michael Spencer must be private — the fiction that Spencer had probably been on the *Mercury* must be maintained. Dickens was supposed to call on Miss Palmer at Princes Square and explain to the brother and sister why they could not have a funeral, only a simple parish burial in Ramsgate. *Better not be seen in Princes Square*, he thought now. He would write and advise them all to go back to Dumpton and stay there.

Logic, though, did not explain what Miss Puss was doing on his doorstep. Safe to go back to the office now, he hoped, but he took a circuitous route back to Wellington Street and was glad to see that no one was hanging about his doorway. The cart had gone, too — just a few feathers from a mattress blowing about with the dust and a chill in the air. And at the back of his neck.

And that wasn't a coincidence, either.

32: MAGICAL THINKING

Jones looked very thoughtful. 'You sure?'

'I am,' Dickens said. And he was. Of course, in the morning he had considered whether he could have been mistaken. He had been thinking of them and he'd seen that poor old woman's terrified face — perhaps she had reminded him of the old housekeeper who had died of fright, but he had looked out of his window to the doorway opposite and in his inward eye, he had seen her, heard her, smelt her. There was no doubt that it had been Puss, but what it meant was something he and Superintendent Jones were now contemplating in the early morning at Jones's house in Norfolk Street.

'They knew you in that pub, and that's not surprising. They want to know what it all has to do with you, and they're dangerous. But, what a risk —'

'Reckless, I'd say, as if they're enjoying themselves —'

'Enjoying!'

'I know. Put it this way — they don't care. Insolent, flippant, even. That moment in the pub when he spat, and she tried to trip me. She showed me that finger guard —'

'She hoped you would see her outside your office.'

'Challenging me — daring us to find them and telling us we can't.'

Jones thought about that. 'They always think they're cleverer than we are, that sort.'

'Exactly — I thought about them last night. This young man with his ridiculous name — as if he is play-acting — how clever to be wicked with such a mild name. That's how he thinks. Dissatisfied with his lot. A tradesman's son, perhaps, without truth, industry, perseverance, or other dull workaday quality, seeks to plume his wings, casts about for some mode of distinguishing himself. The stage? No — there has always been a conspiracy against his kind. Brilliant, of course, but born an outsider. Same with authorship — which he would be a genius at were it not for the conspiracy of those like me who've had it easy. Crime, then. Easy to gain profits, and what power he has over his opium addicts. Even that's not enough — he must exercise power over those who think themselves better than he — a policeman, a wealthy businessman, a rich man's housekeeper — see how they cower before him — how pleasurable is it to have them at his mercy.'

'And her?'

'The same, I should think — her ambitions for the stage thwarted. She'd had a taste of the high life with her viscount, she thought she'd gained stardom, then it all fizzled out. But what a drama is this life of crime — dressed up to the nines and money falls into your lap, and power, too.'

Jones frowned. 'What you said about authorship and her being an actress — you couldn't know them, could you?'

'I'd remember his eyes — they know me, though.'

'They asked Dag about the toff before they murdered him. Perhaps she thought then that she knew you. Kitty Lovell — the theatre — that might be the connection.'

'I suppose it could be. I meet a lot of theatrical folk.'

'And they saw you with the police — they may think you've something to do with Mornay. Then you are in danger, if your theory about them is true — they'd think that they could get away with murdering you.'

'I daresay they would — a chilling thought, Superintendent.' Dickens attempted a grin.

'You need a new office doorman.'

'That's not a question, I take it.'

'No, Stemp — minus his earrings and cutlass and with a clean face — will be ensconced in your lobby. No one will get in without your say-so. Mr Wills will know the regular callers and Stemp will have their description. He'll be your shadow should you wish to go anywhere without me.'

'I could give my office boy a week off.'

'Scrap, you're thinking?'

'He'd like to be useful.'

'Doing what?'

'Keeping his eye on me — taking the post, errands — keeping his eyes open.'

'I don't know, Charles — they might have seen your office boy and note the change.'

'Scrap could wear Tom's suit and cap — they're about the same size. It could be handy, having Scrap about the streets nearby.'

'All right — you go back to Wellington Street and let your boy off and tell Mr Wills about Stemp, and I'll go and get Scrap. I'll need to talk to him — I don't want him doing anything but watching.'

Harry Wills had looked pained when Dickens told him about the office boy and Stemp, and the arrival of Superintendent Jones and the boy, Scrap, did nothing to quieten his mind. He remembered all too vividly a terrible night when Dickens had received an anonymous letter and had gone haring off to St. Bartholomew's Church to rescue Scrap. He remembered the Superintendent's face when Wills had told him that Dickens had gone and not come back, and the long wait through the night — and a man had been shot. Now, there was danger again. Still, he looked at Constable Stemp and felt a bit better.

No one would get past him, he thought, and he would make sure that no one went up those stairs to Dickens's rooms without Harry Wills scrutinising the visitor first — and a constable was to keep watch at night, too.

'It'll be all right, Harry. Don't look so worried.'

'But last time —'

'See, Mr Wills, you ain't ter be worried. Me and Mr Stemp, we'll 'ave our eyes peeled. We'll know 'em — a girl an' a man with pale eyes — stand out a mile.'

Jones smiled at Stemp — suddenly the property of Scrap who was in charge of the whole matter. Stemp grinned. He didn't mind. He'd got fond of that lad. He remembered the night of the shooting, too. He'd look after the boy. Mr Jones needn't worry. And Mr Dickens? Stemp was fond of him as well.

When all was arranged to the Superintendent's satisfaction, Dickens and he had time for the incarcerated wizard.

'Of course, he remembered, but he never saw her again. His wife lived at Kingston and he had rooms in Wormwood Street — convenient for the city. He had a taste for the theatre and picked her up at The Royal Britannia Saloon —'

'Hoxton. That's a decent place. I've been a few times.'

'Maybe that's where she saw you.'

'She wasn't acting there?'

'No, behind the bar, but willing to give it up, I don't doubt. Anyhow, he installed her in his rooms and went home at weekends, leaving her to her own devices. But when he was taken up, that was it. He didn't see her again. His solicitor dealt with the rooms and the landlady. He never knew if his wife had been told about Kitty Lovell. He didn't see his wife again, either.'

'So we're to see the landlady.'

'You are — I'll be with you, of course, just across the street. No talk of murder — just find out if she knows what happened to Miss Lovell. Use your magic.'

'"As polite a gentleman as ever did walk this earth, sir. I was never more astonished, sir, as I was when I found out. Near eight thousand pounds, sir, stolen, sir, and spent on that hussy."'

'Ah, Kitty Lovell, I presume,' Jones said, listening to Dickens's rendition of Mrs Alice Taylor's account of her dealings with Mr Merlin and his lady — who wasn't a lady, as it turned out — not that Mrs Taylor had ever thought she was. She had always thought Mr Merlin — as fine a gentleman as ever there was — had been trapped by the impudent piece.

'Mrs Taylor is in a state of outrage still — more, I think, about Kitty Lovell than the fraud — who, Mrs Taylor assured me, had no doubt been behind the whole business — the scheming minx — Mr Merlin paid for all them jewels — as good-natured a gentleman —'

'Yes, I get the drift — you needn't enact the whole drama, Mr Macready, the gist will do.'

'Just lending verisimilitude to the narrative, Mr Jones — however, I will be brief for your nerves — like Mrs Taylor's, are in rags, I see. Kitty Lovell was presented to Mrs Taylor as our magician's wife, but Mrs Taylor found out the truth when she saw the real Mrs Merlin in court — name of Guinevere, no doubt —' Dickens, interrupted by Jones's striding off towards somewhere away from Wormwood Street, it seemed, hurried after him and took up his tale as they walked along Broad Street. 'And while Kitty was disporting herself at some gin palace — Mrs Taylor's opinion — Mrs Taylor packed up her goods and put them on the doorstep — in two hempen homespun sacks which had once held coal —'

Jones did laugh out loud now. 'You made that up.'

'No, I swear, coal sacks, and Mr Merlin's solicitor, name of Morgan — not Le Fay — to whom Mrs Taylor had, in a passion of moral indignation, revealed the sordid truth, came immediately to take back the jewels and valuables which he deemed were the property of the forsaken Guinevere.'

'And when Miss Puss returned?'

'Mrs Taylor refused to open the door and threatened to get a policeman, at which Miss Puss departed with diverse threats and imprecations — such language as was not fit for a Christian lady to 'ear nor to repeat — the which I did not ask her to, knowing that you might very well guess at such.'

'She doesn't know where Miss Puss went, I take it.'

'Alas, no — and good riddance.'

'So, an entertaining tale, but of no earthly use, but then I keep you for your entertainment value.'

'Ah, Sammy, be not ye bitter as wormwood —'

'Very funny.'

'For I knowest that thou keepest thy friend also for his bright eyes and sharp ears.'

Jones stopped in mid-stride and looked at Dickens narrowly. 'And the rest?'

'A pair of chops and a glass of ale might loosen my wounded tongue.'

'Oh, all right — where?'

'The George and Vulture's not a league away, and since you appear to be wearing your seven league —'

But Sammy was gone again, striding towards Cornhill.

The chops and the ale ordered, Jones repeated his question. 'And?'

'Well, two things, neither what you might call of direct assistance. The first is that Mrs Taylor had a son who was somewhat in thrall to Miss Puss's black eyes, despite being pledged to a very nice damsel, and after the combat of the coal sacks, he vanished, and neither Mrs Taylor nor the very nice damsel — in distress — has seen him since.'

'Ran away with Kitty Lovell?'

'That is what Mrs Taylor thought, but if he did, he's not Millikin, that's certain, for she told me what a tall, handsome, dark-haired young man he was. But I can imagine Kitty Lovell inveigling him away for revenge on Mrs Taylor.'

The chops and a good deal of gravy arrived, and Jones thought while he ate, and having thought, asked, 'Finished him off with opium?'

'Do you know, Sam, I wouldn't be surprised. Ruined him at the very least.'

'Revenge, though — cold-blooded business.'

'A dish best served cold — not so this gravy, alas. She's a nasty piece of work. "Impudent bitch", my actor friend called her.'

'You said there was a second thing.'

'There was an Irish man who came in and went upstairs — the new occupant of Merlin's cave. Mrs Taylor extolled his virtues — of aristocratic lineage, she is certain — as noble a gentleman as —' Dickens noted that Jones was toying with his knife and ended lamely — 'etcetera.'

Jones grinned and put down his knife. 'Irish — go on.'

'Montclair Frankland is an Irish peer — so is Sir Marmion—'

'Grex. Paul Grex.'

'Montclair Frankland served in the Light Dragoons — I read

it in those newspapers. I didn't think of it then — too bedazzled by Miss Puss.'

'Paul Grex's regiment. I'll drink to that.' Jones swallowed a gulp of beer. 'Grex might know Kitty Lovell.'

'Shall we ask him?'

Jones drank up. 'Not yet. I'd like to know more about Mr Grex, and who better to ask than Mr Jonathan Mornay?'

'We can't go to Pole Court. Grex might very well be there.'

'True — that is why you must write to Jonathan Mornay asking him to meet you in Rochester tomorrow at the Bull Inn. You have some business in the town and wish to see him — to enquire after his and his sister's welfare. The details of the narrative I leave to you. And you can ask about that will.'

'Ever thought of writing fiction? And you will be…?'

'Invisible, but not far away, contemplating the ghosts of Mr Pickwick and Mr Jingle. I don't want young Mornay to see me. Find out what you can about Grex and his friends, his financial affairs.'

'Anything else while I'm at it — boot size? Collar size?'

'Why not? You've a nose for that sort of thing. A nose formed to ferret.'

Dickens put his finger to his nose. 'Roman, I've always thought — but wait a moment, Mr O'Jones, yer honour, surr —' Jones was already getting into his coat — 'I've thought of another ingredient for our Irish stew.'

Jones stood still, one arm half in his sleeve. 'What?'

'The Viscountess Montclair Frankland — according to those newspapers, she sued for legal separation, and at the time of the trial she lived in Grosvenor Square. I wonder if she knows Grex.'

'Pity you don't know her.'

'But I do know a Miss Mary Boyle and her brother,

Cavendish — army man — and relations of the Earl of Cork. They're bound to know of the Franklands — and if Mary knows her, I can get an introduction. I'll send a note to Captain Boyle — see if I can go tomorrow evening after we've seen Jonathan Mornay.'

'By the way,' Jones said as they walked away from Cowper's Court, 'Mrs Merlin's name was Enid.'

'Not entirely wrong, then,' Dickens said, his eyes glinting with mischief.

'You never are — entirely.'

33: MR CHEESE RISES TO THE OCCASION

On the train back to London after Dickens had met Mr Jonathan Mornay, he had much to tell about Paul Grex.

'Am I to be brief, or would you like more than a paragraph?'

'Pages, Mr Dickens, whole chapters if you like. You have all of this journey to tell it.'

'Good. Mr Jonathan Mornay, who, by the way, is an artless sort of fellow, was most gratified by my concern, and, rather adroitly, I say with a modest blush, I asked after his sister and Mr Grex — who is not there at the moment, but in town — and hoped that they were both well enough.'

'Miss Mornay, seriously though, she is well enough?'

'I think so, though the matter of the delayed funeral is distressing, but I assured Jonathan Mornay that until you find the murderer, there can be no advertisement of their father's death.'

'It will come out if it turns out Grex is involved.'

'I'll tell you what I found out. Mornay does not know him very well — after all, he went off to Antwerp and before that he was in London. Not much at home and not much interested in his sister, except to wonder what attracted her to Grex. She had been interested in good works, visiting the poor, close friends with the curate's sister —'

'Curate?'

'Quick off the mark, ain't ye? Yes, a young man — limited means, but a thoroughly good sort. He — Mr Jonathan, not the curate — thought that the reverend gentleman was keen on Miss Fanny and she on him. Rather thought they'd make a pair. Then Grex comes galloping in.'

'Literally?'

'Quite so — good horseman, good family. Next thing, Mornay hears that sister Fanny is engaged to Grex. Surprised, but doesn't think much about it except to rather regret the curate, whom he thought —'

'A good sort.'

'So he did. However, Mr Mornay senior seemed very satisfied. The title in exchange for the money.'

'Which Grex still gets — as you said, twenty-five thousand is not to be sneezed at — and more if that will wasn't signed. What did Jonathan Mornay say about that?'

'Mr Goodbody, the solicitor, went down to Pole Court to tell him. They went through all Cornelius Mornay's papers, but there was no sign of any second will.'

'Grex was always at Pole Court. I suppose he could have found out.'

'I'll bet he could — he had the run of the place. Easy enough to snoop about — maybe he wanted to know how much Fanny Mornay was getting once Mornay was dead — the man was obviously unwell. And he found less than he was bargaining for in the shape of a second will — not yet signed.'

'What about Grex's friends?'

'Jonathan Mornay was invited to a club or two with the Grex faction, as we might call them — young men about town, fellow officers, scions of titled families, cards, champagne, toasting the ladies — that sort of thing — off to the music hall — the minor theatres —'

'Interesting. Any particular ones?'

'In the East End, you mean? I asked, but Mornay didn't know details. He wasn't keen on all that. He is a good fellow, I think, Sam, not experienced in the ways of the world, and like his pa, inclined to think Grex and his set a cut above.'

'Money?'

'Enough to suggest that Grex didn't need money immediately, which rather contradicts the idea of his being so poor that he needed to find out how much Miss Fanny might get. Always flush, Grex — quite the spender, so no apparent anxieties there.'

'But your friend, Lord Lytton, spoke of Sir Marmion's financial difficulties.'

'I know — maybe Grex had something from a maiden aunt, mother, uncle, fairy godmother.'

'And was prepared to spend it, knowing he had Fanny Mornay's money coming. It's not much to go on, is it? I mean, he had no immediate financial worries. Suppose he just wants to settle down with Miss Mornay and lead the life of a country squire, do up his castle — or whatever it is — in Ireland, breed horses —'

'Get an heir. I wish we knew more about Miss Mornay and her feelings for him, or his for her. Jonathan Mornay wasn't much help.'

'You could still find out whether there is a connection between Grex and Frankland — that would be worth knowing, even if only to eliminate the idea of Grex knowing Kitty Lovell.'

'I'll go to Captain Boyle's house this evening — by cab.'

'Stemp will take you to the cab stand.'

'In handcuffs?'

When Jones returned to Bow Street, Constable John Gaunt was waiting to tell him about a man they'd picked up who was selling opium at The Shakespeare's Head. Bold had him at the police station. The man claimed that he had bought his supply from a man who worked at the docks — he didn't know the name, of course. Didn't know what the man did at the docks — hadn't asked. Bold had tried him with the name Millikin and Milk, but the opium man had said he didn't know. Did Superintendent Jones want to come down? Bold thought that a Superintendent from Bow Street might loosen the opium seller's tongue.

'Inspector Bold didn't want to tell him too much. He knows it's all hush hush about Mr Mornay, and if our opium man hasn't anything to do with Milk or murder then he can't talk. Someone will have seen him with us in that pub — you can bet on that. Even the ale glasses have ears there.'

The opium man, a ground-down, harassed-looking individual in a worn-out shiny suit, ragged at the sleeves, with a piece of cloth tucked in his jacket to hide the fact that he hadn't a shirt, looked as if he might have been a clerk in a former life — a better life, perhaps. He looked cowed when the tall Superintendent from Bow Street came in, but he stuck to his story — a story he couldn't stop telling once he'd started, as if he'd been waiting to tell it, to unburden himself of his misery. *Poor devil*, thought Jones as he listened.

Yes, he'd bought the stuff — he knew it was probably stolen. Everything you bought round here was stolen — even the milk in your tea. He had to get opium for his wife. Couldn't do without it, see — after the baby. It died. All that pain for nothing, she'd said. Doctor had given her laudanum — now she had to have it. Not a stick in the house. She sold everything — even the shirt off his back. What was he supposed to do? He knew where you got opium cheap. At the docks, see. She had to have it and when the bloke offered him enough to sell, he'd done it — last few quid.

'You don't want to be in that game,' Bold said gruffly, 'however much you make. There's bigger fish than you in it. Dangerous fish.'

The man burst into tears. He was almost at the end of his tether, thought Jones, but he pressed on. 'Inspector Bold is right. There are those who would kill you if you tread on their toes, which is why I'm looking for this Mr Millikin, sometimes known as Milk. You must tell me if you know him.'

The man turned his ruined, blotched face to the Superintendent. He looked a hapless creature — God help him if he did know Milk and his lady love. Jones hoped he did not.

'I don't, sir, swear to God. I only did it for a few days — just in the pubs.'

'Then get out of it — take your money and move on.'

'My wife —'

'Poor devil,' said Bold after they'd let him go.

'He's lucky to be alive. Only the workhouse now, I suppose.'

'I don't believe they're still here — Milk and his girl. Not a sign of them, but that young fellow's better out of it. Shouldn't be out on his own, that one. Though what he can do, I don't know. Had a decent job at the docks — clerk or something, until his missus took to opium.'

'It's a poison in more ways than one. Though I want to find Milk, I'm glad that poor fellow didn't know him. I'd best get back to Bow Street. We've some other leads — connections of Cornelius Mornay's to follow.'

John Gaunt came in. 'Mr Cheese is here, sir, has some information —' he looked at Jones anxiously — 'you need to hear this, Superintendent Jones.'

Ajax Cheese came in, very much out of breath, still dusty, and looking very worried, too. There was blood on his shop coat. He was very glad, very glad indeed to see the Superintendent. He had come straight away as soon as he had heard.

'Heard what?' Bold was impatient.

Ajax Cheese heard the Inspector's tone and became suddenly brisk. 'A girl — from Bluegate Fields — came to the shop not half an hour ago, beaten up by her man. I don't know what the row was about, but she told me he was going up to town on a robbery — spite, I suppose, on her part. Anyway, some toff they had it in for — she said the name "Dickens" — I thought —'

'They?' asked Bold, but Jones was out of the door with Rogers at his heels.

Bold heard a name he knew. 'After 'em, Gaunt. Give 'em the names.'

34: SCHOOL FOR SCANDAL

By indirect and crooked ways, Dickens arrived at Norfolk Street to report to Jones. He had been everywhere by cab and if Miss Puss or her saucer of Milk had followed him, they must have had wings on their feet. But, by the Lord, he was weary.

The cab to which he had been followed by his shadow, Constable Stemp, had deposited Dickens in Upper Berkeley Street at the house of Captain Cavendish Boyle, who was not yet at home. His great-aunt, Lady Juliana, would, the servant said, be happy to receive him. Now this was a mixed blessing. Lady Juliana Boyle knew everybody and everybody's business, but she had a rather circuitously eccentric way of telling it so that her listener had to be very quick off the mark to put in a question.

After the usual pleasantries and the serving of tea, and as there was no sign of Captain Boyle or his wife, Dickens took the plunge and asked about Viscountess Frankland. Lady Juliana's eyes gleamed with cheerful malice. The name was enough. She didn't ask why he wanted to know. Scandal was just what she liked. She put down her china cup in order to tell him that the Viscountess — poor ill-used creature — was in Ireland with her children.

His other children? No one knew. Two different mothers. As to his scandalous conduct — well, one saw him, of course — a title tended to open doors — look at Waterford — the Marquess — two illegitimate sons with Irish seats in Parliament. Blood, of course, told much —

Lady Juliana, whose father had been an Earl of Cork, expiated on blood — one saw blood in a nose — one met it in the chin — there it was — that was blood. Cork — which one, Dickens was not sure — had said he'd rather be knocked down by a man who had blood in him rather than be picked up by a man who hadn't — clever, what? Dickens, who preferred not to be knocked down at all, merely nodded —

One could hardly not see Frankland — one of those very tall men — red hair, too, as if a fire blazed near the ceiling — oh, very tall, and a good thing in its way since one could see him and avoid him. She never liked him. No one liked him. It did not do for a respectable woman to be seen actually talking to the brute. One might well be ruined —

Dickens doubted that — Lady Juliana was well beyond ruin — unless it were debts or drink — or drugs. She was an ancient dowager of the Regency age with a high-nosed, aristocratic face, a good many diamonds, plenty of old lace, and very sharp hazel eyes —

— tainted, at least, to be sure. There were those, of course, who were prepared to countenance him — blood, of course, and Frankland was well-off, too, unlike some of the other Irish peers — Cork was all right, naturally —

In the brief pause when Lady Juliana sipped her tea, Dickens mentioned Sir Marmion Grex —

Poor Grex — dreadfully embarrassed in that draughty old castle — cold, too — blood, though. The son? Oh, well, yes, things were looking up — engaged to a fabulously wealthy young woman from China whom nobody had ever seen. Bound feet, they said. Could hardly walk at all —

Dickens was too late to leap to poor Fanny Mornay's defence. His mouth was full of tea —

Of course, Lady Juliana didn't believe it — people would say anything — but plenty of money. Money went a long way these days. Young Grex had the blood. Didn't matter what she was — the bride would be kept in Ireland, no doubt — Grex was a young man who liked his pleasures — thick with Frankland at one time. At least she wasn't an actress — did Mr Dickens remember that actress who'd stolen his jewels? Young Grex was a little too fond of actresses, she'd heard — and dancing girls —

Dickens sat back in his chair. So Grex could have known Kitty Lovell. His ears caught something else —

— and debts, of course — still, he'd have to settle down for a while — until an heir —

He managed to repeat the word "debts", and off she went again — Grex came into money some time ago — she didn't know where from — some relative, perhaps — godmother or something — useful types, godmothers — she should know, she was one — expensive business — but blood —

Captain Boyle came in with his wife and apologized for their lateness, but Dickens said he had been well entertained by Lady Juliana, who looked very gratified and was quite ready for Captain Boyle to take Dickens away to his library and leave Lady Juliana to her sherry and Mrs Caroline Boyle. Lady Sale? He heard her ask as they went out. Lady Sale's lovers were food for the gossips. Sold to the highest bidder, some wag had said.

Dickens told Captain Boyle that Lady Juliana had given him some information he needed about Paul Grex.

'Grex — what do you want to know about him for?'

'Crime — not his — I'm sure —'

'Good Lord — you do get involved in some queer things.'

'I know — it's to do with Frankland's set and that actress in the court case.'

'That was years ago.'

'Yes, but — well, I can't tell you the details.'

'Ah, your friend, the Superintendent — good man. Grex was part of that lot. Frankland's an incorrigible wretch — lives with another woman now, I'm told, but one sees him about. Blood, according to Aunt Juliana.'

'So she told me. You never knew a Mr Millikin in that set, did you?'

'Not a name I recognize. There's a barrister fellow, I know — Phineas Phelan — Irish, of course. He used to go about with Grex. A few years back. Respectable now, though. He's getting married, too. Lincoln's Inn.'

His cab trotted off to Lincoln's Inn Fields. John Forster was at home. Yes, Forster knew him. Phineas Phelan lived round the corner in Whetstone Place. If not there, then to be found at The Athenaeum. Yes, decent fellow. No, Dickens couldn't stay. He had an appointment with Superintendent Jones. Forster's bushy brows rose to reveal a frown. He did not approve of all this dashing about investigating murder, but Dickens was down the stairs and whirling away to Whetstone Place without an answer. Forster was his closest friend, apart from Sam Jones, but he could be irritating — and too loud in his opinions sometimes.

Phineas Phelan was in his shirtsleeves and had a hammer in his hand as he opened his door. There was a sound of something falling.

'Shelves,' he said. 'No matter. We'll have a drink instead.'

Dickens offered his card, which the good-humoured Mr Phelan waved away. 'Know who you are, Mr Dickens. Read your stuff, of course — we all do. Come in, come in.'

Cheerful, curly-headed, smiling Phineas Phelan was so good-humoured, it seemed, that it was open house. He didn't ask what Dickens wanted, but just opened his door wider and Dickens stepped into a jumble of packing cases, trunks, scattered papers, books, an overturned chair and the empty bookshelves which had fallen down.

'Just moved in?' Dickens asked.

'Moving out — to be married, and matrimony demands a house — a more respectable neighbourhood. Whetstone Place is not — well, I like it. Can't be helped — too late to...' His smile faded to a wry grimace. Not happy about his matrimonial prospects, perhaps.

Dickens raised an interrogative eyebrow. 'You are not making a mistake?'

'I rather think I am.' He looked about Dickens in a rather bewildered way. 'Can't be helped.' He looked at the hammer as if he didn't know what it was and put it down on a heap of papers, on which an empty glass already stood by a half-eaten sandwich.

'Can't you —'

'Mr Justice Maitland's daughter.'

Ah, the formidable Miss Abigail Maitland about whom Dickens's friend, a successful barrister called Henry Meteyard, had spoken rather entertainingly. Thirty-five if she was a day. The judge had rather approved of Henry Meteyard — not so Miss Abby. Henry's father was a butcher in Limehouse. Not the right sort of blood, clearly. Thank the Lord, Henry had said. But obviously not a joking matter for Phineas Phelan. 'How did that happen?'

'To be honest, Mr Dickens, I'm not at all sure. I was too — I am too easy going — easily led — let me get you a drink. I've some beer in the kitchen.'

Easily led — *by the nose as asses are*. Poor fellow. Had he been easily led into Frankland's set, wondered Dickens as he waited. Not that he knew how to broach the subject. What a muddle the room was. He hoped the engaging Mr Phelan was better organized in court than at home — or in his love life. He'd have to be if he went before Mr Justice Maitland — known for his excoriating summings-up, usually at the expense of some hapless young barrister.

Phelan came back with a glass and a jug of beer. 'I had a glass somewhere.'

'On those papers with your sandwich.'

'Oh, yes, couldn't face food. Thought I might drink myself to death.'

'With beer?'

Phelan laughed. 'All I had — Miss Maitland's turned temperance.'

'Oh, Lord, that is serious.'

'Deed it is, sir. Marriage, it's —'

'An affair of house and furniture, of liveries, servants, equipages — money.'

'That's about it — can't be helped. I haven't any — money, that is, so —' Phelan's face fell — 'no disparity in marriage like unsuitability of mind and purpose — that's what your David Copperfield said. Miss Maitland sniffed, as I recall.'

'The mistaken impulse of an undisciplined heart?' Dickens quoted back his own words.

'Ah, heart — no, I'm ashamed to say — and I am ashamed —' Phineas Phelan drank his beer in one long, uninterrupted swallow like one parched in a desert. Dickens drank some of his own and waited for Phelan to resume — 'Breach of promise, though. It'll be the ruin of me — Maitland's a brute. Can't be helped.' He poured more beer and offered the jug to Dickens, who declined.

'Oh, it's no use talking about it. I haven't asked you what I might do for you, Mr Dickens. Police not after you, I hope?'

'Not that I know of —' unless Jones was about Lincoln's Inn — 'it's about an acquaintance of yours — Lord Frankland.'

'Now, there is a fool. Perfectly lovely wife, title, money, children, and he sets up with a couple of painted harridans — and that actress —'

'Kitty Lovell.'

'The very one. Served him right. Not that I liked her, or any of 'em, really, but you get involved. My father's the Frankland family doctor away in Kilkenny at Castle Frankland.'

'Do you know Paul Grex?'

'I did — no money there, but he liked the high life. Don't see much of him these days. Gambler with Frankland. Liked the actresses, too.'

'Kitty Lovell?'

'Wouldn't be surprised, but that was ages ago. He's engaged now — to a Miss Mornay. Pots of money there, by the way. He has a heart — I hope.' Phelan sighed.

'Do you remember a man called Millikin — very pale, cold eyes — no colour in them, and —' Dickens remembered a red mouth pursed up, ready to spit — 'little mouth — almost feminine.'

'Don't remember that name, but I know those eyes. Name of Holy — no, that can't be right — Holly, maybe. Hanger-on, don't know how he knew Frankland. Grex, I suppose — they seemed to know each other quite well. There were always people about, especially in the clubs. The Coal Hole was one we went to — supper, dancing. You met some queer folk there — the swell mob included. A couple of cracksmen were pointed out to me once. Drinking champagne and dressed to the nines as if they hadn't a care in the world —'

'They probably hadn't. They could buy and sell you on their takings from house-breaking.'

'A man was stabbed once in a brawl — dead as a fish on a slab. That finished it for me. My father paid my debts — and he hasn't much. I thought of him in his poor old age and me dead in a rowdy brawl over a card game or some such.'

'You don't remember a connection between Kitty Lovell and the man Holly, or whoever he was?'

'I don't know, Mr Dickens. Why do you want to know?'

'It's complicated — and rather serious, but you'll have to trust me, I'm afraid, and keep our conversation quiet, if you will oblige me.'

'Oh, I will do both. I've read your books and those pieces in your magazine. Holly, or whatever his name was, a parson's son, I heard, from Kent, if that's any help.'

Kent. By the pricking of my thumbs, Dickens said inwardly as he stood up. 'I must go, Mr Phelan. Thank you for your help.'

'I'll light your way downstairs.'

At the front door of the building, Dickens shook Phelan's hand and looked into the young man's eyes, rather reddened from the beer. 'I shouldn't do it, you know. A very grave error — for you both.'

'I don't know how,' Phelan said miserably.

'Courage — do the honourable thing. Give the young lady the chance to break it off. Let her tell her friends that she found you — unsuitable. Go back to Ireland.'

'But my work —'

'The price you have to pay — cheap compared to the price of a life sentence of misery for two.'

Dickens walked away down by Lincoln's Inn Fields. It was dark. Where had the time gone? A solitary cab was waiting, a cab with no lights, looking rather too much like that funeral hearse he had seen near Sam's house. He turned in to the fields and went towards Holborn Row, where several well-dressed people were getting out of another cab. He heard cheerful voices and another voice reply, 'Thankee, sirs.'

'Norfolk Street,' he said, getting in.

35: DAY OF RECKONING

Mr Charles Matthews took his bow. The audience applauded and cheered. His leading lady, Miss Oliver, took hers and they cheered again. She deserved it. 'Charming' and 'Graceful', the papers said next day — not what they had said about Miss Lovell either at The Royal London, or in Whitechapel, where such words were not much in vogue.

The audience had enjoyed their evening at the Royal Lyceum, just opposite the office of *Household Words*. You went into your box under the six Corinthian columns of the facade on Wellington Street — the pit door was in Exeter Court. Lord Frankland, of course, had engaged a box for himself and Mrs Fenton — not quite a painted harridan. Painted, yes, and rather overdone for Lady Julia's taste, but pretty enough and new.

Lord Frankland was not interested much in the theatre. The melodramatic extravagances of Mr Planche's *The Day of Reckoning* had held no interest for him. The first piece, a comedy, *Only a Clod*, had been mildly amusing. Miss Oliver was a pretty piece. Good figure. Nevertheless, he liked to be seen — he enjoyed the gossip about him, and he hoped his wife — the miserable bitch — would hear it. And he liked to see. His opera glasses had roved over the audience, pausing here and there on a pair of white shoulders or a particularly voluptuous bosom. He had lingered a few moments on the opposite box where a young couple sat. Something about her, he thought, but only briefly for Mrs Fenton squeezed his thigh and when he looked again, they were gone. The audience was rising. There would be a crush in the street, but his carriage would be waiting on the Strand.

Carriages and cabs blocked the street as the occupants of the boxes spilled out. The offices of *Household Words* were in darkness. Only behind in the alley was there movement — stealthy and silent as if shadows walked.

Experts, of course. They had watched number sixteen Wellington Street. Dickens had seen Kitty Lovell — not that she had known. And if she had, she wouldn't have cared. Dickens had also seen a cart broken down in the street; he had seen a carter with a surly face and a threadbare man bending down to pick up his household goods, but he hadn't known that the surly man dealt in horseflesh or that the threadbare man had the peculiar ability to wriggle himself up any drainpipe or through any narrow space, or that Toby Quick knew their names.

The screeching woman had no name, but she was quite prepared to screech anywhere for a few bob. She didn't remember much about it and the few bob went on gin, and if she had remembered, she wouldn't have cared. And the child? Nobody's child. No surprise that it — girl or boy was never known — had looked with wondering eyes. It had no idea where it was or who were these people on the cart. Picked up in a street in Wapping and left howling on an abandoned cart by the door of St. Andrew's Charity School in Hatton Garden. It was doubtful whether this was any act of charity by the kidnappers, or indeed their irony — irony was probably not their forte. Nobody's child. The cart was soon stripped of its contents. No one wanted the child. The screeching woman certainly didn't. And nobody missed it in Wapping.

There was a coal chute in the yard behind the offices of *Household Words* down which a man with limbs seemingly made of wax might slide into the coal hole, through which he might crawl to a door that led into a cellar. Of course, the windows were barred, but the building had been there since the last century and the bars on one window were a bit rusty. A man with a stout rope and a piece of wood could easily bend them apart sufficiently for a broad-shouldered man to get through — loop the rope around two bars, insert the wood, and twist until the tension bent the iron. The door to the cellar would be locked. But a door plate was simple enough to unscrew. A turn of the knife and you'd be in. Quiet and easy.

Because they were experts, Horsemeat and Bendy Butler, former associates of Captain Blood whose death made no ripple on the surface of their lives. They'd work with anybody — for money. They were to take what they could — there'd be a safe, of course, but they had a peter-cutter which fastened into the keyhole of the lock; they had picklocks, chisels, knives, oil — the same kit they'd taken to a house in Wellclose Square and that would have been easy, but for Blood and his gun. They didn't use guns — too much noise. A blade was better — nice and quiet.

And the third man from a box at the Lyceum who had slipped through the crowd to come through the window on that silent night? A man with cold eyes who wanted to put the frighteners on the man who would be sleeping upstairs, a man who'd been thick with old Dag. Not that they cared about Dag. If Blood's pal wanted to do something for himself, then that was all right. As long as they got the money.

Easy, the man with cold eyes had said — you've seen for yourselves. Offices close at five — everyone goes out and the toff — name of Dickens — lives upstairs. Watch for his lights to go out. I'll find you round the back.

Scrap had turned out the gas lamps. He preferred the dark so that he could watch the street through the crack in the shutter which was not quite closed. He would watch until Mr Dickens came back in his cab. Before the theatre came out, he hoped — Mr Dickens could get lost in the crowd.

He watched the theatre crowd mill about in the street, looking for a carriage or a cab. He heard laughter and voices calling, but Mr Dickens didn't come and then the street was quiet. Occasionally a cab rolled by, but none stopped outside. He heard the nearby clock strike the hour and other clocks answering chime for chime. In the quiet that followed, he heard footsteps and squinted out to see a policeman on his beat. Good. The street was quiet again. Something moved in the opposite doorway. He froze. Then he heard raucous laughter, and a man and a woman emerged from the doorway — the woman was smoothing down her skirts.

The street was quiet now. Scrap gave up his watching — it wouldn't make Mr Dickens come any quicker, and he had a crick in his neck. He sat back in his chair. He'd hear Mr Dickens's cab and Mr Stemp would open the door. Scrap's eyes closed and he fell into an uneasy sleep until something woke him.

Constable Stemp was on duty — in his uniform. If anyone were to see him going in, the Superintendent had reasoned, they might well be put off visiting unannounced. Policemen were often called in to check on premises. He'd checked the windows and doors. He had made sure the cellar door was locked. Scrap was upstairs — he'd be watching, no doubt. Scrap would not sleep until Mr Dickens came back. He heard the noise outside. Someone banged on the door — not Mr Dickens's knock. There was laughter outside. Some drunk, he supposed. The theatre crowds were disappearing. He heard the cabs roll away and the footsteps fade.

He listened for a cab drawing up outside, but there was nothing. However, he'd wait for the sound of a double knock on the door which would signal Mr Dickens's presence outside. From his seat he could see the front door, the cellar door and up the stairs. He went to the front door again. Nothing. But then he thought he heard — a sound like the scrape of a foot on stone. He looked up the stairs, but all was quiet. He put his ear to the front door again. Then he went to the cellar door and waited.

And at that moment he heard the sound of a cab draw up. He went to the door and slid back the bolt, but he waited for the double knock. Then the cellar door flew open. He cried out and ran just as a man erupted from the cellar and struck him in the face with a chisel. It pierced his cheek and he stumbled, was pushed backwards, and hit the ground with a great thud.

'Copper!' shouted Horsemeat. 'Copper!'

Milk was suddenly beside him, knife in his hand. Stemp groaned and Milk placed his foot on Stemp's throat. Bendy appeared at the cellar door as Milk raised the knife.

36: PROVIDENCE

Jones's house in Norfolk Street was in darkness. Dickens didn't dare knock. Not fair to wake them all up, and the news about Milk would keep. They were hardly going to be able to do anything about him tonight. But a parson's son. Good Lord — or not. Back to Wellington Street, then.

His cheerful cabbie obliged. It would have been quicker to walk, as Oxford Street was thick with traffic and it was worse in Bow Street. Ah, he thought, just in time for the theatres finishing. Traffic from Covent Garden, traffic from Drury Lane, traffic coming up from the Lyceum. He was tempted to get out, but he thought of Sam Jones. No, just wait, he told himself. Stemp would be watching for him, and Scrap would be at the upstairs window. They ought not to see him walking alone down the street, and Sam would, rightly, be angry at his taking a foolish risk because he hadn't the patience to wait. 'You might be the Inimitable,' Sam had said once, 'but you're not immortal.' And Sam had enough on his plate with the Prime Minister and haughty Richard Mayne at his back. It would not help to have Charles Dickens spirited away by some criminal gang — or worse. They wouldn't be able to keep that out of the papers.

'Leave 'im,' Horsemeat warned. 'Time ter gerrout.'

Too late. The front door burst open. Jones took in the scene. Stemp on the floor, the blood, the knife glittering. 'Rattle,' he shouted, flinging himself forward. Rogers was at the door. The high-pitched roaring split the air. Horsemeat lunged at Jones, the chisel catching his cheek. Milk leapt down the cellar steps.

Rogers's rattle fetched a blow on the back of Horsemeat's head. Jones had staggered but lunged again and landed a satisfying punch on Horsemeat's nose.

'Cellar,' Jones gasped as the beat constable rushed in. Horsemeat wasn't done yet. His elbow caught Rogers in the face, and he flew at Jones again. Then something seemed to drop from the sky. There was the crack of bone as something hard hit Horsemeat on the back of the legs. He went down with a great bellow of pain and fell like a lopped tree. They heard the smack of his face on the flagged floor.

'Got 'im,' a triumphant voice yelled. Scrap with a poker in his hand. Scrap who had heard the noise, snatched the poker, seen it all from the stairs, and jumped from the banister right by Horsemeat, the back of whose knees had felt the iron blow.

'Horsemeat, I presume,' Jones said drily as he looked down at the groaning man.

'Man stabbed,' a voice cried from the cellar.

Rogers handcuffed Horsemeat — just in case. 'Watch him,' Jones said to Scrap. Scrap was delighted to do so. *'Orsemeat*, he thought — that's all 'e woz fit fer. Scrap couldn't resist standing over him and caressing his poker, which sight astonished Mr Dickens as he came rushing in, having abandoned his cab at the corner of Tavistock Street where the traffic was still busy. He had seen light coming from his front door and had heard the noise of the rattle. He heard the shouts as he dashed across the road.

'What the devil —' A groan interrupted him, and he turned to see Constable Stemp trying to sit up. There was blood on his cheek. 'Constable Stemp —'

'I'll live — Mr Jones — cellar — someone stabbed.'

'Have this.' Dickens handed him his flask and went downstairs. Scrap was obviously all right — seemed very pleased with himself.

Rogers was kneeling by a man on the floor — a man covered in coal dust — a handkerchief pressed to the man's neck. More blood, and more when he looked at Jones's cheek, but Jones only said, 'Get a doctor — Stemp all right?'

'He's conscious.'

Dickens flew upstairs and out the door to rush back to Tavistock Street and hammer on the door of Doctor Thomas Best — fortunately, Dickens knew him — who answered, having not long walked back from the theatre where he had been much entertained by *The Day of Reckoning*. At the words "stabbing" and "emergency", he went back inside for his bag and they were down in the cellar where, within minutes, Doctor Best was examining the man on the floor.

'He'll live — just a flesh wound. Always a lot of blood. I'll bandage it. What do you want to do with him?'

'Bow Street if he's fit.'

'Should be all right.'

The doctor opened his bag and went to work on the man whom Jones assumed was Bendy Butler from the description Gaunt had given him. Gaunt had speculated that where Horsemeat was going, Bendy Butler would go too. Jones knew who had stabbed him. He had known Milk as the man who had stood over Stemp with his knife. Of course, he had got away, stabbing Bendy Butler in the neck so he could get through the twisted window bars first. Jones had sent the beat constable to have a look about, but Milk would be long gone.

'My constable upstairs,' he said to the doctor.

'You, too, Superintendent, that's a nasty gash.'

Stemp was on his feet, however, but suffered the doctor to look at his wound and to apply iodine. Jones submitted, too, and the doctor went to look at Horsemeat, who still groaned, but whose eyes were shut. Jones saw, with some satisfaction, that his unlovely nose had bled profusely.

'A bucket of water,' the doctor said.

Scrap was up the stairs and back again with the water while the doctor examined the bloody nose and the back of the head. 'Be my guest,' he said, getting to his feet and stepping back. Scrap flung the water on Horsemeat's face. That woke him up.

Jones went up to Bow Street with Stemp to get a wagon and some more constables. Stemp's instructions were to go home and to get his wife to send for a doctor immediately if there were complications.

Dickens was left staring at Rogers. 'What on earth…?'

And Rogers told him, and Scrap, as chief witness to the affray — and hero — made his statement.

'Got 'im in the legs — poker, see. 'Andy thing, a poker.'

The wagon had been and gone, the prisoners taken away, Rogers and the Superintendent had departed again, Milk, no doubt, had vanished to whatever lair he called home, Constables Feak and Dacres were guarding the office of *Household Words*, and the editor and his henchman were seated by the fire upstairs.

Not being able to prise his fire iron from the hero, Dickens had to make do with the coal tongs to get a fire going. He felt cold.

'Evidence, see,' Scrap declared, hugging his weapon of choice close, 'blood on it.'

'There never is.'

'Well, I'll bet bits o' skin an' cloth from that great 'ulk's knees — that brought 'im down a peg or two.'

Scrap was in high spirits again — just what he liked, being in the thick of it. 'An', well — Mr Jones coulda —' He stopped then, suddenly realizing what it might have all meant. He saw Dickens's face. 'No, 'e wouldn't — Mr Rogers an' Mr Stemp, they woz all right — an' you came. You'd 'ave —'

'I suppose I might — I hope, but Scrap, it was dangerous, and you did bring him down, only don't say —'

'Ter Mrs Jones — yer knows I niver do, but she'll see his face.'

'Just caught during the arrest.'

'Right.' But Scrap still looked shocked.

Dickens changed the subject and they talked about the Exhibition for a while. Scrap made him laugh about the Koh-I-Noor — and the ladies in bloomers. Dickens had made hot tea and put some brandy in it. Eventually he saw that Scrap's eyes were closing. He sent him to bed in his spare room — *let him sleep on it*, he thought. Dickens was glad, for he had something he wanted to do. He wanted to consult *The Clerical Dictionary*, where he would find a clergyman whose name was Hollow, or Holly, or some such. He hoped that Phineas Phelan had it right — it could be another name altogether, and they'd be no further on. Horsemeat and Bendy Butler weren't likely to know that Milk was a parson's son.

There was a Hollow — he pictured a tall, gaunt-faced, ascetic parson — but no, alas, the Reverend Hollow was in Shropshire — no need of a man from Shropshire. Holly, he read — a prickly fellow from Essex. Canon Hollier resided in Lancaster; the one with a 'y' was attached to the cathedral in Gloucester. He looked back up the list. The Reverend Holiday was no good. Enjoying himself, Dickens hoped.

His jaw dropped. Great Heavens: St Mary's Church, Sheldwich. Near Faversham, Kent. The Reverend Ernest Holiest — Holiest. Holiest. Holiest. It could not be. It could not be. Milk could not, surely, be the son of a man whose name was Holiest who served the parish of Sheldwich — under their noses, so to speak, all the time. His name could not be Holiest — what a joke. Milk would enjoy that.

But there it was — the village in which Cornelius Mornay had lived at Pole Court, where Miss Fanny Mornay lived now, where Paul Grex visited. To where Paul Grex had galloped and displaced the poor curate. Had he galloped from the rectory at St. Mary's Church, where he was a guest of The Reverend Ernest Holiest and his son whom he had met in the dissolute company of Lord Frankland?

Perhaps Miss Mornay had met Milk — perhaps she knew him as the son of their clergyman. Perhaps he'd brought his friend to tea, a friend in need — of a wife — of a moneyed wife. And yet Grex had plenty of money. Did that come from crime? Was he in cahoots with Milk and Puss?

He thought of Grex and that short meeting they had had. Grex who had been absent for what seemed to Miss Mornay a long time. Fifteen minutes? Perhaps longer? Time enough to make contact with someone about Mornay? The connection was there. It was just that the money was a puzzle.

And Milk? A parson's son. Not a humble clerk as he had speculated. His theory in pieces. Still, there were plenty of poor parsons with sons for whom they could do nothing.

Superintendent Jones came back just as dawn was breaking. Horsemeat — in truth, Clarence Corney, but still a brute beast — and his pal, Bendy — the only name he knew — Butler, were in the cells. They would be before the magistrate in a few hours. They knew Milk only as Milk because, as Horsemeat had put it so eloquently, ''E was a bloody teetotaller.'

'Now, that does make sense. Think of Blood and all those drink-sodden folk at The Shakespeare; our Milk would never lose control — I'll bet he never took opium. And think of the sense of superiority he must have. They're all fools and knaves but him. I wonder if he drank only milk.'

'It was his idea, of course. Rich pickings, he'd told them — money, jewels, silver.'

'In the office of a magazine?'

'He knew they were fools — greedy beggars. They could take what they wanted. Milk was after the toff upstairs.'

'Thank the Lord for the traffic. My cab couldn't get down Bow Street. If I'd —' Dickens changed his mind — 'but your face, it looks painful.'

'It is. It'll heal. No use dwelling on it. Stemp's all right.'

'Made of timber, that one.'

'Scrap all right?'

'Yes, elated at first — hero of the hour and all that, but he realized afterwards what it all meant.'

'Good lesson — make him think in future — and you.' Jones was uncharacteristically sharp.

Shock, thought Dickens. He went to get some brandy. 'Here, drink this.' And then he waited. Neither Mrs Gamp nor Sam Weller was wanted here. Silence was the better wisdom sometimes, but he watched Sam looking into the flames. His face looked swollen where the chisel had cut, but elsewhere it was very pale. He looked gaunt, his shoulders hunched under the coat about which Dickens had teased him.

Then he looked up. 'Sorry, Charles, I know you kept to the rules. It was finding out that they were on their way to you — gave me a turn, I can tell you, and Rogers.'

'How did you find out?'

Jones told him about the opium man and Ajax Cheese. 'You can imagine what I felt on that train to Fenchurch Street and then a cab. John Gaunt told us about Horsemeat and Bendy —

I had a horrible feeling that Milk was behind it.'

'Providence, though, that you came just in time.'

'I hope so — we could do with something on our side. Get any sleep?'

'I've been reading this.' Dickens held out *The Clerical Dictionary*.

'Spiritual guidance — bit late for that.'

'I was looking for a reverend gentleman by the name of Holiest.'

'Now that I do not believe.'

Dickens told him what he had found out from Phineas Phelan.

'In Sheldwich?'

'Providence, eh?'

'Tomorrow after the magistrates' court.'

'Today, rather.'

37: HOLIER THAN THOU

St Mary's Church, not far from Pole Court, was a fine old building with a large handsome rectory set in well-kept gardens. Dickens thought it all looked very prosperous. A handsome living for the Reverend Mr Ernest Holiest. Perhaps he deserved it, or had another living elsewhere, or a stall at Canterbury Cathedral. Probably only the curate was poor. They often were. No wonder Cornelius Mornay had preferred Paul Grex. Maybe Milk really was a toff — not just aping his betters.

However, the Reverent Holiest did not at all look it. He looked well-fed, sleek as a cat with what looked like cream on his whiskers. He was taking a substantial tea in his garden. He did not rise, and they saw that his foot rested on a cushioned stool. The reverend dabbed at his beard with a finicky touch of lawn napkin. Dickens recognized Milk's feminine mouth, which formed into an oily smile. The eyes were pale in the fleshy face. Dickens disliked him on sight.

'Mr Charles Dickens, what a very great pleasure to meet you, though what you can want with a humble country parson I know not. And a policeman from Bow Street, dear me.'

He invited them to take tea. Both declined, Dickens because he recoiled from those fat fingers hovering over a silver pot, and Jones because he was in a hurry, but they did sit down — all the better to watch the Reverend Holiest.

'Your son, sir.'

'Son? You mistake, my dear Superintendent, I have no son. I am not married — or rather married to the Church.'

'I'm looking for a young man whose name I am led to believe is Holiest —'

Lord, Dickens thought, *I hope Phelan isn't wrong — that would be a blow, especially to Sam.*

'You must mean my nephew, sirs, Mr Walter Holiest. I am afraid I cannot help you. I have not seen him for a year or so — we are not — well, not sympathetic.'

'Do you know if he is a friend of Mr Paul Grex?'

'Why, yes — Walter brought Mr Grex here — a most successful enterprise. Mr Grex, an army man — a title to come, of course — is to marry Miss Fanny Mornay of Pole Court. You know the great house, Mr Dickens?' The policeman wouldn't — of course.

'No.'

'Pity, pity — a lovely house — it was my childhood home. My grandfather, Sir Jerome, built it. Mr Mornay is very gracious. I can walk in the grounds at any time — though, at present my foot —'

'Gout?' Dickens couldn't resist.

'A turned ankle,' Holiest said. Dickens noted a glitter of anger in those pale eyes.

'Your childhood home, sir?' Jones asked.

'Yes, my elder brother inherited the estate, though, alas he died young, and it passed out of our hands as these things do. I must perforce take in my nephew — a troublesome youth. Headstrong — but Grex, I thought most suitable as a friend. I had entertained hopes of a match between Walter and Miss Mornay — a pleasing young woman, quiet and ladylike — though trade, you know. Not beautiful, perhaps, but, as I say, very suitable. My nephew prefers London.'

'What is his occupation there?'

'Tea — you won't take some? But a moment to bring a maid.'

'You mean your nephew is in the tea trade?'

'So he tells me. Trade, alas, but he must make his living. I cannot spare anything, of course. Tch, Tch — he might have married well and lived in the dear old house. Still, I am content; I have my calling, and my simple needs are met —' Dickens looked at the table heaped with cakes and cream — '"Trust not in uncertain riches", so the Psalms tell us. What did you want Walter for, by the way?'

'Just enquiries.' Jones had prepared his tale. 'A series of robberies at bachelor rooms at the Albany where your nephew was mentioned as having resided, but he seems to have moved on. Who was his employer in the tea trade?'

'I have no idea. I doubt that he ever told me. I never know where he is, I am afraid.'

They left him to his tea. Dickens glanced back as they crossed the lawn. The Reverend Mr Holiest had forgotten them. He was tucking into a large piece of cake already.

'Humbug,' said Jones.

'Bah, too.'

'Walter Holiest looking from a distance at his ancestral home.'

'And loathing his situation — not a humble background, but one which kept him subordinate and fed his resentment, perhaps.'

'Mr Holiest, the elder, left debts, I'll bet, but his holiness there kept hold of his money — devoted to the Church, my foot — to his stomach, more like.'

'Pole Court and Miss Mornay now, I presume?' Dickens asked.

'Why didn't Milk — I cannot say Holiest — marry Miss Mornay?'

'She wouldn't have him? Cornelius wouldn't have him? Didn't like what he saw. Milk wouldn't have liked that.'

Miss Mornay seemed to have shrunk. Dwindled to a shadow in her deep mourning dress. Half drowned in black crepe. Dickens couldn't imagine her married to anyone, never mind the robust Paul Grex. They were shown into her boudoir and even in that small room, she looked more insignificant than ever, perched on her velvet sofa as if she were a nervous visitor or a governess summoned for an interview.

Jonathan Mornay came in and Jones asked to speak to him privately. Perhaps Mr Dickens could keep Miss Mornay company? Fanny Mornay looked to her brother, who told her that it was best — the Superintendent might wish to talk about... His voice trailed away miserably, and Jones took him out. Dickens had his orders.

He suggested that they might walk on the terrace, and they went out to walk as they had done on the first occasion that Dickens had visited Pole Court.

'My brother met you at Rochester,' she began.

'Yes, I had business there and thought to ask after you both.'

'You are very kind to take the time, Mr Dickens. You must be very busy.'

'Not at all. I was concerned.'

They walked on to the end and looked over at the woods, beyond which Dickens could see the church spire. 'We have just been to the rectory to speak to the Reverend Mr Holiest — about — his nephew. He is a friend of Mr Grex, I believe.'

She did not ask why they should be interested in Walter Holiest or Mr Grex, but it was not the indifference of the parson. He could tell by her stiffness and her fixed gaze at the trees that she wanted to tell him something.

'My father —' she breathed out shakily. 'I should like to walk in the woods. It will be cooler.'

She did look flushed suddenly. He hoped she wouldn't faint, so he took her arm and they walked across the lawns to the cool trees. There in the shade she seemed to breathe more easily.

'Your father?' Dickens asked gently.

She saw how he looked at her with great tenderness and sympathy. She thought she could tell him anything and he would know and understand. Mr Grex seemed to be avoiding her. Jonathan looked evasive, as if he knew more than he was telling. She'd had no one to turn to — not since Mama had died. She thought of Papa, who had always been distant. 'I couldn't tell you then — before — Mr Grex had been so good, but — there was something I ought to — that worried me —' she took a deep breath — 'Mr Grex had quarrelled with my father — before I went to his aunt's house. I heard them. When I went into the library, I knew. My father's face was very red. Mr Grex was angry, too. I think it was about money. Some time before, Mr Grex had confessed to me that he was in debt. He wanted — he asked me to approach my father — he thought my father might give me some money for myself — for my trousseau, for dresses. I couldn't lie to my father. I never asked for money. I go to London for my dresses — the account is — was — settled by my father … so I…'

'It must have been very difficult for you, torn between your father and your fiancée. Was Mr Grex angry with you?'

'Oh, no, not angry, more disappointed in me, I think. He said he hoped I could trust him — he could not bear a life without trust on both sides. I felt unworthy, and so I gave him an emerald bracelet — I never wore it. He promised that I should have it back — he only needed to raise some money to ease a temporary difficulty until he received some money from a relative who had died.'

'And did he bring it back?'

'Oh, yes. I thought all his difficulties were over, but then the quarrel with my father happened. I couldn't understand it.'

'Your father didn't tell you?'

'Oh, no, but he seemed very displeased. He told me that he would have to reconsider the matter of Mr Grex and our engagement. He seemed very distracted — and not at all well, Mr Dickens — and then he said I should go to Mr Grex's aunt's house. He had matters to look into in London, and we would still meet at the Exhibition on that first day.'

'When did this happen?'

'I went to his aunt's house on April the twenty-fifth. I didn't want to go — all those people — I feel out of place there, Mr Dickens — I'm not used to — to grand people —'

Grex's set, Dickens thought. She'd be a fish out of water. He wondered if she'd met Frankland and his cronies. The sort of people Kitty Lovell, the cobbler's daughter, felt at home with — ironically, but Kitty Lovell had all the confidence of a woman of fortune. He nodded to show he understood.

'But my father said he was busy. If I liked it there, he would make up his mind about the marriage. The quarrel was a couple of days before I went.'

'Did Mr Grex take you up to his aunt's?'

'Yes, he came back for me — he went up to see his aunt on the day of the quarrel.'

'Did Mr Grex speak of the quarrel?'

'No, but he asked me if I would be true to him — I said I would, but I was afraid that my father might — and then he was gone — and I have wondered —' She looked him in the eye for the first time. She might be timid; she might be the pawn of two powerful men, but she wasn't a fool. 'I have wondered about the quarrel; I have wondered about the visit of Superintendent Jones. I am now wondering about what he has to say to my brother. Do you — does he — think that Mr Grex — knows —'

She didn't need to finish her sentence. Dickens thought rapidly. 'I do not know, Miss Mornay. The Superintendent must explore all sorts of connections.'

'Is that why you wished to see Reverend Holiest about his nephew?'

'Yes, what can you tell me about Walter Holiest?'

'He brought Mr Grex here on several occasions, and then Mr Grex came on his own, and my father liked him so —'

'Your brother mentioned that you might have once been fond of someone else before.'

Miss Mornay blushed. 'I — oh, you mean Walter Holiest? No, no — Reverend Holiest tried — he suggested — asked if I might become fond of his nephew. I supposed he imagined that Walter would like to live in his family home again, but I could not...' She walked away from him.

Poor child — all that money and property bringing these cold-hearted young men and their grasping relatives to trade for her. He went after her.

'What was it about Walter Holiest?'

'I knew he could never care for me — there is something cold in him, I think. His eyes — he can smile, but —' *and smile and be a villain*, Dickens thought — 'it never reaches his eyes. They seem just blank sometimes. You know he doesn't mean what he is saying. It was my money, Mr Dickens. My father knew that — the house, too. I knew that — I am not — I have not anything else.' She turned away.

'And Mr Grex?'

'I liked him. He is so good-humoured, and he seemed to like me. I thought he would protect me — that he would be a kind husband — I wanted to please him. I don't know what else a wife should feel. It was only the debts that made me anxious, and then after my father disappeared, he was so kind. He did everything. I cannot believe that he had anything to do with my father's death.'

They walked back and saw Superintendent Jones and Jonathan Mornay waiting on the terrace. Before they went up to meet them, Fanny Mornay touched Dickens's arm and stopped.

'I like Mr Grex. I do believe in him, but I have thought over everything and I know that I cannot marry him. I shall release him. I do not belong in that world. And there are too many secrets.'

'One piece of advice, Miss Mornay. Talk to your brother about your father. You are right. There can be too many secrets. Start afresh and decide upon the life you want.'

On the London train, Jones began, 'I think Milk approached Cornelius Mornay in the Park — Mornay knew him as Walter Holiest. That's why he went with him.'

'And Walter Holiest was there quite legitimately with a season ticket. Piece of luck, that. Remember at first only the invited were to have attended the first day and then there was a to-do about it and all those extra tickets sold. Three pounds and he was in.'

'In cahoots with Grex, I'll bet. Grex feared that the engagement would be called off —'

'An engagement that Milk had connived at,' Dickens continued. 'Milk knew he hadn't a chance with Miss Mornay. Cornelius Mornay saw what he was after. But his friend might have a chance. Milk would expect a finder's fee, so to speak, and whatever followed in the way of perks from that marriage, especially after the death of Cornelius Mornay. Nothing to stop him moving in the best society — well, best as he saw it — Viscount Frankland's kind. Phineas Phelan said Milk was a hanger-on, so with Grex in his pocket along with plenty of cash, he'd be very well-placed. Grex finds out about the second family — is that what they quarrelled about? Grex asks Mornay for a loan — advance on the dowry, or he'll spill the beans about the bastard children.'

'Mornay calls his bluff — he doesn't care if Grex knows. Tells him about the second will and how Fanny's legacy is to be reduced — even says that Grex can give up Fanny if that's what he wants. Certainly, he, Mornay, will have to reconsider.'

'Twenty-five thousand pounds gone. But wait, there's the bracelet Miss Mornay mentioned to me — Grex gave it back — and the talk of a legacy.'

'Not enough, perhaps, to pay off all his debts — something on account, maybe, to whoever he was borrowing from.'

'So he might have faced ruin if the engagement was broken off, but if Mornay quarrelled with him, why let Miss Mornay go to Grex's aunt's house?'

Jones thought for a few moments. 'Cornelius Mornay wanted her out of the way — he had all the business of Michael Spencer and Doctor Winslow to deal with. He had to go to Fort Pitt to fetch him to take him to London. Nor could he cancel the visit to the opening — too many questions to answer — the matter of Grex could wait.'

'But let's suppose Grex couldn't — the marriage could only certainly take place if Mornay was dead. Enter a murderer, maybe.'

'Walter Holiest, for whom murder had become a habit and who also bore a grudge against Cornelius Mornay.'

'How did they manage it?'

'That business of queueing for the lemonade — Miss Mornay didn't know how long Grex had been away. If, as you say, Milk had a season ticket, he could have had his eye on them all the time. And it wouldn't matter if Mornay saw him — he had every right to be there. Grex slips out of the queue to meet him. Milk's outside the refreshment room. Milk follows Cornelius Mornay into the retirement room, back to the refreshment room and outside —'

'Grex queued twice — I remember now. Miss Mornay told me she felt better, but he did go to get her another drink.'

'Making sure that Milk had picked up his quarry.'

'Something in Mornay's lemonade? Grex had the opportunity. Something that made Mornay feel faint and head towards those trees.'

'It didn't matter where Mornay went. Milk was on hand to approach him as Walter Holiest, to offer to help, to slip him another dose.'

'Michael Spencer, Sam — we've forgotten about him. He wasn't with Doctor Winslow, so where was he while Mornay was at the Exhibition?'

'When did you say Miss Mornay went up to the aunt's house?'

'April twenty-fifth — but Grex was up in London on April twenty-fourth — at his aunt's, supposedly. He went back to Pole Court on the twenty-fifth.'

'So time to contact Milk. Grex must have known that Cornelius Mornay would be in town on April twenty-ninth — perhaps he knew that Mornay was off to Chatham on the twenty-eighth — but how?'

'Grex told him? If we're right and Grex knew about the second family, did he set Milk to follow him — find out all about it?'

'I don't think the details matter much at this point — we've a glimmer of a motive for Grex and we can connect him with Milk.'

'Did Grex know anything about Milk's other avocations as a murderer or the opium dealing?' wondered Dickens.

'Not necessarily, but he knew Milk well enough to ask him to dispatch Mornay and promise him his share. Milk had reason to loathe Mornay.'

'Hm —' Dickens looked out of the window — 'You know, Sam, there's something almost childlike in them. They can only see the immediate gain, like children who tell a wildly improbable lie to get out of trouble, but they have no imagination to compass the horror of what they plan or the consequences of the deed. Grex thinks only of his ruin by debt — he cannot imagine the rope that might be hung round his neck.'

'Milk?'

'Much worse, I think. Power, as I said before, over those who have wronged him by having what he has not, and he cannot imagine being caught — too clever. He laughs at the idea of the rope — not him, he tells himself, not him. Grex is a fool — Milk is a monster, but still a kind of child in his contemptible egotism.'

'All very well, Charles Dickens, but it doesn't bring him any nearer. Jonathan Mornay knew Milk, of course, as Walter Holiest. Unsurprisingly, he didn't like him, but he couldn't tell me anything of him except that he knew Grex.'

'Tea — Kitty Lovell told Lizzie Mitchell that her husband was in tea. Our fat friend said his nephew was in the tea trade. I wonder —'

'If Francis Hope knew him.'

'I asked about Mr Millikin — lor, Sam, he's not going to believe in a Mr Holiest.'

'He's read your books.'

38: WALTER SAID

It wasn't at all surprising that Francis Hope had met Walter Holiest who had been in the tea trade — albeit briefly. There were at least a dozen tea brokers in the Fenchurch Street and Mincing Lane area, as well as the opium brokers and all the spices from India and China. Francis Hope had been trading in tea in Fenchurch Street for nearly twenty years.

He looked weary when Charles Dickens and a Superintendent from Bow Street were announced, and Dickens felt sorry to have to disturb him again. Francis Hope told them that he had met Walter Holiest, who was employed by Edward Goad whose premises were just down in Mincing Lane.

'I met Walter Holiest just once and I have not forgotten. You have met him, Mr Dickens?'

'I have.'

'Then you will remember his eyes.'

'I do — made of ice.'

'Just so, but it is more than that. He asked me a question — he asked me where I came from — he thought I looked foreign. And he asked about my wife. Mr Goad had mentioned that my father-in-law is Mr Bathe of the London Tavern. These questions were not meant kindly. They were meant to put me in my place.'

'Mr Bathe is a gentleman,' said Dickens.

'I know that, but it suited Mr Holiest to suggest that I didn't belong and that my wife is the daughter of a common publican.'

'What did Mr Goad think?'

'I did not refer to it. Mr Goad is a good-hearted man. He was proud of his apprentice — good family; a gentleman, he had told me, uncle a parson and a grandfather who had been a country squire.'

'Did you meet Holiest again?' Jones asked.

'No, Mr Goad told me that Mr Holiest had given up tea. He was disappointed and he suspected him of theft — a silver inkwell, a gold pen and money had disappeared at the same time as Walter Holiest's departure.'

'He didn't report it?'

'He had no proof, and he couldn't be sure. I think he felt a fool.'

'When was this?'

'The end of eighteen forty-nine, a bit before Christmas. I take it, Superintendent, that all this is to do with Cornelius and Michael?'

'It may well be, Mr Hope. Walter Holiest seems to have taken to a life of crime.'

'I'm not surprised, Superintendent — he was not interested in tea, I'm certain. I had an impression that trade was beneath him, though not crime, it seems.'

'Is Mr Goad still trading?'

'He is — at thirty-five Mincing Lane.'

Only twenty minutes later, Dickens and Jones came out of Goad's premises. They didn't speak until they were inside the East India Arms. Mr Goad had confirmed Francis Hope's information and had somewhat reluctantly admitted that he suspected Walter Holiest of theft. He had not told Mr Cornelius Mornay, for he could not prove anything. Mr Goad had no idea where Mr Holiest had gone — to the devil, he hoped.

'Brandy, Samivel, what one might call a stiffener — in the circumstances.' He went off to the bar. 'Well,' he said, gulping down his drink, 'good Lord, I felt as surprised as Crusoe when he saw that footprint —'

'It's not all that surprising when you think about it. A favour to the Reverend because Mornay didn't want our Milk as a son-in-law. Writes a letter of recommendation to a tea dealer in Mincing Lane — not Hope's in Fenchurch Street, of course. Goad — respectable firm of long standing. Nothing easier.'

'Not that a favour would make any weight against Milk's grudge against Cornelius. Recommended to trade by the Pole Court usurper. Probably made it worse.'

'Now, what I'm thinking is whether Milk in his perambulations up and down Mincing Lane and Fenchurch Street ever saw Cornelius Mornay entering Francis Hope's tea shop.'

'Oh, Sammy, my lad, I've just remembered summat — Cornelius Mornay took his daughter, Jane, to Francis Hope's. Now what might that look like to a mind of Mr Milk's bent? When Jonathan Mornay saw his pa with a young woman on his arm, he thought that —'

'She was his mistress — did Grex think to try a little blackmail? Milk would have been hot to tell him.'

'The holes are aligning.'

'What?'

'Francis Hope showed me a Chinese puzzle ball — ivory balls within balls, fantastically carved. He said you have to align the holes in order to see into the mystery within — the Chinese call them the devil's work ball.'

'There's a few holes still in this case, but I see your meaning. We've some pieces to match up as yet.'

'Milk, the devil's work, indeed — what's your plan? Approach Grex?'

'I think it's time. Even if he wasn't in on the murder, he has questions to answer. And I'm going to ask some very hard ones. Jonathan Mornay told me that Grex is with his aunt in Richmond when he's on leave — which he is, apparently — family bereavement.'

'Grieving son-in-law, forsooth.'

Not so much grieving as distinctly frightened, Dickens thought, certainly pale and with a smell of whisky on his breath. Taken to drink, he wondered.

Sir Marmion Grex's sister, Mrs Monthaven, lived in a fine house, the lawns of which sloped down to the river. They found her in the garden gathering roses.

Her maid went to tell her, and she turned, lifted her hand to her eyes and came towards them. They went through the rigmarole of introductions and the expressions of pleasure and surprise that Mr Dickens should call. Like Charles the first's head, David Copperfield came in and went out, Uriah Heep made a brief appearance with Mr Micawber and Mr Murdstone. 'A sort of murderer,' she said, 'I suppose.' And red petals splashed like blood on the grass as she handed her flowers to the maid.

'You want to see Paul — have you found Mr Mornay? What a dreadful business — Paul has taken it badly. I've told him that he must get down to Pole Court and comfort that poor girl — I don't know if it will come to anything now — nice little thing, Miss Mornay. Trade, Marmion said — as if it mattered. He's as poor as an Irish cottager. Cornelius Mornay's hardly a fishmonger. My husband's a banker, too. Marmion hasn't a bean, and Paul won't have anything if he doesn't marry. I don't mean — well, I daresay you know what I don't mean, Mr Dickens. I did think he cared for her. It was Miss Mornay I wasn't sure about. She never seemed comfortable here. Still, you'll find him inside — in the library — moping.'

The maid took them into the house. She knocked on the library door and opened it at the invitation of Grex's voice. Dickens looked over her shoulder as the maid announced them and he caught, just fleetingly, the expression of terror that flashed in his face before he stood to meet them. He couldn't hide it. Guilt was written in every lineament of his drawn and ravaged face. He had had sufficient time to know what it was he had connived at. Superintendent Jones was determined to make him tell it. Dickens noted how Grex's hand trembled as he put down his glass.

Jones waited for him to ask and Grex had to, though his eyes slid to the open glass doors which led into the garden. He licked his lips. They heard the catch in his throat as he asked, 'Mr Dickens, Superintendent, you have news of Mr Mornay?'

'I do,' Jones said, his tone hard. He was ready to take a risk. 'But perhaps you know already what happened to him — you and Mr Walter Holiest.'

Paul Grex's face took on the hue of impure wax — a kind of sickly greyish white. Dickens thought he would collapse and stepped forward to say, 'You ought to sit down.' Jones saw that there was water on a silver tray beside the whisky. He gave a glass to Grex and they waited.

'You've seen him.'

'I have.' It was quite true. Superintendent Jones had seen Milk at Wellington Street. If Paul Grex thought he meant that Milk had talked, then that was his mistake. They watched the changing expressions on his face: the brief thought of bluffing it out; the glance again at the open door; the guilt; and at last the defeat which showed in the slump of his shoulders. Dickens remembered how healthy and vigorous he had looked beside Fanny Mornay. Grex had shrunk, too.

The silence became too much for him. He looked up miserably. And child that he was, he tried to get out of it. 'He was old — dying. What did it matter? A few weeks. If he hadn't rowed with me — the hypocrite. He had a mistress and yet he told me —'

'Who told you he had a mistress?'

'Walter said — Mr Holiest — he'd seen them in Mincing Lane or somewhere. Thought I ought to know. Chinese girl — some foreign whore, Walter said, and Mornay accused me of dishonesty —'

Dickens was about to ask a question, but Jones signalled: let him talk. He knew it didn't make sense — yet.

'I asked Walter what I should do — Mornay was going to call off the marriage. I'd promised I'd look after Walter. He took me to Pole Court — I sort of pushed Walter out with Fanny, but Walter was decent. He said it was all right. He knew the old man'd prefer a title. But if the marriage didn't happen, we'd both be ruined. Mornay was sick — Walter said we could hurry it up and then it would all be over.'

'Why did Mr Mornay accuse you of dishonesty?'

'I borrowed money and he found out.'

'Borrowed from whom?'

Grex put his hand in his coat pocket and handed Jones a piece of paper which had been cut from a newspaper. Dickens looked at it. He'd seen such things before.

MONEY: £40,000 ready to be immediately ADVANCED upon the personal security of noblemen, gentlemen, heirs to entailed estates, officers on full pay; also upon freehold or funded property, annuities, reversions under wills or marriage settlements. This emanates from a party of the highest respectability. Address: Mr T.W. Wilkinson, 38 Throgmorton Street, City.

'The City — Mr Mornay found out,' Dickens guessed.

'The money lender told him — seems Mr Mornay knew him in the city — the bank.'

'You borrowed forty thousand pounds on your expectations of a marriage settlement and your future wife's inheritance?' Jones asked.

'Walter said — well, it was no harm. A lot of fellows do it — in the regiment. It was going to be mine —' he saw their faces — 'mine and Fanny's. I was fond of her — she's a good sort.'

'What was the money for?'

'My debts, my father's debts — he's bankrupt. The castle's falling about his ears — we have nothing. I'd have nothing, but Mornay — he had millions. A clockmaker from Clerkenwell, my father said.'

Jones went very carefully. 'When Mr Mornay quarrelled with you, did he say anything about his will?'

'His will?'

'Yes, you said he was dying. Did Mr Mornay talk about his daughter's legacies?'

'No, I knew she was to receive fifty thousand pounds and some property.'

'And after the quarrel, you went to Mr Holiest and asked his advice. You told him that you would all be at the Exhibition?'

'Walter said I should leave it to him.'

'And what did you understand him to mean by that?'

Paul Grex's face was suffused with crimson. He hung his head.

'Mr Grex?'

'I thought —'

Jones was relentless. 'You understood. You knew.' The words dropped hard as stones on the bent head.

'If you like.'

'I do like. When you went to queue for the lemonade, you slipped out and met Walter Holiest. You had to be sure he was waiting. You knew.'

Grex looked as though he had been slapped, but he didn't deny it. He just stared at the Superintendent as if he were Nemesis. Jones turned the knife. 'And you put something in that lemonade so that Mr Mornay would feel faint and disoriented — easy then for Mr Holiest to play the good Samaritan.'

'I didn't —'

'You did, and I want you to tell me — precisely — what you thought Mr Holiest would do when he had Mr Mornay in his clutches.'

Grex licked his lips. They saw him swallow. 'Give Mr Mornay something.'

'Poison.'

'I suppose so.'

'And Mr Mornay was found poisoned by opium in the river at Wapping and you know it all.'

'He was dying already — I didn't think —'

'So it would seem. And Mr Mornay's son?'

'Jonathan — what has he to do with it? He hardly knew Walter.'

'Mr Cornelius Mornay had another son from a previous marriage. He was murdered, too, in Broadstairs. What do you know about that?'

If Dickens had felt like Robinson Crusoe seeing Friday's footprint, then Paul Grex looked as stupefied as a man who had received the sentence of death. He opened and closed his mouth, but no words came. However, he heard the ominous implication of Jones's next words.

'Where is Mr Walter Holiest now?'

39: PIGEON'S LOFT

'I need air,' Jones said. 'Let's take the steamer.'

Paul Grex had gone as meek as a lamb to the slaughter with Sergeant Rogers and Constable Feak to the waiting cab. He would be kept in a cell at Bow Street until the murderer had been found and they could listen to Milk's version of the story in which, no doubt, Paul Grex would be cast as the villain. Mrs Monthaven had simply stared.

'The young fool — to throw all his chances away.'

'You said he was a child — "Walter said, Walter said" — not an idea in his head but money. But, for all he's a child and a fool, he knew very well what Milk would do to Cornelius Mornay.'

'But it didn't mean anything to him. None of the Mornays meant anything to him — they were a means to an end. Fanny was a good sort — it was easy to be kind to her to get what he wanted. I don't suppose he would have done anything without Milk.'

'Shot himself, I wouldn't be surprised. Weak as water and as cold-blooded. Greed, Charles, and a sense of entitlement because of his name.'

'Using it to borrow on his expectations, and Mornay found out — and quite by chance.'

'And the will has no bearing on it — I wonder if it exists at all. Maybe Mornay had thought about what his lawyer said and changed his mind, or decided to make a new one altogether without bringing in Ah Say.'

'And Grex knew nothing about the three other children. He should have apologized to Cornelius, come clean about his and his father's debts, sworn his devotion to Miss Mornay and Cornelius might have let the marriage go ahead.'

'Too much hard work, all that thinking — and anyway, Walter said. I want him now.'

'I saw that empty place when Rogers and I were going about after the opium dealers.'

But the cuckoos from Mr Pigeon's nest in Church Row by the church of St Katherine Coleman had flown. The downstairs shop was empty apart from some dusty apothecary's jars on the counter, one labelled arsenic powder and with its stopper missing. There was a set of tarnished scales on the bare shelves and a grey shop coat reminiscent of that worn by Ajax Cheese which lay on a chair as if Henry Pigeon had taken it off after his day's work and gone upstairs to die. Poisoned himself with the arsenic, Dickens wondered.

They stood and listened, inhaling the dust and the faint smell of carbolic before Jones went over to open the door behind the counter. It made no noise. Beyond was another, smaller room filled with packing cases and more bottles, and through the next door they came upon the staircase, up which they tiptoed. A creaking stair might very well alert someone who might be up there.

However, the first room was empty. There were two open doors leading from it. Jones picked up a knife from the table. There was congealed butter on the blade and Dickens noticed the bread half-buttered on a plate beside a cup, which Jones touched. 'Cold,' he said and picked up a bottle of wine. There was a plate with some cheese and cold meat, and a branched candlestick with burnt-out candles and some scattered papers.

'They've gone — and in a hurry.' He indicated a turned-over wine glass and the red stain that had dripped into the rug.

'Came back from wreaking havoc at my premises and Miss Puss had a nice little supper waiting. She'd have expected him to be hungry after a spot of murder.'

'The Mannings were.'

'Sitting down to roast goose after setting about O'Connor with a ripping — sorry, Sam.'

Jones fingered his bruise. 'Chisel — sickening, ain't it?'

'And this pair just as callous.'

'Well, we're both here to tell the tale. Let's have a look through that door.'

The open door showed them a tiny windowless room, the sort a servant might sleep in. There was a little truckle bed on which a blanket was carelessly thrown over a thin mattress. And a plate with some crusts left on it. There was an upright chair and a small table on which a bowl of water stood.

'Good God, Sam —'

Jones was holding up a piece of rope that had been coiled on the chair seat. 'They kept Michael Spencer here, I'll bet. They must have done.'

'Between May the first and the fourth when they took him to Broadstairs. He was their prisoner for three days and they tied him up. Dear Lord, Sam, the cruelty of it. That poor young man.'

Jones was examining the items on the table. 'Look here —'

Dickens looked at the razor and the scummy water. 'They shaved him, tried to make him look presentable for the trip to Broadstairs.'

'Laudanum, too — to keep him quiet.'

'He wouldn't have had a clue who they were or what they wanted with him.'

'They'd have told him his father had sent them. And this —' Jones picked up a piece of cloth. It had been used as a gag.

'They're not human.'

'And he'd believe them. Perhaps he'd known restraint before. One could weep.'

'I know, but that won't help. Have a look at those papers in the other room and I'll take the next room. See if there's anything that might indicate where they've gone.'

Dickens looked at the papers — Milk's accounts were very organized. Neat columns in a neat little hand to record a neat little profit. He thought of a pair pale eyes gleaming with satisfaction and a pair of impudent black eyes laughing. Of course, there were no names or letters — no convenient letter from Paul Grex. Nothing to give a clue as to where they had gone. A pair of neat black gloves of the softest kid. Kitty's, no doubt. Expensive. Well, they would be. Underneath the gloves there was a crumpled theatre programme for the Lyceum — opposite his office.

Dear Lord, cool as you like, enjoying the comedy before the raid. The prologue to the tragedy that Milk had written, but it was, fortunately for Jones and Stemp and Scrap and for him, unfinished — as yet. There was a walking stick leaning against one of the chairs. They had left in a hurry. He picked it up — a Malacca cane with a silver top. A gentleman's accoutrement, of course. Oh, they were a pair of swells — the type Phineas Phelan had described. They'd probably taken a box at the theatre. He noticed that the silver knob was not quite true to the cane and at his touch it rattled. Ah — he unscrewed it and drew out the sword. The steel blade glittered. He ran his finger lightly along the edge. A deadly thing. Had Milk threatened poor Michael Spencer with it? Sickened, he put the blade back in its sheath.

There were more papers and cards on the mantelpiece. He went over and looked in the mirror above — an old, cracked thing, tarnished in places and greenish so that it was like looking into still water.

What secrets did it keep? The images of those who had been here before. Mr Henry Pigeon poring over his accounts? Some long dead apothecary scratching his wig over his scales, measuring out his powders, pouring his oils into deadly green vials, grinding his herbs: henbane, hemlock, belladonna, seeds of strychnine, monk's hood, Othello's mandragora, poppy seeds, opium?

A glitter in the mirror, a breath, a footfall. Dickens whipped round, taking the stick from the table and calling for Jones. Then he was at the door, at the top of the staircase. No one was running down.

'What?' Jones was with him on the landing.

'He was here. I saw a glint in the mirror, heard a breath, a footstep.'

'Rogers is outside. Stemp's across the road — Milk couldn't —' Jones went down the stairs two at a time, shouting for Rogers.

There was a door at the end of the landing, a half-sized door under a heavy beam — a door to the roof space, perhaps? These old buildings — sometimes one roof space led into another, into a quite different house. Just the sort of thing Milk would know about. Dickens pushed at the door. It was just a bare chamber, but there was enough light from the grimy skylight to see the footprints in the dust. He looked at the nearest one — the imprint of a narrow foot — small. It might have been a woman's. Had that been Kitty in the mirror?

But, no, her wide skirts would surely have disturbed the dust. He remembered Milk's little red mouth — he'd have small feet and small hands — big enough, however, to hold a knife or sword. He had been here, but when? And, if a moment ago, where had he gone? There were no doors that he could see, and the skylight was so begrimed, it surely had not been opened in a hundred years.

'Anythin?' It was the voice of Sergeant Rogers. 'Mr Jones has gone round the back and Stemp's having a look about.'

'There are footprints. He's vanished — if he was there. I don't know now. Maybe I imagined it. Oh, wait a minute, they stop by the wall — just stop.'

They looked as if a ghost had walked by and vanished through the wall. Dickens followed the trail, his feet in Milk's footsteps — an uncanny thought — and, sure enough, there was a door, flush to the wall, another ancient beam abutting it. Dickens pushed it open into a small space. You couldn't call it a room.

'Bring your lamp, Rogers, if you will.'

Rogers shone his lamp into the space, its light showing up thick cobwebs clinging to more ancient beams criss-crossing the ceiling. There was another footprint just by what looked like a trap door, which Dickens lifted to see a void below. Rogers angled the light, but it looked like just another little room.

'I'll go down and have a look. Throw the stick after me.'

Dickens sat at the edge of the trap, using his hands to lever himself up for the jump. It wasn't a big drop.

Well, it was. There was a great fountain of dust and the sound of the rending of plaster and lath. Rogers looked down in astonishment and horror. Mr Dickens had vanished. There was a hole. And darkness beyond.

40: TRAITOR'S GATE

Dickens was in a bed — what had been a four poster, though, luckily, the canopy had gone. Its hangings were strips of moth-eaten brocade and he was lying on a rancid-smelling straw mattress. *A palliasse*, he thought, winded. As if it mattered. The sword stick had followed him, landing handily bedside him. Rogers had dropped it.

'Mr Dickens.' He heard Rogers calling from above. 'Mr Dickens — what's happened?'

'I'm all right. Landed on a bed.'

'Thank God, sir, but be careful. I'll find Mr Jones and Stemp.'

'I'll have a look about — can you drop the lamp?'

Rogers could, having closed its shutter, and it landed harmlessly on the bed and was followed by the loose matches which bounced on the floor. Dickens scrambled for it. 'He hasn't been this way,' he shouted up. The dust was undisturbed. No one had been here since the last person had lain in that bed. Not the old apothecary. Dickens was sure he was in another house. He lit the lamp, and he opened the door which led to a staircase of a decidedly Jacobean style. The staircase turned halfway down and then he was in another room.

No door — just a jumble of brick and stone as if someone had simply sealed up this ancient part of a house and forgotten it. *Plague*, he thought. It had started in Fenchurch Street. Pepys had said so — "his good friends and neighbours in Fenchurch Street". Pepys had seen that poor Doctor Burnett's door was shut. That bed upstairs — had Pepys's friend breathed his last agonizing breath on that straw? For the first time, Dickens felt nervous. Entombed in a plague house, doomed to wander in a labyrinth of rooms in ever shrinking circles, himself dwindling to a shadow.

Fool — Rogers would come back. Jones would come and they would get him out — a rope ladder would be handy. In the meantime, it was worth having a look at what was down the passage running by the staircase. Milk had not come this way. The dust was thick on the floor — that which was not up his nose, in his eyes and down his throat. Lord — the dust of dead men — and women for that matter. He hoped the plague wasn't catching after all these centuries.

There was a door under the stairs which opened to reveal a set of stone steps. Cold air came up to meet him and he thought he heard the sound of running water — one of those underground rivers. The Langbourne — an offshoot of The Walbrook which fed into the Thames. A secret way out to a boat — to escape plague, fire, or later, the Bow Street Runners, or now, the police. But Milk hadn't been this way. The bull's eye lamp cast shadows down there. A glint of water. He didn't fancy drowning. Not a sewer, though. It smelt damp and earthy like the grave.

Hampered by the sword stick and the lamp, he thought to leave the stick behind; something fluttering about his heart warned him. He slid the sword from the stick, tied his cravat about his waist and fashioned a knot through which he threaded the sword. Only a short flight of steps and he was in a tunnel with a trickle of water beneath his feet. The walls dripped and the smell of the grave caught in his throat. The water was deeper and the wind blowing colder. Somewhere, there was an opening.

At first the roof was high enough for a man to walk upright, but gradually it was lower and Dickens had to bend his head. The water splashed as he put down his feet. Then it was drier, and he felt the stone and the roof was lower still. He hunched his shoulders and went on, shining his light ahead. He almost tripped over something. Lowering the lamp, he saw what looked like human bones. Dear Lord, it was a grave. And then, leering at him was a skull — the eye sockets black holes flickering in the lamplight and the mouth seeming to grin. "Doctor Burnett, obliged, sir" — not that he felt like laughing. He stopped and listened, holding his breath, but there was no sound except for the occasional splash where the water dripped somewhere into a puddle. He felt the wind again. There must be a way out.

Just an iron grille — like a small version of Traitor's Gate but shut fast. He peered out into more darkness. He lifted the lamp and saw the impress of fingers in the rust and broken stems of ivy. Someone had tried to get out. Had Milk come this way?

Cursing himself for a fool, he untangled the sword — as a young man he had taken lessons in fencing. A head full of duels, drawling aristocrats and lovely ladies stooping to conquer. Not that he fancied tackling Milk, but it might scare him off if he were anywhere about. He walked back along the tunnel and eventually he could stand upright where the roof was higher. He breathed out. He'd be glad to be out of it.

Upstairs, Sam Jones was staring into the hole through which Dickens had vanished, Constable Feak beside him with his lamp. Rogers was with Stemp, still searching for another way in.

'I'll go down,' Feak offered. Jones saw him land safely on the bed.

A few minutes later, he returned and shouted up, 'Place is all blocked up. No way out but steps down to a cellar, I think. Mr Dickens musta gone that way.'

Cursing Dickens for a fool and himself for a bigger one — too big for what he was about to do — Jones launched himself down to the bed. It didn't collapse as he had feared, but it groaned and shuddered. Jones was off it in a trice with Feak's helping hand. Relief — only one set of footprints.

Silence in the tunnel. But there was no other way Dickens could have gone. Feak disappeared into darkness as if swallowed into his grave. Then Jones saw the flickering of the light and caught up with him and they groped their way along. Something shifted in the darkness beyond. A shadow? No, a light. Feak placed his hand over the glass of his lamp and eased the shutter closed. They stood, not daring to move, hardly daring to breathe. Feeling the wind and hearing the drip of water. And then they heard something else.

And so to bed, Dickens thought, groping his way along, upright at least, though somewhat clumsily with the drawn sword in his right hand and the lamp in his left. Hadn't Pepys said that all the time? He'd wait. Rogers would be back by now, so even if Milk… His hand came to the edge of a wall. Another tunnel. He hadn't seen that as he had passed. Too late. Something reared out — a shadow filling the air around him. Something monstrous and dripping. A terrible white face, two glittering eyes. A white hand. And a blade, its edge like ice in the lamplight.

Dickens recoiled instinctively, felt something move under his foot, felt himself sliding, reached out to save himself, dropped his lamp, felt the touch of stone under his hand and retreated. But there was nowhere to go. The thing didn't move. He heard breathing in the dark, as if some creature was preparing to attack. It had to be Milk — those eyes. He waited, listening to the quick breathing and hearing the water drip, but the shadow remained motionless. He chanced another tentative step back to give himself room. Something else moved under his foot — old bones, he thought. The noise sounded loud in the dark. He raised the sword.

The shape leapt towards him and snatched up the lamp. The light flickered. 'Ah, Mr Charles Dickens.' The lamp went out, but not before he saw the devil's face. The devil's work.

Dickens stepped back again. 'Ah, Mr Walter Holiest. I wondered where you'd gone.'

'There are ways.'

'But not out, even for you.'

There was silence after Dickens's voice. The question was: when to act? Milk would have a knife, Jones was sure. And Dickens defenceless in the dark before a ruthless killer. But they shouldn't show a light. Feak inched forward, his hand on the wall. They waited again. Absolutely still and barely breathing. Jones felt his heart beating — a clock ticking away the seconds which felt like hours. He fingered his truncheon. Nothing moved. The silence pressed in on them.

'The grave's a fine and private place.' Milk's voice. Mocking.

'And none I think do there embrace.' Dickens sounding eerily calm.

'The question is: which of us is destined to arrive first?'

'After you.'

Milk laughed. He didn't seem to be able to stop, and the sound echoed about the tunnel, bouncing back, and shadows leapt as though a legion of devils danced. Madman. Jones caught him on the back of his head with the truncheon, and down he went into what was left of the old River Langbourne.

Feak turned him over so that his mouth wasn't in the water. Jones wanted him alive. He fetched the lamp and they looked down at the white face. He was breathing, but his eyes were closed. He looked nothing, Dickens thought, just a young man asleep with his mouth partly open. Just a mouth. What would he see when he opened those eyes again? When he opened them in a prison cell?

Jones saw the sword in Dickens's hand. 'D'Artagnan, eh?'

'Monsieur Treville.'

They went up to find Rogers and Stemp waiting — with a rope ladder.

'Let him sweat,' Jones said when they were seated in the East India Arms. 'I'm in no hurry. I might club him with my truncheon if I see him any sooner.'

'Where did he spring from? That gave me a fright, I can tell you. There were no footprints where I went down.'

'I've asked Feak to have a look in that other tunnel while Rogers goes for the police van. Stemp's in charge of the prisoner. He's going nowhere — well, to Newgate, I hope.'

'He'd been in my tunnel — he'd tried to get out but there was an iron grille.'

'He heard you and tried going back to the way he went in? Somewhere else from that roof space, perhaps? The place has more holes than a Dutch cheese. Wherever he went in, he found more water than he bargained for.'

'Pity he didn't drown — poetic justice, that.'

'No, I want it all cleared up — I want him to say he did it.'

'Mayne, eh?'

'Exactly.'

'Glad it wasn't Mattinson?'

Jones breathed out a sigh of relief and took another sip of his brandy. 'I am — I didn't like the man or his money, but I certainly didn't want to tell Lord John that Mattinson was a murderer. I don't want to know what he would have done — what Mayne, Grey, the Mattinsons, Sir Francis Baring would have done.'

'No — but there'll be justice for Cornelius Mornay and poor Michael — even Dag. He didn't deserve that death.'

'That's our job. Milk's off the street and so is his opium —'

'Kitty Lovell?'

'Let's see what Milk has to say about her.'

'They'd been to the theatre before Milk came to Wellington Street. The play was *Only a Clod*.'

Jones grinned. 'What Mayne thinks about me, I daresay.'

'Well, now you mention it — there's straw on your coat. Jack Straw, eh? Come up from Kent, as thee, zir?'

41: PENNY DREADFUL

Nothing was written on that face. Nothing white and ravaged as Paul Grex's face had shown. Just something about the mouth puckered up in that insolent smile. He was the same as he had been in The Shakespeare's Head — his eyes glittering in a pale, narrow face. He might have been a handsome young man had it not been for those eyes — a handsome boy, perhaps, whose mother had indulged him.

'Well, well, the celebrated author comes from slumming it in Wapping to hear the condemned man's final words — oh, I've had my eye on you. You've a taste for Newgate, as I recall. The prisoner realizing that in two hours he will be dead — oh, the horror! Not me, Mr Dickens, not me. And the Superintendent, too, the chief of men. How is your face, sir? Mr Horsemeat is a clumsy fellow. Now, what might I do for you both?'

'Cornelius Mornay, Michael Spencer, and a man known as Uncle Dag — you are responsible for their deaths.'

'Come, come, Mr Jones, don't be squeamish. I murdered them. That old man was dying anyway — I merely hastened the inevitable. All that money — he had my house, why should I not have some of his fortune? There, I have confessed it all. No more to be said. I'll bid you both farewell.'

'I need more than that.'

'No doubt you do, but I am not obliged to tell you — either of you.'

'No, indeed, Mr Holiest, but I should like to know more,' Dickens said.

'You want to know it all, Mr Dickens, so you do. It's quite a three-volume affair. I'd thought of writing it down for you to serialise in your magazine. You might bridle at that, Mr Dickens, I daresay. You prefer to print only your own best-sellers, but you're not the star of my story — regrettably only a minor role for you. Mr Reynolds will take it, I'm sure. More than equal to his *Mysteries of London.*'

'A Penny Dreadful, then?' Dickens tempted him. Milk would believe his tale to be more than a mere blood-soaked melodrama. And it was. It was worse. Because it was real and his victims, dead and alive, had suffered and would continue to suffer, but the story had no redeeming features. It taught nothing. It was a sordid tale of greed, envy, resentment, and ice-cold cruelty, told by a man of monstrous vanity. That rogue George Reynolds would like it, no doubt. Probably print it.

Milk ignored the barb. *'The Mystery of Pole Court* — a fortune at stake, murder, madness, opium, Chinese ritual, bastard children born in the mystic East —'

'You knew about Mr Mornay's second family?' Jones couldn't be bothered with all this fencing with words.

'First family, I believe, Superintendent. Of course I knew. I made it my business to know about Mornay. He put me in Mincing Lane — and I was to be grateful, no doubt. Tea, forsooth — in trade. Not good enough for that whey-faced girl, of course. That house is mine, by rights, by birth. Oh, no, but the future Lord Grex, though — an Irish bumpkin without a brain in his potato head —'

'Mr Grex has proved most eloquent.'

Milk's eyes glittered. 'First time, then. However, there old Mornay was one day. I saw him going into Hope's tea business in Fenchurch Street with a young woman. Mistress, I thought, the sly dog — Chinese girl — and I, not good enough for his daughter, tasteless as a dish of curds. I dogged him like his murderer, as the poet has it — well, as his murderer, and there he was in Wapping visiting Old Cheng. Opium, too, I thought, but no, it seems that the old miser was paying them a stipend. Likes his money, does old Cheng — thirty pieces of silver and I had all the details about the little family in Princes Square.'

'Ah, Princes Square,' Jones said. 'A robbery took place there. An old woman died — of fright.'

'Things that go bump in the night, eh?'

No point in pursuing that now, Jones thought. Milk had no conscience about an old woman. 'You told Mr Grex that Mr Mornay had a Chinese mistress.'

'He could have that titbit — the other stuff was mine to know.'

'A little bit of blackmail on your own account,' Dickens said.

'So virtuous, Mr Dickens, so high-minded — I daresay you've secrets you wouldn't want known. Wish I'd thought of that. It was a great pity that Mornay found out about Grex's scheme for enriching himself before the event, as it were. I should have had a clear run at Mornay myself — no need for murder if he'd paid up. Still, necessity had to be the mother of invention. The marriage was in jeopardy — Grex challenged Mornay about the mistress. Mornay told him to go hang — if you'll pardon the expression — and I had a feeling that my attempt at blackmail over the bastards wouldn't work. So, nothing for it — the old miser had to disappear —' he snapped his fingers — 'Still listening, Mr Dickens? I hope you are taking it all down — in shorthand.'

'And Michael Spencer?'

'Oh, the mad boy — well, he was rather in the way. Grex came bleating up to London on account of the quarrel — all in a lather about his debts, so, having nothing particular to do, I took a pleasant little railway trip to Chatham — just keeping my eye on Mornay. Mornay brought the fellow back with him and put up at a nice little inn on the Hampstead Road.'

'Where?' asked Jones.

'I don't care to tell you. Then some Chinese fellow entertains them to lunch at York Gate. Oh, the company Mornay kept, and dear Lord, the heat, you can't imagine — all that dashing about. I was quite worn out. Next day, I'm to pick up my man at the Exhibition while —' he stopped suddenly. His eyes went blank. Fanny Mornay had noticed that. Perhaps he had nearly given himself away to her — almost caught out.

'While someone else collected Michael Spencer from The Spaniards Inn, perhaps?' Dickens made a guess. The Spaniards, on the Hampstead road, was well known and always busy and far enough from town for Cornelius Mornay's discreet purposes.

'It might have been.' The insolent tone was belied by a flicker in Milk's eyes. Even he couldn't hide everything. Dickens knew he was right.

'Who?' Jones asked.

'That's for me to know and for you to investigate, Superintendent. Perhaps Mr Dickens's invention can supply a narrative.'

'Kitty Lovell, known as Puss, an actress — of sorts.'

'Is she, indeed? Not my type of girl at all.'

'You were seen with her at The Shakespeare's Head in Wapping. I saw her outside my office in Wellington Street. You broke in. Kitty Lovell collected Michael Spencer from The Spaniards Inn and you kept him somewhere until I found him on the beach at Broadstairs.'

Milk laughed. 'Oh, I wish I'd seen that.'

'Yes, I reported it to the coastguard, and I found this —' Dickens held out the gold finger guard — 'which I had seen on Kitty Lovell's finger in The Shakespeare's Head.'

Jones pressed on. 'We saw the doctor at the infirmary in Ramsgate. He confirmed that Michael Spencer died of an overdose of opium, as did his father. You deal in opium.'

'He was a half-wit — scarcely able to dress himself. I could hardly leave him where he was. Anyway, he wanted to go to Broadstairs to see his friend, someone called Miss Palmer — he rather went on about her, so I took him.'

'And killed him. Two murders, Mr Holiest — you'll hang for them, and for Mr Dag, whom you enlisted to get rid of Cornelius Mornay's body.'

'Perhaps I will. If so, do let me extend an invitation to both of you. I should like to think you'll be there. Walter Holiest — the crowd will like that. I shall pray, of course, express my contrition. They'll pity me and hate the man who sent me to the gallows. I shall go to my death with godly courage, however — the reputation of the Holiests intact. We fought at Agincourt when your ancestors, Mr Dickens, were no doubt grubbing in the dirt. Perhaps my noble uncle would like to officiate at the gallows.'

They left him in his cell and walked away down the cold corridor. He wouldn't break, Dickens thought. He was still on his stage. Perhaps when he heard the bell of Saint Sepulchre tolling at ten minutes to eight on the day of his hanging, heralding his appearance on that last stage of all — the gallows. For that sullen bell would toll, Dickens had no doubt of that.

'Kitty Lovell at The Spaniards Inn?' Jones interrupted his musings as they reached the great door which would let them out. 'Let's hope that's the place.'

42: ILL-OMENED EYES

'Hampstead Heath, The Spaniards,' Jones told the cab driver.

Dick Turpin, thought Dickens. The highwayman was supposed to have roistered at The Spaniards Inn and kept his eye on the passing coaches. Dick Turpin who had bowed his way to the scaffold in his new frock coat and plumed hat — and had died a hero. He thought again of the roaring rabble that would pack into the streets by Newgate. Not Milk.

'I doubt if it will help us find her, but I want to know if she was there. I want to know about Michael Spencer. At the very least I want her name blazoned in the headlines as his accessory.'

'She'll not be the heroine of this trial,' Dickens said.

'Good — if we find her, she won't hang, but she'll be inside for a very long time.'

'Where be your gibes now? Your gambols? *Hamlet*,' he said, seeing Jones's face.

'Oh, yes, by the graveside, I remember. Same for him — his swell's clothes burnt, his body in a rough deal box, scattered with quicklime. Buried under Dead Man's Walk.'

'Mourned by none — Kitty Lovell will be concentrating on her own survival.'

'And the Reverend Holiest on his cakes.'

Up the leafy lane where birds sang, and green trees overhung the path and there were flowers starring the mossy bank, Dickens and Jones walked in search of a hard-faced girl to whom murder meant a kind of twisted pleasure. The Spaniards tea garden was full of people enjoying the May sunshine. Not a highwayman in sight. Nor Mr Pickwick's adversary, Mrs Bardell who'd taken tea here before being taken to the Fleet Prison. Newgate seemed a world away, but it was from here, perhaps, that a bewildered young man had been kidnapped and taken to his death.

'How sweet the country is, to be sure,' Dickens observed in the manner of Mrs Bardell's friend.

'I doubt that Kitty Lovell noticed the landscape.'

Neither Dickens nor Jones was astonished. Crusoe's footprint was not invoked. The landlady's account of the clergyman who had brought a nurse to look after Mr Cornelius Mornay's son produced only a mild further enquiry by the Superintendent from Bow Street and his bespectacled companion. *Them detectives*, she thought, didn't wear uniforms, so they said. Looked a bit 'ot, the younger one in his long black coat. Queer thing ter wear in this weather. She wanted to ask why they wanted to know about Mr Mornay, but something about the Superintendent stopped her. Queer, though.

'Tell me all you can about them, Mrs Locke, if you will.'

The landlady remembered Mr Cornelius Mornay and his son. Mr Mornay had booked a bedroom and sitting room for three nights — she consulted her book — the twenty-ninth of April to the first of May.

It fitted. Cornelius Mornay's appointment with Doctor Winslow had been for May the second. Then he perhaps had hoped he could return his son to Fort Pitt.

'A quiet gentleman and his son,' the landlady continued, 'took meals in their sitting room, but they strolled out in the evening when the gardens was quieter. You could talk to Mrs Rose — a widow lady staying here. I saw her chatting to them one evening.'

'Did anyone come to see them?'

'No, I don't think so — only, as I says, the clergyman as came on the morning of May the first after Mr Mornay had left for town.'

'Name?' asked Jones in a further tone of mild enquiry.

'The Reverend Mr Ernest Holiest —' The Superintendent did not blink. His companion's face was a blank — 'brought the nurse for Mr Michael Mornay — the son.'

'He was ill?'

'I'm not sure, sir. Mr Holiest said they'd been sent by Mr Mornay to take care of the young man who was to see a doctor on account of his nerves and the nurse was to look after him until the Reverend should return — he had some business, he said.'

'And did he return?'

'Oh, he must have, cos when my girl went up to ask about lunch, the nurse and the young man was gone — I didn't see him, mind, but it was a busy morning in the garden — lots o' folk wantin' breakfasts and sandwiches an' such — 'tis the weather, see, an' the Exhibition o' course, but you might ask Mrs Rose — her rooms is next door to Mr Mornay's. She's in the garden — I'll take you.'

They found Mrs Rose, a kindly-faced, bright-eyed elderly lady sitting in the shade of a tree with her cup of tea and a book. The landlady explained what the visitors wanted, and they sat down at her invitation. Jones noted the title of her book. He had no desire to welcome Mr Micawber's, or Murdstone's, or anybody's head into their discussion — however tempted the author might be. He swiftly introduced himself and Constable Feak and asked about the departure of Mr Mornay's son and the nurse. Constable Feak took out a notebook.

'Yes, I saw them leave. It was about nine-thirty, I think. I stopped to say goodbye to the young man — not that he said very much, just smiled and nodded. A very retiring young man, Superintendent. His father had intimated to me that he had suffered from a nervous collapse and was to see a doctor, so I wasn't surprised to see the nurse.'

'What was your impression of her?'

'It was a brief meeting, Mr Jones. I can hardly say — she was rather abrupt, I suppose. I thought she must be rather anxious to be off. I only had time to shake the poor young man's hand.'

'How did he seem?'

'Bewildered, I think. I did feel sorry for him. He looked so lonely. I —' her blue eyes clouded — 'I had a boy, Superintendent, a lovely, fragile boy. He died — oh, years ago. I haven't forgotten. He was only thirty — consumption. I think that is why I was so struck by poor young Mr Mornay, who seemed so delicate and —'

'Yes?'

'Confused, but then, perhaps he hadn't met the nurse before. I went downstairs after them. She kept a very firm grip on his arm. He looked back — I supposed for his father. I did wonder where Mr Mornay was. I gave him an encouraging smile, but he just seemed — rather frightened, now I think of it. Oh, dear,' she faltered, 'do you want Mr Mornay for something, Superintendent?'

Mrs Rose's bright eyes looked alarmed now, and Jones thought quickly about what to tell her. He'd need her as a witness. 'I shall have to ask for your confidence, Mrs Rose, but first can you describe the nurse?'

'Conjure up her face for us, Mrs Rose — see her in your mind's eye,' Dickens said.

She closed her eyes. 'A young woman — in her twenties, I should guess, dressed in sober grey as one might expect, a black bonnet, dark hair, I think — and —' she stopped suddenly and looked at Dickens — 'Good advice, young man. I do see her, and now I think of it, an impertinent face. I said "abrupt" before, but I see her differently now — something nasty about her. It was her eyes — black and hard. A cold young woman, I should say, not what one would hope from a nurse.'

'She wasn't a nurse,' Jones said. 'I have asked for your confidence, Mrs Rose. The young woman you saw is wanted in connection with a serious criminal matter —'

'Has she done something to that poor young man?'

'I think she has. Mr Mornay's son disappeared on the day that he was taken from here, and his father, too. I cannot tell you any more just now, I'm afraid, but I may need you to be a witness should the matter come to court.'

Mrs Rose looked at the policeman's serious face and sympathetic grey eyes. She felt that she could trust him. A good man, she thought. 'I shall ask no more, Superintendent, and you may rely on me should you need me. Such wickedness. That young man was like a child, I think —' she pointed to her book — 'like poor little David Copperfield in the hands of Miss Murdstone and her villainous brother — ill-omened black eyes, both of them. I should have known.'

Jones forbore comment on her literary allusion, nor did he look at his constable, whose eyes were fixed on his notebook; he only reassured her that she could not have known anything was wrong with the nurse. He asked if Mrs Rose had seen the clergyman, but she had not, and then they departed.

'Ill-omened eyes, indeed,' Jones said as they walked down the lane, 'and where are they now, I wonder?'

'She'd have enjoyed that — masquerading as a nurse, but she couldn't disguise the truth of herself. "If thine eye be evil, thy whole body shall be full of darkness" — not a text for our false Reverend. Play-acting, the pair of them.'

'It's evidence, though, all adding up — Kitty Lovell took Michael Spencer away; the ropes and laudanum at Pigeon's premises; the evidence of Horsemeat and Bendy — her name will be in the papers. Someone will remember Kitty Lovell and Lord Frankland, and someone will know where she is.'

43: A DIVIDED DUTY

'Don't tell me,' Maggie Chester said, changing her mind after she had asked Dickens what he wanted Kitty for.

Dickens didn't blame her. He hadn't wanted to tell her. Kitty's daughter, Tilly, had let him in and asked eagerly if he had news of Auntie Kitty.

Maggie Chester continued, looking at him anxiously, 'If I don't know, I can't tell her.' She pointed upstairs to where she had sent the girl. 'And don't ask me to tell you if Kitty — Tilly's own mother — whatever Kitty's done, she's still my — don't tell me, just don't —'

Her red hand went to her mouth and he saw the tears in her eyes. A decent, hard-working, loyal woman, who'd taken in a child, had saved a child from a dreadful life with a mother who wouldn't have cared a straw, who would have thought a child an inconvenience, an obstacle to her ambitions. Kitty Lovell had abandoned them all after Mr Merlin's defalcations.

He couldn't blame Maggie Chester. Jones had warned him once about betrayal — how murder taints everyone, how the father must betray his son; the mother her child; the lover his mistress; the childhood friend his bosom companion. It might be an inadvertent betrayal, but it was betrayal, and it might lead to the gallows. Dickens had known what it was to be torn. He had been told a secret — a secret he kept — and it might have helped solve a case sooner. His duty had been to Sam Jones, but a beautiful woman had dazzled him. Her secret had not mattered in the end, but he had felt the anguish of a divided duty.

'I won't tell you and I won't come back unless you ask me.' He gave her his card and two sovereigns. 'For Tilly,' he said. She understood him and he went away.

Maggie Chester looked at the card which told her that the gentleman with the kind eyes was Charles Dickens. And when she read the phrase *Household Words*, she realized who he was. Her neighbour had given her a copy of the magazine. Not that she had time to read it — or the inclination, but she had seen that it was "conducted by Charles Dickens" and she had heard of him.

She sat down. Oh, yes, she had heard of Charles Dickens. Her father had talked of him and he had read them some parts — they came in green covers, she remembered — parts of a story about an orphan boy. Oliver Twist — the boy who had asked for more. She had been entranced, but she couldn't remember if her father had ever finished it.

She remembered the quiet Sunday afternoon in the little house — the firelight and the red glow of sunset and the frost on the window. Now she thought about it, that was the last time she had felt safe. Kitty had been bored. She'd been about ten then and wanting to be off. Not even a thrashing could keep her indoors. And she had run off. She'd not come back until the next morning. And that began it, she supposed. Her father had been a strong-willed man, but Kitty had defeated him. He had not understood that beating did not cast out badness. Badness went underground. Kitty's badness was insolence, slyness, hardness — hardness that their father had never fathomed. Kitty Lovell had no conscience.

What did the police want her for? She thought about Charles Dickens's solemn face and the pity in his eyes when she had begged him not to ask. It was serious, then. She sat looking at the name on the card and thought about what she would do if

Kitty came visiting.

No use thinking. She threw it in the fire.

There was no news for Superintendent Jones at Bow Street. Inspector Bold and John Gaunt had tried all the theatres from Wapping to Greenwich. They'd questioned Cheng and his wife, but they only wanted to know what had happened to their daughter. Bold did not enlighten them. He could get nothing from them about Kitty Lovell, and as for Cornelius Mornay, they admitted that he had been brought to their shop but swore that he had been taken away alive by the man they knew as Mr Millikin and the man called Uncle Dag. Bold couldn't shift them on that. Mr Millikin had assured them that he was taking Mr Mornay to his friends in Princes Square. Whether they would be fit to appear as witnesses, he very much doubted, but that would be up to Superintendent Jones. He and Gaunt tried Sally Quick again, but she knew nothing. She was too far gone in opium to remember much now. She didn't ask about her brother. They'd tried various lodgings and brothels in Bluegate Fields, even The Shakespeare's Head. Kitty Lovell had vanished.

But her name was once again in the newspapers. Milk's trial came on. The prisoner was charged with the murders of Mr Cornelius Mornay and Mr William Dagnall — known familiarly as Uncle Dag.

The death of Michael Spencer would remain a mystery. He had been buried quietly in Ramsgate churchyard. Only Miss Anne Palmer had attended. Jonathan Mornay had agreed — by letter — with James and Jane Spencer that no purpose would be served by identifying Michael. His history, as a patient at Fort Pitt, and as the son of Cornelius Mornay by his Chinese wife, would not be told.

The Home Secretary and Mr Mayne had agreed to this subterfuge. Superintendent Jones had shown the Prime Minister the correspondence between Jonathan Mornay and Charles Dickens and between the Spencers and Jonathan Mornay. Cornelius Mornay was buried quietly, too, at Sheldwich Church. The curate officiated. He and his sister were much with Jonathan and Fanny Mornay afterwards. Mr Ernest Holiest intended to retire abroad.

As far as the accessory to the murders, Sir George Grey had looked as if he thought it better that Kitty Lovell remain unfound. Holiest was undoubtedly guilty — he'd not be allowed to speak in his own defence. Sometimes a defendant could, but the least said by that villain the better, so opined Sir George. And Grex — well, he was a fool, but was prepared to give evidence for the prosecution. He'd denied to his own solicitor that he'd had any idea of Holiest's murderous intentions —

'He admitted to me that he knew,' Superintendent Jones interrupted. He did not mention Dickens.

'Well, he's changed his mind.' Sir George Grey wanted the matter done with as speedily as possible. 'A weak young man, I grant you, but Holiest — damned silly name — is the murderer here.'

Jones wondered what convolution of argument would be presented by Grex's barrister to persuade the jury. He couldn't think of anything. The prosecution, in the form of Henry Meteyard, would tear him to pieces. He was on remand at any rate — plenty of comforts, however, for him. Sir Marmion Grex and Mrs Monthaven believed in him. No one had visited Milk to bring any comforts. The Reverend Ernest Holiest's Christian charity did not extend to his disgraced nephew.

But all that was by the way. There was no doubt that Milk would be found guilty. But Kitty Lovell. He looked Sir George in the eye, Sir George who was repeating his idea that the sooner the matter was dealt with the better. It was enough that the murderer of Cornelius Mornay had been found without any inconvenient discussion of the opium trade or security at the Great Exhibition.

'A family matter, Superintendent — the accused bore a grudge against his victim and inveigled the daughter's fiancé into a money-making scheme. Nothing to do with China or the Exhibition. The accused had a season ticket. The police could hardly be expected to make enquiries into the private circumstances of every ticket holder.'

'Opium?'

'Mr Mornay was a retired banker — his Chinese connections are not relevant. He was in China over twenty years ago. It is only to be expected that the accused visited these unsavoury places — no doubt he took his victim there and paid the creature Dag to help him dispose of the body, but whether it was an opium den or a brothel is not pertinent.'

'Holiest dealt in opium.' Jones was determined to have his say.

'No doubt,' Richard Mayne intervened, 'but it is not illegal. He is charged with murder and he will hang as he deserves to. That is the outcome we all want. And as for the girl — before you raise the matter again — if she turns up, action will be taken, of course, but I cannot sanction the time and resources, and I do not want you to encourage —'

Sir George gave Mayne a warning glance. Jones wondered if Mayne were about to mention Dickens. Sir George filled the gap. 'If she has taken refuge in the East End, then Inspector Bold can deal with the matter.'

And that was it. Dismissed. The Home Secretary had the courtesy to thank him for a successful investigation. Richard Mayne had merely nodded. Superintendent Jones knew what his duty was to his masters, but there was duty to justice, too. He was determined to try to find her.

44: SENTENCE OF DEATH

From *The Morning Post*

Mr Justice Crewell then put on the black cap and addressed the prisoner as follows: Walter Jerome Holiest, you have been convicted of the crime of murder. You have been found guilty upon evidence, which I will venture to say, could leave no rational doubt in the mind of any human being who heard it. A verdict of guilty is the only one which the jury could conscientiously return upon the perpetrator of the most appalling instances of human wickedness which the annals of this court could furnish.

It has been suggested that the deceased, Mr Cornelius Mornay, a respectably retired banker, led a vicious course of life and that he was a frequenter of a vile opium den, the resort of criminals. That these are lies the evidence of the witnesses has shown all too clearly. It has been averred that the victim, Mr William Dagnall, was a criminal murdered by his own associates. Again, the evidence brought to this court shows that you and your paramour and partner in these foul deeds — who has yet to be brought to justice — murdered Mr Dagnall in a most vicious and cruel manner. The court has heard of your attempt on the life of a police constable in the course of an attempted robbery at the offices of the celebrated author, Mr Charles Dickens, whose enquiries into the disappearance of the shoe-black boy brought him to your vindictive notice. Mr Dickens, well known for his philanthropy, had sponsored one of the shoe-black boys who sought the aid of the author when his fellow shoe-black vanished.

You have shown not an atom of remorse for your crimes. Therefore, I cannot hold out the slightest hope of a commutation of the sentence which I am about to pronounce, and I am bound to tell you that, as far as my judgement goes, your doom is irretrievably fixed when that sentence is passed. Having given you this warning, it remains only for me to pronounce the dread sentence of the law which is that you be taken hence to her Majesty's gaol and thence to the place of execution; and there be hanged by the neck until you be dead; and that afterwards you be buried within the precincts of the gaol, and may the Lord have mercy on your soul.

Would He? Dickens paused in his reading. He thought of Milk in his cell as they had last seen him. He couldn't imagine Milk praying for mercy, as had the Psalmist who believed that the Lord would not turn His mercy away. Without remorse, could there be mercy for such a wretch?

He read on. Let's see what the reporter had to say about the prisoner.

The prisoner listened to the learned judge's words with the same indifference he had shown all through the trial, but at the sentence of death he seemed to smile at judge and jury as if he mocked them. He bowed to the judge and showed perfect composure as he was led away...

Would that icy composure ever crack? Would that insolent smile turn to terror? Perhaps when the Reverend Ordinary began to read the words from the burial service. Perhaps when he was pinioned by the hangman. Perhaps when he was led down Dead Man's Walk, when he saw that hideous perspective of narrowing archways through which he must walk, each one closing, closing, until the last as narrow as a coffin. The dead end. Perhaps when he had that last glimpse of the sky above the netting in the space called the birdcage. Perhaps when he heard the great roar of the crowd. Not the genteel audience at the Lyceum. A horde of yelling, jeering, crazed beasts with no more pity than he'd had himself. He'd see the scaffold with its black draperies; he'd see the noose and the trap door, and he'd feel Calcraft's strong arm on his.

"And none I think do there embrace", Dickens had quoted to Milk in that tunnel. The last creature to hold him would be the hangman. The Reverend Holiest would not be there. Then Calcraft would place the hood over his head. The world blotted out. Then he'd know it was real — he'd feel the terror that the old lady had felt, the terror that Cornelius Mornay had felt, Michael Spencer had felt, and poor old Dag. He would know then that it was not the drama in which he'd starred with his leading lady.

Ah, here she was in the concluding remarks of the article:

Mr Justice Crewell adverted to the prisoner's accomplice and paramour. Our readers will no doubt remember the name of Kitty Lovell who several years ago made a sensational appearance at the Central Criminal Court, accused of theft by the noble Viscount Montclair Frankland. She was acquitted of that crime and for a short period appeared on the stage. It is to be hoped that we may see her again ere long in the court before the learned judge to answer for her crimes. The evidence against her is as compelling as that against the condemned prisoner, Mr Walter Jerome Holiest.

"Ere long" — it looked like it might be a long time. Jones had told him Sir George's instructions. They would have to rely on Inspector Bold and his men and Jones would go down to Wapping whenever he could. Dickens thought about Kitty Lovell — and he thought that she would turn up. She'd take a risk. That's what she liked. At the hanging, maybe — to see the last act. And she wouldn't feel a thing.

45: THE PLAY'S THE THING

The Chinese man had got into the Exhibition right under the noses of the police — right under the royal nose. Someone could get in here. And the Queen was coming — it couldn't happen again, surely. Entrance was by ticket only, but as Sir George had pointed out about the Exhibition, the authorities could hardly enquire into the private lives of every ticket-holder — especially the kind of people who were expected here tonight. The "haut ton", as the newspapers liked to say — a term Superintendent Jones felt ought to have gone out with the Prince Regent.

Superintendent Jones was contemplating the extensive gardens at the back of Devonshire House in Piccadilly, Berkeley Street to his right and Berkeley Square behind. At the end of the garden, he could make out Stemp stalking about some fancy kind of temple. A folly, he believed you called it. Folly, to be sure, to be here at all. He looked back at the house where servants were coming and going through several doors. At the front of the vast mansion — palace — whatever it was — were carriage houses, stables, servants' quarters, all kinds of service places. Carriages were already rolling up and Sergeant Rogers and Constable Feak were keeping an eye on those.

Superintendent Jones had never seen the woman he was watching for. 'Might be dressed as an orange seller,' Dickens had told him. Jones had asked what on earth for. 'Mad,' Dickens had said, 'mad as Bedlam.'

So he was looking out for a mad woman carrying a basket of oranges which Dickens feared might at the very worst be chucked at the Queen — at the very best at Dickens himself while he was acting his heart out on the stage at Devonshire House. Wearing a sword again, though this time for histrionic purposes. Milk's swordstick was safely in a cupboard at Bow Street. The lady in question was a lady, it seemed, Lady Rosina Bulwer-Lytton, estranged wife of the playwright, Sir Edward Bulwer-Lytton, bent on revenge for his alleged cruel treatment of her.

She had declared her disruptive intentions in a letter to the Duke of Devonshire, in which she had suggested she might sell her oranges at the gates of Devonshire House on the opening night of her husband's play. She had written to Dickens along the same lines: her husband was "Sir Liar Coward"; Dickens the "Autocrat of Blackguards"; and the Queen "Pig-headed" and worse. Even the Duke was debased by his association with the "scoundrels". She had declared her intention of attending the "Fooleries" in order to distribute her pamphlets exposing their villainy. And if that wasn't sufficient, she had published an advertisement excoriating her husband, his play, and the Guild of Literature and Art, the charitable endeavour for which the performance was to raise money.

Dickens had asked Jones if he could provide a plain clothes man or two in the hall who could divert the lady to an exit if she were, as Dickens feared, to have acquired a ticket by nefarious means. Jones, who had had quite enough of the great and the good, and even of the Queen and her potential attackers — Chinese acrobats or mad aristocrats — had agreed, only for Dickens's sake. Therefore, his own Inspector Grove would be in the reception area with Henry Wills, Dickens's sub-editor, who would recognise the lady. Rogers and Feak were outside to keep an eye on the carriages in case the lady should shout her abuse at the Duke of Wellington or the Prime Minister or hurl a rotten orange.

And Superintendent Jones? He had a ticket in his pocket. His wife had a ticket — Mrs Elizabeth Jones was to come with Mrs Dickens in her carriage. Superintendent Jones was not on duty. But they were his men, and the Queen was coming, and a Chinese man had got as close to her as an assassin. And Sir George Grey was not coming. Mr Richard Mayne was not coming. Not invited, perhaps. If there were a disturbance — if her Majesty were showered with orange peel or curses — and the Superintendent were found to have been lolling in the audience, aping his betters, without a thought for security — well, he could imagine what might be said.

He heard cheering — the Duke had arrived, probably. With his characteristic military precision. Time to go in. He gave Stemp a sign to indicate his departure and went round the front. The Duke was descending from his carriage with various other dignitaries. Jones slipped in under the portico to see Inspector Grove and Henry Wills waiting near the entrance to vet the guests. The Duke of Devonshire's footmen were examining the tickets. He took a position at the foot of the grand marble staircase with its gilded balustrade and glass handrail — the crystal staircase, they called it. *Frippery*, Jones thought, though the Duke of Devonshire had been very gracious to him. Good thing Sir George Grey had not seen that encounter. The staircase led up to a gallery fitted up as a temporary theatre from where he could hear voices and laughter. The entrance hall was filling up. The Duke and his party passed by, followed by the Prime Minister and Lady Russell. Lord John nodded slightly to him as he mounted the steps.

And then there was a parting of the crowd in the pillared entrance hall. Her Majesty, the Prince Consort, and their distinguished guests were arriving. Jones went partway up the stairs for a better vantage point. The hall was adazzle with the light from enormous crystal chandeliers with hundreds of candles reflected in gleaming silver mirrors in pierced golden frames, and scented by a blaze of flowers, fresh from Chatsworth House in Derbyshire. However, he could make out Inspector Grove and Henry Wills bowing with everyone else. The Royal Party was greeted by the Duke of Devonshire, who began to lead them towards the staircase. Jones came down quickly to stand out of sight at the side of the staircase. The Queen and her party passed up the stairs, followed by the rest of the crowd. He saw Mrs Dickens and Elizabeth, and there were a few other faces he recognized, but the impression was a blur of colour, and candlelight on diamonds and gold, broken up by the black suits of the men. A footman closed the doors.

Inspector Grove remained on duty in the hall as Henry Wills and Jones made their way up to the gallery. They slipped in at the tail-end, Henry Wills to take his seat on one of the chairs nearer the front. Jones found a place at the end of one of the benches at the back. While he waited, listening to the music, he scanned the audience. He hoped the lady had not slipped by Henry Wills and Grove, but everyone seemed good-humoured in anticipation of the comedy.

And even Superintendent Jones felt the tightness in his chest dissolve when he heard the familiar voice ask in the drawling manner of an eighteenth-century man of fashion, 'Any duels today?' He couldn't help laughing. Duels, indeed. But it seemed that Lord Wilmot, clearly the hero of the piece, had no such events in his diary, according to Smart, his valet. Mr Wilkie Collins in the part. Jones didn't know him but he — and the laughing audience — recognized the diminutive journalist, Douglas Jerrold, playing the improbably named Mr Shadowly Softly, some kind of follower of the noble Lord — aping his better, it appeared. Mr Forster played Mr Hardman, a politician — Jones recognized him by his powerful voice. Mr Mark Lemon whom Jones knew was very convincing as Sir Geoffrey Thornside — his bulky form filled out the part very well.

And it was very funny. Her Majesty was obviously enjoying it. He could see her quite clearly seated in the specially constructed royal box canopied by gold fringe and tasselled curtains and bedecked with flowers. Comfortable chairs — thrones, no doubt — a backrest to the bench would have been welcome. The Queen applauded enthusiastically, as did her party and the rest of the audience. No one seemed about to lob anything at the box or the stage. The Iron Duke looked a bit glum — comedy not in his line, perhaps.

The plot was somewhat convoluted, Jones thought — he wasn't always sure who Dickens, in his various disguises, was meant to be, but then he couldn't help keeping his eye on the audience. *The Silent Lady of Deadman's Lane* baffled him completely. Elizabeth could explain the finer points later. Now Dickens was back, this time as the fashionable young lord again — he'd been the scribbler, Curll, a moment ago. Jones watched, marvelling at that energy undimmed by the events of the last weeks. So much at ease on the stage — but he wasn't surprised at that — he made a very convincing constable sometimes, or a lawyer, or a bent old man. But the cases were never just play-acting for Dickens. Jones couldn't have stood that. Milk and his partner had been the players at murder.

He shook his head to banish the thought of Kitty Lovell. No point in dwelling on that tonight, even though it was like an itch that needed scratching.

Mrs Emmeline Compton was the leading lady in this play — and here was Dickens declaring his love for the beautiful heroine after the various disguises and stratagems. It seemed that he had loved her all along. Not so bad as he seemed. Hardman was cut out but bore it nobly. Not so bad as he seemed either, and Shadowly Softly won his fair lady, Barbara, too.

And then it was over to cheers and loud applause, and by God, it was way after midnight. Jones prepared to make a quick exit, but of course the Queen must go out first. Well, Inspector Grove was at his post, Rogers and Feak would still be outside watching the carriages and Stemp would still be in the garden.

Jones managed to make his way down the crowded stairs. At the half-way point, he saw Elizabeth going towards the front doors. Mrs Dickens would be waiting for her husband — still in the theatre, perhaps. Elizabeth would wait for him under the Portico. At last, he found her. She turned a shining face up to him. She had obviously enjoyed it as much as the Queen had. He took her arm, glad that they did not have to wait for a carriage. They would walk home. At that moment, he caught sight of Rogers struggling through the press of carriages, servants, drivers and waiting guests. He knew from the strained and anxious face that something had happened. His heart thumped. Good God, no — not her Majesty.

He murmured to Elizabeth, 'Something's up. We'll have to wait.'

Rogers gained the portico and hurried to them, red-faced and perspiring, putting his mouth to Jones's ear to whisper, 'Saw her, sir, Lovell, comin' out in the crowd.'

'Sure?'

'As I can be — all dressed up in white and jewels an' that, but I knew that face.'

'Where's she gone?'

'Didn't see.'

'On her own?'

'Think so.'

'Get Feak — go round the back for Stemp. I'll send Grove. See if you can spot her. I'll find Mr Dickens.'

Elizabeth knew by his face that something was wrong. 'What can I do?'

'Come back in and wait. I'll send if I need you.'

Elizabeth sat on a window seat, trying to look as if she were waiting for someone or a carriage. The entrance hall was still full of chattering, laughing people. Jones pushed through as politely as he could, trying to smile and look calm. The heat was stifling now, and he could feel the sweat at his neck and on his back. The damned coat felt tighter than ever. Navigating the staircase was more difficult — swimming against the tide. Some fool stopping to light a cigar. A lady blocking the way with her elaborate flounces, standing to wave to someone below. A man with a stick, tottering on the edge of a step. *Don't you fall*, Jones thought. A couple snatching an intimate moment. Some purple-gowned dowager bearing down on them. She gave him a filthy look.

But he made it to the top, steadied himself, took a breath, arranged his face into a mask of calm, and went back into the theatre where the Duke of Devonshire was still talking to people from the audience. He glimpsed Mrs Dickens talking to Henry Wills, but she didn't see him. No one noticed as he went onto the stage and through the wing to what he thought must be the green room.

He avoided John Forster — he wouldn't keep his voice down; he almost tripped over little Wilkie Collins, who was removing a boot; then he was eye to eye with Sir Geoffrey Thornside, who was taking off his coat. Mr Mark Lemon, editor of *Punch*. A sensible man.

'Looking for Charles?'

'Yes, I've something important —'

'He's gone out — a message, he said — something about Mrs Dickens — fainted, I think.' Mark Lemon saw the Superintendent's face. 'What's up?'

'When?'

'A minute or so ago.'

'Who brought the message?'

'House Steward, I recognized him — in the Duke's livery. Charles went with him — that way. There are stairs.'

'To the back of the house?'

Lemon didn't answer; he just took Jones's arm and led him away to the back staircase, down which they hurried. Now Lemon spoke. 'Something wrong about Charles?'

'Mrs Dickens is still in the theatre with the Duke. One of my men saw someone —'

'Not Lady Rosina?'

'Worse — Kitty Lovell. You know the name.'

'By God, I do. You've other men here?'

'Yes, they're searching. Charles didn't say where he was going?'

'No — I thought he looked a bit alarmed — I was going to go with him, but you know he'll never wait. Off like a shot. It reminded me of when his daughter died — a message came to the dinner. He must have thought —'

They were out into the garden. Nothing moving, but Jones saw a light in the temple he'd seen before. She? Or he? Waiting. 'Over there,' he whispered to Mark Lemon.

'I'll go — she doesn't know me. Just one of the actors — still got the wig. And if it's Charles, I can tell him about Mrs Dickens.'

'I'll come with you.' They hadn't noticed Wilkie Collins —

he was in his stockinged feet. 'We'll go for a cigar. Most natural thing in the world.'

Jones watched them go, tall Mark Lemon's hefty arm on the little man's shoulder — both staggering slightly as if they'd taken a drink or two. Most natural thing in the world. Of course, they were actors.

They went into the temple. Just then, he saw a woman in white going along the gravel walk towards the building. Kitty Lovell. Must be, though he couldn't really make her out — unless it was some other lady bent on a tryst with a gentleman. He thought of that girl with her lover on the stairs and the ill-tempered dowager. If it were not Kitty Lovell, then he was wasting time.

He heard a scream — not of fright, but of rage. He ran. Dear Lord, she looked like a harpy, her face contorted in spitting, hissing fury; all fangs and claws as burly Lemon was trying to pinion her arms behind her back. His wig was askew, and Collins was taking off his cravat — ready to tie her. His nose was bleeding. She spat at Jones as he approached. *Wildcat*, he thought. Despite the white satin and the paste jewels and the tiara, she couldn't disguise what she was. Alley cat.

He snatched the cravat from Collins and rushed to tie her arms. The release of Lemon's pressure almost loosed her. She fought like one possessed, screaming the most unutterable filth as she did. Jones grappled with her. Her dress tore and the diamonds scattered, but she wouldn't give in. Jones felt a kick on his shins and Mark Lemon grabbed her again by the waist. Collins, feeling the hurt where she'd struck him, punched her in the face. That shut her up. Lemon let go and she fell at their feet.

The Superintendent and Mr Lemon looked at him, astonished. For a little man, he could pack a punch. 'She wasn't a lady,' Collins said. 'I'd not have —'

'Egad, what's this? The epilogue?' an eighteenth-century voice drawled from the door. Only Superintendent Jones caught the tremor in it.

Dickens had to laugh. Mark Lemon, still in his wig and pantaloons with greasepaint smudged about his eyes and mouth, Wilkie with a torn shirt and a bloody handkerchief to his nose, and Sam Jones with his bruised face and cravat all awry. They looked like three actors at the end of a farce. The actress had been taken away by Inspector Grove and Constables Stemp and Feak. Rogers had come back to report that she was safely gagged and cuffed. She could scream all night if she wanted, he had said — plenty of drunks to join her at Bow Street.

'I nearly sent for a straitjacket,' Jones said.

'How's the nose, Wilkie?' asked Dickens.

'Bloody.'

'But unbowed. You finished her off.'

'Fought like a tigress,' Lemon observed, 'Wilkie, too.'

They were back in a little anteroom off the green room. Lemon had found a bottle of brandy — *steady our nerves*, he'd said.

'Now, tell the rest,' said Dickens, who had heard the account of the message and the sighting of Kitty Lovell.

Collins removed the handkerchief from his nose. 'Well, Lemon here grabbed her and I said, "What's the game?" and —' he grinned at Dickens, who'd snorted at that — 'it just came out — anyway, she stood still for a moment —'

'I think we both thought what if it were the Duchess —' Lemon added.

'Coming to look at her pelargoniums or something.' Wilkie

was enjoying himself. Brandy and shock, Jones thought, looking at his wide eyes behind the spectacles.

'But we thought she wouldn't know us dressed as we are —'

'She had seen the play, Sir Geoffrey,' Dickens interposed, laughing, too.

'True, my lord — in any case, we knew almost straightaway that it was the guttersnipe when she started screeching —'

'Bless me, such language,' Wilkie said piously.

'As was not fit for any Christian to 'ear nor repeat,' Dickens and Jones spoke together.

'We'd heard of — er — that side of her nature before,' Dickens explained. 'But do go on.'

'Fearful struggle,' Lemon said, 'a lot of spitting and kicking — hence Wilkie's nose.'

'For which I paid her handsomely.'

'She'll have a nice black eye in the morning.' Rogers, who had been listening to all this with great enjoyment, added his bit.

'Serves her right. But what we want to know is, where were you when we were exchanging fisticuffs with the harpy?'

The question sobered them when they remembered the danger that might have been for Dickens if he had arrived before them.

'The Duke's steward brought the message —'

'Who was it supposed to be from?' Jones asked.

'Mrs Cavendish Boyle.'

'The cunning devil,' Lemon said.

'So she is. I went down those back stairs — quickest way to the temple, which was all in darkness. The steward had given me a lantern, so I had a quick look.'

'Lucky you left the lamp there,' Jones said.

'I put it down without thinking. I just thought Catherine

must have been taken somewhere else, so I went back to go in under the portico — thinking to find the steward — and I saw your Elizabeth, Sam, and she told me that you'd gone up to the green room — something amiss, she told me. She looked anxious, so I flew up the stairs —'

'More than I managed.'

'Well, they know me, and there weren't so many people by then. They made way for Lord Wilmot, of course. I saw Catherine talking to the Duke, so I knew something was wrong — naturally, I thought of Lady Rosina. Forster told me you'd gone out with Mark, so down I came — just in time for the final curtain.'

'Not yours, thank the Lord. What was she going to do to him, Superintendent, do you think?' Lemon asked.

'She had a knife — only a small one,' Rogers said.

'That's consoling, I'm sure.'

'You still had your sword,' Lemon pointed out.

'Good Lord, so I did.'

'Any duels today, sir?' Wilkie asked in the voice of cockney Smart.

It was a relief to joke about it, a relief to know they'd got her, Jones reflected, as more brandy was poured. He didn't want to think about what Kitty Lovell might have done, but Dickens was a fighter. He would have fought her off, and Lemon and Collins would have got there in time. And Superintendent Jones.

Dickens was speaking. 'She's not as clever as she thinks she is — mistimed her entrance, and she hadn't given a thought to the lighting. She was never any good.'

'Every bit as bad as she seemed.' Lemon finished his drink.

46: INTO THE LIGHT

Dickens stood on the cliff at Broadstairs on the spot where he had watched the storm and had heard the ship's bell from the sinking *Mercury*. How changed the scene was this evening. He looked up to the sky, radiant with the softened glory of the sunset. Long lines of purple and crimson fading to green and gold touched the horizon. Above, the sky glowed with rose, showing a few early stars, a sight at once beautiful and melancholy. Down on the beach where poor Michael Spencer had lain, the pools were burnished with gold and the sands lay still under the now fading light. He could hear the soothing shush and shift of the sea coming in on silken feet and receding with a whisper. He took comfort in the peace, but the melancholy touched him, too. The end of this day, but herald of the next. Time could not stand still. Change would come — and decay. Death and Life. Loss and hope.

Hope. He smiled at a memory. He had walked over to see Miss Palmer in Dumpton. He found that he knew the house — not at all like Betsey Trotwood's, except for the green field in front. The donkey browsing serenely there had looked as though it belonged, however. It was the large round green fan in the window next to the drawn back muslin curtain that he had given to Betsey Trotwood — he had not known where it came from. No doubt, he had seen Miss Anne Palmer that time in her lavender dress and gardening gloves and heard her talking to her servant, Janet — the same Janet who had let him in and bobbed him a blushing curtsey. She'd known, too. He almost blushed to think that Miss Palmer had known.

And there she had been, as brisk and forthright as before, to tell him her news that tentative relations had begun between the Spencer and Mornay children. No second will had been found, but Jonathan Mornay intended to honour its terms. He had grown up, Dickens had thought. Pole Court was to be sold, and all its treasures.

'A good thing, too,' Miss Palmer had opined. 'What did Cornelius want with all that frippery? That poor child, Fanny Mornay, hadn't any use for it. She's to take a small house and live with the curate's sister. Marriage, forsooth, she ought to take up gardening. Good for the soul.'

Toby Quick and Lily Cheng had not turned up at Dover to see Mr Fullerton — not that Dickens had held out much hope for that, but her two thousand pounds would be waiting if he ever heard from them again. Anne Palmer would write to him if she heard anything.

Life would go on for all of them. Miss Palmer had been very brisk about that. 'We must live misfortune down. Some good will come of it, you'll see, for those brothers and sisters. It will be done by the sisters — good hearts there — sensible girls. And you'll write another book, Mr Charles Dickens, you can't help yourself, I daresay —' She gave him a sly smile. 'Though David Copperfield will always be my favourite child.'

'Mine, too,' he had answered, shaking her hard hand. He walked away, hearing her final words in his head.

'Hope, Mr Dickens, hope to the end.'

He heard footsteps. He knew who it was. The one face he wanted just at this moment.

'All settled?' he asked. Sam Jones and his family, and Scrap, of course, had come down at last to Broadstairs and were lodging not far from Fort House.

'Settling — they are all so excited. Scrap's directing operations. Told me to come and see if you were all right.'

'Brought his poker?' Dickens had given the weapon to Scrap as a souvenir.

'He wanted to — might be robbers in that Broadstairs, he said, but I managed to persuade him that there were no such beings at the seaside.'

'What's the story?'

'Guilty and a long sentence, as we hoped. Nothing mentioned about Devonshire House. Mr Mayne and Sir George saw to that — the Queen and so forth. They'd have looked fools.'

'But how did she get in? Did she tell?'

'Not us — but her sister went to see her in Newgate when she was on remand. That young woman's a saint. She came to see me, though, to tell me about Kitty's latest tale — not that she believed it. Kitty, it seems, was not at all grateful for Maggie Chester's company or comforts. She was expecting a ladyship to come and rescue her and to speak for her at the trial.'

'Do I know the name of this ladyship?'

'You do. From what I gather — and it was all a bit garbled by Maggie Chester — Kitty Lovell saw Lady Rosina's newspaper piece about the play and the Guild, and the folk associated with it. She wrote to the lady with a story about being wronged by Charles Dickens — seduced and abandoned and all that —'

'Thank the Lord that wasn't mentioned in the trial.'

'Her lawyer advised against it — the trouble was that she thought it would be a re-run of the Frankland case, with Kitty, the wronged heroine, swooning in the dock. The details of the murders and robberies and the collusion with the hanged Mr Holiest sealed her fate. She didn't give evidence — the lawyer knew she'd condemn herself as soon as she opened her mouth.'

'And the ticket?'

'Lady Rosina gave it to her — how the ladyship got it we don't know. We never will. It's done, Charles, there are always loose ends —' he grinned — 'an unaligned hole in our Chinese puzzle. It's good enough for me.'

'And me. You're right — better for Bulwer-Lytton for us to leave it alone. At least she didn't turn up to disgrace him.'

'Or you, or the good Mr Lemon and the pugnacious Mr Collins. I felt like cheering when he punched Kitty Lovell in the face. Enjoy your triumph. The Queen loved the play, as did everyone.'

They watched as the sun began to disappear below the horizon, the colours fading, the sky darkening, and night falling as a curtain on an empty stage. They watched the stars brightening and listened to the murmur of the eternal sea, dark and unknown, but for which all the currents of our lives are desperately bent, so Dickens reflected, feeling that touch of mournfulness again.

'Time rolls on,' said Dickens, 'time — and change — and decay.'

'Give over — decay, you?' Jones was smiling, his face touched by the last glow of the sunset.

They stood unspeaking for a while. Then it was dark, and Dickens felt the pressure of a strong hand on his shoulder as Sam Jones turned them away from the cliff's edge.

They walked back. The North Foreland light showed from the hill behind the village.

HISTORICAL NOTES

Dickens did serve on the Central Committee of the Working Classes, the aim of which was to widen access for the poorer classes to the Great Exhibition which opened on May 1st, 1851. The members of the committee were to be men known for their promotion of the welfare of working people and workers' leaders. You only have to read any one of Dickens's novels to understand why he was approached. Lord Ashley was another member, as was Dickens's fellow novelist, William Thackeray.

I wasn't surprised, however, to discover that Dickens made the first move to dissolve the committee. He was angry that the General Committee, running the affairs of the Great Exhibition, were nervous that Prince Albert, who came up with the idea of the Exhibition, might somehow be tainted by association with the workers. In the event, shilling days were established and there was universal praise of the good conduct of the working-class visitors — Dickens had known that there would be all along.

The newspaper article concerning the supposed Chinese Ambassador did intrigue me. Captain Hesing was the man, and his adverts proclaimed 'Under Royal Patronage.' The Chinese junk was one of the sights of London from 1848, and Dickens did visit it as well as the Exhibition, which he found overwhelming. However, some of the things he saw perhaps found their way into the book that was on his mind during that year, 1851. There was an exhibition of dinosaurs in their swamp, and it's interesting to note the appearance of the Megalosaurus in the opening chapter of *Bleak House*. In the novel, there is also a reference to the Chinese puzzle ball which Francis Hope shows to Dickens. In *Bleak House*, Lawrence Boythorn uses the reference to show his defiance of Sir Leicester Dedlock over a boundary dispute. Boythorn doesn't care if there are a hundred Chesney Wolds (the seat of the Dedlocks) 'one within another, like the ivory balls in a Chinese carving.' He still won't give in. I couldn't help wondering if Dickens had seen one at the Great Exhibition. Perhaps he had seen the pictures of tea production in China which appear on the walls of Esther Summerson's room at Bleak House. And of matters Chinese and opium-related, there is the character of Nemo in *Bleak House* who dies of an overdose — though this is probably the imported opium from Turkey or Egypt rather than the opium exported from India to China.

I found the reference to the shoe-black brigade in an 1888 biography of Lord Ashley, the philanthropist, who with John MacGregor, barrister and ragged schoolmaster, founded the brigade. The idea was to provide employment for orphaned and abandoned boys and prevent them from turning to or returning to crime. Another book about the Ragged School Movement, *Sixty Years of Waifdom*, gave me the astonishing detail about the shoe-black boy Smike whom Dickens sponsored. I knew then that a shoe-black boy would be a very good witness. The same book gave me the detail about the boy who still had a bullet in his neck, so he became Toby Quick, but I couldn't resist a cameo appearance by Smike.

There was at the time a good deal of controversy about the opium trade to China run by the East India Company, and, given the agitation about the potential dangers to the Exhibition in the form of revolutionary groups and foreign agents, I did wonder what might have happened if a China merchant disappeared. The story of the Mornay family and their connection to China is based on the Huguenot Magniac family, who were goldsmiths and clockmakers in Clerkenwell at the end of the eighteenth century. In the early nineteenth century, Francis Magniac sent his eldest son, Hollingworth, to Canton to supervise the trade in clocks and watches. Hollingworth went into partnership with another merchant, Daniel Beale. After Beale's retirement, the company became Magniac and Company, eventually merging with Jardine Matheson, on which company I based Johnstone Mattinson. The history of these companies is found in *The Thistle and The Jade*, which tells the story of the Jardine Matheson company — still going in Hong Kong.

Hollingworth's two brothers, Charles and Daniel joined the company. Charles had children by his Chinese mistress and died on his way home to England. Daniel resigned after he married his Chinese mistress. Charles's illegitimate son was sent to England and became a tea merchant in Fenchurch Street, and I found the advertisements for Daniel Hope's tea business in the British Newspaper Archive. He did submit a Denization Petition in 1837, which allowed him the right to own property. One of Daniel's sons was confined to a mental hospital and died a pauper lunatic later in the nineteenth century — he profited nothing from all that wealth acquired by the opium trade.

Dickens visited an opium den for his research for the unfinished novel, *The Mystery of Edwin Drood*. This was in 1864. However, there were records of Chinese in the East End of London in the 1840s and 50s. A man called Yahee and his English wife are mentioned in accounts of opium dens in the 1860s, and Yahee had lived there as a tobacconist and opium seller for over twenty years. There were Chinese servants in the houses of the former Canton and Hong Kong merchants. The story of John Fullerton and his agent, Mr Li Shen, is based on the true story of a former director of the East India Company. There were Chinese sailors in the East End and various troupes of Chinese performers appearing in theatres all over the country, including the irrepressible Captain Hesing, whose acrobats performed nightly on the Chinese junk.

Dickens wrote to Mrs Gaskell in May 1851, thanking her for her piece entitled *Disappearances*, which inspired the story of Cornelius Mornay's secret life. Dickens wrote that it 'is very curious and interesting, and I can't help writing to thank you for it at once.' And, as to the play, *Not So Bad as We Seem*, by Dickens's friend, Sir Edward Bulwer-Lytton, it was performed before Queen Victoria at Devonshire House, for the purpose of raising money for the Guild of Literature and Art, a charitable foundation established by Lytton and Dickens, and it was true that Lytton's estranged wife threatened to disrupt the proceedings. Kitty Lovell is the potential disrupter in my novel — she was based on an actress named Alice Lowe, who did steal jewels and trinkets from her aristocratic lover.

Truth is very often stranger than fiction, or at least, as strange, as I keep finding out in my constant searches through The British Newspaper Archive. Did I tell you about Dickens's friend who was shot by his mistress's husband? In Paris, too. Now that is another story. *A Shot in the Dark*, at the moment — in more ways than one!

A NOTE TO THE READER

Dear Reader,

It is astonishing into what curious by-ways research takes a writer. Of course, a good deal of the background information doesn't find its way into the novel — and it shouldn't. The interested reader can find out all about The Great Exhibition and The Opium Trade in the history books. Only those details which lend authenticity and colour are necessary. The reader needs enough historical detail to be convinced that the writer has done the work, and the writer needs to immerse herself into the world in which her characters live.

Some discoveries are of no immediate use at all, but you can't help following a lead for its own sake. So, although the Chinese detective I discovered could play no part in my story — he was conducting his investigations in seventh-century China — I did find the parallels with all the detective stories I've read very thought-provoking. Judge Dee appears in Robert van Gulik's translation of an eighteenth-century Chinese novel and in his own novels featuring the judge/detective, which were first published in the 1950s and based on original Chinese plots from the seventh century.

Judge Dee has the penetrating intellect of a Sherlock Holmes. He sees evidence that others miss and is very skilled at fitting the puzzle pieces together. He has his Watson in the person of Sergeant Hoong, who, like my Sergeant Rogers, is very good at inveigling himself into the confidence of unsuspecting witnesses.

The methods of ancient Chinese murderers are not so different from any murder we might read about in the paper or

351

in our favourite detective novels: knife crime was a very popular method of dispensing with enemies in seventh-century China, as in *The Double Murder at Dawn* — not much change there. *The Case of the Poisoned Bride* speaks for itself — the judge thinks arsenic might have been used. Dickens was very familiar with that poison. There seems to have been a veritable arsenic epidemic in the 1840s. In Judge Dee's story, the culprit is a snake which lives in the rafters — positively Holmesian. There's a mysterious poison in Van Gulik's *Murder in Canton* which originates from the Ti-yang-kuei mountain tribe. Of course, I thought of those mysterious Russian names, Novichok and Polonium — very high-tech, no doubt, but poison just the same. There's the familiar blow to the back of the head inflicted by a handy block of wood, or an iron hammer as in *The Monkey and The Tiger*, and strangulation appears to be popular, often with the bare hands. These ancient crimes are disturbingly familiar, too: murder, robbery, drug-dealing, smuggling, kidnapping, rape, and the trafficking of young women into prostitution. There's even a locked room mystery in *The Chinese Maze Murders* from 1962.

Dickens always asked of his characters; what's his motive? In an essay on capital punishment, he identifies four motives for murder: rage, revenge, gain and elimination. Of the last, he writes of murders committed, 'for the removal of an object dangerous to the murder's peace — murders done to sweep out of the way a dreaded or detested object', and he identifies 'the corroding, growing hate' which drives the murderer to eliminate his or her enemy.

And the same motives drive Judge Dee's perpetrators. Adulterers seek to remove the hated spouse; jealous lovers of both sexes seek to destroy their rivals; ambitious politicians and merchants plot to destroy their competitors for power or wealth; and avaricious relatives are quite ready to murder their grandmothers, or any family member for money.

Human nature does not seem to have changed much in two thousand years — grim thought — whether in seventh-century China or Victorian London, or in the twenty-first century world. However, there are some good people, too, thank goodness. Like Dickens and Jones, Judge Dee seeks justice for the innocent victims, risking his life and often his career in the process, and there are honest witnesses who want right to be done and demonstrate wisdom, love and loyalty. And when the detective's work is complete, justice is served and order restored — until the next case, of course.

I hope that you enjoyed reading my 'Chinese' novel, and I thank you for taking the time to do so. Reviews are really important to authors, and if you enjoyed the novel, it would be great if you could spare a little time to post a review on **Amazon** and **Goodreads.** Readers can connect with me online, on **Facebook (JCBriggsBooks)**, **Twitter (@JeanCBriggs)**, and you can find out more about the books and Charles Dickens via my website: **jcbriggsbooks.com,** where you will also find Mr Dickens's A-Z of murder — all cases of murder to which I found a Dickens connection.

Thank you!

Jean Briggs

Sapere Books is an exciting new publisher of brilliant fiction and popular history.

To find out more about our latest releases and our monthly bargain books visit our website: **saperebooks.com**

Made in United States
North Haven, CT
01 November 2022

26183651R10196